Sarah Perry is the author of *Essex Girls*, *Melmoth*, *The Essex Serpent* and *After Me Comes the Flood*. She has been the UNESCO City of Literature writer-in-residence in Prague and a Gladstone's Library writer-in-residence. Her work has been translated into twenty-seven languages.

The Waterstones Book of the Year 2016
Shortlisted for the 2016 Costa Novel Award

'A work of great intelligence and charm, by a hugely talented author'
Sarah Waters

'A joyous and beguiling book that wrapped itself around me'
Cathy Rentzenbrink

'Had Charles Dickens and Bram Stoker come together to write the great
Victorian novel, I wonder if it would have surpassed *The Essex Serpent*? No
way of knowing, but with only her second outing, Sarah Perry establishes herself as one of the finest fiction writers working in Britain today' John Burnside

'A Victorian-era Gothic with a Dickensian focus on societal ills, Perry's
second novel surprises in its wonderful freshness. There's a sense of
Llareggub about close-knit Aldwinter, its flint church, historic oak and
ribby shipwreck instantly present, while the tapestry of voices that results
from the use of letters amplifies the *Under Milk Wood* echo. Perry's singular
characters are drawn with a fondness that is both palpable and contagious,
and the beautifully observed changing seasons permitted space to breathe,
all making for pure pleasure' Stephanie Cross, *Observer*

'I loved this book. At once numinous, intimate and wise, *The Essex Serpent* is
a marvellous novel about the workings of life, love and belief, about science
and religion, secrets, mysteries, and the complicated and unexpected shifts
of the human heart – and it contains some of the most beautiful evocations
of place and landscape I've ever read. It is so good its pages seem lit from
within. As soon as I'd finished it I started reading it again' Helen Macdonald

'Perry is a wonderful descriptive writer with a remarkable talent for making
the familiar strange . . . Her accounts of open-heart surgery carried out half
a century before antibiotics, or an autistic child questioning the nature of
sin, or a soldier's wedding in the phthisic slums of Bethnal Green, snatch
the breath in your throat. Perry bleeds light into darkness and back again
with a mastery born of her deep professional acquaintance with the Gothic
tradition' *The Times*

'A lovely book . . . it sets out unashamedly to lift the spirits . . . The writing has a gorgeous lilt . . . The method is itself Victorian – an omniscient
narrator scattering sackfuls of sympathy – but the message never gets old:
the world is poorer if we don't put ourselves in each other's place once in a
while' Anthony Cummins, *Spectator*

'*The Essex Serpent* is a work of historical fiction, set in the 1890s, which, for originality, richness of prose and depth of characterisation is unlikely to be bettered this year ... it is Perry's ability to conjure up a sense of entire lives unfolding before our eyes that is most impressive. Filled with wisdom about human behaviour and motivations, and written in a distinctive, stylish prose, *The Essex Serpent* is one of the most memorable historical novels of the past decade' Nick Rennison, *Sunday Times*

'An irresistible novel ... Perry's Victoriana is the most fresh-feeling I can remember ... Her prose is often beautiful ... the tone is a masterstroke ... You feel the influences of Mary Shelley, Bram Stoker, Wilkie Collins, Charles Dickens and Hilary Mantel channelled by Perry in some sort of Victorian séance. This is the best new novel I've read in years. It's the kind of work that makes you alive to the strangeness of the world and of our history' Charlotte Runcie, *Daily Telegraph*

'*The Essex Serpent* is a thing of beauty inside and out. When it comes to historical fiction, Perry's achieved the near impossible; she's created a novel and within it a world that seems to have sprung complete and fully formed directly from the period in question – a long-lost fin-de-siècle Gothic classic – but her characters are as enticingly modern as they are of their period ... Perry also showcases the most beguiling evocations of landscape ... For only a second novel it's a stunning achievement' Lucy Scholes, *Independent* online

'Sarah Perry has written an exquisitely absorbing, old-fashioned page-turner peopled by memorable characters, particularly the magnificent, stubborn and wilful Cora. Perry also captures a society on the brink of a profound shift, uncomfortably reassessing its view of the world through the prism of scientific progress. *The Essex Serpent* is shot through with such a vivid, lively sense of the period that it reads like Charles Dickens at his most accessible and fans of *Jonathan Strange & Mr Norrell* will also find much to love in this engaging, entertaining Gothic novel' Charlotte Heathcote, *Daily Express*

'The result is a novel that somehow embodies the exhilaration and ecstasies – of body and mind – its characters stumble into, suggesting not just the ferment of its times but something of the ferment of our own. And, no less impressively, it exults in the possibility that inheres in the liminal spaces that its titular serpent inhabits – between land and sea, old and new, even life and death. Agile, unconventional, wonderfully weightless, it is a delight' *The Australian*

THE
ESSEX
SERPENT

SARAH PERRY

This paperback edition published in 2022
First published in Great Britain in 2016 by Serpent's Tail,
an imprint of Profile Books Ltd
29 Cloth Fair
London
ECIA 7JQ
www.serpentstail.com

1 3 5 7 9 10 8 6 4 2

Designed and typeset by Crow Books
Printed by CPI Group (UK) Ltd, Croydon CRO 4YY

A CIP record for this book can
be obtained from the British Library

ISBN 978 1 78816 962 2
eISBN 978 1 78283 204 1

For Stephen Crowe

If you press me to say why I loved him, I can say no more than because he was he, and I was I.

Michel de Montaigne, *On Friendship*

NEW YEAR'S EVE

A young man walks down by the banks of the Blackwater under the full cold moon. He's been drinking the old year down to the dregs, until his eyes grew sore and his stomach turned, and he was tired of the bright lights and bustle. 'I'll just go down to the water,' he said, and kissed the nearest cheek: 'I'll be back before the chimes.' Now he looks east to the turning tide, out to the estuary slow and dark, and the white gulls gleaming on the waves.

It's cold, and he ought to feel it, but he's full of beer and he's got on his good thick coat. The collar rasps at the nape of his neck: he feels fuddled and constricted and his tongue is dry. *I'll go for a dip*, he thinks, *that'll shake me loose*; and coming down from the path stands alone on the shore, where deep in the dark mud all the creeks wait for the tide.

'*I'll take a cup o' kindness yet*,' he sings in his sweet chapel tenor, then laughs, and someone laughs back. He unbuttons his coat, he holds it open, but it's not enough: he wants to feel the wind's edge strop itself sharp on his skin. Nearer he goes to the water, and puts out his tongue to the briny air: *Yes – I'll go for a dip*, he thinks, dropping his coat on the marsh. He's done it before, after all, when a boy and in good company: the brave tomfoolery of a midnight dip as the old year dies in the new year's arms. The tide's low – the wind's dropped – the Blackwater holds no fear: give him a glass and he'll drink it down, salt and seashell, oyster and all.

But something alters in a turn of the tide or a change of the air: the estuary surface shifts – seems (he steps forward) to pulse and throb, then grow slick and still; then soon after to convulse, as if flinching at a touch. Nearer he goes, not yet afraid; the gulls lift off one by one, and the last gives a scream of dismay.

Winter comes like a blow to the back of his neck: he feels it penetrate his shirt and go into his bones. The good cheer of drink is gone, and he's comfortless there in the dark – he looks for his coat, but clouds hide the moon and he's blind. His breath is slow, the air is full of pins; the marsh at his feet all at once is wet, as if something out there has displaced the water. *Nothing, it's nothing*, he thinks, patting about for his courage, but there it is again: a curious still moment as if he were looking at a photograph, followed by a frantic uneven motion that cannot be merely the tug of the moon on the tides. He thinks he sees – is *certain* he sees – the slow movement of something vast, hunched, grimly covered over with rough and lapping scales; then it is gone.

In the darkness he grows afraid. There's something there, he feels it, biding its time – implacable, monstrous, born in water, always with an eye cocked in his direction. Down in the deeps it slumbered and up it's come at last: he imagines it breasting the wave, avidly scenting the air. He is seized by dread – his heart halts with it – in the space of a moment he's been charged, condemned, and brought to judgment: oh what a sinner he's been – what a black pip there is at his core! He feels ransacked, emptied of all goodness: he has nothing to bring to his defence. Out he looks to the black Blackwater and there it is again – something cleaving the surface, then subsiding – yes, all along it's been there, waiting, and at last it's found him out. He feels a curious calm: justice must be done, after all, and he willingly pleads guilty. It's all remorse and no redemption, and no less than he deserves.

But then the wind lifts, and tugs the covering cloud, and the shy moon shows her face. It's a scant light, to be sure, but a comfort – and there, after all, is his coat, not a yard away, muddy at the hem; the gulls return to the water, and he feels completely absurd. From the path above him comes the sound of laughter: a girl and her boy in their festival clothes – he waves and calls 'I'm here! I'm here!' *And I am here*, he thinks: here on the marsh he knows better than his home, with the tide slowly turning and nothing to fear. *Monstrous!* he thinks, laughing at himself, giddy with reprieve: as if there were anything out there but herring and mackerel!

Nothing to fear in the Blackwater, nothing to repent: only a moment of confusion in the darkness and far too much to drink. The water comes to meet him and it's his old companion again; to prove it he draws nearer, wets his boots, holds out his arms: 'Here I am!' he yells, and all the gulls reply. *Just a quick dip*, he thinks, *for auld lang syne*, and laughing slips free of his shirt.

The pendulum swings from one year to the next, and there's darkness on the face of the deep.

I

STRANGE
NEWS
OUT OF
ESSEX

JANUARY

I

One o'clock on a dreary day and the time ball dropped at the Greenwich Observatory. There was ice on the prime meridian, and ice on the rigging of the broad-beamed barges down on the busy Thames. Skippers marked the time and tide, and set their oxblood sails against the north-east wind; a freight of iron was bound for Whitechapel foundry, where bells tolled fifty against the anvil as if time were running out. Time was being served behind the walls of Newgate jail, and wasted by philosophers in cafes on the Strand; it was lost by those who wished the past were present, and loathed by those who wished the present past. Oranges and lemons rang the chimes of St Clement's, and Westminster's division bell was dumb.

Time was money in the Royal Exchange, where men passed the afternoon diminishing their hope of threading camels through a needle's eye, and in the offices of Holborn Bars the long-toothed cog of a master clock caused an electric charge to set its dozen slave clocks chiming. All the clerks looked up from their ledgers, sighed, and looked down once more. On Charing Cross Road time exchanged its chariot for buses and cabs in urgent fleets, and in the wards of Barts and of the Royal Borough pain made hours of minutes. In Wesley's chapel they sang *The sands of time are sinking* and wished they might sink faster, and yards away the ice was melting on the graves in Bunhill Fields.

In Lincoln's Inn and Middle Temple lawyers eyed their calendars and saw statutes of limitation expire; in rooms in Camden and Woolwich time was cruel to lovers wondering how it got so late so soon, and in due course was kind to their ordinary wounds. Across the city in terraces and tenements, in high society and low company and in the middle classes, time was spent and squandered, eked out and wished away; and all the time it rained an icy rain.

At Euston Square and Paddington the Underground stations received their passengers, who poured in like so much raw material going down to be milled and processed and turned out of moulds. In a Circle Line carriage, westbound, fitful lights showed *The Times* had nothing happy to report, and in the aisle a bag spilled damaged fruit. There was the scent of rain on raincoats, and among the passengers, sunk in his upturned collar, Dr Luke Garrett was reciting the parts of the human heart. '*Left ventricle, right ventricle, superior vena cava*,' he said, numbering them off on his fingers, hoping the litany might slow his own heart's anxious beating. The man beside him glanced up, bemused, then shrugging turned away. '*Left atrium, right atrium*,' said Garrett, beneath his breath: he was accustomed to the scrutiny of strangers, but saw no reason to court it unduly. The Imp, they called him, since he rarely came higher than the shoulders of other men, and had a loping insistent gait that made you feel he might without any warning take a leap onto a window ledge. It was possible to see, even through his coat, a kind of urgent power in his limbs, and his brow bulged above his eyes as if it could barely contain the range and ferocity of his intellect. He affected a long black fringe that mimicked the edge of a raven's wing: beneath it his eyes were dark. He was thirty-two: a surgeon, with a hungry disobedient mind.

The lights went out and relit, and Garrett's destination came closer. He was due within the hour to attend the funeral of a patient, and no man ever wore his mourning clothes more lightly.

Michael Seaborne had died six days before of cancer of the throat, and had endured the consuming disease and the attentions of his doctor with equal disinterest. It was not towards the dead that Garrett's thoughts were now directed, but rather to his widow, who (he thought, smiling) would perhaps be brushing her untidy hair, or finding a button gone on her good black dress.

The bereavement of Cora Seaborne had been the strangest of all he'd seen – but then, he'd known on arrival at her Foulis Street home that something was awry. The atmosphere in those high-ceilinged rooms had been one of confirmed unease seeming to have little to do with sickness. The patient at that time had still been relatively well, though given to wearing a cravat doubling as a bandage. The cravat was always silk, always pale, and often very slightly stained: in such a fastidious man it was impossible to imagine that it was done unconsciously, and Luke suspected him of trying to make his visitors ill at ease. Seaborne had managed to convey the impression of height by being extremely lean, and was so quietly spoken it was necessary to come near in order to hear him. His voice was sibilant. He was courteous, and the beds of his nails were blue. He'd endured his first consultation calmly, and declined an offer of surgery. 'I intend to depart the world as I entered it,' he said, patting the silk at his throat: 'Without scars.'

'There's no need to suffer,' said Luke, offering unsought consolation.

'To suffer!' The idea evidently amused him. 'An instructive experience, I'm sure.' Then he'd said, as if one thought naturally followed from the other: 'Tell me: have you met my wife?'

Garrett recalled often his first meeting with Cora Seaborne, though in truth his memory of it was not to be trusted, having been made in the image of all that followed. She'd arrived at that moment as if summoned, pausing at the threshold to survey her visitor. Then she'd crossed the carpet, stooped to kiss her husband's brow, and standing behind his chair held out her hand. 'Charles Ambrose tells me no other doctor will do. He gave me your article on the life of Ignaz Semmelweis: if you cut as well as you write, we'll all live forever.' The easeful flattery was irresistible, and Garrett could do nothing but laugh, and bow over the offered hand. Her voice was deep, though not quiet, and he thought at first she had the nomad accent of those who've never lived long in one country, but it was only that she had a faint speech impediment, overcome by lingering on certain consonants. She was dressed in grey, and simply, but her skirt's fabric shimmered like a pigeon's neck. She was tall, and not slender: her eyes also were grey.

In the months that followed Garrett had come to understand a little the unease scenting the Foulis Street air alongside sandalwood and iodine. Michael Seaborne, even in extremities of pain, exerted a malign influence that had little to do with the invalid's usual power. His wife was so ready with cool cloths and good wine, so willing to learn how to slip a needle into a vein, that she might have memorised a manual on a woman's duties down to its last syllable. But Garrett never saw anything passing for affection between Cora and her husband. Sometimes he suspected her of actually willing the brief candle out – sometimes he was afraid she'd take him aside as he prepared a syringe and say, 'Give him more – give him a little more.' If she bent to kiss the starved saint's face on the pillow, it was cautiously, as if she thought he might rear up and tweak her nose in spite. Nurses were hired to dress, and drain, and keep the bed-sheets clean, but rarely lasted a week; the last of these (a Belgian girl, devout) had passed Luke in the corridor and whispered '*Il est comme un diable!*' and shown him her wrist, though there was nothing there. Only the unnamed dog

– loyal, mangy, never far from the bed – had no fear of its master, or at any rate had grown accustomed to him.

In due course Luke Garrett grew familiar with Francis, the Seabornes' black-haired silent son, and with Martha, the boy's nanny, who was given to standing with her arm about Cora Seaborne's waist with a possessive gesture he disliked. Cursory appraisal of the patient was hurriedly got out of the way (after all, what was there to be done?), and Luke would be taken away to survey a fossil tooth Cora had received in the post, or to be interrogated at length as to his ambitions for advancing cardiac surgery. He practised hypnosis on her, explaining how once it had been used in war to ease the removal of soldiers' limbs; they played games of chess, which ended with Cora aggrieved to find her opponent had marshalled his forces against her. Luke diagnosed himself to be in love, and sought no cure for the disease.

Always he was aware of a kind of energy in her, stored up and waiting release; he thought when the end came for Michael Seaborne her feet might strike blue sparks on the pavements. The end did come, and Luke was present for the last breath, which had been laboured, loud, as if at the last moment the patient had set aside the *ars moriendi* and cared only to live a moment longer. And after all Cora was unchanged, neither mourning nor relieved: her voice broke, once, when reporting that the dog had been found dead, but it was not clear whether she was about to laugh or to cry. The death certificate signed, and all that remained of Michael Seaborne resting elsewhere, there was no sound reason for Garrett to make his way to Foulis Street; but he woke each morning with one purpose in mind, and arriving at the iron gates would find himself expected.

The train drew in to Embankment, and he was borne along the platform with the crowd. Grief of a kind came to him then, though it was not for Michael Seaborne, nor for his widow: what troubled him most was that this might mark the last of his meetings with Cora – that his final view of her would be as he looked over his shoulder while mourning bells tolled. 'Still,' he said: 'I must be there, if only to see the coffin-lid screwed down.' Beyond the ticket barriers ice melted on the pavements; the white sun was in decline.

Dressed as the day demanded, Cora Seaborne sat before her mirror. Pearl drops on gold wires hung at each ear; the lobes were sore, since it had been necessary to pierce them again. 'So far as tears go,' she said, 'these will have to do.' Her face was powdered pale. Her black hat did not suit her, but had both a veil and a black plume of feathers, and conveyed the proper degree of mourning. The covered buttons on her black cuffs would not fasten, and between the hem of sleeve and glove a strip of white skin would be seen. The neckline of her dress was a little lower than she'd have liked, and showed on her collarbone an ornate scar as long as her thumb, and about as wide. It was the perfect replica of the silver leaves on the silver candlesticks that flanked the silver mirror, and which her husband had pressed into her flesh as though he were sinking his signet ring into a pool of wax. She considered painting it over, but had grown fond of it, and knew that in some circles she was enviously believed to have had a tattoo.

She turned from the glass and surveyed the room. Any visitor would pause puzzled at the door, seeing on the one hand the high soft bed and damask curtains of a wealthy woman, and on the other the digs of a scholar. The furthest corner was papered with botanical prints, and maps torn from atlases, and sheets of paper on which quotations were written in her large black capitals (NEVER DREAM WITH THY HAND

ON THE HELM! TURN NOT THY BACK TO THE COMPASS!). On the mantelpiece a dozen ammonites were ranked according to size; above them, captured in a gilded frame, Mary Anning and her dog observed a fallen fragment of Lyme Regis rock. Was it all hers now – that carpet, these chairs, this crystal glass that still gave off the scent of wine? She supposed so, and at the thought a kind of lightness entered her limbs, as if she might come untethered from Newton's laws and find herself spread out upon the ceiling. The sensation was decently suppressed, but all the same she could name it: it was not happiness, precisely, nor even contentment, but relief. There was grief, too, that was certain, and she was grateful for it, since however loathed he'd been by the end, he'd formed her, at least in part – and what good ever came of self-loathing?

'Oh, he made me – yes,' she said, and memory unfurled like smoke from a blown candle. Seventeen, and she'd lived with her father in a house above the city, her mother long gone (though not before she'd seen to it that her daughter would not be damned to samplers and French). Her father – uncertain what to do with his modest wealth, whose tenants liked him contemptuously – had gone out on business and returned with Michael Seaborne at his side. He'd presented his daughter with pride – Cora, barefoot, with Latin on her tongue – and the visitor had taken her hand, and admired it, and scolded her for a broken nail. He came again, and again, until he grew expected; he brought her slim books, and small hard objects of no use. He'd mock her, putting his thumb in the palm of her hand and stroking, so that the flesh grew sore, and it seemed her whole consciousness dwelt there at the touching place. In his presence the Hampstead pools, the starlings at dusk, the cloven prints of sheep in the soft mud, all seemed drab, inconsequential. She grew ashamed of them – of her loose untidy clothes, her unbraided hair.

One day he said: 'In Japan they'll mend a broken pot with drops of molten gold. What a thing it would be: to have me break you, and mend your wounds with gold.' But she'd been seventeen, and armour-clad with youth, and never felt the blade go in: she'd laughed, and so had he. On her nineteenth birthday she exchanged birdsong for feathered fans, crickets in the long grass for a jacket dotted with beetles' wings; she was bound by whalebone, pierced with ivory, pinned by the hair with tortoiseshell. Her speech grew languid to conceal its stumble; she walked nowhere. He gave her a gold ring which was too small – a year later another, and it was smaller still.

The widow was roused from her reverie by footsteps overhead, which were slow, and measured out as precisely as the ticking of a clock. 'Francis,' she said. She sat quietly, waiting.

A year before his father died, and perhaps six months after his disease had first appeared at the breakfast table (a lump in the throat restricting the passage of dry toast), Francis Seaborne had been moved to a room on the fourth floor of the house and at the furthest end of the passage.

His father would've had no interest in domestic arrangements even if he'd not at that time been assisting Parliament with the passage of a housing act. The decision had been made wholly by his mother and by Martha, who'd been hired as nurse when he was a baby, and never, as she herself put it, quite got round to leaving. It was felt that Francis was best kept at arm's length, since he was restless at night and made frequent appearances at the door and even, once or twice, at the window. He'd never ask for water, or for comfort, as any other child might; only stand at the threshold holding one of his many talismans until unease raised a head from the pillow.

Soon after his removal to what Cora called the Upper Room, he lost interest in his nightly travels, becoming content with accumulating (no-one ever said 'stealing') whatever took his fancy. These he laid out in a series of complex and baffling patterns that changed each time Cora made a maternal visit; they had a beauty and strangeness she'd have admired if they'd been the work of somebody else's son.

This being Friday, and the day of his father's funeral, he'd dressed himself. At eleven years old he knew both one end of a shirt from the other, and its usefulness in spelling ('It is NECESSARY that the shirt has one Collar, but two Sleeves'). That his father had died struck him as a calamity, but one no worse than the loss of one of his treasures the day before (a pigeon's feather, quite ordinary, but which could be coiled into a perfect circle without snapping its spine). When told the news – noting that his mother was not crying but was rigid and also somehow blazing, as if in the midst of a lightning strike – his first thought was this: *I cannot understand why these things happen to me.* But the feather was gone; his father was dead; and it seemed he was to attend church. The idea pleased him. He said, conscious of being quite affable given the circumstances: 'A change is as good as a rest.'

In the days following the discovery of Michael Seaborne's body it was the dog who'd suffered most. It had whined at the sickroom door and could not be consoled; a caress might've done it, but since no-one would sink their hands into its greasy pelt, the laying-out of the body ('Put a penny on his eye for the ferryman,' Martha said: 'I don't think St Peter will trouble himself...') had been accompanied by that same high keening. The dog was dead now, of course, thought Francis, patting with satisfaction a little wad of fur collected from his father's sleeve, and so the only mourner was now itself to be mourned.

He was uncertain what rituals attended the disposal of the dead, but thought it best to come prepared. His jacket had a number of pockets, each of which contained an object not sacred, precisely, but well suited, he thought, to the task. An eyeglass which had cracked, offering a broken view of things; the wad of fur (he hoped it might still contain a flea or tick, and within that, if he was ever so lucky, a bead of blood); a raven-feather, which was his best, being bluish at the tip; a scrap of fabric he'd torn from Martha's hem, having observed on it a persistent stain in the shape of the Isle of Wight; and a stone with a perfect perforation in the centre. Pockets packed, and tapped, and counted out, he went down to find his mother, and at each of the thirty-six steps to her room incanted 'Here – to*day* – gone – to*morrow*; here – to*day* – *gone*.'

'Frankie –' How small he was, she thought. His face, which curiously bore scant resemblance to either parent, save for his father's rather flat-seeming black eyes, was impassive. He'd combed his hair, and it lay in ridges flat against his scalp: that he had troubled to make himself neat moved her, and she put out her hand, but let it fall empty to her lap. He stood patting each of pockets in turn, and said: 'Where is he now?'

'He will be waiting for us at the church.' Ought she to take him into her arms? He did not look, it must be said, much in need of comfort.

'Frankie, if you want to cry, there is no shame in it.'

'If I wanted to cry, I would. If I wanted to do anything, I would.' She didn't chastise him for that, since really it was little more than a statement of fact. He once again patted each of his pockets, and she said, gently, 'You are bringing your treasures.'

'I am bringing my treasures. I have a treasure for you (*pat*), a treasure for Martha (*pat*), a treasure for Father (*pat*), a treasure for me (*pat, pat*).'

'Thank you, Frankie ...' – all at a loss: but there at last was Martha, brightening the room as she always did, dissipating by nothing more than her presence the slight tension which had taken the air. She lightly touched Francis on the head, just as though he had been any other child; her strong arm circled Cora's waist; she smelt of lemons.

'Come on then,' she said. 'He never did like us to be late.'

The St Martin's bells tolled for the dead at two, rolling out across Trafalgar Square. Francis, whose hearing was pitilessly acute, pressed gloved hands to each ear and refused to cross the threshold until the last peal died, so that the congregation, turning to see the late-coming widow and her son, sighed, gratified: how pale they were! How very fitting! And would you take a look at that hat!

Cora watched the evening's performance with an interested detachment. There in the nave, obscuring the altar – in a coffin resting on what resembled a butcher's trestle – was her husband's body, which she did not recall having ever seen in its entirety, only in small and sometimes panicked glimpses of very white flesh laid thinly over beautiful bones.

It struck her that really she'd known nothing of him in his public life, which was carried out in (she imagined) identical rooms in the Commons, and in his Whitehall set, and in the club which she could not attend, having the misfortune to be female. Perhaps he dealt elsewhere with kindness – yes: perhaps that was it – perhaps she'd been a kind of clearing-house for cruelties deserved elsewhere. There was a kind of nobility in that, if you thought about it: she looked down at her hands as if expecting the notion to have raised stigmata.

Above her, on the high black balcony which seemed in the dim air to float several feet above the columns which bore it up, was Luke Garrett. *Imp*, she thought: *look at him!* and her heart seemed almost to move towards her friend, pressing against the bars of her ribs. His coat was no more fitting to the occasion than his surgeon's apron might have been, and she was certain he'd been drinking long before he came, and that the girl by his side was a recent acquaintance whose affection was out of his budget; but despite the darkness and distance there came down to her, in one black glance, an incitement to laugh. Martha felt it too, and administered a pinch to her thigh, so that later, when glasses of wine were poured in Hampstead and Paddington and Westminster it was said: 'Seaborne's widow gasped with grief just as the priest declared *though he were dead, yet shall he live*; it was beautiful, you know, in a way.'

Beside her, Francis went on whispering, his mouth pressed to his thumb, his eyes tightly closed; it made him babyish again, and she put her hand over his. It fit within hers perfectly still, and very hot, and after a while she lifted her own and laid it again in her lap.

Afterwards, as black cassocks flapped like rooks between the pews, Cora stood on the steps and greeted the departing congregation, who were all kindness, all solicitude – she must consider herself to have friends in Town; she was welcome, with her handsome boy, at any supper she chose; she'd be remembered in their prayers. She passed to Martha so many visiting-cards, and so many small posies, and so much in the way of little books of remembrance and black-hemmed samplers, that a passer-by might have mistaken the day for a wedding, albeit a sombre one.

It was not yet evening, but frost thickened on the steps with a hard glitter in the lamplight, and fog enclosed the city in a pale tent. Cora shivered, and Martha came a little nearer, so that she could feel warmth rising from that compact body in its second-best coat. Francis stood some distance away, his left hand foraging in the pocket of his jacket, his right smoothing fitfully at his hair. He did not look distressed, precisely, or either woman would have drawn him between them, with the murmurs of comfort which would have come so easily if they'd been sought. Rather, he looked politely resigned to disruption in a cherished routine.

'Christ have mercy on us!' said Dr Garrett, as the last of the mourners departed, black-hatted, relieved it was over, turning to the night's entertainment and the morning's business. Then, with the swift transition to the serious which was so irresistible in him, he grasped Cora's gloved hand. 'Well done, Cora: you did well. Can I take you home? Let me take you. I'm hungry. Are you? I could eat a horse and its foal.'

'You can't afford a horse.' Martha only ever spoke to the doctor with a show of annoyance; Imp had been *her* name for him, though no-one remembered it now. His presence in the house at Foulis Street – first a matter of duty, then one of devotion – was an annoyance to Martha, who felt her own devotion to be more than adequate. He'd dispensed with his companion, and had put into his breast pocket a handkerchief edged in black.

'I'd like more than anything to go for a long walk,' said Cora. Francis, as if detecting her sudden weariness and seeing in it an opportunity for gain, came quickly to stand at her feet and demand they travel home by Underground. As ever, it came not as a childish request that if granted, would give him pleasure, but as a bald statement of fact. Garrett, who'd not yet learned to negotiate the boy's implacable will, said, 'I've already had enough of Hades for one day,' and gestured towards a passing cab.

Martha took the boy's hand, and out of sheer surprise at her audacity he let it lie there in her glove. 'I'll take you, Frank: it'll be warm, and I can't feel my toes – but Cora, you surely cannot walk all the way – it is three miles at least?'

'Three and a half,' said the doctor, as if he himself had laid the paving stones. 'Cora, let me walk with you.' The cab driver made an impatient gesture, and received an obscene response. 'You shouldn't do it. You can't go alone . . .'

'Shouldn't? Can't?' Cora took off her gloves, which were no more proof against the cold than a cobweb. She thrust them at Garrett. 'Give me yours – I can't think why they make these, or why women buy them – I can walk, and I will. I'm dressed for walking, see?' She lifted her hem and displayed boots better suited to a schoolboy.

Francis had turned away from his mother, no longer interested in the turn the evening might take; he had a great deal to do, back in his Upper Room, and a few new items (*pat, pat*) which required his attention. He pulled his hand from Martha's and set off towards the city. Martha, throwing a mistrustful look at Garrett and a rueful one at her friend, called out a farewell and slipped into the mist.

'Let me go alone,' said Cora, pulling on the borrowed gloves, so threadbare they were scarcely warmer than her own. 'My thoughts are so tangled they'll take a mile or more to unravel.' She touched the black-edged handkerchief in Garrett's pocket. 'Come tomorrow, if you like, to the grave. I said I'd go alone, but perhaps that's the point; perhaps we are always alone, no matter the company we keep.'

'You ought to be followed about by a clerk making a record of your wisdom,' said the Imp, satirically, letting her hand fall. He bowed extravagantly, and retreated into the cab, slamming the door against her laughter.

Marvelling at his ability to bring about such total reversions in her mood, Cora turned first not west towards home, but towards the Strand. She liked to find the place where the River Fleet had been diverted underground, east from Holborn; there was a particular grating where on a quiet day you could hear it running out towards the sea.

Reaching Fleet Street, she thought that if she strained hard enough into the grey air she might hear the river running through its long tomb, but there was only the noise of a city which no frost or fog could dissuade from work or pleasure. And besides, she'd once been told that it was scarcely more than a sewer by now, swollen not by rainwater leaching down from Hampstead Heath but by humanity massing on its banks. She stood a while longer, until her hands ached with the chill, and the punctured lobes of her ears began to throb. She sighed, and set out for home, discovering that the unease that once accompanied the image of the high white house on Foulis Street had been left behind, dropped somewhere beneath the black pews of the church.

Martha, who'd anxiously awaited Cora's return (little more than an hour later, with freckles blazing through white powder and her black hat slipped), put a great store on appetite as evidence of a sound mind, and watched with pleasure as her friend ate fried eggs and toast. 'I'll be glad when it's all over,' she'd said. 'All these cards, these handshakes. I am so bored of the etiquette of death!'

In his mother's absence the child, mollified by the Underground, had gone wordlessly upstairs with a glass of water and slept with an apple core in his hand. Martha had stood at his door and seen how black his lashes were against his white cheek, and felt her heart soften towards him. A scrap of the wretched dog's fur had found its way to his pillow; she imagined it seething with lice and fleas, and stooped over the boy to take it and leave him safely sleeping. But her wrist must've touched the pillowcase; he came fully alert in the time it took a breath to leave her; seeing the fur in her hand he gave a kind of wordless scream of rage, so that she dropped the greasy wad and ran from the room. Coming down-stairs, she thought, *How can I be afraid of him: he's nothing but a fatherless boy!* and was half-inclined to return and insist that he hand over the unsavoury little keepsake, and perhaps even submit to a kiss. Then a key was fitted noisily to the lock, and there had been Cora, demanding a fire, throwing down her gloves, holding out her arms for an embrace.

Late that night, the last to bed, Martha paused at Cora's door: it had been her habit these past few years to content herself that all was well with her friend. Cora's door stood half-open; a log in the fireplace spat as it burned. At the threshold Martha said, 'Are you sleeping? Should I come in?' and receiving no answer stepped onto the thick pale carpet. All along the mantelpiece were visiting cards and mourning-cards, black-edged, close-written; a bunch of violets tied with a black ribbon had fallen onto the hearth. Martha bent to pick them up, and they seemed almost to shrink away from her and hide again behind their heart-shaped leaves. She stood them in a little glass of water, set them where her friend would see them on first waking, and stooped to kiss her. Cora murmured, and shifted, but did not wake; and Martha recalled first coming to Foulis Street to take up her post, antici-pating some haughty matron with a mind enfeebled by gossip and fashion, and how wrong-footed she'd been by the changeable being who'd come to the door. Infuriated and entranced, Martha found that no sooner had she grown accustomed to one Cora, another would emerge: one moment a girl who seemed a student over-pleased with her own intelligence, the next a friend of long years' intimacy; a woman giving suppers of stylish extravagance, who'd swear once the last guest was gone, take down her hair, and sprawl laughing beside the fire.

Even her voice was a matter for confused admiration – that

odd half-lilt, half-impediment, which would appear when she was tired, and certain consonants gave her trouble. That behind the intelligent charm (which, Martha wryly observed, could be turned on and off like the bathroom tap) there were visible wounds only made her dearer. Michael Seaborne treated Martha with the kind of indifference he might've reserved for the hat-stand in the hall: she was entirely inconsequential – he did not even meet her eye on the stairs. But watchful Martha let nothing pass her by – overheard each courteous insult, observed each concealed bruise – and only with a great effort prevented herself from plotting a murder for which she'd've cheerfully been hanged. Just less than a year after arriving at Foulis Street – in the small hours, during which no-one had slept – Cora had come to her room. Whatever had been done or said had caused her to tremble violently, though the night was warm; her thick untidy hair was wet. Without speaking Martha had raised the cloths that covered her, and taken Cora into her arms; she drew up her knees to enclose her entirely, and held her very tight, so that the other woman's trembling entered her. Unlaced from the conventions of whalebone and cloth Cora's body was large, strong; Martha felt the blades moving in her narrow back, the soft stomach which she cradled against her arm, the sturdy muscles of her thighs: it had been like clinging to an animal which would never again consent to lie so still. They'd woken in a loose embrace, wholly at ease, and parted on a caress.

It heartened her now to see that Cora had not taken to her bed in mourning, but with her old habit of looking over what she called 'her Studies', as if she were a boy cramming for college. On the bed beside her was the old leather file which had been her mother's, and which had lost the gilt from its monogram, and which smelt (so Martha insisted) of the animal it once had been. And there also were her notebooks, written in a small clear script, the margins covered, the pages interleaved with pressed stems of weeds and grasses, and a map of a section of coastline marked with red ink. A spill of papers lay all around her and she'd fallen asleep clutching her Dorset ammonite. But in her sleep she'd held on much too hard: it had crumbled to pieces, and left her with a muddy hand.

FEBRUARY

I

'I mean: take jasmine, for instance.' Dr Luke Garrett swept papers from his desk as if he might find beneath them white buds popping into bloom, and discovering instead a pouch of tobacco set about rolling a cigarette. 'The scent is so sweet that it's both pleasant and unpleasant; people recoil and go nearer, recoil and go nearer; they're not sure whether to be disgusted or seduced. If only we could acknowledge pain and pleasure not as opposite poles but all of a piece, we might at last understand . . .' He lost the thread of his thought, and cast about for it.

Accustomed to these lectures, the man who stood beside the window sucked at his beer and mildly said, 'Only last week you concluded that all states of pain are evil, and all states of pleasure are good. I remember your words exactly, because you said it so many times, and in fact wrote it down for me, in case I forgot. I might actually have it on me –' He patted ironically at each pocket, then flushed, never having quite got the hang of affectionate mockery. George Spencer was all that Garrett was not: tall, wealthy, fair, shy, with feelings deeper than his thoughts were swift. Those who'd known both since their student days joked that Spencer was the Imp's good conscience, severed from him somehow, always running to keep up.

Garrett shoved himself deeper into his armchair. 'Of course it *seems* completely contradictory and wholly unjustifiable, but then the best minds can hold two opposing thoughts at once.' He frowned, an expression which caused his eyes almost to vanish below his black eyebrows and blacker fringe, and drained his glass. 'Let me explain . . .'

'I'd like that: but I'm supposed to be meeting friends for dinner.'

'You don't *have* any friends, Spencer. Even I don't like you. Look: it's useless denying that causing or experiencing pain is the most repulsive of human experiences. Before we knocked the patient out cold, surgeons would vomit in horror at what they were about to do; sane men and women would shorten their lives by twenty years rather than endure the knife – so would you – so would I! But all the same – it is impossible to say what pain actually *is*, or what is truly felt, or if what pains one pains another: it is more a matter of the imagination than of the body – so you see then how valuable hypnosis ought to be?' He narrowed his eyes at Spencer and went on: 'If you tell me you're burned and in pain, how can I know whether the sensations you report bear any resemblance to what I'd feel if I suffered the same injury? All I can safely say is that we each experienced some physical response to an identical stimulus. True, we might both yelp, and splash about in cold water for a bit and so on, but how can I know that you are not actually experiencing a sensation that, if I were to experience it, might have me yelping to an entirely different tune?' Wolfish, he bared his teeth and went on: 'Does it matter? Would it alter the treatment a physician might give? If you begin to question the truth – or I suppose the value – of pain, how could you resist withholding or dispensing care according to some measure which you admit yourself is completely arbitrary?'

Losing interest, Garrett stooped to collect the fallen papers from the floor, and set about sorting them into neat files. 'Doesn't matter in the least, to all practical purposes. The thought just occurred to me, that's all. Things occur to me, and I like to talk about them, and I haven't anyone else. I ought to get a dog.' Spencer, noting his friend's plunge into gloom, took out his cigarette, and ignoring the ticking of his watch sat in a bare-seated chair and surveyed the room. It was fanatically clean, and the parsimonious winter sun could not pick out a speck of dust, no matter how it tried. It contained two chairs and a table, with two upended packing cases making do elsewhere. A length of fabric nailed over the window was washed thin and pale, and the white stone fireplace gleamed. There was a strong scent of lemons and antiseptic, and over the fire were black-framed photographs of Ignaz Semmelweis and John Snow. Pinned above the little desk there was a drawing (signed LUKE GARRETT AGE THIRTEEN) of a serpent coiled about a staff and testing the air with its split tongue: the symbol of Asclepius, who was cut from the womb of his mother on her funeral pyre and grew up to be the god of healing. The only food and drink Spencer had ever seen up those three flights of whitewashed stairs were cheap beer and Jacob's crackers. He looked down at his friend, conscious of the familiar battle between frustration and affection which he always roused.

Spencer could recall with perfect clarity their first meeting in the lecture rooms of the Royal Borough, the teaching hospital where Garrett proved himself to have leaped ahead of his tutors in theory and understanding, bearing their tutelage with ill grace save when studying cardiac anatomy and the circulatory system, when he'd become so boyish and enthused he was suspected of mockery and often tossed out of class. Spencer, who knew the only way to conceal and overcome the limits of his own intelligence was to study, and study hard, avoided Garrett. He suspected no good could come of being seen with him, and besides was a little afraid of the black glitter set behind his eyes. Encountering him one evening, long after the laboratory was emptied and its doors ought to have been locked, he thought at first he must be in deep distress. He was seated with a drooping head at one of the scored and Bunsen-burned benches, staring intently at something between his outspread hands.

'Garrett?' he'd said: 'Is that you? Are you all right? What are you doing here so late?'

Garrett hadn't answered, but turned his head, and the sardonic grin with which his face was usually masked was gone. Instead he gave the other man a frank smile of such happy sweetness that Spencer thought he must have been mistaken for a friend; but Garrett gestured and said, 'Look! Come and see what I made!'

Spencer's first thought was that Garrett had taken up embroidery. This would not have been so strange: each year there was a contest among the graduate surgeons to see who could sew the finest stitches on a white silk square, and some claimed to have practised with cobweb. What had been holding Garrett's attention was a beautiful object that resembled a Japanese fan in miniature with an intricately woven tassel at the handle. It measured no broader than his thumb, and was worked in such fine patterns of blue and scarlet on dense yellowish cream that he could barely see where the threads looped through the silk. Stooping to look closer, his vision sharpened and shifted, and he realised what it was; an exquisitely cut portion of the lining of a human stomach, sliced thin as paper, injected with ink to show the tracing of the blood vessels and set between glass slides. No artist could have matched the fine loop and twist of vein and artery, which had no pattern at all, but in which Spencer thought he saw the image of bare-branched trees in spring.

'*Oh!*' He caught Garrett's eye, and they shared a look of delight that was a stitch neither ever severed.

'You made this?'

'I did! Once when I was young I saw a picture of something

like this, made by Edward Jenner, I think – I told my father I'd make one of my own, though I doubt he believed me – and here we are and here it is. I broke into the morgue. You won't tell?'

'No – never!' said Spencer, entranced.

'I believe for most of us – for me, certainly – what's below the skin is more worth looking at than what's outside it. Turn me inside-out and I'd be quite a handsome man!' Garrett placed the slide in a cardboard box, secured it with string, and placed it in his breast pocket, reverent as a priest. 'I'm going to take it to a framer and have it set in ebony. Is ebony expensive? Pine, or oak – I live in hope of one day knowing someone who'll think it as beautiful as I do. Shall we have a drink?'

Spencer had looked at the exercise books he'd carried from his rooms, then down at Luke's face. It occurred to Spencer for the first time that he was certainly shy, and probably lonely. 'Why not?' he said. 'If I'm going to fail the exam, I might as well not care about it.'

The other man had grinned. 'I hope you've got some money, then, because I've not eaten since yesterday.' Then he'd loped ahead down the corridor, laughing at himself, or at Spencer, or at an old joke he'd only just remembered.

It was apparent Garrett had not yet found a fit recipient for his handiwork, for there – years later – was the slide in its box, placed reverently upon the mantelpiece, the white cardboard darkened at the edge. Spencer rolled the cigarette between his fingers, and said: 'Has she gone?'

Looking up, Garrett considered pretending he misunderstood, but knew himself bettered. 'Cora? She went last week. The blinds are down at Foulis Street and the furniture's covered in dust-sheets. I know, because I looked.' He scowled. 'She'd gone by the time I came by. That old witch Martha was there and wouldn't pass on the address: said she needed rest and quiet and I'd hear from her in her own good time.'

'Martha is one year older than you,' said Spencer mildly. 'And admit it, Garrett: peace and quiet are two qualities which are not often linked with you.'

'I am her *friend*!'

'Yes, but not a peaceful or a quiet one. Where has she gone?'

'Colchester. Colchester! What is there at Colchester? A ruin and a river, and web-footed peasants, and *mud*.'

'They're finding fossils on the coast: I read about it. Smart women are wearing necklaces of sharks' teeth set in silver. Cora will be happy as a schoolboy there, up to her knees in mud. You'll see her soon.'

'What good is *soon*? What good is *Colchester*? What good are *fossils*? It's been hardly a month. She should still be mourning.' (At this, neither met the other man's eye.) 'She should be with people who love her.'

'She is with Martha, and no-one ever loved her more.' Spencer did not mention Francis, who'd several times beaten him at chess: it did not somehow seem feasible to suggest the boy loved his mother. His watch ticked louder, and he saw in Garrett the slow burning of a furious temper. Thinking of the dinner that awaited him, and the wine, and the warm deep-carpeted house, he said – as if the thought had just occurred – 'I meant to ask: how's your paper coming along?' Dangling the prospect of academic approval in front of Garrett generally had much the same effect as showing a dog a raw bone, and lately little else could turn his mind from Cora Seaborne.

'Paper?' The word came out like something unpleasant eaten. Then, a little mollified: 'On the possibility of replacing an aortic valve? Yes, all right' – almost without looking, he deftly retrieved half-a-dozen sheets of dense black script from midway through a stack of notebooks – 'Deadline's Sunday. Might as well crack on with it. Get out, would you?' He turned away, folded himself over the desk, and began sharpening a pencil with a razorblade. He unfolded a large sheet of paper which showed a vastly enlarged transverse section of a human heart, with cryptic markings in black ink, and sections of script crossed out and reinstated with a series of exclamation marks. Something in the margins caught his eye; it excited or irritated him: he swore, and began scribbling.

Spencer withdrew a banknote from his pocket, set it silently on the floor, where his friend might mistake it for one he himself had dropped and forgotten, and closed the door behind him.

2

Having scoured its river for kingfishers and its castle for ravens, Cora Seaborne walked through Colchester with Martha on her arm, holding an umbrella above them both. There'd been no kingfisher ('On a Nile cruise, probably – Martha, shall we follow them?'), but the castle keep had been thick with grave-faced rooks stalking about in their ragged trousers. 'Quite a good ruin,' said Cora, 'But I'd have liked to've seen a gibbet, or a miscreant with pecked-out eyes.'

Martha – who had little patience for the past and eyes fixed always at some brighter point several years distant – said, 'There's suffering, if you're really determined to find it,' and gestured towards a man whose legs ended above the knee and who had stationed himself opposite a cafe, the better to induce guilt in tourists with overfilled bellies. Martha had made no secret of her discomfort at being plucked from her city home: for all that her thick fair plait and strong arms gave her the appearance of a dairy-girl with a fondness for cream, she'd never before been much east of Bishopsgate, and thought the oaky Essex fields sinister and the pink-painted Essex houses the dwelling-places of half-wits. Her astonishment that coffee could be had in such a backwater had been matched only by her disgust at the astringent liquid she'd been served, and she spoke to anyone they met with the extravagant politeness reserved for a stupid child. All the same, in the fortnight since they'd departed London – Francis retrieved from school, to the unspoken but evident relief of his teachers – Martha had almost come to love the little town for its effect on her friend, who removed from London's gaze had abandoned her dutiful mourning and receded ten years to a merrier self. Sooner or later, she thought, she'd gently ask how long Cora intended to live in their two rooms on the High Street, doing nothing but walking herself weary and poring over books, but for now she was content to witness Cora's happiness.

Adjusting the umbrella, which had done nothing more than channel the weak rain more efficiently into the collars of their coats, Cora followed Martha's pointing hand. The crippled man was doing a far better job than they of tricking the weather, and judging by the satisfaction with which he examined the contents of his upturned hat, had made a good day's takings. He was sitting on what Cora first took to be a stone bench, but which on looking closer she saw was a piece of fallen masonry. It measured at least three feet broad and two deep, and the remains of a Latin phrase emerged to the left of the beggar's limbs. Seeing the two women in their good coats observing him from across the road he immediately adopted an expression of craven misery; this he swiftly discarded as being too obvious and replaced with one of noble suffering, with the suggestion that though he found his occupation odious he could never be accused of shirking. Cora, who loved the theatre, tugged her arm from Martha's and slipping behind a passing bus stood gravely at his feet, sheltered a little by a shallow porch.

'Good afternoon.' She reached for her purse. The man cast his eyes up at the sky, which at that moment split and displayed an astonishing blue interior. 'It isn't,' he said. 'But it might yet be: I'll give you that.' The brief brightness illuminated the building behind him, which Cora saw had been torn apart as though by an explosion. A section to her left remained more or less as its architect intended – a several-storeyed building that might have been a great house or town hall – but a portion to the right had sheared away and sunk several feet into the ground. A bulwark of poles and planks kept it from tumbling across the pavement, but it was treacherous, and she thought she could hear above the slow traffic the creak and grinding of iron on stone. Martha appeared at her side and Cora instinctively took her hand, unsure whether to step backwards or hitch up her skirt and take a closer look. The same appetite that made her break stones in search of ammonites until the air reeked of cordite propelled her forward: she could see up to a room with its fireplace intact, and a scarlet scrap of carpet lolling over the edge of the broken floor like a tongue. Further up, an oak seedling had taken hold beside the staircase, and a pale fungus that resembled many fingerless hands had colonised the plaster ceiling.

'Now steady on, miss!' Alarmed, the man shuffled across his stone seat and gripped the hem of Cora's coat. 'What d'you want to be doing that for? No, a little further back, I should think . . . and a little further . . . safe enough now, yes; and don't do it again.' He spoke with the authority of a gate-keeper, so that Cora felt rather ashamed of herself and said, 'Oh, I am sorry: I didn't mean to alarm you. It's just I thought I saw something move.'

'That'll be the house martins and they needn't trouble you a bit.' Forgetting for a moment the demeanour of his profession, he tugged at his scarf and said, 'Thomas Taylor, at your service. Not been here before, I take it?'

'A few days. My friend and I' – Cora gestured towards Martha, who stood a little distance away in the shadow of her umbrella, stiff with disapproval – 'Are staying on awhile, so I thought maybe I'd better say hello.' Cora and the cripple both examined this statement for logic, and finding none let it pass.

'You've probably come about the earthquake,' said Taylor,

gesturing behind him to the ruins. He gave the appearance of a lecturer taking a last look at his notes, and Cora – always ready to be educated – indicated that she had. 'Could you enlighten us?' she said: 'If you have the time.'

It had come (he said) eight years back, by his reckoning, at eighteen minutes past nine precisely. It had been as fair an April morning as any could remember, which later was counted a blessing, since most were out-of-doors. The Essex earth had bucked as if trying to shake off all its towns and villages; for twenty seconds, no more, a series of convulsions that paused once as if a breath were being drawn and then began again. Out in the estuaries of the Colne and the Blackwater, the sea had gathered into foaming waves which ransacked the shore and reduced every vessel on the water to splinters. Langenhoe Church, known to be haunted, was shaken almost to bits, and the villages of Wivenhoe and Abberton were hardly more than rubble. They felt it over in Belgium, where teacups were knocked from the table; here in Essex a boy left sleeping in a cot beneath the table was crushed by falling mortar, and a man cleaning the face of the town hall clock was knocked from a ladder and his arm broke clean off. Over in Maldon they thought someone had set dynamite to terrorise the town and ran screaming in the streets, and Virley Church was beyond repair and had no congregants but foxes, no pews but beds of nettle. In the orchards the apple trees lost their blossom and grew no fruit that year.

Come to think of it, thought Cora, she did recall the headlines, which had been a touch amused (to think that modest little Essex, with barely a pleat in its landscape, should have shuddered and broken!). 'Extraordinary!' she said, delighted: 'It's all Paleozoic rock under our feet, this part of the world: to think of it, laid down five hundred million years before, shrugging its shoulders and bringing down the steeples on the churches!'

'I don't know about that,' said Taylor, exchanging a glance with Martha which had in it a degree of understanding. 'At any rate, Colchester did badly, as you see, though no lives lost.' He gestured again with his thumb to the gaping ruin, and said 'If you're minded to go in step careful, and keep your eyes skinned for my legs, on account of them being not fifteen yards away.' He tugged at the fabric of his trousers, and tucked the empty cloth closer; Cora, whose pity was very near the surface, bent and with a hand on his shoulder said: 'I'm so sorry to have been the cause of your remembering – though probably you never forget it, and I'm sorry for that, too.' She reached for her purse, wondering how to convey that it was not done in the spirit of alms, but of payment.

'Well now,' said Taylor, taking a coin, and managing to do so with the air of having done her a favour, 'There's more!' The lecturer's manner departed, and he took on the appearance of a showman. 'I daresay you've heard tell of the Essex Serpent, which once was the terror of Henham and Wormingford, and has been seen again?' Delighted, Cora said that she had not. 'Ah,' said Taylor, growing mournful, 'I wonder if I ought not to trouble you, what with ladies being of a fragile disposition.' He eyed his visitor, and evidently concluded that no woman in such a coat could be frightened by mere monsters. 'So then: in 1669 it was, with the son of the traitor king on the throne, a man could scarcely walk a mile before coming up against a warning pinned to an oak or a gatepost. STRANGE NEWS, they'd say, of a monstrous serpent with eyes like a sheep, come out of the Essex waters and up to the birch woods and commons!' He buffed the coin to brightness on his sleeve. 'Those were the years of the Essex Serpent, be it scale and sinew, or wood and canvas, or little but the ravings of madmen; children were kept from the banks of the river and fishermen wished for a better trade! Then it was gone as soon as it came, and for nigh on two hundred years we had neither hide nor hair of it 'til the quake came and something was shook loose down there under the water – something was set free! A great creeping thing, as they tell it, more dragon than serpent, as content on land as in water, that suns its wings on a fair day. The first man as saw it up by Point Clear lost his reason and never found it again and died in the asylum not six months back, leaving behind a dozen drawings he made with bits of charcoal from the grate . . .'

'Strange news!' said Cora. 'And stranger things in heaven and earth . . . tell me: was any picture ever taken of it – did anyone think to make a report?'

'None that I know of.' He shrugged. 'Can't say as I put much store on it myself. Essex folk are over-keen on this sort of thing, what with the Chelmsford witches, and Black Shuck doing the rounds when he's tired of Suffolk flesh.' He surveyed them a while, and appeared to grow suddenly weary of their company. He put the coin in his pocket, and patted it twice. 'Well then, I've made my living today, and more besides, and I'll be fetched home soon to a good meal. Besides' – he looked wryly at Martha, whose impatience shivered in the spokes of her umbrella – 'I think you'd best be off wherever you're going, though mind the cracks in the pavements, as my daughter'd tell you, since you never know what's between.' He waved them away with a grand gesture that would have sat well on a statesman dismissing a secretary, and hearing a young couple laughing through the wet air turned away and assembled his expression of pleading.

'Somewhere in there,' said Cora, returning to Martha's side, 'All in the rubble and dust, there's a pair of his shoes and probably the bones of the legs he's lost . . .'

'I don't believe a word of it: look, the lights are coming on, and it's past five. We should get back and see to Frankie.' This was true: they'd left Francis in bed, wrapped tight and rigid as a mummy, tended to by a landlord who'd raised three sons of his own and thought Cora's a docile thing whose cold could be drowned by soup. Francis, wrong-footed to encounter a man who viewed him not only without suspicion but barely with any interest, had consented to a brusque kindliness his mother could never have provided. He'd been seen to give the landlord one of his treasures (a piece of iron pyrite which he half-hoped would be mistaken for gold), and had taken to reading Sherlock Holmes stories. Cora wondered how it was possible to feel anxious for her son (when ill his face grew luminous and girlish and broke her heart) yet relieved at their enforced separation. Living in those two small rooms had brought all his little rituals to her door, and his indifference to her anger or warmth could not be ignored; her day of freedom by the castle keep and the bare willows down by the River Colne had been a delight, and she was loath to end it. Martha, who had a trick of voicing Cora's thoughts even before they'd formed, said: 'But look, your coat's dragging in puddles and your hair's wet through: let's find a cafe and wait for the rain to pass.' She nodded towards a dripping awning beneath which a pair of windows bulged with cakes.

Cora said, tentatively: 'Besides, he'll be sleeping by now, don't you think? And he's so cross when he's woken . . .' Complicit, they headed across wet pavements made bright by a low sun, and had reached the awning's shade when Cora heard a familiar voice.

'Mrs Seaborne, I declare!' She peered into the dim street and said, 'Has someone seen us?'

Martha, resentful of further intruders on their time, tugged at the strap of her bag. 'Who can know you here? We've been here less than a week: can't you ever just be overlooked?'

The voice came again – 'Cora Seaborne, as I live and breathe and have my being!' – and with a cry of delight she plunged onto the pavement and raised her arm. 'Charles! Come over! Come over and see me!' Coming towards her beneath a pair of umbrellas so large they commandeered the street, Charles and Katherine Ambrose were an unlikely sight. Once a colleague of Michael Seaborne – undertaking one of the many Whitehall roles Cora was never able to fathom, and which seemed to entail twice the politician's power with none of the responsibility – Charles had become a regular feature of Foulis Street life. The brightness of his waistcoats, and his insatiable appetite for all things, shielded a shrewdness which went undetected by most; that Cora had picked it out on first meeting had made him more or less her slave. Perhaps surprisingly, he was entirely devoted to his wife, who was diminutive where he was large, and who found him ceaselessly amusing. The pair of them were generous, benevolent, and interested in the lives of others; when they'd insisted that no doctor but Garrett would do for the ailing Seaborne, it had seemed impossible to refuse.

Cora gave her companion's waist a mollifying squeeze. 'You know I'd rather it was just you and me and our books. But it's Charles and Katherine Ambrose: you met them, and liked them – no: really, you did! – *Charles!*' Cora made a deep ironic curtsey, which might have been elegant if the toe she extended hadn't been concealed in a man's boot mottled with mud. 'You know Martha, of course?' Beside her, Martha unfurled to her full height and gave an unwelcoming nod. 'And Katherine, too – I'd no idea you knew England extended past Palmer's Green: are you lost? Can I lend you my map?' Charles Ambrose looked with disgust at the muddy boot, and the Harris tweed coat which was cut too broad across the shoulders, and the strong hands with their bitten nails.

'I would tell you it's a pleasure to see you, though I never saw

anyone look more like a barbarian queen bent on pillage: is it
necessary to emulate the Iceni just because you're on their turf?'
Cora – who refused to wear anything that might restrict her waist,
who'd raked her hands through her hair and stuffed it into a hat,
who hadn't worn jewellery since she tugged the pearls from her
ears a month before – was not offended. 'Boudicca would be
ashamed to be seen like this, I'm sure. Shall we go in, and have
coffee, and wait for the clouds to break? You're pretty enough
for the pair of us.' She tucked her hand in the crook of Katherine
Ambrose's elbow, and they winked at each other, and watched
Charles's velvet back make an impressive entrance into the cafe.

'But how, actually, *are* you, Cora?' Katherine paused at the
threshold, and taking the younger woman's face between her palms,
turned it to the light. She surveyed the high-boned face, and the eyes
which were like slate. Cora didn't answer, because she was afraid to
betray her shameful happiness. Katherine, who'd suspected more of
Michael Seaborne's dealings with his wife than Cora ever guessed,
found her answer, and stood on tip-toe to plant a kiss on her temple.
Behind them, Martha feigned a cough; Cora turned, stooped to
pick up her canvas holdall, and whispering 'Just another half-hour,
I *promise* . . .' hustled her companion inside.

'Well: what *are* you doing here? I associate you both so much
with Whitehall and Kensington that I supposed I imagined you
evaporating at the borders of town!' Cora surveyed the table with
satisfaction. Charles commanded an awestruck girl in a white
apron to bring at least a dozen of the cakes she personally liked
best, and a gallon of tea. She evidently favoured coconut: there
were macaroons, and speckled shortbread, and lozenges of cake
doused in raspberry jam and rolled in coconut flakes. Cora, who'd
walked several miles that morning, placidly ate her way towards a
centrepiece of madeleines.

'Yes,' said Martha, with a glint of steel she intended to be seen: 'What *are* you doing here?'

'Visiting friends,' said Katherine Ambrose. She shrugged neatly out of her little coat, and gazed about the dim, fragrant interior with an air of wonder. Something in the green tasselled cloth that fell into their laps evidently amused her; she fondled it, suppressed a smile, and said: 'Why else would anyone come? There's no shopping to be done, not one department store. Where do the locals get their wine and cheese?'

'The vineyard and the cowshed, I imagine.' Charles handed his wife a plate on which he had set a small cake vivid with icing. She'd never been seen to eat cake, but he liked now and then to play the tempter. 'We're trying to persuade Colonel Howard to stand for Parliament next election. He's due to retire, and . . .'

'. . . and is *Really Good News*,' finished Cora, serving Charles one of his own well-worn phrases. Beside her, Martha had grown a little tense, possibly preparing for one of her diatribes on public health, or the need for housing reform. (Wrapped in a blue paper bag, tucked in the canvas holdall, was an American novel that described in the most approving terms a future utopia of communal city living. Martha had waited weeks for its English publication, and was impatient to get home and make a study of it.) Cora, though appreciative of her friend's tender conscience, was too weary to watch battle commence over the teacups. She added a madeleine to Katherine's plate, but it was pushed away and replaced with the map Martha had placed on the tablecloth.

'May I?' Katherine unfolded its pages until Colchester appeared in black-and-white, with sites of interest marked approvingly and illustrated with photographs. Cora had ringed the Castle Museum, and a tea-stain blotted the spire of St Nicholas.

'Yes,' said Katherine. 'We thought we'd get to the Colonel

before the *others* do: he's made no secret of his ambitions, but never lets on in which direction they lie. I think Charles convinced him there'll be a change of government next election; says we must all lay money on it. The old boy's got the strength of a man half his age and is stubborn to boot: we might see the oldest Prime Minister yet.' It was not necessary for her to name Gladstone, who was to the Ambrose family a combination of eccentric saint and beloved relation. Cora had once met him – she standing rigid at her husband's side as his sharp-tipped fingers perforated the flesh on her upper arm, Gladstone a touch stooped as he greeted a procession of guests – and been startled by the savage intelligence blazing beneath eyebrows that cried out for a pair of scissors. It had been evident, from the ice that had entered his voice as he greeted Michael Seaborne, that the statesman had loathed her husband with an implacable hatred, and though Gladstone's greeting to her had been correspondingly chill, she had always felt, in the years that followed, as if he were an ally.

Martha said, 'Still gadding about with hookers, is he?' doing her best to disgrace herself; but Charles was beneath being shocked and grinned over the rim of his teacup.

Hastily Katherine said: 'So much for us – but what are you doing in Colchester, Cora? If you wanted the sea you could have used our house in Kent: here it's little but mud and marsh for miles and the sight of it would depress a clown. Unless you've got it in your head to search the garrison for a new husband, I can't see the appeal.'

'Let me show you.' Cora drew the map towards her, and with a forefinger which Katherine observed was none too clean, traced a line south from Colchester towards the mouth of the River Blackwater. 'Last month two men were walking at the foot of the Mersea cliffs and were almost knocked out by a landslip. They had the wit to take a look at the rubble and found fossil remains – a few teeth here and there, the usual coprolites, of course – but also a small mammal of some kind. It's been taken up to the British Museum for classification: who knows what new species they might have discovered!'

Charles looked warily at the map. For all his liberality and his determined attempts at worldliness, he was at heart profoundly conservative and would not keep the works of Darwin or Lyell in his study for fear they carried a contagion that might spread throughout his healthier books. He was not an especially devout man, but felt that a common faith overlooked by a benevolent God was what kept the fabric of society from tearing like a worn sheet. The idea that after all there was no essential nobility in mankind, and that his own species was not a chosen people touched by the divine, troubled him in the hours before dawn; and as with most troubling matters he elected to ignore it, until it went away. What's more, he blamed himself for Cora's adoration for the geologist Mary Anning: she'd never shown the least interest in grubbing about among rocks and mud until finding herself at an Ambrose dinner party seated beside an elderly man who'd spoken with Anning once and been in love with her memory ever since. By the time Cora had heard his tales of the carpenter's daughter who grew strong after a lightning strike, and of her first fossil find at twelve, and her poverty, and her martyrdom to cancer, she too was in love and for months afterwards talked of nothing but blue lias and bezoar stones. If anyone had hoped her passion would dwindle they did not, Charles thought wearily, know Cora.

Eyeing the last of the macaroons, he said: 'Surely it's best left to the experts, by now: we're not in the dark ages, reliant on crackpots in petticoats crawling about with a tack-hammer and paintbrush. There are colleges and societies and grants, and so on.'

'Well? What d'you expect me to do? Sit at home planning supper and waiting for a new pair of shoes to arrive?' Cora's temper, which burned slow, made itself seen first in a hardening of her grey eyes to flint.

'Of course not!' Thinking he detected an edge to her look, Charles said: 'No-one who knows you would expect that. But there are things that matter *now* that could use your time and your mind, not scraps of animals that meant nothing while living and less when dead!' As evidence of his desperation he gestured towards Martha. 'Could you not join Martha's society – whatever it's called – and sort out the plumbing in Whitechapel, or the orphans in Peckham, or whatever it is she goes in for these days?'

'Yes, Cora. Couldn't you?' Grinning at Charles, knowing that he disapproved as much of her political conscience as of Cora's muddy boots, Martha made her blue eyes into pools of appeal.

'Meant *nothing*!' Cora drew a breath to deliver a well-rehearsed speech on the significance of her beloved scraps of animals, but Katherine placed a cool white hand on hers and said, as if oblivious to the past few minutes: 'And you intend to make your way there and find a beast of your own?'

'I do! And I will: you'll see! Michael never' – at the name she faltered, and unconsciously touched the scar at her neck – 'He thought it a waste of time, and that I'd be better off reading *The Lady* to see what shape skirt I ought to wear to the Savoy.' She thrust her plate away in disgust. 'Well: I can do what I like now, can't I?' She eyed each of them in turn, and Katherine said: 'Darling child, of course you can: and we are very proud of you. Aren't we, Charles?' There came a humble nod. 'And what's more, we can help: I know just the family for you!'

'Do we?' Charles looked dubious. His only friend in Colchester was the choleric Colonel Howard, and he felt certain that the sight of Cora might deliver the final blow to his battle-battered health.

'Charles! The Ransomes! Those gorgeous children and that awful house, and Stella with her dahlias!'

The Ransomes! Charles brightened at the thought. William Ransome was the disappointing brother of a Liberal MP of whom the Ambroses were fond. Disappointing, because at an early age he'd decided to hitch his considerable intellect not to the law or to Parliament, or even to the service of medicine, but to the church. What was worse, the natural ambition that generally accompanies a good mind was so lacking he'd consented to spend the past fifteen years shepherding his small flock in a bleak village down by the Blackwater estuary, marrying a fair-haired sprite and doting on his children. Charles and Katherine had stayed there once after a journey to Harwich had gone awry and come away devoted to the Ransome brood, Katherine clutching a paper packet of dahlia seeds which promised to produce black blooms. She turned to Cora.

'I tell you, you never saw a more perfect family. The good Reverend Ransome and little Stella, no bigger than a fairy and twice as pretty. They live down at Aldwinter, which is almost as bad as it sounds – but on a bright night you can see right across to Point Clear, and in the mornings watch the Thames Barges off with their cargo of oysters and wheat. If anyone could show you your way round the coast there, it's them – don't look at me like that, dear, you know perfectly well you can't go trudging off with nothing but a map.'

'It is a foreign shore, mind: you may require a phrasebook. There are kissing-gates and croats, and acres of tidal land they call the saltings.' Charles licked sugar from his forefinger, and contemplated another pastry. 'Will once walked me through Aldwinter churchyard and showed me the graves they call broken-backed: the villagers reckon if you die of TB the earth sinks down into the coffin.'

Cora attempted to conquer her scowl. Some bull-necked country curate all Calvin and correction, and his parsimonious wife! She could not, off-hand, think of anything worse, and inferred from Martha's rigidity at her side that her feelings were shared. But still – it would be useful to have some local knowledge of Essex geography. What's more, it was not necessarily the case that a man of the cloth would be ignorant of modern science: among her favourite books was a thesis from an anonymous Essex rector on the high antiquity of the earth, which crisply dispensed with notions of calculating the date of creation from Old Testament genealogies.

She said, tentatively, 'Perhaps it would be good for Francis. I spoke to Luke Garrett about him, you know. Not that I think there is anything wrong with him!' She flushed, because nothing shamed her as much as her son. Acutely aware that her unease in the presence of Francis was shared by most who met him, it was impossible to exculpate herself; his remoteness, his obsessions, must be her fault, for where else could she lay the blame? Garrett had been uncharacteristically quiet, soft-spoken; he'd said, 'You cannot pathologise him – you cannot attempt to make a diagnosis. There is no blood test for eccentricity, no objective measure for your love or his!' Perhaps, he conceded, he might benefit from analysis, though it was hardly recommended for children, whose consciousness was barely formed. There was little she could do but continue to watch over him, as best she could; to love him, as far as he would let her.

The Ambroses shared a glance, and Katherine said hastily: 'Fresh air would be the best thing for him, I should think. Won't you let Charles write to the Reverend, and make an introduction?

Aldwinter's barely fifteen miles from here – I've known you walk further! – and you could at least spend an afternoon there, and let Stella give you tea.'

'I'll write to William, and give him your address – you're staying at the George, I assume? You'll all make fast friends, I'm sure, and find piles of your wretched fossils.'

'We're staying at the Red Lion,' said Martha. 'Cora thought it looked authentic, and was disappointed not to find straw on the floor and a goat tethered to the bar.' *Reverend Ransome*, she thought, scornfully: as if some slow-witted parson and his fat-cheeked children could interest her Cora! But kindness shown to her friend always earned her loyalty, and so she tipped the last of the cakes onto Charles's plate and said quite sincerely: 'I've so enjoyed seeing you again: d'you think you might come back to Essex soon, before we go?'

'Probably.' He took on an air of noble suffering. 'And by then we expect a whole new species to be discovered and anatomised, and ready for the Seaborne Wing at Castle Museum.' With a little gesture to his wife that signalled they should depart, he reached for his coat, and then with an arm arrested mid-sleeve said 'Oh!' and turned grinning to Cora. 'How could we forget! Have you heard of this strange beast that's been putting the fear of all the gods into the local populace?'

Katherine laughing said: 'Charles, don't tease: it's just some game of Chinese whispers that went a little too far.'

Struggling with his jacket, Ambrose ignored his wife. 'Now here's a mystery of science for you – put that appalling hat down and listen! Three hundred years ago or thereabouts a dragon took up residence in Henham, twenty miles north-west of here. Ask at the library and they'll show you the leaflets they nailed up round the town: eye-witness accounts from farmers, and a picture of some kind of leviathan with wings of leather and a toothy grin. It used to lie about basking in the sunshine and snapping its beak (its *beak*, mind you!), and no-one thought much of it until a boy got his leg broken. It vanished soon after, but the rumours never did. Every time crops failed or the sun eclipsed, or there was a plague of toads, someone somewhere would see the beast down on the riverbank, or lurking on the village green. And listen: *it's back*!' Charles looked triumphant, as if he'd personally spawned the beast for her benefit, so that Cora regretted diminishing his delight by saying, 'Oh Charles, I know – I heard! We've just been treated to a lecture on the Essex Earthquake – haven't we, Martha? – and how it shook something loose out there in the estuary. It's all I can do to prevent myself from heading there now with notebook and camera and seeing it for myself!'

Katherine consoled her husband with a kiss, and said placidly, 'Stella Ransome wrote and told us all about it. On New Year's Day a local man was washed up on the Aldwinter saltings with his neck broken. Drunk, I should think, and got caught in the tide, but the whole village is up in arms. There've been several sightings just off the coast, and someone swore they saw it moving up the Blackwater at midnight with murder in its eyes. There, Charles, you were right: did you ever see anyone so excited?'

Cora shifted like a child in her seat, and pulled at a lock of hair. 'Just like Mary Anning's sea-dragon, all those years ago! Every six months a paper's published setting out ways and places extinct animals might still live on – imagine, just imagine, if we were to encounter one in so dull a place as Essex! And imagine what it might mean: further evidence that it's an ancient world we live in, that our debt is to natural progression, not some divinity –'

'Well: I don't know about that,' said Charles, 'But it will interest you, no doubt. And if you visit Aldwinter you must ask the

Ransomes to show you their very own Essex serpent: one of the pews in the parish church has a winged snake making its way up the arm-rest, though since the latest sightings the good rector has been threatening to take it off with a chisel.'

'That settles it,' said Cora. 'Write your letters, as many as you like: we'll suffer the attentions of a hundred parsons for the sake of one sea-dragon, won't we, Martha?' Leaving Charles to attend to the bill, and dispense the immense tips with which he salved his conscience, the women stepped out onto the High Street. The rain had receded and the declining sun sent the shadow of St Nicholas across their path. Katherine gestured across to the broad white façade of her hotel. 'I'll go upstairs right away and find some headed paper, and warn them you'll bring trouble, with your London ideas and your disgraceful coat.' She plucked at Cora's sleeve, and said: 'Martha, can't you do anything about this?'

Since half her pleasure in adopting such a ramshackle appearance lay in her friends' disgust, Cora turned up her collar against the wind, tilted her hat like a boy, and stuck her thumbs in her belt. 'The wonderful thing about being a widow is that, really, you're not obliged to be much of a woman anymore – but here comes Charles, and I can tell by that look he's in need of his evening drink. Thank you, *dear* both.' She kissed them, and pressed Katherine's hand much too hard. She'd have liked to say more, and explain that her years of marriage had so degraded her expectation of happiness that to sit cradling a teacup with no thought for what waited behind the curtains on Foulis Street seemed little short of miraculous. Smiling a farewell, she stepped briskly across the road towards the Red Lion, wondering if it was Francis's face she saw at the window, and whether he might be pleased to see her.

20th February

My Dear Will,

I trust you are all in good health, and hope it won't be long before we see you again. Katherine asks me to tell Stella that her dahlias did very well, but turned out blue rather than black – perhaps it was the soil?

I am writing in order to introduce to you a very great friend of ours, who I think would benefit from meeting you both. She is the widow of Michael Seaborne, who died early this year (you might recall having kindly prayed for his return to good health, but the Almighty's will evidently lay elsewhere).

We've known Mrs Seaborne for many years. She is an unusual woman. I think of her as having an exceptional – really I might even say a masculine! – intelligence: she is something of a naturalist, which Katherine tells me is the latest fashion among society women. It seems harmless enough, and seems to bring her pleasure after a time of great sadness.

She has recently come to Essex together with her son and companion in order to study the coastline there (something about fossil bird remains at Walton-on-the-Naze, I believe), and has been staying in Colchester. Of course I told her about the legend of the Essex Serpent and the rumours of its return, and about the curious carving in All Saints church, and she was most intrigued, and plans to visit.

If she comes to Aldwinter (and knowing Cora, she will be already planning her journey!) perhaps you and Stella could make her welcome? She has given me permission to supply details of her current address, which I enclose here together with our good wishes, as ever —

Yours faithfully,

CHARLES HENRY AMBROSE

3

The Reverend William Ransome, Rector of Aldwinter Parish, returned the letter to its envelope and propped it thoughtfully on the windowsill. He could never think of Charles Ambrose without a smile – the man had a limitless appetite for making friends, often (though certainly not always) out of genuine affection, and it was not at all surprising that he should have taken so fondly to a widow – but despite the smile the letter unsettled him. It was not precisely that newcomers were unwelcome, but one or two phrases (*society women ... masculine intelligence ...*) were calculated to trouble any diligent minister of the church. He could picture her as precisely as if her photograph had been included in the envelope: entering the lonely final stages of life bolstered by yards of taffeta and a half-baked enthusiasm for the new sciences. Her son was doubtless down from Oxford or Cambridge, and would bring with him some secret vice which would either thrill Colchester, or make him completely unsuited to civilised company. She probably lived on a diet of boiled potatoes and vinegar, hoping Byron's diet might improve her silhouette, and would almost certainly have Anglo-Catholic tendencies, and deplore the absence of an ornate cross on the All Saints altar. In the space of five minutes he furnished her with an obnoxious lap-dog, a toadying companion with no flesh on her bones, and a squint.

His sole consolation was that Aldwinter was so resolutely unpicturesque a destination that he couldn't imagine a society woman – even a bored and meddlesome widow – troubling to visit. Each spring a few ardent naturalists arrived to document the handful of seabirds that passed through the salt-marshes, but even these tended to be the drabbest species imaginable, their muddy feathers so indistinguishable from their surroundings they often passed without notice. Aldwinter had only one inn and two stores, and though its village green was occasionally considered the longest, if not the largest, in Essex, there was very little to recommend it even to its own inhabitants. Aside from the church's curiosities – which were in truth a minor embarrassment to each successive incumbent – the only item of interest within five miles was the blackened hull of a clipper which could be seen when the Blackwater estuary lay at low tide, and which the village children decorated each harvest in a kind of pagan rite of which he dutifully disapproved. The train line terminated seven miles to the west, so that the farmers still relied on barges to carry oats and barley to the mills at St Osyth, and onward to London for sale. Perhaps the best that could be said for Aldwinter was that if it was neither wealthy nor beautiful, it was at least not particularly poor. It was not in the Essex character to succumb miserably to change and decay, and when John Barleycorn came under threat from cheap imports one or two tenant farmers had tried their hand at caraway and coriander, and shared the hire cost of a threshing-engine which not only increased their output to a startling degree, but gave the entire village a festive air as the children gathered to marvel at its size, its thunderous voice, and its gusts of steam.

Will felt an ill temper settle on him, and resisting the urge to toss the envelope onto the fire hid it behind a sheet of paper presented to him that morning by John, the youngest of his boys. It was a drawing which might've been of an alligator which had acquired a set of wings, but might equally have been a greatly enlarged caterpillar eating a moth. His mother was convinced it was the latest demonstration of his genius, but Will was unconvinced: he remembered his own childhood spent filling notebooks with engines and devices so complex he'd clean forget their purpose from one page to the next, but what had come of that?

And it was not only the threat of a probably harmless widow that dampened his mood, but the trouble that had lately settled on the parish. He surveyed John's drawing, and this time took it for a winged sea-dragon approaching the village. Since the discovery on New Year's morning of a drowned man down on the Blackwater marshes – naked, his head turned almost 180 degrees, a look of dread in his wide-open eyes – the Essex Serpent had ceased to be merely a device to keep children in check, and had begun to stalk the streets. On Friday nights in the White Hare drinkers claimed to have seen it, children playing on the saltings needed no urging to come home before dark, and no amount of reasoning on Will's part could persuade them the drowned man was a victim of nothing more than drink and the tides.

He resolved to shake himself into a better frame of mind by walking a circuit of the parish – looking up a few folk as he went, quelling rumours of a sea-dragon wherever they arose. He took up his hat and coat, and there was whispering at the study door (the children were forbidden entry, but were not above trying the handle); he bellowed threats of bread-and-water for a fortnight, and made his habitual escape through the window.

Aldwinter that day was aptly named: frost lay on the hard earth, and black oaks clutched the pale sky. Will thrust his hands into his pockets, and set out. The red brick house behind had been new the day he'd first crossed the threshold, Stella coming slowly up the tiled pathway with her swollen belly cradled in her hands, and Joanna bringing up the rear trailing an invisible pet (species never established) on a length of string. Bay windows on both floors gave the impression of shallow turrets on either side of the front door, above which a fanlight in coloured glass caught an hour of light each afternoon. The largest house on the single street which passed through the village, leading south from Colchester and terminating at the small dock where a single barge now lay at anchor, it had a bright hard look entirely out of keeping with the rest of the village. He never thought there was much to recommend it save good insulation and a garden large enough to lose the children for hours at a stretch, but knew himself blessed: at least one of his peers endured a house which seemed to be sinking into the ground, and in which fungus the size of a man's hand grew in the upper corners of the dining room.

Coming onto the street they called High Lane in deference to its slight elevation above sea level, Will bore left where it passed through common ground. A few sheep grazed listlessly under the Aldwinter oak, said to have once sheltered troops loyal to the traitor Charles, and which appeared so black it might have been burned to charcoal. Its lower branches had sunk beneath their own weight, and curving down thrust into the earth and after a while up again, so that in the spring the tree appeared surrounded by saplings. The down-curved branches formed seats where in summer lovers sat, and as Will passed a woman spread her red skirts and tossed out a few scraps for the birds. Beyond the oak, set back from the road behind a mossy wall, All Saints with its modest tower made its usual call on him: he ought, really, to sit there awhile on a bare cold pew and wait for a cooling of his temper, but someone might be waiting in the shadows for blessing or censure. In the year past, with the coming of the Essex Serpent (which he took to calling 'the Trouble', reluctant to christen a rumour), claims on his time had grown steadily greater. There was a feeling – mostly unspoken, at least in his presence – that they were all under judgment, doubtless well-deserved, from which only he could deliver them; but what comfort could he offer which would not also affirm their sudden fear? He could not do it, any more than he could say to John, who so often woke at night, *you and I will go together at midnight and slay the creature that lives under your bed*. What was built on deceit, however kindly done, would not withstand the first blow. And time enough for pulpit and pew tomorrow, when the sun rose on the Lord's Day; for now he felt such an urgent desire to look out on the saltings and fill his self with the empty air that he almost ran.

On past the White Hare ('My dear Mansfield, impossible for a man of the cloth, as I think you know!') and past the neat small cottages with cyclamen on the windowsill ('She's very well thank you: the 'flu has gone, praise God …') to the place where High Lane sloped down to the quay. Hardly that, of course, simply an inlet on the Blackwater bolstered with stonework that only ever seemed to last a season and was re-made each spring out of whatever fell to hand. Henry Banks, who racketed up and down the estuary in his barge, conveying who-knew-what to who-knew-where beneath his sacks of corn and barley, sat cross-legged on the deck mending his sails, his cold hands livid as the cloth. Seeing Will, he beckoned him over, saying 'Still no sign of her, Reverend: still no sign,' pulling dolefully at a hipflask. Some months had passed since Banks had lost a rowing-boat, and been refused his insurance on the grounds that he'd failed to make it fast to the quay, being probably drunk at the time. Banks felt the grievance deeply, and told anyone who'd listen that it had been stolen away in the night by oystermen from over Mersea way, and that he'd always been a truthful man, as Gracie would've witnessed, had she still been living, God rest her. 'No? I'm sorry for it, Banks,' said Will sincerely: 'Nothing's harder to bear than injustice. I'll keep a lookout, mind.' He refused a nip of rum, gesturing ruefully at his collar, and moved on – past the quay, the low water always to his right, where up ahead on a slight incline a row of bare ash trees were like so many grey feathers stuck in the ground. Beyond the ashes was the last Aldwinter house, which for as long as he could remember they'd called World's End. Its bowed walls were bound together with moss and lichen, and over the years it had been added to so that by degrees of lean-to and annex it had doubled in size, and seemed a living thing feasting on the hard earth. The portion of land around it was fenced off on three sides; the fourth gave directly onto the grasses of the salt-marsh, and from there down to the pale stretch of mud riddled with creeks that glistened in the weak sun.

As Will approached World's End, its sole resident was so nearly camouflaged against the walls of the house that when he emerged it was as if by a charm. Mr Cracknell seemed made of the same stuff as his home: his coat green as moss and quite as damp, and his beard reddish as the clay tiles that fell from the roof. He held in his right hand the small grey body of a mole, and in his left a folded knife. 'Stand back a little, Reverend, for the good of your coat,' he said, and Will obeyed, seeing that strung all along the fence were a dozen moles or more; but these were skinned, and their hides hung from their hindquarters like a shadow. Their pale paws, so like the hands of children, reached blindly for the earth. Will inspected the body nearest. 'Quite a haul; and a penny apiece?' Man's dominion over animals notwithstanding, he'd never been able to shake a fondness for the little gentlemen in their velvet jackets, and wished the farmers' war of attrition could be ended by kinder means.

'A penny apiece, that's right, and warm work besides.' He laid the creature out, and deftly cut a loop at wrist and ankle.

'Twenty years an Aldwinter man, and still your customs surprise me. Is there no better way of keeping moles from the crops than by scaring them off with their slaughtered brethren?'

Cracknell frowned. 'Oh, I've a purpose in mind, Parson; you know that: you see I have a purpose in mind!' Delighted, the man slipped a forefinger between flesh and skin and tested the ease with which he could part them. 'I am aware that in *some quarters* I am considered not as they say the full shilling, not that I've lately seen a shilling, being content with such pence as might now and then come my way' – and here a pause, and a direct glance at Will's pockets, then down again to the task at hand – 'And yet there you stand, God's own man, and ask if I have a purpose!'

'I felt it,' said Will, gravely, 'as if by instinct.' The tearing of skin from flesh was like that of paper. Cracknell lifted his handiwork, inspecting it, well pleased with his skill; a ribbon of steam unfurled from the hot bare body in the cold air.

'Scaring them off, *oh* yes –' his jovial mood fractured, he busied himself with a length of wire, which he ran through the animal's pink nose, nostril to nostril, and looped three times around the fencepost. 'Scaring them off, says he! Though of what I might be scaring off there mightn't be knowing now nor later I daresay, when a voice is heard of weeping and lamentation for our children, because they are not, and we will not be comforted ...' His hand on the wire trembled a little, and Will was appalled to see that so also did his lower lip. His first impulse, which came as much from training as from instinct, was to offer a word of comfort – but hard on its heels came a flash of irritation. So the old man too had succumbed to whatever trick of the light had the whole village taken in! He thought of his daughter running home weeping in terror at what might be creeping upriver towards them, and of notes slipped in the collection box urging he preach repentance of whatever sins had brought judgment to their door.

'Mr Cracknell' – briskly, with a little humour perhaps; let him see that there was nothing to fear but a long winter and a tardy spring – 'Mr Cracknell, I may not quite be episcopal material, but I know misquoted scripture when I hear it. Our children are in no more danger now than they have ever been! Where are your wits? What have you done with them?' Reaching out, he made a show of patting the other man's pockets. 'You don't mean to tell me you've strung up these poor beasts to fend off some – some rumoured sea-serpent in the Blackwater!'

Cracknell was coaxed into a smile. 'Gentlemanly of you to allude to my wits at all, Parson, on account of the general disbelief that I ever was in possession of such a thing as wits.' He patted the mole on its stripped back with a fond gesture. 'For all that, though, I do say and always have said that caution is the side best erred on; and if man or creature were minded to make their approaches here at World's End my little scarebeasts here would give them pause.' He jerked his thumb towards the rear of his dwelling, where a pair of tethered goats industriously cropped a circle of grass. 'I've Gog and Magog here for companionship, you understand, in addition to providing the milks and the cheeses which Mrs Ransome is so kind as to enjoy, and I'll not risk their loss! Not I! I'll not be left alone!' There was the trembling again, but here Will felt on firmer ground: three times in three years he'd stood with Cracknell at the graveside: first wife, then sister, then son.

He clasped the old man by the shoulder: 'Nor shall you; I have my flock, and you have yours, and the same Shepherd has their care.'

'That's as maybe, and I thank you for it; but I'll not be darking your church door tomorrow all the same. I made my stand,

Parson: take Mrs Cracknell and the Almighty will have to make do without me, you recall were my words; and I'll not be dissuaded come high or low water.'

He wore now the mulish expression of a stubborn child, which was so greatly preferable to the threat of tears that it took Will an effort not to laugh, and instead to say, quite gravely, and conscious of the cost of a bargain struck with God: 'You made your stand, and I've no right to come between a man and his word.'

Out on the saltings water crept towards the house and the lowering sun was cold. Beyond the marsh Aldwinter's outlook was not of some other village on the far bank of the Blackwater, but of a broad horizon where the estuary met the North Sea. Will saw the lights of a fishing vessel headed home, and thought of Stella – tired by now, her small hands busy with the children – drawing back the curtain to look past Traitor's Oak and see him coming. Longing for her, and for the sound of children at his study door, gave him a sudden distaste for the mossy house sinking into its patch of land; then he remembered Cracknell at the graveyard throwing a clod of earth onto a small pine coffin, and stood a while longer at the gate. 'A minute more, Reverend,' said Cracknell, 'I have something for you.' He was absorbed again into the side of the house, then emerged a moment later with a brace of handsome bright-eyed rabbits, newly caught, and thrust them at Will. 'With my compliments to Mrs Ransome, who needs her strength, on account of the child-bearing years, which as Mrs Cracknell said tends to a thinning of the blood.'

The pleasure of giving illuminated him, and Will took them graciously, feeling a restriction in his throat. Quite a pie they'd make, he said; and Johnny's favourite, as it happened – then, as if he wanted to give something in return, he hung the rabbits from his belt, in the farmer's fashion, and said: 'Mr Cracknell, tell me what you've seen, because I cannot think whom to believe, or when. A poor man drowned: but after all drowning's not so rare in winter. A sheep was gutted I'm told, but foxes must make their living too, and the child they said was lost overnight was found in the morning in a linen cupboard eating her mother's sweets. Banks brings strange news on his barge from St Osyth and Maldon, but you and I know him for a liar, do we not? Then there are whisperings in doorways and outside the Inn, and they say a baby was snatched from a boat at Point Clear, but whoever took an infant to sea when the days are short and cold? Tell me you have yourself witnessed something to fear, and then perhaps I'll believe it.' He fixed his gaze on the old man's eyes, which could not quite seem to meet his; they slid over his shoulder to the empty horizon behind.

Knowing the value of silence, Will refused to speak, and in a moment Cracknell – sighing, shrugging, busying himself with his knife – said, 'The point is not what I *see*, but what I *feel*; I cannot see the ether, yet I feel it enter and depart, and depend upon it. I *feel* that something is coming; sooner or later, my words be marked. It has been before, as well you know, and it will come again, if not in my lifetime in yours, or in your children's, or in your children's children's, and so I will gird my loins up, Parson, and if I might make bold a moment, I would recommend that you do similar.' Will thought of the church with its carved remnant of the old legend, and wished (not for the first time) that he'd taken hammer and chisel to it on the morning of his arrival.

'I have always put great store on you, Mr Cracknell, and will continue to do so; perhaps you can consider yourself the Aldwinter watchman, out here at World's End, and set a beacon in your garden for a warning. – The Lord make his face to shine upon you, whether you want it or not!' said Will, and on this light blessing turned and left for home.

He imagined himself walking just a little faster than the night, so that he might arrive at the door a moment before darkness. Cracknell's scarebeasts and his visible fear had given him pause, not because he thought some aberration lay waiting in the Blackwater biding its time, but because he felt it a failing of his that his parish could have succumbed to such godless superstition. No-one could agree on its size, form or origins, but there seemed a consensus that it favoured the river and the dawn. There had been no witness to any attack, but in the weeks since the end of summer the unseen thing had been blamed for every mislaid child and every broken limb. He'd even heard it said that its urine poisoned the water-pump down at Fettlewell, and caused the sickness which had left three dead on New Year's Eve. Resisting Stella's gentle suggestion that he speak directly from the pulpit, he'd instead chosen a brisk refusal to acknowledge the Trouble, not even when he discovered that each Sunday morning the congregation – with unspeaking unity – would not sit in the pew with the serpent carving, as if being near it put flesh and bones on their terror.

The night at his heels, he walked on, turning once to see the white moon rising with its marred face. The wind strengthened in the reeds, which gave out a single mournful note, and Will felt a quickening just behind his ribs that was very like fear, and laughed: there – how easy it was to turn your face from nothing more than a shadow. And perhaps it would be wise to make use of the Trouble, if it proved impossible to ignore – few things turned the heart to eternity more surely than fear. The Aldwinter lights appeared up ahead, and somewhere among them his family waited – their bodies solid, warm, soap-scented, each with the fine fair down on their cheeks he'd carried as a boy; wholly real, impossible to deny, never for a moment quiet or still, so that no shadow could contain them – and he felt such a rush of joy that he gave a quiet shout (and was it also one of warning or challenge, in case there was after all a wild dog loose?), and ran the half-mile home. John was waiting, standing one-footed on the gatepost in his white nightclothes. Seeing Will he roared, *'By the pricking of my thumbs!'* and buried his face in his father's coat. Feeling the rabbit fur on his neck, he said: 'You've done it! You've brought me a pet!'

Cora Seaborne
c/o The Red Lion Inn
Colchester

14*th* February

My dear Imp!

How are you? Are you keeping warm? Are you eating properly? How's your cut – have you healed? I'd've liked to have seen it. Did it go very deep? You must keep your scalpels sharp and your wits sharper. Oh dear: I do miss you!

We are well, and Martha sends her – oh, you won't believe that, will you? Francis doesn't send his love at all, but I don't think he'd mind seeing you again, if you were to come down, and that's as much as any of us can hope for. WILL you come down? It's cold, but the sea air is good, and Essex nowhere near as bad as they say.

I've been over to Walton-on-the-Naze and out to St Osyth and I haven't found my sea-dragon yet – not even a bit of crinoid sea-lily! – but you know I don't give in easily. The man who owns the hardware store here thinks me mad as a hatter, and has sold me two new hammers and a kind of suede belt to hang them from. Martha says I never looked odder or uglier, but you know I've always thought beauty a curse and am more than happy to dispense with it completely. Sometimes I forget that I'm a woman – at least – I forget to THINK OF MYSELF AS A WOMAN. All the obligations and comforts of womanhood seem to have nothing to do with me now. I'm not sure how I am supposed to behave and I'm not sure I would, if I knew.

Talking of distinguished: you'll never GUESS who accosted us in the High St just as we were looking for a civilised place to wait out *the rain? Charles Ambrose, looking just like a parrot in a flock of pigeons, bustling about in his velvet coat! He's adamant I need an Essex friend, to keep me from broken limbs out on the mudflats or worse (he tells me the River Blackwater is menaced by a beast, but I will tell you all about it when I see you next). He has threatened to put me in touch with some rural vicar, and though I'm half tempted to take him up on the offer purely for the pleasure of shocking whatever poor old fellow he has in mind, I really would rather be left to my own devices. WON'T YOU COME DOWN, DEAR? I miss you. I don't like to do without you. I don't see why I should.*

Love,

CORA

Luke Garrett MD
Pentonville Rd
N1

15th February

CORA –

Hand better, thanks. The infection was useful – I tested out my new Petri dishes and made some bacterial cultures. I thought you would have liked them. They were blue and green.

Coming down with Spencer probably next week. See you then. Hold off the rain if you can.

LUKE

PS: Technically, that was a Valentine. Don't deny it.

4

Five miles east of Colchester, Cora walked in fine rain. She'd set out with no destination in mind and no thought to how she'd come home, only wanting to get out of the cold room in the Red Lion where Francis had cut his pillow to retrieve and count the feathers. Neither she nor Martha had been able to explain why it was that he ought not to have done it ('Yes but you can pay for it, and then it will all be mine . . .'), and rather than listen to her son's patient totting up – *one hundred and seventy-three* as the door had closed – she'd belted up her coat and run downstairs. Martha heard her call 'I'll be home before it's dark – I have money with me – I'll find someone to bring me back,' and sighing had returned to the boy.

Colchester had dwindled behind her in a matter of half an hour, and she'd walked east, almost persuading herself she could reach the mouth of the Blackwater before she grew tired. She skirted around a village: she wanted neither to be seen nor spoken to, and favoured overgrown paths that ran along the rim of oakwoods. Traffic was sparse and slow, and no-one spared a glance for the woman walking on the verge. When the rain set in, she delved deeper between the trees, turning her face to the featureless sky. It was a uniform grey, without shifting of clouds or sudden blue breaks, and no sign at all of the sun: it was an unwritten sheet of paper, and against it the bare branches were black. It ought to have been dreary, but Cora saw only beauty – birches unfurled their strips of bark like lengths of white cloth, and under her feet wet leaves were slick. Everywhere bright moss had taken hold, in dense wads of green fur swaddling the trees at their foot, and fine pelts on broken branches that lay across the path. She tripped twice on brambles that held scraps of white wool and little feathers grey at the tip, and swore at them without malice.

It struck her that everything under that white sky was made of the same substance – not quite animal, but not merely earth: where branches had sheared from their trunks they left bright wounds, and she would not have been surprised to see severed stumps of oak and elm pulse as she passed. Laughing, she imagined herself part of it, and leaning against a trunk in earshot of a chattering thrush held up her arm, and wondered if she might see vivid green lichen stippling the skin between her fingers.

Had it always been here – this marvellous black earth in which she sank to her ankles, this coral-coloured fungus frilling the branches at her feet? Had birds always sung? Had the rain always this light touch, as if she might inhabit it? She supposed they had, and that it had never been very far from her door. She supposed there must have been other times when she'd laughed alone into the wet bark of a tree, or exclaimed to no-one over the fineness of a fern unfolding, but she could not remember them.

The past few weeks had not always been so happy. At times she remembered her grief, and for long stretches in which it was necessary to teach herself again how to draw breath she would feel a cavity open behind her ribs. It was a kind of draining sensation, as if a vital organ had been shared with the man who'd died and was atrophying slowly from misuse. In those cold minutes she would recall not the years of unease, in which she'd never once successfully judged his mood or circumnavigated the methods of his wounding, but their first few months, which were the last of her youth. Oh, she had loved him – no-one could ever have loved more: she'd been too young to withstand it, a child intoxicated by an inch of drink. He had been imprinted on her vision, as if she'd glanced at the sun and closing her eyes found a pinprick of light persisting in the darkness. He had been so sombre that when attempts at levity made him laugh she'd felt an empress in command of an army; he was so stern, and so remote, that the first moment he embraced her had been a battle won. She'd not known then that these were the common tricks of a common trickster, to cede a skirmish and later lay her waste. In the years that followed, her fear of him was so very like her love – attended by the same fast-paced heart, the same broken nights, the same alertness to his footstep in the hall – that she was drunk on that, too. No other man had touched her, and so she could not tell how strange it was to be subject to pain as much as pleasure. No other man had loved her, and so she could not judge whether the sudden withdrawal of his approval was natural as the tide and as implacable. By the time it occurred to her that she ought to divorce him, it was too late: at that stage Francis could not tolerate so much as an altered lunch-hour, and any change would have risked his health. Besides, the boy's presence – for all his troublesome rituals and inscrutable tempers – had given Cora the single sensation in life about which she felt no confusion at all: he was her son, and she knew her duty; she loved him, and sometimes suspected he loved her, too.

The scant wind paused, the oakwood held its tongue; Cora again was twenty, and her son was come bawling into the world with his fists clenched. They'd wanted to take him from her and swaddle him in white cloth; she'd roared, and wouldn't let them. He'd crawled blindly from belly to breast and sucked so strongly the midwife marvelled, and said what a good boy he was, and a clever one. Hours it had been, surely, of their gazes meeting, his eyes fixed intently on her, the dark hazy blue of evening; *I have an ally*, she thought: *he will never let me go*. Days passed, and she felt herself split down the middle, a wound that would never heal, and which she would never regret: because of him her heart would always be exposed to wind and weather. She worshipped him with many small acts of devotion, wondering at his marvellous foot, its skin like the thin silk covering of a cushion; she passed hours in stroking it with the tip of her finger and seeing how he spread his toes in delight – that he could take pleasure! That she could give it! His curled hand was a cockleshell warmed by the sun – she held it between her lips – she was astonished by him, that those small hands, those feet, contained such multitudes. But it had been only a matter of weeks before the blinds went down, the eyes (she sometimes thought) actually clouding over. If she nursed him, it appeared to cause him pain, or at least a rage he could not contain; if she held him he struggled, flailed, cut her eyelid with the sharp little nail on his thumb. Their days of adoration seemed remote, impossible – bewildered by this second rejection of her love she began to withhold it out of shame. Her failure was a source of amusement to Michael, who said that after all it was vulgar to be entertained by one's own children, and she'd best leave him to nurses and tutors. Years passed: she learned his ways, and he hers. If their relationship bore little resemblance to the careless warmth she witnessed between other mothers and their sons, it was serviceable enough, and it was theirs.

On she walked, and though the cold rain and the black earth ought to have dispirited her, she could not summon up her widow's grief. A kind of gurgling bubbled from her throat and came out in a shameless peal of laughter, which startled the silent birds into speech. She was ashamed of it, of course, but was used to feeling that she lived in a state of disgrace, and felt certain she'd concealed her growing happiness from everyone but Martha. At the thought of her friend (sitting scowling in a coffee-shop no doubt, to escape

Frankie's latest obsession, or passing the time by enchanting the proprietor of the Red Lion) the laugh subsided, and Cora lifted her arms up a little, imagining seeing her coming towards her under the dripping trees. At night they lay back to back under a thin quilt with knees drawn up against the cold, sometimes turning to murmur a fragment of remembered gossip or say *goodnight*, sometimes waking cradled in the crook of an arm. The simplicity of it had sustained Cora when everything else had sent her flying, and if Martha had been afraid that she'd be no longer needed now Cora stood on firmer ground, she'd been mistaken.

Coming to her eighth mile and growing tired, Cora found herself on a slight rise where the trees began to thin. The drizzle subsided, and cleared the air, and without any sunlight breaking through the low white canopy the world flushed with colour. Everywhere reddish banks of last year's bracken glowed, and above them gorse thickets burned with early blooms of yellow. A little aimless flock of sheep with purple ink splashed on their haunches looked up briefly from their grazing, and shrugging turned away. The path on which she stood was bright Essex clay, and a little further down the incline a fallen tree had been overtaken by a thick covering of vivid moss. The change of scene was like a change in altitude: it took her breath, and she paused for a moment to adjust herself to it. In the silence a curious sound reached her: it was a little like a child crying, but a child old enough to know better. She could not make out any words, only an odd choking, whinnying noise, which fell silent for moments at a time then started up again. Then another voice joined it, and it was the voice of a man – crooning, patient, deep – wordless also, though (she listened harder) not quite: *now . . . now . . . now . . .* After a pause – during which her heartbeat thrummed, although she later claimed she'd never been afraid – the man's voice set up again, only this time at a higher, rougher pitch; she could not quite divine the words, but thought in among the frantic urging was *Oh, damn you! Damn you!* Then there was the sound of something heavy striking something soft, and another choked little bray.

At this, she hitched up her coat, which was too long and had grown heavy with mud at the hem, and followed the sound. The clay path led over the slight rise and down again, between high pale green hedges on which twisted black seed-pods rattled as she passed. A little further down and she saw an acre of that russet bracken opening before her, with a few sheep nosing at the earth. To her left, overlooked by a bare oak, there was a shallow lake. Its water was thick with mud, and speckled with rain; no reeds grew, and there were no birds busy on the bank. It was entirely featureless, except that on the nearer bank a man stooped struggling over something pale, which made frantic movements and gave out another weak cry. The sound of it struck and sickened her, and there was something familiar in the wretched imploring movements it made, so that when she gathered pace and began to run what she had hoped would be an imperious 'Stop that! Stop!' came out as a shriek.

The man may have heard her, or he may not: he neither lifted his head, nor stopped whatever he was doing. His voice had lowered again to the curious deep crooning noise she first had heard, only now it seemed to her appalling that he should be so tender when he was causing so much harm. As she drew nearer, she saw his feet planted firmly in muddy water, and his back in a dark winter coat splashed with mud. Even from that distance she saw that he was shabby and rough-looking: everything about him was dirty, from the thick wet fabric of his clothes to the damp curls falling over his collar. If the old stories were right, she thought, and man had been first made from a handful of dust, here was Adam himself: all mud, ill-formed, without the full powers of speech. 'What are you *doing*? Stop!' At this he half-turned, and she saw that he was not much above medium height, and bulky. Smears of mud on his face gave the impression of a beard, and from the filth a pair of eyes blazed at her. He might have been sixty, or he might have been twenty. He had rolled his sleeves to his elbows, and his forearms were thickly corded with muscle, and as if deciding she'd neither help nor hinder he shrugged, and turned back to his task. Nothing infuriated Cora more than being ignored: she gave an exasperated cry and ran the few remaining yards. Reaching the water's rim she saw that the pale thing struggling beneath the man was a sheep dumbly struggling in the shallows, and she was rinsed with relief: whatever horror she'd imagined, it was not this.

The sheep rolled its stupid eyes at the newcomer, and bleated. Its hindquarters were blackened to the waist with mud, and with frantic workings of its rear legs it contrived to sink a little deeper. The man had his right arm hooked beneath its left foreleg and around its back, and with his left he was attempting to grasp its flank, the better to haul it to safety, but his feet could not find a purchase on the slick earth. The movement frightened the animal, which had closed its eyes for a moment, as if resigned to its own end; it bleated and struggled again, and with its left foreleg flailed out and struck the man across his cheek. He yelped, and Cora saw a wound open beneath the mask of mud.

The sight of blood roused her from a reverie: she said, 'Let me help,' and he gave a breathless grunt of assent. *Man's a halfwit!* she thought, already wondering how to tell the tale to best please her friends. Again the sheep went limp, exhaling a long kind of sigh that plumed in the air, and allowed the man to clasp both arms behind its back. In their embrace the two sank together into the mud, and looking furiously over his shoulder the man said, 'Well:

come on!' Not quite a halfwit, then, though with slow Essex vowels. Cora reached for her belt, which was broad and meant for a man. Her fingers were stiff and slow, and she fumbled with the buckle, as the sighing sheep slipped further down. Then she tugged it free, and dashing forward looped the belt across the animal's back where it would catch in the crook beneath its forelegs, forming a kind of bridle. The man released his grip and tugged the strap from her hand, and the animal felt the loss of his grasp and panicked; it gave a convulsive movement that threw Cora into the mud. The man showed her no concern, only grunted 'Up! Get up!' and, gesturing that she should take the belt, again resumed his grip on the sheep's flank. There was a long moment in which their matched strength slowly worked against the sucking mud, and Cora felt the bones of her shoulders straining in their sockets, then all at once the sheep's rear legs appeared above the water's surface, and it propelled itself forward onto the bank. Cora and the man fell back, and she turned away to conceal her breathlessness: she would not have minded the mud, and the pain in her wrists, had the man not been an oaf, and the sheep not such a witless beast. Some distance away the sheep's companions looked warily up, showing no pleasure, awaiting the lost one's return. It ought to have felt, she thought, like a triumph, but instead the pleasure of the day had gone, and even the banks of bracken had lost their colour.

When she turned back the man was regarding her above his sleeve, which he had pressed to the cut on his cheek. He had put on a knitted hat, which was so poorly made he might well have put it together himself from scarlet scraps, and pulled it to his eyebrows, which were thick with mud and almost obscured his eyes. He said, 'Thanks,' a little curtly, again with that flattening of the vowels that marked him out as a country man. *A farmer then*, she thought, and without accepting the gratitude so grudgingly given she said, gesturing to the exhausted sheep: 'Is it going to be all right?' It mouthed at the air, and rolled its eyes again.

He shrugged. 'Should think so.'

'One of yours?'

'Ha! No. Not my flock.' The idea evidently struck some chord of slow humour in him, and he began to chuckle.

A vagrant, then, poor soul! It was in her nature to think well of folk until they gave her cause to do otherwise, and besides: she'd shortly be home to Martha and their clean white sheets, and who knew but that he might be making his bed in the bracken with nothing but a half-drowned beast for company. Smiling, she decided to bring good London manners to their conversation. 'Well: I must be home. It was very nice to meet you.' She gestured towards the dripping oaks, and the pond where little eddies from their struggle still moved, and wishing to be generous said: 'Essex. Nice part of the world.'

'Is it?' His voice was dampened by the sleeve still pressed against his cheek, on which she could see blood mixed in with dirty water. She wanted to ask if he would be all right, if he'd make it safely home, if there was anything she could do; but it was his territory, not hers. It occurred to her, as she saw the first thickening of the shadows at dusk, that of the pair of them she was most at a loss, miles from her bed and with only a vague sense of where she stood. With a fair attempt at maintaining what she felt was the upper hand, she said: 'Tell me: am I far from Colchester? Where can I fetch a cab home?'

The man lacked the wit to be surprised. He nodded towards the further bank, where she could make out a breach in the line of oaks, and behind it an open stretch of land. 'Out onto the road – bear left, five hundred yards. There's a pub: they'll fetch it for you.'

Then, with a motion extraordinarily like that of a man dismissing an inferior, he turned and trudged away through the mud. His shoulders were so stooped against the cold that the weight of his filthy coat made him seem very like a hunchback. Always more easily moved to mirth than rage, Cora could not prevent herself from laughing: perhaps he heard, because he paused on the path, half-turned towards her, then thought better of it and went on his way.

Cora tugged her coat closer, and heard all around her the gathering of birds for evensong. The sheep had dragged itself a yard or two further onto the bank; it had raised itself into a kneeling position and was nudging the earth in search of a blade of grass. The light was fading, and a fine white mist rose up from the cold earth and spilled over the rim of her boots. Beyond the last of the oaks a grass verge dropped a little to the roadside, and in the near distance a half-timbered pub with bright-lit windows beckoned to passing travellers. The sight of the gleaming panes, and the thought that she was still so far from home, and that she did not know the way, brought on a weariness so sudden it struck her like a blow. When she reached the threshold and saw a woman leaning on the bar and smiling a welcome beneath a high coil of bright hair, Cora paused to adjust her clothes. Smoothing her coat, she found in the buckle of her belt a little scrap of white wool, and on it – gleaming in the lamplight as though it were fresh – a smear of blood.

5

Joanna Ransome, not quite thirteen, tall as her father and wrapped in his newest coat, held her hand over flames. She brought her palm as near the flicker as she could, then withdrew it slow enough to preserve her pride. Her brother John watched solemnly, and would've liked to have thrust his own hands into his pockets, but had been instructed to leave them to grow as cold as he could bear. 'We are making a sacrifice,' she'd said, leading him to the stretch of land just beyond World's End, where the marshes gave way to the Blackwater estuary, and beyond that, the sea: 'And for there to be a sacrifice, we must suffer.'

Earlier that day she'd explained to him, whispering in cold corners, that something was rotten in the village of Aldwinter. There was the drowned man, for one thing (naked, they said, and with five deep scratches on his thigh!), and the sickness at Fettlewell, and the way they all woke from dreams of wet black wings. And there was more: the nights should've grown lighter by now – there should be snowdrops in the garden – their mother should not still have a cough that woke her at night. There should be birdsong in the mornings. They should not still shiver in their beds. It was all because of something they'd done and forgotten and never repented, or was because the Essex earthquake had let something loose in the Blackwater, or perhaps it was because their father had lied ('He said he's not afraid, and there's nothing there – but why won't he go down to the sea after dark anymore? Why won't he let us play out on the boats? Why does he look tired?'). Whatever the cause and wherever the blame, they were going to do something about it. Long ago in other lands they'd cut out hearts to bring the sun up: surely it wasn't too much to ask that they try out a little spell for the sake of the village? 'I have it all worked out,' she'd said: 'You trust me, don't you?'

They stood between the ribs of a clipper which had pitched up there a decade ago and never shifted from the shore. In the harshness of the weather it had worn down to little more than a dozen black curved posts that looked so much like the opened chest cavity of a drowned beast that visitors took to calling it Leviathan. It was near enough to the village for the children to reach it without censure, and far enough out of sight for no-one to notice what they did there. In summer they hung their clothes from its bones, and in winter they lit small fires in its shelter, always afraid the hulk would burn, and dismayed when it didn't. Love notes and curses were cut in the wood with penknives; pennies were stacked on the posts and were never spent. Joanna's little fire was set some distance away from the wreck in a circle of stones, and had taken hold nicely. She'd looped it with lengths of bladderwrack, which gave off a clean scent, and pressed into the coarse sand seven of her best shells.

'I'm *hungry*.' John looked up at his sister and immediately regretted his lack of resolve. He'd turn seven before summer, and felt firmly that it was high time he matched his increasing years with increasing courage. 'I don't mind though,' he said, and capered twice around the fire.

'We have to be hungry because tonight's the night of the Hunger Moon, isn't that right, Jo?' Red-haired Naomi Banks crouched with her back to Leviathan and looked beseechingly at her friend. As far as she was concerned, Reverend Ransome's daughter had the Queen's authority and God's wisdom, and she'd cheerfully have stepped barefoot in the flames if the other girl had commanded it.

'That's right: the Hunger Moon, and the last full moon before spring.' Conscious of the need to be both stern and benevolent, Joanna imagined her father in his pulpit, and mimicked his stance. In the absence of a lectern, she raised both her arms and said in a chanting voice which had taken some weeks to perfect: 'We are gathered here on the day of the Hunger Moon to beseech Persephone to break the chains of Hades and bring spring to our beloved land.' Wondering if she'd struck quite the right note, and a little concerned that she was playing fast and loose with the education her father insisted upon, she glanced quickly at Naomi. Her friend's cheek was flushed, and her eyes were bright: she pressed a hand to her throat and Joanna, bolstered, went on: 'Too long have we suffered winter winds! Too long have the dark nights concealed the river's terrors!' John, whose determination to be brave was unequal to his dread of the beast probably lurking not a hundred yards away in the water, squealed. His sister frowned, and raised her voice a little. 'Goddess Persephone, hear us!' She nodded briskly at her companions, who chorused: 'Goddess Persephone, hear us!' They made their supplications to numerous gods, genuflecting deeply at each name; Naomi, whose mother had been of the old religion, crossed herself fervently. 'And now,' said Joanna, 'we have to make a sacrifice,' and John – who'd never forgotten the story of how Abraham had tethered his son to an altar and got out his carving knife – squealed again, and bolted twice round the fire.

'Come back, stupid boy,' said Joanna. 'Nobody's going to hurt you.'

'The Essex Serpent might,' said Naomi, coming at the child with claws, and receiving a look of such censure in return that she flushed, and took John's hand in hers.

'We give you the sacrifice of our hunger,' said Joanna, whose stomach burbled shamefully (she'd concealed breakfast in a napkin and fed it later to the dog, and pleading a headache avoided lunch). 'We give you the sacrifice of our cold.' Theatrical, Naomi shivered. 'We give you the sacrifice of our burning. We give you the sacrifice of our names.' Joanna paused, forgetting for a moment the ritual she'd prepared, then putting her hand in her pocket took out three pieces of paper. Earlier that day she'd dipped the corner of each sheet in the font of her father's church, alert to the possibility he'd find her there, and with several lies prepared in her defence. The damp corners had dried in ripples, and as she handed them to her fellow celebrants they crackled audibly. 'It is necessary for us to commit to the spells,' she said, sombrely, 'to give a part of our own nature. We must write our names, and in writing them vow to whichever gods hear us that we give of our own being, in the hope that winter will be gone from the village.' She examined her words as she said them, and pleased with her phrasing, was struck by a new thought. Stooping to pick up a broken twig, she put it in the fire and let it burn a while, then blowing out the flame scrawled her name on the paper with the charcoal. It was not quite extinguished, and the paper scorched and tore, and the goddesses would need celestial vision to make out more than her initials from so great a distance, but the effect was gratifying. She handed the stick to Naomi, who scored her paper with a capital N, and helped John make his mark. The boy was proud of his handwriting, and scuffled and elbowed at the girl, determined to manage on his own.

'Now,' said Joanna, collecting up the pieces of paper and tearing them into fragments: 'Come to the fire with me. Are your hands cold? Are they full of winter?' *Full of winter*, she thought: *what a line!* Perhaps she'd be a vicar like her father when she grew up. John looked at the tips of his fingers and wondered whether he might soon see the first black flecks of frostbite. 'I can't feel anything.'

'Oh, you will,' said Naomi, grinning. Her hair was red and so was her coat, and John had never liked her. 'You'll feel something all right.' She tugged him to his feet, and they joined Joanna by the flames. Someone stood on a string of bladderwrack and made it pop, and some distance away the tide was turning.

'Now,' said Joanna. 'You're going to have to be brave, John, because this is going to hurt.' She tossed the scraps of paper into the fire, and followed them with a scattering of salt from her mother's silver shaker. The flames burned briefly blue. Then holding out her hands to the fire, with an imperious nod that her companions should do the same, she closed her eyes and held them, palm down, above the fire. A damp log spat sparks and scorched her father's sleeve; she flinched, and fretting for the white skin on her brother's wrist tugged his hands upward an inch or more. 'We don't need to hurt ourselves badly,' she said hastily, 'we just have to let our hands warm up quickly and it'll burn like it does when you come in from the snow.'

Naomi, chewing a coil of hair, said, 'Look: you can see my veins.' And it was true: she had a little webbing of flesh set deep between each of her fingers, and was proud of her defect, having once heard that Anne Boleyn had had something similar and caught herself a king, nonetheless. In the firelight a ruddy glow passed through the thin flesh and threw into blue relief a vein or two. Joanna – impressed, but conscious of the need to maintain the upper hand – said: 'We have come here to mortify our flesh, Nomi, not take pride in it.' She used the nickname of their babyhood to show that the girl was not in disgrace, and in response Naomi flexed her fingers and said, very seriously, 'Oh, it really hurts, I can tell you that. It's prickling like nettles.'

The girls looked at John, whose hands wavered with his courage. Something was evidently going on, since his fingers were a vivid red and even, Joanna thought, swollen at the tips. Either the low-hanging smoke the fire gave out had stung his eyes, or he was trying not to cry. Torn between her certainty that the gods would look kindly on a sacrifice from so small a celebrant, and equal certainty that her mother would be justifiably outraged, she nudged the boy and said, 'Higher, silly boy, higher: d'you want to burn yourself to stumps?' At this, his held-back tears overspilled, and just at that moment (or so Joanna later told it, huddled under a school table with Naomi nodding at her side and an audience awestruck at her feet), the full moon passed out of a low blue cloud. All around them the pebble-specked sand took on a sickly cast, and the sea – creeping at them over the salt-marsh as their backs were turned – glistened.

'A sign, you see!' said Joanna, removing her hands from above the fire then hastily replacing them at Naomi's raised eyebrow: 'A portent! It is the goddess' – she cast about for the name – 'The goddess Phoebe, come to acknowledge our petition!'

John and Naomi turned towards the moon, and looked a long while on its downcast face. Each of them saw, in the high mottled disc, the melancholy eyes and curved mouth of a woman sunk in sadness.

'D'you think it worked?' Naomi could not believe that her friend might have been mistaken in so serious a matter as the summoning of spring, and besides: she'd felt the pain in her hands and she had not eaten since bread-and-cheese the night before; and had she not also seen her own name on its christened piece of paper go up in a shower of sparks? She buttoned her coat a little higher, and looked out over the salt-marsh and the sea, half-expecting to see an early sunrise, and with it a flock of swifts.

'Oh Nomi, I don't know.' Kicking aimlessly at the sand, Joanna found herself already a little ashamed of her display. All that waving of her arms about and chanting! Really, she was much too old for all this. 'Don't ask *me*,' she said, forestalling further query: 'Not done it before, have I?' Pricked with guilt, she knelt beside her brother and said gruffly, 'You were very brave. If it doesn't work it won't be your fault.'

'I want to go home. We'll be late and there'll trouble and there won't be dinner left and it was going to be my favourite.'

'We won't be late,' said Joanna. 'We said we'd be home before dark, and it's not dark, is it? It's not dark yet.' But it was almost dark, and it seemed to be coming, she thought, from across the sea beyond the estuary, which had taken on the appearance of a black and solid substance across which she might walk, if she cared to try. She'd lived all her life here at the margin of the world, and never once thought to mistrust its changing territory: the seeping of salt water up through the marshes, and the changing patterns of its muddy banks and creeks, and the estuary tides which she checked almost daily against her father's almanac, were all as untroublesome as the patterns of her family life. Before she could ever have recognised them on paper she could sit on her father's shoulders and point, and proudly name Foulness and Point Clear, St Osyth and Mersea, and the direction of St Peter's-on-the-Wall. It was a family trick to spin her a dozen times and say: 'She'll always come out facing east, to the mouth of the sea.'

But something had changed in the course of their ritual: she had a curious impulse to glance backward over her shoulder as if she might catch out the tide in reversing its direction, or see the waters split open as once they had for Moses. She'd heard, of course, the rumours that something lived now in the estuary depths, and was responsible for the taking of a lamb and the breaking of a limb, but thought little of it: childhood was so rife with terrors that it was use-less giving more credence to one thing than to another. Wanting to see again the sad pale face of the lady in the moon, she looked up, and there was only the gathering of dense clouds stacking up above the marsh. The wind had dropped, as it often did at dusk, and up on the road above them the earth would be hardening with frost. John, evidently feeling his own unease, forgot his increasing years and put his hand in hers; and even Naomi, who'd never once been seen to look afraid, sucked fretfully at her coil of hair and drew closer to her friend. As they made their silent way past the dying embers of their fire, and past Leviathan as it shored itself deeper for the night, they glanced repeatedly over their shoulders at the black water creeping closer across the mud. '*Girls and boys come out to play*,' sang Naomi, not quite managing to keep a tremor from her voice: '*The moon does shine as bright as day . . .*'

Much later – and only when pressed, since it had all seemed to be a part of a ritual of which the children felt strangely ashamed – each claimed to have seen a curious thickening and rising of the water in a particular place, just where the salt-marsh ended and the riverbed shelved steeply down. There'd been no sound, and nothing as comfortingly frightening as a long limb or rolling eye; only a movement that was too swift and directionless to be the casting of a wave. John claimed that it had had about it a whitish look, but Joanna thought that was only the moon peering out and brightening the surface with her gaze. Naomi, the first to speak up, embellished the event with such a flourish of wing and snout that it was generally accepted she'd seen nothing at all, and her testimony was discarded.

'How long until we're home, Jojo?' John, tense with a longing to run home to his mother and the dinner he imagined going cold on the table, tugged at his sister's hand.

'Nearly there: look, see the smoke from the chimneys and the sails on the boats?'

They had reached the path – their teeth chattering, with the sudden chill and with unease – and up ahead the oil lamps set in the windows of World's End had the charm of a Christmas tree. They could see Cracknell making his rounds for the night, cuffing Gog and Magog into their pen, and pausing at the gate to bid them goodnight.

'*Girls and boys come out to play*,' he sang, having heard them coming, thudding the gatepost for emphasis: 'And though I note it's a full-face moon you'll have no daybright shining what with the light being borrowed only, and that paid back at interest, and losing its value month by month, which accounts for the dimness of the thing. Eh?' Pleased with this line of thought he grinned, then beckoned them closer, and closer still, so that they smelt the earthy dampness rising from the pockets of his coat, and saw the stripped bodies of the moles hanging by their heels.

'Keen to get home, ain't he?' Cracknell nodded at John, who was an old friend of his, and would not usually pass up the chance to sit astride Gog or Magog and circuit the shack, and after eat honey straight from the comb. John, who by now imagined his supper being passed to the dog, scowled, and it was perhaps this that made the old man scowl in return, and grasp the boy's ear. 'Listen up then, the three of you – it's not just girls and boys come out to play in these times which I do wonder but might well be the last and you'll hear no regrets from me on that score, *even so come quickly Lord Jesus* as I might have said when I had truck with such talk ... *join your playfellows in the street*, as the song says but it's a strange playfellow you made down there in the Blackwater black water, don't think I don't know and haven't seen it myself twice or thrice when the moon's bright ...' He gripped John's ear a little too tight, and the boy yelped. Cracknell looked at his own hand in surprise, as if it had operated without his permission, and released John, who rubbed his face and began to cry. 'Well, then. Well, then: what's this noise for?' Cracknell patted his several pockets, but found nothing that might placate a child in need of his mother's lap, and a hot meal. 'I only speak kindly, only kindly, as always I hope I do, and wouldn't wish the snapping and the creeping and the watching on any of you or any of yours.' John had not yet stopped crying, and Joanna feared for a moment that the old man might cry also, out of shame and something she suspected was fear. She reached over the mole-strung fence and patted the greasy sleeve of his coat twice, and had begun to cast about for something soothing to say when Cracknell stiffened, thrust up his arm, and roared: 'Halt, now! *What goes there?*'

The children flinched: John buried his face in his sister's waist; Naomi spun on her heel, and gasped. A dark misshapen creature was coming at them along the path, moving slowly, making a low sound in the depths of its throat. It did not creep, but stood on hind legs; it almost had the shape of a man – it held out its arms – it might have been a threat, but the noise it made seemed almost laughter. It *was* a man, surely; indeed, there was something in the unhurried gait that was almost familiar – nearer it came to the light cast by Cracknell's lamps; it paused, and she saw its long coat shedding thick flakes of mud, and its heavy boots. The face was obscured by a hat pulled low to the brows, and by a heavy scarf – everything about the creature was coated in mud that showed black with damp in places and dried pale in others; only there were parts of the filthy hat which showed the original scarlet of the wool.

'Don't you know me? Am I such a sight?' Again the man held out his arms, then tugged off the knitted cap, and a thicket of untidy curls the same russet shade as her own long plait gleamed in the lamplight.

'Daddy! Where have you been? What have you done – how have you cut your cheek?'

'John, lad: and don't you know your own father?' With a child in the crook of each arm, the Reverend William Ransome reached out to cuff Naomi kindly on the shoulder, and nodded at Cracknell, who said, 'And a sight for sore eyes you represent as ever, Parson; and if I could suggest the littl'uns be taken home and kept there, I'll bid each a goodnight.' Bowing to them all – and most deeply to John – the old man retreated into World's End and slammed shut the door.

'And why are you all out so late, might I ask? We shall all of us answer to your mother for this; and as for you, Miss Banks, what will I tell your father?' He tweaked Naomi's cheek, and propelled her home towards a grey stone cottage that overlooked the quay. The girl looked once over her shoulder at her friends, then hurried inside, and they heard the door bolted.

'Yes – but Daddy, where have you been? What have you done to your face? Do you need a stitch?' (This said eagerly, since Joanna had a private longing to wield the surgeon's knife.)

'Never mind that: why is John crying, and he as old as the hills!' Will tightened his hold on the boy, who swallowed the last of his sobs. 'As for me: I have been out rescuing sheep, and frightening ladies, and I must say' – they'd reached the chequered garden path, and the borders where snowdrops gleamed in the dark – 'that I haven't enjoyed myself so much in a long time. Stella! We're home, and we need you!'

MARCH

Stella Ransome
All Saints Rectory
Aldwinter
11th March

My dear Mrs Seaborne —

I write in the hope that a note from me won't seem a note from a stranger, since Charles Ambrose assures me you're expecting to hear from the Ransome family, of Aldwinter, Essex — and behold: here we are!

But first, I hope you will accept the most sincere condolences from my husband and myself on your recent bereavement. We hear little of London, and yet Mr Seaborne's name reached us via Charles, and sometimes even in The Times! *We know him to have been a man greatly admired, and I'm sure greatly loved. You have been in our prayers, and most of all mine, as I think I can imagine best a wife's grief at her husband's loss.*

And now: to the matter at hand. Charles and Katherine Ambrose will be here next Saturday for supper, and we would be delighted beyond measure if you would join us. I understand you are accompanied by your son, and by a companion of whom Charles speaks very fondly, and we would be pleased to meet them also. There is no occasion to be marked, only the chance to see old friends and make new ones.

Our address is as you see it, and we are easily reached from Colchester: I'm afraid there's no train, but it's a pleasant enough journey by cab. You must stay with us, of course: we have room, and you will not want to travel home so late. I will await your response, and in the meantime plan what dainty dishes I can set before a woman with London tastes!

Yours very sincerely,

STELLA RANSOME

PS – As you see, I could not resist sending you a primrose, though I was too impatient to press it well, and it has stained the page. I never could learn to bide my time! – S.

Dr Luke Garrett surveyed his room at the George Hotel, Colchester, with grudging pleasure: it was clear that Spencer had spared no expense. His fingertip, having been swept across each surface, remained spotless. 'I could perform an appendectomy in here,' Luke said, with what his friend rightly took to be an air of wishing disease on passers-by. The cleanliness of the room established, Garrett flicked open the brass fastenings of his suitcase and withdrew a pair of crumpled shirts, several books with pages folded down, and a sheaf of paper. This he set on the dressing-table, reverently surmounted with a white envelope on which his name was written in a neat decisive hand.

'She's expecting us?' Spencer nodded at the envelope: he knew Cora's handwriting well, since his friend had lately been in the habit of passing him each of her letters, the better to examine the meaning behind each phrase.

'Expecting? Expecting! I wouldn't have come, left to my own devices – I've far too much to do. Not to put too fine a point on it, Spencer, the woman begged. "I miss you, dear" she said' – he gave his wolfish grin, and above it his black eyes shone – ' "I miss you, dear"!'

'Will we see her tonight?' Spencer said this carelessly. He had motives of his own for this display of impatience, but having successfully concealed them even from Garrett's forensic gaze was unwilling to show them. Too absorbed in re-reading Cora's letter (mouthing *dear!* to himself twice), his friend noticed nothing, only said, 'Yes: they're at the Red Lion; we'll see them at eight – at eight on the dot, if I know Cora, which I do.'

'Then I will go for a walk. It's too fine a day to be cooped up, and I want to see the castle. They say you can still see ruins from the Essex earthquake – will you come?'

'Certainly not. I hate walking. Besides, I have here a report of a Scottish surgeon who is convinced he can relieve paralysis by the exertion of pressure on the spinal column – I think often, you know, that I would have been better off in Edinburgh than in London: there is such courage there among medical men, and the miserable climate suits me . . .' Spencer and the castle already forgotten, Garrett sat cross-legged on the bed and spread before him a dozen sheets of fine black type punctuated with drawings of vertebrae. Spencer, a little relieved to be granted an afternoon's solitude, buttoned up his coat, and left.

The George Hotel was a fine white inn that overlooked the broad High Street. The proprietors plainly fancied their position as the best establishment in town, and displayed these credentials by means of a thicket of hanging-baskets in which daffodils and primroses jostled bad-temperedly for space. The day was fine, as if the sky regretted the slow release of winter's grip: the high clouds hurried on to pressing business in another town. Ahead, the spire of St Nicholas glittered, and there was a great deal of birdsong. Spencer, who could differentiate between a sparrow and a magpie only if pressed, found himself bewildered and delighted by it, and by the whole merry town with bright striped awnings above the pavements and cherry blossom speckling the sleeve of his coat. When he encountered a ruined house, and at its threshold a crippled man seated like a sentinel off-guard, this too seemed to him a charming sight: the house displayed an interior gone over to ivy and saplings of oak, and the cripple had taken off his coat to bask like a cat in eddies of light.

The embarrassment of his riches made Spencer absurdly generous, and wanting to share a little of the day's joy he emptied his pockets into the man's upturned hat. The weight of the coins dented the shabby felt; the man raised it level with his eyes, peering as if suspecting a practical joke, then, evidently satisfied, bared a row of superb teeth in a grin. 'Looks like I can knock off for the day then, don't it?' He reached behind his stone perch for a low wooden trolley on four iron wheels, and with a practised movement swung himself into it, and drawing on a pair of leather gauntlets to protect his palms propelled himself deftly towards the pavement. The trolley, Spencer saw, was extremely well-made, with designs of knot-work cut into it: a Celtic warrior felled in battle might have been content with such a vehicle, so that whatever natural pity he might have felt for the man's infirmity seemed an affront.

'Fancy a look, then?' With a lift of his chin the man indicated the gaping ruin of the house behind, conveying the impression that he held authority over its broken walls. 'Worst of the earthquake, this, and a danger to life and limb if you ask me, which no-one ever does; but there's such a wrangling in the law courts they can't settle who's to foot the bill, and meanwhile there's barn owls in the dining room.' Negotiating a pair of fallen marble slabs on which the remains of Roman lettering were gathering moss, the man led Spencer to the threshold of the house. Much of the front wall had sheared away, leaving the rooms and staircases exposed. Nothing was left but what could not be reached or looted: the lower floors were empty, save for immense carpets in which violets had seeded themselves and grew dense as a mattress, concealing coy blue flowers. On the upper levels paintings and trinkets remained: something silver glinted on the windowsill and at the head of the staircase a chandelier's crystal drops might have been polished that morning for the night's events.

'Quite a sight, isn't it? Look on my works ye mighty and despair, and what have you.'

'You ought really to sell tickets at the door,' said Spencer, hoping to spot the barn owl: 'Surely every passer-by wants a look.'

'They do, Mr Spencer: but they are not always given it.' This voice was not a man's, soft with Essex vowels and coming from below, but was that of a woman, and a London one at that. Spencer would've known it anywhere, and when he turned away from the ruin he knew he was blushing, but could not prevent it.

'Martha. You are here.'

'And so, I see, are you; and you've met my old friend?' Martha reached down, smiling, and grasped the cripple's hand. He shook it, and shook also his well-filled hat – 'Enough here for a leg or two, I reckon!'; then with a gesture of farewell began to wheel himself home.

'There is no barn owl. He only says it to please the tourists.'

'Well: it certainly pleased me.'

'Everything pleases you, Spencer!' She wore a blue jacket, and over her shoulder hung a leather bag from which protruded several peacock's feathers. In her left hand she held a white magazine, and on it Spencer saw *An Englishwoman's Review of Social and Industrial Questions* printed in elaborate black type. Trying his hand at gallantry, he said, 'Well: seeing you pleases me, at least,' but of all women Martha was the last to approve such a ploy. She raised an eyebrow, and rolling up the magazine struck him on the arm.

'Enough of all that: come and see Cora. She'll be so glad you came. The Imp is with you, I suppose?'

'He is reading up on paralysis, and what to do about it, but he'll join us later.'

'Good: I want to speak to you about something' – she shook the magazine – 'and it is impossible to be serious about anything with that man in the room. How was the journey?'

'A child cried from Liverpool Street to Chelmsford, and only stopped when Garrett told him he'd lose all the water from his body, shrivel up, and be dead by Manningtree.'

Martha snorted. 'How either you or Cora can stand his company is a mystery to me. Is this your hotel?' She surveyed the pale façade of the George, and its hanging-baskets. 'We're at the Red Lion, a little further on: I didn't think we'd stay so long, only Francis has taken a liking to the landlord, and so life has been calm of late. Feathers are the latest fad: you'd think he was trying to make himself a pair of wings, though there's not much angelic about that boy.'

'And Cora – is she well?'

'I've never known her happier, though sometimes she remembers she ought not to be, and puts on her black dress, and sits in the window looking like an artist's idea of grief.' They passed a flower-seller closing her stall for the night, and selling daffodils by the armful for a penny. Retrieving the last coin or two from his pockets, Spencer relieved her of her stock, and clasping a dozen bunches of the yellow blooms said: 'Let's take spring to Cora. We'll fill up her rooms and she'll forget she was ever sad about anything.' He glanced quickly at his companion, afraid he'd spoken out of turn: perhaps it was best to keep up the pretence of a decent woman decently mourning.

But Martha said, smiling, 'She'll thank you for it, too; all month she's been going out walking looking for signs of spring, and coming home muddy and bad-tempered; then one day there it was, on the stroke of noon, as if someone had summoned it.'

'And has Essex yielded any fossils? I saw in the papers some new species was unearthed up on the Norfolk coast after a winter storm: sometimes I think we must be walking on shoals of bodies without realising it and all the earth's a graveyard.' Spencer, who rarely voiced his flights of whimsy, flushed a little and prepared for one of Martha's parries, but none came.

'A toadstone or two, she says, but nothing more. But she has high hopes for the Essex Serpent – look: here we are.' A little distance on, Spencer saw a timber-framed inn from which hung an iron sign emblazoned with a red lion rampant.

'The Essex Serpent?' said Spencer, glancing down as if expecting to see an adder on the pavement.

'It's all she talks about these days – didn't she write to the Imp, and tell him? Some legend kept going by village idiots, about a winged snake seen coming out of the estuary and menacing villages on the coast. She's got it into her head it's one of these dinosaurs they say might've survived extinction – did you ever hear the like?' They'd reached the threshold of the inn, and saw through its thick mottled panes of glass a fire in the hearth. There was a strong scent of spilled beer, and a joint roasting somewhere out of sight. 'What can you expect, of poor country folk who can't read or write?' Her Londoner's contempt was magnificent, taking in the spire of St Nicholas, and the paltriness of the earthquake, and the Red Lion, and everyone in it. 'But Cora has a hive of bees in her bonnet: she says it's likely a living fossil – she will tell you the names for them: I can never remember – and she's determined to seek it out.'

'Garrett always says she'll not rest easy until her name's on the wall in the British Museum,' said Spencer. 'I can believe it might happen, too.'

At the doctor's name Martha snorted, and pushed open the door. 'Come up to our rooms, and see Francis: he'll remember you, and won't mind your coming.'

Luke, arriving late having attempted to replicate a human vertebra in papier-mâché, found his friends seated on a thinning rug, their clothes studded all over with feathers. In a window-seat Martha turned the pages of a magazine, and watched Francis silently threading feathers from gulls and crows through the weave of Spencer's coat until he looked like an angel dismayed by its fall. Cora had come off relatively lightly, with a peacock plume sticking up from the back of her dress and the contents of a pillow dusting her shoulders. No-one noticed the Imp arrive, so that he turned and re-entered noisily – 'What is going on? Have I come to the insane asylum? Where are *my* wings then, or must I be earth-bound – Cora, I have brought you books. Spencer, get me something to drink – you have something on your coat.'

Cora, giving a little yell of delight, leaped up and kissed the newcomer on each cheek, holding him at arm's length: 'You've come! Have you grown? Half an inch at – no that was cruel, I'm sorry, only you're late, you know. Frankie, say hello (Francis has a new hobby as you see, and we're all being very patient about it). You remember Luke?' The boy did not look up, but sensing a change of air to which he had not agreed began silently to retrieve each fallen feather from the carpet, counting in reverse.

'*Three hundred and seventy-six – three hundred and seventy-five – three hundred and seventy-four . . .*'

'Now our play is ended,' said Cora ruefully, 'Though he'll be quiet enough now so long as he reaches *one . . .*'

'You look dreadful,' said Luke, who would've liked to touch one by one the freckles newly arrived on her forehead. 'Don't you brush your hair out in the sticks? Your hands are dirty. And what are you wearing?'

'I've freed myself from the obligation to try and be beautiful,' said Cora: 'And I was never more happy. I can't remember when I last looked in the mirror –'

'Yesterday,' said Martha. 'You were admiring your nose. Good evening, Dr Garrett.'

This was said with so penetrating a chill Luke shivered, and might've attempted a wounding response if the landlord had not arrived, and with an admirable refusal to acknowledge the feather-strewn room and the chanting boy left a tray of beer upon the sideboard. This was followed by a platter of cheese and cold beef marbled with yellow fat, and a plaited white loaf, and a dish of pale butter sprinkled with salt, and lastly a cake studded with cherries and giving off the scent of brandy; and such was the impossibility of maintaining a bad temper in the presence of the feast that Luke gave Martha the sweetest smile he could manage, and tossed her a green apple.

Spencer, sitting beside Martha on the window-seat to watch the passers-by on the wet black pavements below, took up her maga-zine and said, 'You were going to tell me about this – may I see – what've you been reading?' He leafed through the booklet, which contained bewildering statistics on London's over-population, and the catastrophic consequences of urban clearance.

Martha surveyed him with the temporary warmth of wine. Truth be told, he roused in her a kind of reflexive loathing which took an effort to suppress. Certainly he seemed kindly enough, and gentle; she'd seen him make attempts with Francis no other visitor had ever done (all those swift games of chess ending in Spencer's defeat!), and she admired his efforts to keep the Imp in check. More – and most importantly – he treated Cora with a courteous friendship which never once transgressed into attempts to know her any better than he ought. But she saw his wealth and privilege coat him like furs. What little she knew of his circumstances (the possession of more property than he could find use for – the liberty to train in medicine as a kind of hobby while women contented themselves with bedpans and broth) ranked him among those she had all her life counted as the enemy.

Martha's socialism was no less ingrained than any inherited faith still clung to past childhood fervour. Community halls and picket lines were her temples, and Annie Besant and Eleanor Marx stood at the altar; she had no hymn book but the fury of folk songs setting English suffering to English melody. In the kitchen of their Whitechapel rooms her father – hands reddened with brick dust, the whorls of his fingertips worn smooth – counted out his wages and set aside his Union fees, and in his careful handwriting joined the petitioning of Parliament for a ten hour limit on the working day. Her mother – who'd once stitched stoles and copes with golden crosses, and pelicans pecking out their hearts – cut cloth for banners held high above the picket line, and eked out the household budget to take beef soup to the striking match-girls at Bryant and May. 'All that is solid melts into air,' her father had said, reverently reciting his apostle's creed: 'And all that is holy is profaned! Martha, don't bow your head to the way things are and always were – whole empires are brought down by nothing but ivy and time.' He washed his shirts in the small tin bath – the water came out red – he sang as he wrung the linen dry: 'When Adam delved and Eve span, who was then the Englishman?' When Martha walked from Limehouse to Covent Garden she saw not high windows and Doric columns, but the labourers toiling behind them. It seemed to her that the city's bricks were red with the blood of its citizens, its mortar pale with the dust of their bones; that deep in its foundations women and children lay head-to-toe in buried ranks, bearing up the city on their backs.

Taking her place in Cora's household had been an act of purest pragmatism: it permitted a degree of social acceptance and a reasonable wage; it placed her firmly outside the class she despised and equally firmly within it. But she had not bargained for Cora Seaborne – after all, who could?

Spencer's long, melancholy face was flushed – she was conscious of his eagerness to please, and it roused her to mischief: '*All that is solid melts into air*,' she said, testing his courage.

'Shakespeare?' he said.

Smiling, relenting, Martha said, 'Karl Marx, I'm afraid, though he was a bard of sorts. Yes, there was something I wanted to tell you' – for the sorry truth was that Spencer and those like him, however despised, were useful sources of influence and income. She spread open the pages and showed him a map on which the poorest of London's housing was overlaid with plans for new developments. They would be sanitary, she said, and spacious: children would have green spaces to play in and tenants would be free from landlord caprice. But (she flicked contemptuously at the paper) to qualify for housing, tenants must demonstrate good character. 'They're expected to live better than you or I ever did to deserve a roof over their children's heads: must never be drunk, or a nuisance to neighbours, or gamble, and God forbid too many children by too many fathers, and had too often. You, Spencer – with your estate and your pedigree – you can drink yourself wretched on claret and port and no-one begrudges you any of your homes; but spend what little you have on cheap beer and the dogs and you've not enough moral standing to sleep in a dry bed.'

Spencer could not rightly claim to have given the capital's housing crisis any further thought than the headlines invited, and felt keenly the contempt for his wealth and status which lay behind her words. But in her indignation she seemed to him more to be desired than ever, and as if her rage were contagious he felt something like anger stir in his belly. He said, 'And if you're given one of these homes, and are later discovered out in the streets breaking a pint glass over your neighbour's head?'

'On the streets you'll stay, and your children, and it'll be no more than you deserve. We are punishing poverty,' she said, pushing away her plate: 'If you are poor, and miserable, and behave as you might well expect a poor and miserable person to behave, since there's precious little else to pass the time, then your sentence is more misery, and more poverty.'

He would've liked to ask what he could do, but felt the presence of his privilege as uncomfortably as if it had been pockets full of chilly gold, and instead fumbled with words of agreement and censure – certainly something ought to be done about it, questions raised and so on . . . '*I'm* going to do something about it,' she said, imperiously; then as if to forestall requests for detail raised her voice, and said: 'Now, Cora: have you told the Imp about your poor Essex parson, and the serpent?'

Cora (who'd been sitting at Luke's feet recounting the tale of how she had rescued a lost lamb from the clutches of an Essex ogre) explained how they'd encountered Charles Ambrose, and how they'd learned of the beast in the Blackwater shaken loose by the earthquake. She showed him photos of a plesiosaur uncovered at Lyme Regis, and gestured to its long tail, and its flippers rather like wings. 'Sea-dragon, Mary Anning called it: you can see why, can't you? Can't you see why?' She snapped the book shut, triumphant, and told him how she planned to go down to the coast, where the Colne and the Blackwater met in their estuary and went out to the sea, and how Charles Ambrose had foisted them on an unsuspecting rural priest and his family. Her friend's appalled laughter threatened to crack in two the black beams that upheld the roof: mirth doubled him at the waist, and he gestured to her man's boots, and the earth beneath her fingernails, and the godless little library on the windowsill. The sweet letter of invitation was unfolded and passed from hand to hand and the primrose crumbled: this Stella Ransome was a darling woman (it was agreed) and ought at all costs to be protected from Cora, who would surely terrify her more than any sea-serpent might.

'I hope the good Reverend's faith is sincere,' he said. 'He'll be needing it.' Only Spencer, silently watching from his window-seat, saw in Luke's hilarity the unease of a man who would've liked to keep Cora only for himself, with no other friend or confidant, even one choked with a dog-collar and slow-witted to boot.

A little later, watching from the window as Spencer guided his friend the short distance to the George, Martha said, 'I like him: I always thought him stupid, but really I think he's just kind.'

Cora said, 'The two things are hard to tell apart, sometimes, and sometimes amount to much the same thing – will you take Francis to his room? I will clear the feathers up, or the maids will think we've held a black mass, and we will lose our reputation.'

2

Stella Ransome stood at the window buttoning her blue dress. It was the view she liked best, taking in the chequered path with its bluebell border, and beyond that the High Road with its cluster of cottages and shops, the sturdy All Saints tower, and the fresh red-brick walls of the school. Nothing pleased her more than feeling that all around her was the bustle of life, and she loved the beginning of spring, when green buds quickened on Traitor's Oak, and the village children were set free from heavy clothes and indoor games. Her usually irrepressible cheer had been dampened by a long winter which had not had the glamour of snow, only been a dreary chill period that not even Christmas could make bearable. The cough which had kept her awake at night had receded as the weather grew warmer, and the grey thumbprints beneath her weary eyes had almost gone. This, too, pleased her: she was not vain, only took delight in her appearance in just the same way she took delight in the scarlet camellia blooming in its black flower-bed down on the lawn. Her white fair hair, heart-shaped face and pansy-blue eyes were a pleasant enough sight in the mirror, but one she took for granted. It was true that Will could no longer circle her waist with his outspread hands, but she took to her new stoutness cheerfully: it was evidence of the five children she'd carried, and of the three who remained.

She heard them downstairs ending their early supper, and closing her eyes saw each as plainly as if she'd gone to the kitchen. James bent over as he drew his fantastic machines, all food disregarded as he sketched another cog or flywheel, and Joanna, the eldest, tending sternly to John, the youngest, who was doubtless embarking on his third slice of cake. Delighted at the prospect of the night's visitors (they adored Charles Ambrose, as all children did, for the depth of his pockets and the colours of his coat), they'd helped set the dining table with every piece of silver and glass in the house, exclaiming over the napkins their mother had sewn with forget-me-nots, and which they were not permitted to use. Only Joanna would be awake to greet the guests, and had promised to gather what gossip she could to entertain the younger children over breakfast. 'I think the widow will be fat as a carthorse and will cry into her soup,' she said, 'and her son will be handsome and rich and stupid, and will ask me to marry him, and I'll turn him down, and he will blow his brains out.'

Stella felt, as she often did, dazed with the good fortune which she knew to be a gift she had done nothing to earn. Her love for Will – which had arrived as suddenly as a fever when she was seventeen and had been just as dizzying – had not abated or diminished, even briefly, in their fifteen years of marriage. She'd been warned by a mother disappointed in almost every aspect of life that she should keep her expectations of happiness low: the man was likely to demand unpleasantness from her which she should bear bravely for the sake of children; he would tire of her quickly, but by then she would be grateful; he would grow fat; he was headed for a country parish and would never be rich. But Stella, to whom the mere existence of William Ransome, with his grave eyes and his sincerity and his deeply buried humour, was a miracle on a par with the wedding at Cana, could not prevent herself from laughing at her mother, and kissing her on the cheek. She felt then, and felt still, a fond pity for any woman who had not had the sense to marry her Will. Her mother had lived long enough to be disappointed in her daughter's failure to be disappointed. The girl had taken to every aspect of marriage with indecent delight, and seemed to be expecting a child the moment she had delivered one; they walked the Aldwinter High Road hand in hand; even the loss of two children had not struck a blow to their love, only settled it more deeply on its foundation. Stella admitted, every now and then, that she might have been happier in London or Surrey, where you could barely cross the road without making some new friend; but she was a kind and indefatigable gossip, and found in Aldwinter sufficient intrigue to sustain her interest in her fellow man without ever being heard to speak ill of anyone.

Will, meanwhile, had not emerged from his study since breakfast. It was a habit of his to see no-one on a Saturday until it was evening, when he eked out as long as possible a single glass of good wine. For all the bemusement of friends and family at his willing exile to this little parish (something most predicted would pall on him within a year) he took his Sunday duties as seriously as if he'd taken instruction at the burning bush. His was not the kind of religion lived only in rule and rubric, as if he were a civil servant and God the permanent secretary of a celestial government department. He felt his faith deeply, and above all out of doors, where the vaulted sky was his cathedral nave and the oaks its transept pillars: when faith failed, as it sometimes did, he saw the heavens declare the glory of God and heard the stones cry out.

Marking morning readings in the prayer book, and composing a prayer for the safety of Aldwinter and all who were in it, he too heard the clamour of children in the room across the passage. It was an unwelcome reminder that his time of peaceful solitude was coming to an end: the clock on the mantel struck six, and a bare two hours remained before the ringing of the doorbell would disturb his peace.

He was not an inhospitable man, though he'd never shared his wife's longing to be always in the company of others. Charles and Katherine Ambrose he loved more dearly than his own brothers, and frequent untimely visits from anxious parishioners were always met with welcome. He loved also to see Stella admired, presiding over the table with her warmth and wit, her beautiful head turning this way and that as she overlooked the pleasure of her guests. But a London widow, and her crone of a companion, and her indulged son! He shook his head, and slammed his notebook shut: he'd do his duty, because he always did, but he would not indulge a wealthy woman's dabbling in the natural sciences, probably to the detriment of her spiritual health. If she were to ask him to chaperone some harebrained attempt to uncover whatever it was she thought lay buried in the Essex clay or lived still out in the estuary, she would receive a polite and implacable refusal. It was all part of the Trouble, he thought, refusing as always to dignify the village's anxious rumours with the name of beast or serpent; they were all to be tried like gold in the fire, and would emerge purified. 'Praise God,' he said, but a little sourly, and went in search of tea.

'You are not at all what I expected!'

'Nor I you – you're so young to be a widow, and so beautiful!'

At ten past eight Stella Ransome and Cora Seaborne were seated side by side on the couch nearest the fire. Within moments each had taken such a liking to the other it was agreed it had been a great shame they'd not met during childhood. Martha, used to her friend's sudden affection and its equally sudden removal, took very little notice, and watched Joanna shyly shuffle a pack of cards. The girl's serious, clever face and thin plait pleased her, and drawing near her she indicated that they should play a game.

'Oh, I'm not beautiful: not at all,' said Cora, delighted by the kind lie. 'My mother always said the most I could hope for was to be thought striking, which suits me fine. Though it's true I've dressed more respectably than usual. I'm afraid you would never have let me over the doorstep if you'd seen me this afternoon.' It was true: at Martha's insistence she'd put on her good green dress, in the folds of which it was possible to imagine every kind of moss growing. She'd covered the scar on her collarbone with a pale scarf, and for once her shoes were intended for a woman. Her hair, given one hundred strokes of the brush by Martha, strained against its hairpins, several of which lay already on the carpet.

'Will is so pleased you've come, and will be so sorry to be late: he was called just now to see one of the parishioners who lives at the end of the village, but he won't be long.'

'I am so looking forward to meeting him!' This also was true: Cora decided that this delightful woman with her fairy's face and white-blonde hair would not be so happy if she shared her life with an oaf of a parson with flat feet. She was more than prepared to like him enormously, and settled happily into the cushions with her glass of wine. 'It was kind of you to invite my son, but he's been unwell, and I didn't want him to travel.'

'Ah!' The other woman's eyes filled with tears, which made their blue remarkable; she swiftly wiped them away. 'To lose a father is very cruel – I am so sorry for him, and of course I should have thought that he wouldn't want to spend an evening with strangers.'

Cora, whose honest disposition could not bear to see tears shed for a grief she suspected had never been felt, said: 'He is bearing it very well – he is . . . an unusual child, and I think doesn't feel things as deeply as you might expect.' Seeing her hostess was puzzled, she was glad to be spared further explanation by a bustle on the doorstep and the sound of boots on the scraper; a large and heavy bunch of keys was fitted to the lock, and Stella Ransome leaped to her feet. 'William – was it Cracknell? Is he taken ill?'

Cora looked up, and saw in the doorway a man stooping to kiss the woman where her fair hair parted. Stella was so little that he seemed to loom above her, though he was not especially tall. He was dressed smartly in a black coat cut well across his shoulders, and showing a breadth and strength that made a curious contrast with the little white collar of his office. His hair was of the kind that is never tidy, unless clipped short to the scalp: it fell in pale brown curls and in the light from the lamps had a reddish look. Having embraced his wife – his hands resting lightly at her waist, the fingers broad and rather short – he turned back to the door and said, 'No, love – Cracknell himself is not sick – and see who I found on the path?' He stood aside, plucking the white collar from his throat and tossing it onto a table; then in came Charles Ambrose in a scarlet frock coat, and behind him Katherine, concealed by a bouquet of hot-house flowers. Their scent was indecent, thought Cora: it went to her stomach, and she could not think why, until she recalled that when last she'd seen lilies they'd been laid all around the trestle where her husband's coffin had rested.

There was a flurry of greeting, in which Cora – glad for once to be forgotten – watched Martha and the girl absorbed in a game of patience. 'The queen is in her counting-house,' said Joanna, and dealt another card. Then the brief peace broke, and the little crowd came in; Charles and Katherine embraced Cora, patting her cheek and exclaiming at the beauty of her dress, and the absence of mud on her shoes. Was she well? Look at her hair, so clean and shining! And there was Martha, and what were her latest schemes, they wondered? And Frankie: did he take well to the country air? What of the sea-dragon – was Cora at last to see her name in the pages of *The Times*? And did they not love Stella already, and what did she make of the good Reverend Will?

At this, a deep quiet voice said – with good humour, but (thought Cora) a decided lack of enthusiasm: 'I've yet to meet our guests – Charles, you blind me with your glory, and nothing else can be seen.' Charles Ambrose stood aside, and raising an arm conducted their host to the couch where Cora sat. She saw, above the open neck of a black shirt, a mouth pressed into a smile, eyes with the grain of polished oak, and a cheek which seemed to have been badly nicked while shaving. In all her long years of society life, she had prided herself on an astute assessment of the status and character of those she met: here the wealthy businessman embarrassed by his own success, there the shabby Lady with a van Dyck on the staircase. But here was a man who'd not be catego-rised, however long she stared at the high polish on his shoes and the sleeves which pulled a little at the bulk of his arm: he was too burly for a desk-bound parson, but his gaze too thoughtful to be that of a man content with farming; his smile was too polite for sincerity, but his eyes glittered with good humour; his voice (and had she heard it before, on the Colchester streets perhaps, or on the London train?) had in it an echo of Essex, but he spoke like a scholar. She stood, and with all the graciousness she could muster while her stomach still turned with the scent of the lilies, held out her hand.

Will, for his part, saw a tall handsome woman whose fine nose was specked with freckles, and whose mossy dress (its value, he rightly guessed, twice that of Stella's entire wardrobe) drew out a greenish cast in eyes which were largely grey. She'd wound a scrap of gauzy fabric around her throat (absurd: did she really think it would keep her warm?), and wore on her wedding finger a diamond which broke the light and threw it against the wall. Despite the grandeur of her clothes, there was something boyish about her: she wore no jewellery aside from the ring, and her face had not been powdered pale, but glowed where the briny Essex air had struck it. When she stood, he saw that she was not the cart-horse his daughter had prophesied, but nor was she slender: she was large, and had substance; her presence would be, he thought, impossible to ignore, however hard one tried.

Whether it was the motion she made as she raised her hand or the realisation that her height matched his completely he was never sure, but at that moment he knew her at once. She was the roaring harridan who'd plunged out of the mist that day on the Colchester road, when together they'd tugged the sheep from its muddy trap and he'd received the cut on his cheek. She did not recognise him, of that he was certain: her smile was warm, though perhaps a little condescending. The pause before he took her hand was surely too brief to have been noticed by their companions, but caused her to look more keenly at her host. Will, who had not ceased laughing at the memory of that absurd encounter by the lake since the night he returned home in his coat of mud, could no longer conceal his amusement, and began to laugh again, touching lightly the reddish mark the animal had made.

Cora, so swift to assess the shifting moods of those around her, was briefly thrown: he put his hand in hers, and it was perhaps something in the pressure of his grasp that caused her to look again at the position of the cut on his cheek, and the curls on his collar, and with a gasp – 'Oh! *You!*' – begin laughing too. Martha (watching the exchange with a sensation very like fear) saw her friend and their host each cling to the hand of the other, helpless with inexplicable merriment. Cora, mindful of her manners, tried now and then to contain herself and explain to a bewildered Stella what it was that had struck them with laughing-sickness, but she could not. It was Will, at last, who released her hand, and giving an ironic bow – one leg extended, as if in the court of the queen – said, 'I'm so pleased to meet you, Mrs Seaborne: might I offer you a drink?'

Composing herself, she said, 'I'd very much like another glass of wine; and have you met my Martha? I never travel anywhere without her.' This effort of manners proved too much: she pressed her lips together to prevent another gale of laughter, then said gently, 'I do feel rather sheepish,' and watched, delighted, as the man could not help another gleeful burst.

Stella – amused, but never keen to feel outside events – said: 'I take it you've met?'

Her voice sobered Will, who drew her towards Cora and said, 'You remember, the week before last, how I came home late, covered in mud, because I'd pulled a sheep from the lake, and how a strange woman helped me? Well: here she is.' He turned to Cora, and said with sudden seriousness: 'I feel I should apologise: I'm sure I was rude, and I don't know what I would have done without you.'

'You were monstrous,' said Cora, 'but you've provided so much entertainment for my friends that I forgive you completely – and here's Martha, and she won't believe me that I thought you a creature that had climbed out of the mud and would certainly climb back into it. Martha, meet the Reverend William Ransome; Mr Ransome: my friend.' She put her arm round Martha's waist, feeling a sudden need to tether herself to what was familiar, and saw her friend give the parson a swift appraising glance which almost certainly found him wanting.

Charles, meanwhile, was applauding, as if the entire affair had been arranged for his pleasure; then urgent matters struck him, and putting a hand pitifully to the splendid curve of his stomach he said to Stella, 'Did I hear you say there is pheasant to be had, and apple pie?' He stood, and offered his left arm to his wife, and his right to his hostess. Joanna, leaping up from her game of cards, remembered the task she'd been set, and flung open the door to the dining room. Light picked out channels cut in crystal glasses and glossed the polished wood of the table, and Stella's forget-me-nots bloomed on their napkins. The room was small, and it was necessary to move in single file past the high-backed dining chairs. There was nothing fashionable in the green wallpaper and the watercolours above the fireplace, but Cora thought she had never seen anything so homely. She thought of the rooms at Foulis Street, with the plasterwork on the high ceilings and the long windows which Michael had forbidden her to hang with curtains, and hoped fervently never to see them again. Joanna, rather awestruck by this magnificent laughing woman in her green dress, gestured shyly to a card on which Cora's name had been written in John's best calligraphy.

'Thank you,' whispered her guest, and lightly tugged the girl's plait: 'I saw you beat Martha at cards: you are far cleverer than me!' (Later, when Joanna took a plate of chocolates to her brothers to recount the night's events, she said, 'She's not old, though she is rich; she has an overnight bag made from crocodile skin; and I don't know why, but she made me think of Joan of Arc. Also – John, don't eat it all – she has an odd sort of voice, with an accent. I don't know where she's from but it must be far away.')

Stella, more intrigued than ever by her guest, watched Cora from beneath her long fair lashes. She'd pictured a lady of studied melancholy, who'd peck at her food, and sometimes fall silent to turn her wedding ring, or open a locket to gaze on the face of the departed. It was bewildering instead to be presented with a woman who ate elegantly, but in great quantities, making smiling apology for her appetite by declaring she'd walked ten miles that morning and would do the same tomorrow. In her presence the conversation veered dizzyingly from the content of Will's sermon ('I know it well – *Therefore will not we fear, though the earth be moved*, and so on? – and how apt for your congregation: how clever of you!') to Charles Ambrose and his political scheming ('Has Colonel Howard succumbed, Charles – Reverend, would you welcome a new MP?'), pausing to briefly take in her scouring of the coast for fossils.

'We told Cora all about your Essex Serpent,' said Charles, peeling the wrapper from a chocolate. 'Both of them, indeed.'

'There is only one that I know of,' said William, with perfect calm: 'And if our guests are interested, they can of course come and see it with me in the morning.'

'It is beautiful,' said Stella, leaning towards Cora: 'A serpent coiled all around the arm of a pew in the church, with wings folded on its back. Will thinks it a blasphemy, and threatens every week to take a chisel to it, but he wouldn't dare.'

'I would like to see it very much, thank you!' The fire burned low, and Cora held her cup close to her breast. 'And tell me: has there been more news of the creature they say's in the river?' Stella, knowing her husband's dislike of any mention of the Trouble, glanced anxiously at him, and prepared to douse the conversation with coffee.

'No news, since there's no creature – though I'm afraid one of my parishioners might disagree! I've been to see Cracknell,' said Will, turning to Stella, 'and either Gog or Magog has given up the ghost.'

'Oh!' said Stella, pouting, resolving to go out the following morning and take the old man a meal: 'Poor Cracknell – as if he's not already lost enough.' She handed her guest a cup of coffee, and said, 'He lives out on the edge of the marsh, and has only just buried the last of his family. Gog and Magog were his goats, and his pride and joy, and keep us well supplied with butter and milk. What happened, Will?'

'To hear him tell it you'd think some monster appeared on the doorstep and snatched one of them out of his arms – no-one believes in the serpent more than Cracknell. But of course it was only that it slipped out of its pen one night and got caught in the marsh, and the tide came in.' He sighed, and said: 'He says he found it frozen solid with terror, frightened – quite literally! – to death. I'm afraid this will do nothing to help put thoughts of this nonsense out of their heads. How can I make them all see how our minds are capable of clever tricks, and that without faith to sustain us we are apt to see' – he flexed his hands, as if grasping for the phrase, and tried again: 'I think it possible to put flesh on the bones of our terrors, most of all when we have turned our back on God.' Conscious of Cora's steady gaze – which was amused, though not contemptuous – he concealed his face behind the steam rising from his coffee cup.

'And you think him insane – you think there can be nothing in what he says?' Cora's pity for the old man did nothing to alleviate her curiosity: here was evidence, of a kind!

The rector snorted. 'A goat, frightened to death? Absurd. No witless beast could comprehend fear to such an extent, even if it could tell the difference between a sea-dragon, or whatever they say it is, and driftwood lying on the marsh. Frightened to death! No: it was on its last legs, and got out of its pen and into the cold. There's no monstrous serpent here, aside from the one carved in the church, and we'd be rid of that, too, if my wife would give me (for once!) my way.'

Cora, ever the devil's advocate, said: 'But you are a man of God, who surely sent signs and wonders to His people: is it so strange, after all, to think He's choosing to do so again, to call us to repentance?' She could not keep the wryness of the sceptic from her voice, and Will, hearing it clearly, raised an eyebrow.

'Now: you do not believe that any more than I do. Our God is a god of reason and order, not of visitations in the night! This is nothing more than the Chinese whispers of a village which has lost sight of the constancy of their Creator. It's my duty to guide them back to comfort and certainty: not to give in to rumour.'

'And what if it is neither rumour nor a call to repentance, but merely a living thing, to be examined and catalogued and explained? Darwin and Lyell –'

Will pushed his cup away impatiently. 'Ah, it is never long before those names come up. Clever men, I don't doubt: I've read both, and there may be much in their theories which later generations will prove to be true. But tomorrow there will be another theory, and another; one will be discredited and the other praised; they'll fall from fashion and be resurrected a decade later with added footnotes and a new edition. Everything is changing, Mrs Seaborne, and much of it for the better: but what use is it to try and stand on quicksand? We will stumble and fall, and in falling become prey to folly and darkness – these rumours of monsters are nothing more than evidence that we have let go of the rope that tethers us to everything that's good and certain.'

'But is your faith not all strangeness and mystery – all blood, and brimstone – all seeing nothing in the dark, stumbling, making out dim shapes with your hands?'

'You speak as if we were in the Dark Ages still, as if Essex still burned its witches! No – ours is a faith of enlightenment and clarity: I am not stumbling – I am running with patience the race that is set before me – there is a lamp on my path!'

Cora smiled. 'I can't tell whether you are using words of your own, or of others: you have me at a disadvantage!' She drank the last of her coffee, which left a coating of bitter grit on her tongue, and said: 'We both speak of illuminating the world, but we have different sources of light, you and I.'

Will, unaccountably elated, feeling he ought to be piqued at this odd woman's grey gaze challenging him at his own table, instead smiled, and went on smiling, and said: 'Then we shall see who first blows out the other's candle,' and raised his cup in a toast. Stella, who could not have taken more pleasure in the exchange if she'd paid for a good seat in the theatre, put her palms together as if she were in the midst of applause; but something caught at her throat, and she began to cough. It seemed too deep a sound to come from so small and fragile a vessel: it shook her body, and she clutched at the tablecloth, and tipped over a glass of wine. Startled at once from his good humour Will crouched at her side, and with little practised taps on her narrow back murmured consolingly in her ear.

'We should fetch hot water – she should breathe in steam,' said Katherine Ambrose; but as soon as the fit arrived it ended.

The woman unfolded, and looked out at them all from wet blue eyes: she said, 'I am sorry – what manners, and you'll all now have the flu, and it takes such a long time to shake off! – will you forgive me if I go up to bed? I've enjoyed myself *so* much' – she reached across the table and clutched Cora's hand in both of hers – 'but you will be here in the morning, and I know we can show you one serpent, at least.'

3

As it turned out the following morning, the All Saints serpent was an innocent-seeming thing on the arm of a Restoration pew. It had been carved in the last days of the Essex Serpent, when rumour had given way to legend, and there were no more warning signs pinned to the oaks and way-posts. Certainly the beast had held no fear for the mischievous craftsman, who'd coiled its tail three times around the spindle with sharp and lapping scales, but omitted either claws or teeth. The wings, Cora conceded, laughing, were a little sinister, looking as if a bat had mated forcibly with a sparrow, and shadows passing over the grinning face gave it the appearance of blinking, but really it was hardly a signifier of the occult. It had endured two hundred years' fondling from affectionate congregants, and its spine was worn smooth.

Joanna, who'd accompanied Cora and her father on their morning walk, ran her finger along a fresh groove in the wood. 'That's where he did it,' she said. 'That's where he was going to cut it off with a chisel, but we wouldn't let him.'

'They hid my toolbox,' he said: 'They won't tell me where it is.' William Ransome looked that morning rather sterner than Cora remembered from dinner in the small hot room, as if he'd put on his office when he put on his collar. It didn't suit him, nor did the blackness of his suit, nor did being freshly shaved, which gave his scarred cheek a raw look. All the same, there lurked deep in his tired eyes a lightness she'd tried to coax out as he'd showed her the small village, and the low-towered church whose flint walls were wet from overnight rain and gleamed in the morning sun.

Cora put the tip of her little finger in the serpent's mouth. *Bite me then I can take it*. 'If you had any sense you'd make a feature of it, and whisper rumours yourself, and thunder from the pulpit, and charge at the door to see the monster.'

'I suppose it might pay for a new window, but Essex is full of horrors, and we can't compete with Hadstock and the Dane-skin door.' Seeing her frown, he said: 'The church door there is studded all over with iron bolts, and under the bolts are scraps of skin. They say an apostate Dane was caught and flayed, and his pelt used to keep the rain out.' She shuddered, delighted, and wanting to give her more he discarded the last of his sternness and said, 'Perhaps they gave him the Viking blood eagle punishment, and cleaved his ribs from his spine and spread them out like wings, and lifted out each lung – oh, you're pale, and I've made Jojo sick!'

The girl gave her father a contemptuous look – *you've let me down: really you have* – and buttoning up her jacket went out to greet the bell-ringers on their morning duty.

'How lucky you are – how *blessed*, you'd probably say!' said Cora, impulsively, watching the girl dart between tombstones and stand beneath the lychgate waving. 'You all seem to have the knack of happiness . . .'

'Don't you?' He sat beside her on the pew, and touched the serpent there. 'You're always laughing; it's contagious, like a yawn!' *We dreaded you*, he thought: *and look at you!* 'You're not what we expected.'

'Oh, lately, yes. Lately – I laugh when I shouldn't. I know I don't give what's expected of me . . . these last few weeks I've thought over and over that there was never a greater difference between what I ought to be, and what I am.' Absurd to talk so freely to almost a stranger, but after all they'd seen each other at their worst, and no conversation could mire them as deeply as that little lake by the Colchester road. 'I am in a state of disgrace, I know it: I always have been, but it was never as visible.' She made such a sudden transition to sadness that he saw, appalled, her grey eyes glaze and brighten, and touching his collar he said (in the grave voice that did so well for these occasions), 'We're taught — and I believe — that it's when we're most lost and feeling most lacking in grace that the source of comfort is nearest ... forgive me, it's not that I mean to impose, only not to say these things would be not to give you a glass of water if I saw you thirsty.' This last phrase was so far out of his usual stock in trade that he looked down at his hands in astonishment, as if to check that it was his own body the words inhabited.

She smiled, and said, 'I'm thirsty, I'm always thirsty — for everything, *everything*! But I gave all this up a long time ago.' She gestured to the high roof with its white stones and the beams that crossed it, and the altar with its blue cloth. 'Sometimes I think I sold my soul, so that I could live as I must. Oh, I don't mean without morals or conscience — I only mean with freedom to think the thoughts that come, to send them where I want them to go, not to let them run along tracks someone else set, leading only *this* way or *that* . . .' Frowning, she ran her thumb along the serpent's spine and said, 'I've never said this before, not to anyone, though I've meant to: but yes, I've sold my soul, though I'm afraid it didn't fetch too high a price. I had faith, the sort I think you might be born with, but I've seen what it does and I traded it in. It's a sort of blindness, or a choice to be mad — to turn your back on everything new and wonderful — not to see that there's no fewer miracles in the microscope than in the gospels!'

'You think — you really think — that it is one or the other: your faith or your reason?'

'Not only my reason — there's not enough of that to set against my soul! – but my liberty. And sometimes I'm afraid I'll be punished for it, but I know punishment, I've learned how to stand it . . .' He didn't understand, and was afraid to ask – but then Joanna came in and stood in the nave while behind her the bell-ringers tugged at their ropes and the bells sounded faintly indoors.

'You are not what we expected,' he said again.

'Nor are you,' said Cora, looking at him as directly as she could in a curious bout of shyness. She thought his collar conferred no more authority than a blacksmith's apron, but even a blacksmith is lord in his forge. 'No, nor are you: I thought you'd be very fat and pompous, and Stella very thin and frail, and your children all horribly devout.'

He grinned – 'Devout!' he said: 'What, traipsing into church in the mornings dripping piety and jostling to get at the bibles!' At that moment Joanna genuflected enormously in front of the altar (a school-friend was a Catholic girl, and Joanna envied her rituals and rosary), and crossed herself three times. Her hair was bound like a halo above her ears; she wore white, and adopted such a prim expression her mouth had all but disappeared. She was so exactly the image of a parson's horrid daughter that Cora and Will looked at each other in delight and could not help falling into another of their fits of laughter.

'I can't find my prayer book,' said Joanna with dignity, not understanding what she'd done and deciding to be offended.

They were laughing still when the congregation arrived to take their minister by surprise. Will went to the porch to greet them as Cora tried once or twice to catch his eye, like a schoolboy wanting a conspirator, but could not: he'd pulled up the drawbridge. The serpent's pew was in a dim corner where she would not be seen, and reluctant to leave the cool quiet church, she thought that she might stay a while.

The small village summoned up a hearty congregation: there was almost (she thought) a kind of festival air, or the good humour brought on by the prospect of a common enemy. Unnoticed in her seat, she heard them whisper of the Trouble, and the serpent, and something seen the night before when the moon had been full and red; certain crops had failed early; there was yet another sprained ankle. A young man who rivalled Ransome for blackness of suit and graveness of aspect put out his hand to any who passed his pew, and made remarks about the Judgment, and the Last Times.

The bells ceased tolling, the people fell silent, and William crossed the nave. When he reached the pulpit steps, a Bible beneath his left arm and (so Cora thought) a look of shyness about him, the door was flung open and there stood Cracknell. He was preceded by such a long dark shadow, and such a powerful smell of damp and mud, that a woman who'd forgotten her glasses shrieked 'It's here!' and clutched her handbag to her breast. Evidently enjoying the effect, the old man paused on the threshold until he could be certain he'd been seen, then walked to the front of the church and sat with folded arms. He'd put on another coat above the mossy one he always wore; it had a fur collar, in which earwigs scuttled in alarm, and many brass buttons.

'Good morning, Mr Cracknell,' said William, without surprise: 'And good morning to you all. *I was glad when they said unto me: let us go to the house of the Lord.* Mr Cracknell, once you're comfortable, we'll begin with hymn number 102, which I know is a favourite of yours. We've missed you, and your voice.' He reached the pulpit, and closed himself in. 'Shall we stand?'

Cracknell, scowling, considered sulking in his seat and refusing to join in, but had always been admired for his sweet tenor and couldn't resist the melody. Since he'd already broken his resolve not to darken the church doors in protest at the hand the Almighty had dealt he might as well be hanged for a goat as for a kid. The loss of Gog a few days before (found tipped on her side, her yellow slotted eyes rolled back in horror and no wound anywhere) had given him a new resolve: the Trouble was no rumour conjured out of air and water, but had flesh and bones, and was nightly creeping nearer. Only that morning Banks reported having seen something black, slick, just beneath the water's surface, and up at St Osyth the day before a boy had drowned on a clear day. For the life of him Cracknell could make no link between the small sins of a small village and divine judgment, but divine judgment it certainly was; and if the vicar wasn't going to give the call to repentance he'd best do it himself.

Fortunately for the Reverend Ransome, Cracknell had chosen a seat warmed by a shaft of sunlight, and between the spring heat and his two coats he sank into a slumber that punctuated the collect with his snores and murmurings.

From her dim corner Cora watched the congregation bow for prayer and stand for song; she smiled at babies held over their mothers' shoulders and pawing at children seated behind; she heard how the preacher's voice altered a little as it moved from prayer to verse. Beside her on the wall a scuffed plaque read *David Bailey Thompson, Choirboy 1868–1871, RIP*; and she thought: Was it that he lived or sang only those three brief years? At her feet the parquet floor lay in the pattern of a herring-bone and the pale wood glowed, and all the stained glass angels had the wings of jays. Something in the second of the hymns – the melody perhaps, or a line or two half-remembered from childhood – touched a place she thought had scarred over, and she began to cry. She had no handkerchief, because she never did; a child saw her tears in astonishment and nudged its mother, who turned, saw nothing, and turned away again. The tears would not stop, and Cora had nothing but her hair to wipe her eyes; only the preacher from his white stone vantage point saw her; saw the deep breaths with which she tried to suppress a sob, and how she tried to hide her face. He caught her eye and held it, and his look was one she could not remember having ever received from a man. It was not amused, or acquisitive, or appalled; had it in no hauteur or cruelty. She imagined it was how he might look at James or Joanna, if he saw them in distress; yet could not have been, because it was a look divided between equals. It was brief, and his gaze moved on, out of delicacy and because the music had ended, and since it was too late to conceal her disgrace Cora let the tears fall.

At the end of the service, her good humour recovered enough that she was able to laugh at herself and at the damp marks on the front of her dress, Cora kept her seat until Will was safely crowded at the door with well-wishers and children. She had no real objection to being seen in her sadness, but was afraid she might be offered pity, and would rather bide her time until she could make her way back to Martha and the safety of her ammonites and notebooks, which had never once made her cry. Deciding it was safe to leave, she slipped out of the pew at its darkest side and encountered – plainly awaiting her – Cracknell in his fur collared coat.

'How do,' he said, delighted at having startled her. 'A stranger in our midst, I see. What're you doing here in them green boots of yours?'

'I may well be a stranger,' said Cora, 'but at least I was on time! Also: my boots are brown.'

'Right enough,' said Cracknell: 'Right enough.' He flicked an earwig from his sleeve. 'You've heard tell of me I expect, and quite rightly too, since the Parson over there's an especial friend of mine and one I cherish somewhat having little else left worth the cherishing.' He gave her his hand, and his name.

'Ah – Mr Cracknell!' she said: 'Certainly I've heard of you, and of your loss last night. I am sorry – a sheep, was it?'

'Sheep, she says! *Sheep!*' He chuckled, and looked about for someone to share in her stupidity, and finding only the jay-winged angels above him bellowed at them 'Sheep!' and laughed a little longer. Then he stopped, as if remembering something, and leaned forward to grasp her by the elbows. His voice dropped, so that quite unconsciously she leaned in to hear him better: 'They've told you then? They've told you and you listened well? About what's out there in the Blackwater by moonlight and lately I'm given to understand by daylight, too, since it was noon when the St Osyth boy got taken and no clouds passing? They've told you, and you've seen it yourself perhaps, *heard* it perhaps, *smelt* it perhaps, like what's on my coatskin now and on your skin also I'll be bound . . .' He drew nearer; his breath had on it both fish and decay; he pressed her deeper back into the shadows. 'Oh I see you know, *Oh I see you know*: you're afraid aren't you? You dream of it, you listen for it, you wait for it, you *hope* for it . . .' and having struck truth where he least expected it brought his mouth very close to her and crooned: 'Oh *what* bit of wickedness it is, knowing the judgment's coming and knowing there's nowhere to hide and in the end you hope for it don't you, *you hope for it*, you can endure it so long as you see it – might it be here now even, you think, having crept up over the threshold while we all bent our heads?' The shadows thickened – the air grew chill – from a little distance Cora heard William Ransome's voice; she searched for him, and could not find him. Cracknell swayed before her, obscuring her vision, crooning 'Oh *he* don't see it, *he* don't feel it, *he* can't help – no good looking over *there*, no good'll come of *that*.'

'Let me go,' said Cora, touching her scarred neck, recalling what she'd said to the rector as they'd sat together where she stood now: *I know punishment, I've learned how to stand it.* Was it punishment she sought – had Michael so mistreated her she hoped for others to do the same – was she malformed now, misshapen, having been pressed and moulded so long? Or was it really that she'd sold her soul and must honour the transaction? 'Let me go,' she said, and put her hand on the pew to steady herself, and found it wet. Her hand slipped; she stumbled against Cracknell and felt the oily pelt of his coat, with its reek of salt and oyster – he stumbled also, and in steadying himself raised up his arms; his long coat opened and spread and showed its leather lining, black, greasy, with the flap of wings. '*Let me go!*' she said, and the door opened, and there stood Joanna at the threshold, letting in the light, and Martha with her, and they were saying 'Who shut the door? Who let the door shut?' – and Cracknell fell into the pew, saying that really he was ever so sorry, only it had been a troublesome few months, what with the one thing and the other. 'I'm coming,' called Cora, then saying it again to be certain her voice came without breaking: 'I'm coming, and we'd better rush, if we're going to catch our train.'

Stella stood at the rectory window, watching children cross the common and hide between the branches of Traitor's Oak. She'd coughed for much of the night, and slept very little, dreaming when she did that someone had come to her room and painted everything blue. The walls had been blue, and so had the ceiling; in place of the carpet were blue tiles vivid with light from the window. The sky had been blue, and so were the leaves of the trees, which bore blue fruit. She had woken distressed to find the same old roses on the wallpaper, and the same old cream linen curtains, and sent James out to pick bluebells from the garden. These she ranged on the windowsill with violets she'd pressed and dried in early spring, and the stem of lavender Will had once put on her pillow. She felt a little hot, though not unpleasantly; and while the bells tolled she carried out a ritual of her own. Touching each bloom with her thumb she said, singingly, over and over, 'Lapis, cobalt, indigo, blue,' but later could not explain why.

II

TO USE
HIS BEST
ENDEAVOUR

APRIL

1st April

Dear Mr Ambrose

As you see, I write from an aptly named establishment in Colchester, where I'm staying for a time with Dr Luke Garrett, who you may recall introduced us last autumn at a dinner in Foulis Street given by the late Michael Seaborne.

I hope you will forgive my writing to you, and seeking your advice. When we met, we spoke briefly about recent Acts of Parliament designed to improve living conditions for the working classes. If I remember correctly, you expressed dismay at the lack of speed with which the Acts are being made into policy.

In recent months I've had an opportunity to learn a little more about the problem of London housing, in particular the crippling rents imposed by absentee landlords. I understand that the work of philanthropic charities (such as the Peabody Trust, for example) is of growing importance in combating the problem of over-crowding, poor accommodation and homelessness.

I am keen to find appropriate ways to make use of the Spencer Trust – I know my father anticipated that I'd do more than simply fund an extravagant lifestyle – and I am very anxious to secure advice from those more knowledgeable than me on how this might be done. I am sure you are already fully aware of the issues, but

*nonetheless I enclose a leaflet from the London Metropolitan
Housing Committee for information.*

*I have recently become acquainted with proposals aiming to
supplement existing provision of new accommodation for the
London poor without placing moral duties on inhabitants –
rewarding the 'good' with safe and healthy homes and leaving the
remainder to their squalor – but rather to bring our fellow men out
of poverty with no conditions attached.*

*I will be in London again in a week or two – if you can spare the
time, may we talk? I'm only too aware that in this matter, as in
most, I am very uninformed.*

I look forward to hearing from you.

Yours sincerely,

GEORGE SPENCER

My dear Stella,

Can it really have been only a week since we met? It feels a month, at least. Thank you again for your hospitality and kindness — I don't believe I've ever eaten so well, or so happily.

I write in the hope I might tempt you up here to Colchester one afternoon. I'd like to visit the castle museum, and thought perhaps the children might come too: Martha has taken such a liking to Joanna that I feel quite jealous. There's a pretty garden, too, with plenty of blue flowers to please you.

I've enclosed a note for the good Reverend, together with a leaflet I hope he'll find interesting . . .

Write soon!

With love,

CORA

Dear Reverend Ransome –

I hope you are well, and write to thank you all for your hospitality and kindness. I am so glad to have met you under more auspicious circumstances than before.

The oddest thing happened soon after we met, and I wanted to tell you at once. We took a trip to Saffron Walden, in order to look at the Guildhall, and visit the museum. Such a lovely town, it would redeem Essex in anyone's eyes: I could almost be persuaded there was the scent of saffron blowing up the streets. And what did I find, in a bookshop on a sunny corner, but this (see enclosed) – a facsimile of that original pamphlet warning of a flying serpent. STRANGE NEWS OUT OF ESSEX, it says: a true relation, no less! One Miller Christy has taken the trouble of reproducing it, and for that we must be thankful. There's even an illustration, though I must say nobody looks very scared.

Watch out for it, won't you? No man bested by a sheep could expect to triumph over such a foe.

Sincerely,

CORA SEABORNE

William Ransome
All Saints Rectory
Aldwinter
6th April

Dear Mrs Seaborne

Thank you for the pamphlet, which I read with amused interest and return here (John thought it another colouring book, I'm afraid, while James entertains himself designing a crossbow to defend the household). I promise as faithfully as my collar allows that if ever I see a monstrous serpent with wings like umbrellas clacking its beak on the common, I'll trap it in a fishing-net and send for you at once.

I enjoyed meeting you. I am often nervous on Sunday mornings and you were a welcome distraction.

Will you stay in Colchester long? You are always welcome in Aldwinter. Cracknell has taken a liking to you, as have we all.

In Christian love,

WILLIAM RANSOME

I

In the last week of April, when all the Essex hedgerows were white with cow parsley and blackthorn flower, Cora moved with Martha and Francis into a grey house beside Aldwinter common. They'd grown tired of Colchester and the Red Lion: Francis had exhausted the landlord's store of Sherlock Holmes (marking inaccuracies in red ink and improbabilities in green), and Cora had grown dissatisfied with the town's civilised little river, which could certainly conceal nothing larger than a pike.

The memory of her encounter with Cracknell – the saline scent on the collar of his coat, how he'd conjured from dark corners the waiting beast in the Blackwater – had made her restless. She felt something awaited her over in Aldwinter, though whether she sought the living or the dead she couldn't quite say. Often she thought herself childish and credulous to be in pursuit of a living fossil in (of all places!) an Essex estuary, but if Charles Lyell countenanced the idea of a species outwitting extinction, so could she. And hadn't the Kraken been nothing but legend, until a giant squid pitched up on a Newfoundland beach, and was photographed in a tin bath by the Reverend Moses Harvey? Besides all that, here was the Essex clay beneath her feet, concealing who-knew-what, biding its time. She'd go out walking with her coat's hem muddy and the rain on her cheek and say, 'I don't see why it shouldn't be me, and shouldn't be here: Mary Anning knew nothing about anything until a landslide killed her dog.'

News of the grey house standing empty on the common had come from Stella Ransome. She'd gone to Colchester to buy bolts of blue cloth and said, 'Won't you come to Aldwinter, once you're tired of the town? The Gainsforths have been looking for tenants for months now, but only someone very strange would go out there to live with us! It's a good house, there's a garden – summer's not long off; you can hire Banks to take you out on the estuary: you'll never find your serpent on the High Street!' She took Cora's hand, and said: 'Besides, we want you near us. Joanna wants Martha, James wants Francis, and we all want you.'

'I *have* always wanted to learn to sail,' said Cora, smiling and taking Stella's small hands. 'Will you put me in touch with the Gainsforths, and vouch for my good character? Goodness, Stella, your hands are hot: take off your coat, and tell me how you are.'

Francis, listening from his newly favoured position under the dining table, approved thoroughly: the move to Colchester had given him new kingdoms to conquer, and he was ready for more. He'd exhausted the town's small store of treasure (the gull's egg he'd blown and preserved, the silver fork which Taylor had let him take from the High Street ruin), and shared his mother's certainty that something was waiting on the Blackwater marsh. In the months since his father's death he had become (he felt) more or less an adult himself: neither Cora nor Martha attempted any more to cosset or coddle him, and certainly he never asked for it. His tendency to arrive unbidden in the night or early morning, watchful at the door or window, was long gone – he didn't know why he'd done it, only that it was no longer necessary. Instead he grew self-contained and contentedly silent, and bore their Aldwinter visits with good grace. The rector's sons treated him with an amiable contempt that suited him perfectly: on the two occasions they'd met the boys had ranged across the common and exchanged perhaps a dozen words in several hours. 'Aldwinter,' he said, trying it out for size: 'Aldwinter.' He liked the three syllables; he liked the declining cadence. His mother glanced down at him and said, with relief, 'Would you like that, Frankie? There, then: it's settled.'

2

In his rooms on the Pentonville Road, sleeping off bad wine, Dr Luke Garret was woken by a tumult beneath his window. A running boy had brought a message, and stood obstinate on the doorstep awaiting a response. Opening the folded sheet of paper, Garrett read:

Suggest attend wards immediately. Patient presents with stab incision left-hand side above fourth rib (police notified). Wound measuring one and one eighth of an inch, penetrating through intercostal muscle to the heart. Primary examination suggests cardiac muscle undamaged; incision to pericardial sac (?). Patient male, twenties, conscious and breathing. Possible candidate for surgical intervention if attended within the hour. Anticipate your arrival and will prepare accordingly – Maureen Fry.

He gave such a bellow of joy that the waiting boy, startled, abandoned all hope for a tip and slipped back into the crowd. Alone among the hospital staff (saving always Spencer), Sister Maureen Fry was Garrett's champion and confidante. Thwarted in her own desire to take up knife and needle, she saw in Garrett's disruptive fierce ambition a proxy for her own. Her long service and formidable intellect, combined with an implacable serenity wielded as a weapon against the arrogance of men, caused her to seem as essential to the hospital's structure as any of its supporting walls. Garrett had grown used to her near-silent attendance in the operating rooms, and suspected (though was never so certain as to be able to thank her) that to have her as ally had permitted him to attempt several operations which might otherwise have been considered too grave a risk. And none came so burdened with risk as this: no surgeon had ever made a successful attempt to close a wound to the heart. The impossibility of doing so had become attended by romance and legend, as if it were a task set by a goddess no-one could ever hope to placate. Less than a year before, one of the most promising surgeons in an Edinburgh hospital, believing he could remove a bullet from a wounded soldier's heart, had lost his patient on the table, and in his shame and grief gone quietly home and shot himself. (He'd aimed, of course, for the heart; but with a shaking hand misjudged the aim and died of an infection.)

None of this occurred to Luke Garrett, there on the sunlit doorstep with the sheet of paper held to his chest. 'God bless you!' he roared at the baffled passers-by, meaning both patient and nurse, and whoever had so conveniently wielded the knife. He put on his coat – he patted his pockets – his money was gone on drink, and there was none remaining for a cab. Laughing, he ran full-tilt the mile to the hospital gate, shedding with each step the last of the night's dreariness, and on arrival found himself expected. His entrance to the ward was blocked by a senior surgeon with a beard the colour and shape of a garden spade, who more or less braced himself in the doorframe. Beside him, looking anxious as he so often did, Spencer stood with his hands raised in a placating gesture, now and then gesturing to the note he held, which Luke saw clearly to have also come from Sister Fry. Behind them both a door was opened and pulled quickly shut, though not before Luke glimpsed a pair of long, narrow feet extended beneath a white sheet.

'Dr Garrett,' said the older surgeon, tugging at his beard: 'I know what you are thinking, and you cannot do this – you cannot.'

'Can't I?' This was said so mildly that Spencer drew back in alarm. There was, he knew, no mildness anywhere in Luke. 'What's his name?'

'I mean that you both cannot, and you must not. His family is with him: let him reach the end in peace. I knew someone would send for you!' He wrung his hands. 'I will not let you bring disgrace on this hospital – his mother is with him, has not stopped talking since she came in.'

Garrett took a step further, and smelt a kind of onion ripeness coming from the surgeon, and above it the consoling reek of iodine.

'Tell me his name, Rollings.'

'You've no use for his name whatever. When I discover who sent for you . . . you're not going in. I will not let you. No-one ever treated a wound of the heart and had the patient live, not all the better men than you. And he is a man – he is not one of your dead toys – and think of the reputation of the hospital!'

'My dear Rollings' – this was said with such exquisite politeness that Spencer fairly recoiled – 'you could not stop me if you tried. I will waive my fee, if they give me permission; and they will, because they will be desperate. Besides: the Royal Borough has no reputation at all save the one I've given it!'

Rollings shuffled in the doorway as if he wanted to swell to fit each corner and turn to steel, flushing such a deep and meaty red Spencer came near in fear that he might faint. 'I am not speaking of *rules*,' he said: 'I'm speaking of a man's life – it is not *possible* – you will ruin your reputation – it is his heart! It is his heart!'

Garrett had not moved, only seemed in the dim corridor to have grown not larger but more massy, more dense: he had not lost his temper, but seemed almost to thrum with a great store of energy barely suppressed. Rollings sagged against the wall: he knew himself bested. Passing him with a look that was almost kindly, Garrett crossed swiftly into a small room, scrupulously clean. The bright antiseptic air smelt of carbolic acid, and of lavender scent rising from the handkerchief drawn through the hands of a woman seated by the patient's bedside. She leaned forward at intervals, confidingly, whispering to the man beneath the white sheet: 'Shouldn't think you'll be long off work – we won't bother them yet.'

Maureen Fry, in a dress starched stiff as card and thin rubber gloves, stood at the window adjusting a cotton blind to let the late sun in. She turned to greet the men with a placid nod: if she'd heard the intemperate wrangling just beyond the closed door it was clear she'd never acknowledge it. 'Dr Garrett,' she said; 'Dr Spencer. Good afternoon. You of course will prepare before examining the patient, who is doing nicely.' She handed Spencer a small file on which was recorded the declining pulse, the peaking temperature. Neither Garrett nor Spencer were fooled by a form of words calculated to convey nothing at all to the mother: he was not doing nicely, and likely never would again. 'His name is Edward Burton,' she said: 'Twenty-nine, and in good health: a clerk in the Prudential Insurance Company. He was attacked by a stranger as he walked home to Bethnal Green; they found him on the steps of St Paul's.'

'Edward Burton,' said Luke, and turned to the man beneath the sheet.

He was so slight that he hardly lifted the white cloth covering him, but tall, so that his feet and shoulders were visible. His collarbones were sharp, and between them the declivity of his throat fluttered visibly. Spencer thought: *He's swallowed a moth*, and felt sick. A high colour spread across the patient's cheeks, which were broad and high, and marked with moles in black clusters. His hair had begun to recede early, leaving a white stretch of forehead on which beads of sweat stood out. He might have been twenty; he might have been fifty; he was probably more beautiful at that moment than he had ever been before. He was conscious, and had about him an air of great concentration, as if the expelling of breath were a skill that had taken years to perfect. Listening carefully to his mother, he interjected where she paused, but only to say something about crows and rooks.

'He was all right a few hours ago,' said his mother, apologetically, as if they'd missed seeing him at his best and would go away disappointed. 'They put a plaster on. Can you show them?' The nurse lifted first the thin arm, and then the sheet. Spencer saw a large square plaster fastened over the left nipple and extending a few inches down. There was no blood or suppuration: it looked as if a cloth had been draped over him as he slept. His mother said, 'He was all right when they brought him in. He was talking. They patched him up a bit. There wasn't much bleeding, there wasn't much of anything. They put him away in here out of sight and I think they forgot about us. He's just getting tired, that's all. Why didn't anyone come? Why can't I take him home?'

Gently, Luke said: 'He is dying.' He left the word in the air a while to see if she'd take it up, but she only smiled uncertainly, as if it had been a joke in poor taste. Luke crouched by her chair, and touched her lightly on the hand, and said, 'Mrs Burton, he's going to die. By morning, he'll be dead.'

Spencer, who knew how eagerly Luke had awaited a wound like this – had seen dogs and corpses cut and probed in preparation, and once let Luke stitch and restitch a long cut of his own to perfect his needlework – saw his friend's patience with astonishment and love.

'Nonsense!' the woman said, and they heard the fabric of her handkerchief tear between her fingers. 'Nonsense! Look at him! He'll sleep it off!'

'His heart is cut. The bleeding is all in there, all in here' – Garrett thumped his own breast – 'his heart is getting weak.' Reaching for words she might understand he said, 'It will get weaker and weaker like an animal bleeding in the forest, and then it will stop and there'll be no more blood anywhere in him, and everything – his lungs and his brain – will starve.'

'*Edward* –' she said.

Luke saw the blows land, and that his prey was weak; laying a hand on her shoulder he said: 'What I mean is – he will die, unless you let me help.'

There was a moment of struggling against the truth, then she began to cry. In a quiet voice that carried through the weeping with more authority than Spencer had ever seen him muster, Luke said, 'You are his mother: you brought him into the world, and you can keep him in it. Will you let me operate? I . . .' – his belief in the possibility of success did battle with his honesty, and reached an uneasy truce – 'I am very good – I'm the best, and I'll do it without payment. It's not been done before and they'll tell you it can't be done, but for everything there's a first time and it's the time that matters most. You want me to promise, I know, and I can't, but can you trust me, at least?'

Outside the door there was a brief commotion. Spencer suspected that Rollings had alerted various administrative authorities, and leaned against the door with his arms folded. He caught the nurse's eye, and each conveyed silently *Oh we are sailing very close to the wind*. The commotion subsided.

The woman said, between gasps, 'What will you do to him?'

'Really, it's not so bad,' said Luke. 'His heart is protected by a kind of bag, like an infant in the womb. The cut is there – I have seen it – I could show you? – yes, perhaps you'd rather not. The cut is there, no longer than your little finger. I'll stitch it up, and the bleeding will stop, and he will – he might – recover. If we do nothing . . .' He spread out his hands in a gesture of dismay.

'Will it hurt?'

'He will know nothing about it at all.'

She began to gather herself piece by piece, beginning at her feet, which she set a little further apart on the floor, and ending with her hair, which she brushed away from her face as if to show off her newly acquired resolve. 'All right,' she said. 'Do what you like. I'm going to go home now.' She did not look at her son, only grasped his foot as she passed the bed. Spencer went out with her, to do as he always did: soothe, and placate, and with the authority conferred by wealth and status protect his friend from the consequences of his actions.

Garrett meanwhile stooped over the bed and said briskly, 'In a little while you'll have a good deep sleep – are you tired? I think you are.' Then he took the man's hand, feeling foolish, and saying, 'I am Luke Garrett; I hope you'll remember my name when you wake.'

'One rook is a crow,' said Edward Burton, 'but two crows are rooks.'

'Confusion's only to be expected,' said Garrett, and replaced the man's wrist on the white sheet. He turned to Sister Fry, and said, 'Are you able to attend?' though it was merely politeness, since it was inconceivable that she would not. She nodded, and in that silent response conveyed such quiet confidence in Garrett's skill that his pulse – not yet settled since running there – began to slow.

When he and Spencer entered the operating theatre, hands raw from scrubbing, the porters had departed. Edward Burton lay high on the bed, eyes fixed on Sister Fry, who'd changed into a fresh uniform and was withdrawing with practised monotony a series of bottles and instruments which she laid out on steel trays.

Spencer would've liked to explain to the patient what was to come next – that the chloroform worked slowly and sickly, and that he should not fight the mask, but would wake (would he wake?) in due course, throat aching from the tube through which the ether passed. But Garrett required silence, and both Spencer and the nurse had come to anticipate what he required next by little more than nods and nudges, and how directed were the black looks he gave above the white mask.

The patient immobile, the rubber tube tugging at his lip to give the impression of a sneer, Garrett removed the plaster and surveyed the wound. The tension of the skin had caused it to open in the shape of a blind eye. Burton had so little fat on him that the grey-white bone of the rib was visible beneath the severed skin and muscle. The opening was insufficient, and having first washed the flesh in iodine Garret took his knife and made it larger by an inch in each direction. With Spencer and Fry attending, to suck and swab and keep clear his view, Garrett saw it would be necessary first to remove a section of the rib that covered the wounded heart. With a fine bone-saw (he'd used it once to amputate a girl's crushed toe, despite her protestations that she couldn't possibly dance in sandals if she was down to just the four) he cut the rib to four inches shorter than creation intended, and put it in a pan held nearby. Then with steel retractors that would not have looked out of place in the hands of a railway engineer he opened up a cavity and peered within. *We're so tightly packed*, thought Spencer, marvelling as always at how bright and beautiful it was. The marbling of red and purplish-blue, and the scant deposits of yellow fat: they were not the colours of nature. Once or twice the muscles all around the opening flexed slowly, like a mouth arrested in a yawn.

And then there was the heart, thrumming in its slick case, the damage seeming so slight. Garrett had promised that the cut was to the case alone and had gone no further, and believed himself truthful, and now with a probing finger saw that he was. The chambers and valves were undamaged: he gave a little cry of relief.

Spencer watched as Luke slipped in his hand – the wrist angled a little, the fingers curved – to cup the heart where he could, to feel it, because (he'd always said, even with the dead ones) it was the most intimate thing, and sensual, and he saw by touch as much as by sight. With his left hand he steadied the heart, and with his right he took from Fry the curved needle threaded with a catgut ligature so fine it would have been fit for wedding silk.

Much later, Spencer would be stopped on the wards and in the corridors and asked: 'How long did it take? How many stitches were there?' and he took to saying 'A thousand hours and a thousand stitches,' though in truth it seemed he barely breathed in and out again before he heard the grinding of the retractor bolts, and the wet slip of the instrument as it was removed; the muscles at the rim of the open cavity slammed shut, and then it was only the skin being stitched over a hollow place where the rib had once been.

They passed a long hour then, moving about the bedside as opiates replaced chloroform and dressings were fitted and nervously watched for slow or sudden bloomings of blood. Sister Maureen Fry, straight-backed and bright-eyed, as if she could happily have done it all again and then again, passed them water which Spencer could not drink, and which Luke took in draughts that almost made him sick. Others came and went, peering curiously around the door, hoping for triumph or disaster or both, but seeing no movement and hearing nothing went away disappointed.

At the beginning of the second hour Edward Burton opened his eyes and said loudly, 'I was just by St Paul's, that was all, wondering how the dome stays up,' then, more quietly, 'I've got a sore throat.' To those who'd seen so much of life in ebb and flow, the colour on his cheek and the attempt to lift his head were as telling as any careful daylong chart of pulse and temperature. The sun had gone down: he'd see it come up.

Garrett turned, and left, and finding one of the many cupboards where linens were stored crouched for a long while in the dark. A dreadful trembling took hold of him, and shook him so violently that only by making a straitjacket of his own arms could he prevent his whole body from throwing itself against the closed door. Then it subsided, and he began instead to cry.

3

William Ransome, walking coatless on the common, saw Cora come towards him. From a distance he'd known at once it was their visitor: she strode like a boy, and seemed always to be pausing to peer at something in the grass, or to put something in her pocket. Low sun lit the long hair loose upon her shoulders; when she saw him, she smiled and raised her hand.

'Good afternoon, Mrs Seaborne,' he said.

'Good afternoon, Reverend,' said Cora. They paused, and smiled, not taking their greeting seriously, as if long years had passed and made the niceties absurd.

'Where've you been?' he said, seeing that certainly she must have walked miles: her coat was unbuttoned, her shirt damp at the neck and marked with moss, and she held a stem of cow parsley.

'I'm not sure: two weeks an Aldwinter woman and still it's all a mystery! I walked west, I know that. I bought some milk, which was the best I ever had; I trespassed on the grounds of a stately home, and frightened the pheasants. My nose is burned – look! – and I fell over a stile, and am bleeding from the knee.'

'Conyngford Hall, I should think' – he did not acknowledge her wounds: 'Were there turrets, and a sad peacock in a cage? You were lucky to get away without being shot for a poacher.'

'A bad squire, then? I should've set the peacock free.' She surveyed him placidly. No man ever looked less a parson: his shirt was loose, and grubby at the cuffs; there was soil beneath his nails. His clean Sunday cheek had given way to a light beard, and where the sheep's hoof had left its curled scar, no hair grew.

'The worst of squires! Trap a rabbit on his acres and he'll have you up before the beak by breakfast.'

They fell easily into step, matching pace for pace; it occurred to him that their legs must be the same length, their height the same, perhaps the span of their open arms. Cherry blossom drifted on the idle wind. Cora felt herself brimming with things to offer, and could not keep herself from giving them: 'Just before I saw you a hare paused right there on the path and looked at me. I'd forgotten the colour of their fur, like almonds just out of the shell – the strength in their hind legs, and how tall they are, as they pelt off over the fields, suddenly, as if they've remembered something they ought to be doing!' She glanced at him – perhaps a country man would think her childish in her delight? – but no: he smiled, and inclined his head. 'There was a chaffinch,' she said, 'and the flash of something yellow, which may have been a siskin – are you any good with birds? I'm not. Everywhere there's acorns splitting open and sending out a root and a stem: a white thing burrowing into the soil where last year's leaves are rotting, and a green leaf beginning to unfold! How did I never see that before? I wish I had one to show you.'

He looked, bemused, into the empty palm she held out. How strange she was, to notice such things, and think of telling him; it sat curiously on a woman whose man's coat could not conceal her shirt's fine silk, its pearl fastenings, the diamond on her hand. 'I'm not as good with birds as I'd like,' he said, 'though I can tell you the blue tit wears a highwayman's mask, and the great tit wears the black cap of the judge that's going to hang him!' She laughed, and he diffidently said: 'I wish you'd use my name. Do you mind? Mr Ransome will always be my father.'

'If you like,' she said. 'William. Will.'

'And did you hear the woodpeckers? I listen for them, always.

And have you found the Essex Serpent – are you come to deliver us from bonds of fear?'

'Neither hide nor hair of it!' said Cora, ruefully: 'Even Cracknell looks cheerful when I mention it. I believe you informed the wretched thing I was coming, and sent it to Suffolk with a flea in its ear.'

'Oh no,' said Will: 'I assure you, rumours abound! Cracknell may put a brave face on for a lady but he never leaves his window without a candle. He's keeping poor Magog indoors, and her milk's dried up.' She smiled; he said: 'What's more, either the folk of St Osyth are careless with cattle or something's taken two calves from their mothers and they've not been seen since.' *Likelier to be theft*, he thought, *but let her have her daydream*.

'Well, that's encouraging, at least. No hope, I suppose' – she spoke gravely – 'that another man has drowned?'

'None, Mrs Seaborne – Cora? – though it pains me to disappoint. Now then: where was it you were going?'

They'd come, by silent consensus, to the rectory gate. Behind them on the common lengthened the shadow of Traitor's Oak; before them the chequered path was bordered by blue hyacinths. They gave out a strong scent, and Cora reeled with it, felt it indecent – it caused a response in her so like unsought desire that her pulse quickened.

'Where was I going?' She looked down at her feet, as if they'd carried her without consent. 'I suppose that I was going home.'

'Must you? Won't you come in? The children are out, and Stella will be glad to see you.' And she was: the door opened without their knocking, as if they'd been awaited, and there was Stella, all her colours vivid in the dim hall – her silver hair loose, her eyes bright.

'Mrs Seaborne – how funny: we talked about you at breakfast – didn't we? – we hoped you'd come soon! William Ransome, don't leave your guest on the doorstep: bring her in, make her comfortable – have you eaten? Won't you have tea?'

'I can always eat,' said Cora, 'always!' She saw how Will stooped to kiss his wife; how lightly his fingers slipped through the fine fair curls above her ear, and marvelled at their tenderness (*I'll fill your wounds with gold*, Michael had said, and pulled one by one the hairs from the nape of her neck, leaving a bald place there the size of a penny).

A little later, in a sunny room, they dawdled over plates of cake, and admired the daffodils blooming on the table. 'And tell me: how is Katherine? How is Charles?' Stella's appetite for the lives of others made her an easy companion, since she wanted only to be spun stories and never much minded embellishment. 'They're both appalled that you're here. Charles says he's going to send a case of French wine and that you'll last a month at most.'

'Charles is much too busy to think of wine – even French wine. You see: he has turned philanthropist!'

Will raised an eyebrow, and drained his tea. The notion seemed unlikely: Charles was good-hearted, but in the fashion of a man devoted to his own happiness, and – always supposing it cost him no great effort – that of those he liked. That he'd exert himself for the benefit of what he was in the deplorable habit of calling 'the great unwashed' was surprising indeed. 'Charles *Ambrose*?' he said. 'No-one was ever fonder of anyone than I am of him, but he troubles himself more over the cut of his shirts than the state of the nation!'

'It's true!' said Cora, laughing. (She'd have liked to defend the man, but knew were he to overhear, slumbering in his velvet seat at the Garrick, he'd surely have nodded, and laughed, and agreed.) 'It's Martha's doing.' She turned to Stella. 'Martha is a socialist. Well: sometimes I think we all must be, when it comes down to it, if we have a grain of sense – but for Martha it's as much a way of life as Matins and Evensong to the good Reverend here. London housing is the loudest bee in her bonnet (which, honestly, contains entire hives): workers damned to slum conditions unless they prove themselves deserving of a roof, and meanwhile land-lords fatten themselves on rent, and vice, and Parliament sits on cushions stuffed with their coins. She grew up in Whitechapel, and her father was a working man and a good one, and they all lived well enough; but she never forgot what was just beyond the doorstep. How was it the newspapers put it, a year or two ago – "Outcast London"! You remember – you saw it?'

It was clear they had not, and Cora – who'd clean forgotten she was not in Bayswater or Knightsbridge, and that what occupies London gossip for months might not filter far from the waters of the Thames – could not help giving each a censorious look. 'Perhaps I know it well only because of Martha, who really, I think, could recite it by now. It was printed and reprinted so often a few years back that you almost expected to find it wrapping your fish and chips.'

'And what was it – what did it say?' said Stella. *Outcast London!* The phrase appealed to her ready pity.

'A pamphlet produced by a group of clergymen I believe – *The Bitter Cry of Outcast London*, and once read not soon forgotten. I thought that I'd seen everything the city had to offer from best to worst, but never anything like that. In one cellar a mother and father living with their children and their pigs – a baby dead and cut open for the coroner right there on the table, since there wasn't any room in the mortuary! And women working seventeen hours a day stitching buttons and buttonholes . . . unable to pause long enough to eat, and never earning enough to keep warm, so that they might as well have been sewing their own shrouds. I remember Martha would not buy new clothes for years, saying she'd not be clothed in her sisters' suffering!'

Stella's eyes brimmed. 'How could we not have heard? Will – isn't it your duty, to know, and to help?'

Cora saw his discomfort, and in the absence of an observer might have sought to worsen it, out of mischief and principle. But it wouldn't do to diminish a man in the eyes of his wife, and she said: 'I'm sorry to distress you! The book did its work – the cry was heard – they've been pulling down the slums, though they tell me what goes up in their place is hardly better. Martha has it in hand. She's enlisted the help of our friend Spencer, who is embarrassingly rich, and who in turn is calling on Charles. I hear there's even a Committee. Well – much good may it do them.'

'I hope it will! I hope it will!' said Stella. To Cora's dismay she dabbed at her eyes, and said, 'All of a sudden I'm tired – Cora, would you forgive me if I went up to bed? I can't shake the flu, and you'll think I'm very feeble, when really until this winter just gone I hardly had a day in bed, not even when I had my babies.' She rose, and so did her guest; Cora kissed her, and felt how hot her wet cheek was.

'But you've not finished your tea, and I know there was something Will had to show you, if you can stay a little longer? Will, play the host! Perhaps' – she showed them her dimples – 'you can talk over your sermon preparation, and Cora can give you her verdict?' Cora laughed, and said that she was in no position to comment; Will laughed, and said that in any case he would not dream of subjecting her to it.

The door closed behind Stella – they heard her footstep on the stair – and it seemed to them both that there came a slight alteration in the air. It was not precisely that the room seemed at once smaller, and more warmly lit – though certainly it did, as the sun fell, and on the table the yellow blooms took on the look of flames burning in their bowl. It was a sensation of freedom, as though the curious liberty both felt as they'd crossed the common had returned. Will also was conscious of feeling mildly aggrieved: he did not for a moment think his guest had set out to make him look foolish, but that had been the effect. With little more than a look she'd made him feel chastised, and rightly so – when had his conscience dwindled down to the scope of the parish boundary? 'Grace,' he said, suddenly. 'On Sunday I'll talk about the quality of grace, which I suppose is a gift of a kind – of goodness and mercy undeserved, and unexpected.'

'That'll do, for your sermon,' she said. 'That's quite enough. Let them go home early and walk in the forest, and find God there.' This was so nearly his own preferred method of worship that his annoyance evaporated; he threw himself into an armchair, and gestured that she should do the same.

'What was it you were going to show me?' In Stella's presence Cora had sat ladylike, neat, her ankles crossed beneath her skirts; now, she curled in the corner of a couch, leaning against the arm and resting her chin in a cupped hand.

'Really,' he said, 'I wish she hadn't mentioned it – it's nothing – only a bit of stuff I found on the saltings last week, and put in my pocket, thinking you might like to see it. Come with me!'

It did not occur to him then that no-one but Stella ever entered his study – that it was neither clean nor tidy, and that anyone caring to look at the litter of books and notes on the desk and floor might've made a guess at the full character of his mind. Not even the children were allowed to enter, unless expressly invited, and then only in order to be chastised or taught; it would seem to him less exposing to relieve himself against Traitor's Oak at noon than to allow anyone across the threshold. But none of this struck him as he opened the door, and stood back to let her pass, nor was he troubled by how immediately her attention turned to his desk, or that her letter was set beside his papers, thin at the folds from being opened and reopened. 'Do sit,' he said, gesturing to the leather armchair which had been his father's; and she did, spreading out her skirts. He reached up to a bookshelf and withdrew a white paper packet, which he placed on the desk and opened very carefully, taking out a pale lump a little larger than a child's fist. Embedded within were several black and pitted fragments, as if a rough plate had been smashed, and concealed for some reason inside a piece of clay. Will picked it up, and showed her, stooping beside her chair; looking down she saw where his hair grew whorled at the crown, and the few white threads which grew thick and gleaming as wire. 'It's nothing, I'm sure,' he said, 'but there it was, broken away from one of the banks down in the creeks; I go down so often, and never saw anything like it before, but then until you came I wouldn't have thought to look! What do you think – ought we to contact the museum in Colchester, and offer to make a donation?'

Cora was not entirely sure: ammonites and toadstones she knew well enough, and the shocking white curl of a shark's tooth biting through its lump of clay; she knew the puffed and spiny echinoid when she saw it, and the flared ribs of a trilobite, and was convinced that once at Lyme Regis she'd struck a seam in which was concealed the bone of a small vertebrate. But she'd learned the humility of scholars: that the more she knew, the more she did not know. Will flexed his hand – the lump rolled in his palm – a piece of clay broke off, and fell between his outspread fingers to the floor. 'Well then,' he said: 'What is the expert's verdict?' He looked both eager and shy, as if certain there was nothing he could show her that might please her, but hoping all the same that he might. She drew her thumbnail across the black surface; it had grown warm from his hand, and was smooth. 'I wonder,' she said, grateful that the thought had occurred, 'if it's a kind of lobster – I'll never remember the name! – *hoploparia*, that's it. I can't tell you the age of it, though several millions of years, I imagine.' (And would he counter this with talk of an earth barely cool from creation?)

'Surely not!' he said, evidently delighted, though attempting to conceal it. 'Surely not! Well – if you say so, Mrs Seaborne: I bow to your knowledge.' And indeed he did bow, standing, and holding the crumbling bit of mud out as he did so, and placing it on the mantelpiece with a reverence that was only partly mocking.

'Will,' said Cora: 'How did you come to *be* here?' She spoke with a kindly hauteur very like that of a minor royal greeting dignitaries at the opening of a library; they both heard it, and smiled.

'Here, you mean?' he said, taking in the uncurtained window which overlooked the lawn, the pot of leaking pens, the several drawings of mechanical devices which served no purpose other than to turn and turn.

'Here, I mean! Here, in Aldwinter – you ought to be elsewhere – Manchester, London, Birmingham – not always fifty paces from a rural church with no equal near to hand! If I met you elsewhere I would think you a – a lawyer, or an engineer, or a government minister – what, did you vow to take holy orders at fifteen, when you were a child, and were afraid to break your promise in case you were struck by lightning for your betrayal!'

Leaning against the windowsill Will surveyed his guest, and frowned. 'Am I really so interesting – did you never meet a clergyman before?'

'Oh – I am sorry – do you mind?' said Cora. 'I have met more clergymen than I care to remember, but you surprise me: that's all.'

He shrugged, elaborately. 'You are a solipsist, Mrs Seaborne – can you really not imagine that I might take a path which differs from yours and be happy walking there?'

No, she thought: *no, I cannot.*

'I'm not an unusual or interesting man. You're mistaken if you think so. For a time I wanted be an engineer, and revered Pritchard and Brunel, and once skipped school and travelled by train all the way to Ironbridge, and made drawings of the rivets and struts; I'd sit bored in class and make plans for box-girder bridges. But in the end it was purpose I wanted, not achieve-ment – you see the difference? I have a good enough mind – if I'd played my cards right I could even now be sitting on the back benches debating some minor point of law – wondering whether it's turbot for dinner and has Ambrose found another parliamen-tary candidate and ought I to go to Drury Lane or the Mall for dinner. But it chills me. Give me an afternoon guiding Cracknell back to the God who never left him over a thousand Drury Lane dinners. Give me an evening with the Psalms on the saltings and the sky breaking open over a thousand walks in Regency Park.' He could not remember having ever spoken so long on the subject of himself, and wondered how she'd contrived to make him do so. 'Besides,' he said, a little irritated: 'I have an equal in Stella.'

'I think it a shame, that's all.'

'A shame!'

'Yes – a shame. That in the modern age a man could impover-ish his intellect enough to satisfy himself with myth and legend – could be content to turn his back to the world and bury him-self in ideas which even your father must have thought outdated! Nothing is more important than to use your mind to its last degree!'

'I've turned my back on nothing – I have done the reverse. Do you think everything can be accounted for by equations and soil deposits? I am looking up, not down.' There again was another of those little alterations in the air, as if the pressure had dropped, and a storm was coming: each was aware of having grown angry with the other, uncertain why.

'You certainly don't seem to be looking outward – I know that at least!' Cora found herself braced against the arms of her chair, wanting to be a little unkind: 'What do you know of England now, of how the roads are laid, and where they're going – of places in the city where children have never seen the Thames – never seen a patch of grass. How content you must be, reciting your Psalms to the air, and coming home to a pretty wife and books that left the press three hundred years ago!' It was unjust, she knew; she faltered a little, wanting neither to retreat nor press on. And if she'd intended to infuriate her host she succeeded; he said, with a sharpness to his voice on which she could have cut herself, 'How perceptive of you, to have my character and motives sketched out on our third meeting.' Their gazes met. 'It is not I who goes grubbing about in the mud for scraps of dead things – it's not I who has run away from London and lost myself in a science I barely understand.'

'True,' said Cora. 'Oh well, true enough!' and smiled; and the effect was to disarm him completely.

'Well then,' he said. 'What are *you* doing here?'

'I am not sure. Liberty, I suppose. I lived so long under constraints. You wonder why I grub about in the mud – it's what I remember from childhood. Barely ever wearing shoes – picking gorse for cordial, watching the ponds boiling with frogs. And then there was Michael, and he was – civilised. He would pave over every bit of woodland, have every sparrow mounted on a plinth. And he had me mounted on a plinth. My waist pinched, my hair burned into curls, the colour on my face painted out, then painted in again. And now I'm free to sink back into the earth if I like – to let myself grow over with moss and lichen. Perhaps you're appalled to think we're no higher than the animals – or at least, if we are, only one rung further up the ladder. But no, no – it has given me liberty. No other animal abides by rules – why then must we?'

If Will was able to set aside the obligations of his office, they were never far away; as she spoke he touched his throat as if hoping to find there the comfort of his white collar. How could he begin to believe that she was content to be as much animal as woman, careless, without a soul, or the prospect of its loss or salvation? What's more, she contradicted herself on every turn: impossible to reconcile an animal Cora with the one who seemed always to be grasping at fresh ideas just beyond her reach. The silence that fell had the effect of a full stop at the conclusion of a long confusing sentence, and it was not broken for a time. Then, with a deliberately relieved glance at the clock – and smiling, because she'd taken no offence, and hoped she'd given none – Cora said, 'I should go. Francis doesn't exactly need me, but he does like to know that come six o'clock there will be dinner on the table, and that I will be eating it. And I am already hungry! I always am.'

'I have noticed.' She stood; he opened the door. 'Then I'll walk with you – I should do my rounds, like a surgeon in a hospital – I must pay calls to Cracknell, and to Matthew Evansford, who took a vow of temperance the day the body was found on New Year's Eve, and has taken to wearing black and getting in a state over the serpent, and the End Times. You may have seen him when you first came to All Saints – all in black, and looking as if he ought to have a coffin on his shoulder.'

Out on the common again, with the sun lowering, and no wind;

they walked with lightness of heart, conscious of having traversed uncertain terrain without serious injury. Cora spoke admiringly of Stella, perhaps by way of apology; Will in turn asked to be taught how it was that fossils were dated by the layers of sediment in which they were found. On the All Saints tower sunlight sparkled on the flint; beside the path the courteous daffodils all nodded as they passed. 'And do you still think – seriously now, Cora – that you might find a living fossil (the ichthyosaur did you say?) in such a dull and shallow place as the Blackwater estuary?'

'I think I might – I believe I might. And I am never sure of the difference between thinking and believing: you can teach me, one day. And after all I can hardly lay claim to the idea: Charles Lyell was firmly of the opinion that an ichthyosaur might turn up, although I admit no-one took him very seriously. Look – I've ten minutes of liberty left – let me walk with you to World's End, and the water. I'm sure we'll be safe: April's too gentle a month for sea-dragons.'

They reached the water – the tide was out – mud and shingle gleamed in the westering light, and someone had wreathed the bones of Leviathan in yellow branches of broom. Sedge grew in soft pale sheaves that shimmered when the wind took them; a little distance away they heard the deep implausible booming of a bittern. The air was sweet and clear: it went in like good wine.

Neither was ever certain who first shielded their eyes against the dazzle on the water, and saw what lay beyond. Neither recalled having exclaimed, or having told the other 'Look – look!' only that all at once both stood transfixed on the path above the saltings, gazing east. There on the horizon, between the silver line of water and the sky, there lay a strip of pale and gauzy air. Within the strip, sailing far above the water, a barge moved slowly through the lower sky. It was possible to make out the separate pieces of its oxblood sail, which appeared to move under a strong wind; there quite clearly was the deck and rigging, the dark prow. On it went, flying in full sail, high above the estuary; it flickered, and diminished, then regained its size; then for a moment it was possible to see the image of it inverted just beneath, as if a great mirror had been laid out. The air grew chill – the bittern boomed – each heard the other breathing swiftly, and it was not quite terror they felt, though something like it. Then the mirror vanished, and the boat sailed on alone; a gull flew below the black hull, above the gleaming water. Then some member of the ghostly crew tugged a rope, or dropped an anchor – the vessel ceased to move, only hung on silent, wonderful, becalmed against the sky. William Ransome and Cora Seaborne, stripped of code and convention, even of speech, stood with her strong hand in his: children of the earth and lost in wonder.

29th April

Dear Mrs Seaborne –

I write, as you see, from the Reading Rooms at the British Museum. My collar got me my pass, though when I came to the desk they looked me up and down, since I had soil beneath my nails from planting out broad beans. I've come to cram for something I must write on the presence of Christ in the 22nd Psalm, but instead find myself determined to get to the bottom of what we saw last night.

You recall we agreed (once we'd regained the powers of speech) we couldn't possibly be seeing the Flying Dutchman, or any other supernatural apparition? You wondered if it were a mirage of some kind, like those lakes that appear in the desert and deceive dying men with promises of water. Well – you were not far off the mark. Are you ready for a lesson?

I believe we witnessed a Fata Morgana illusion, named for the fairy Morgan le Fay, who set about bewitching sailors to their death by building icy castles in the air above the sea. Cora, you'd be amazed how much of it there is about! I copy out here an extract from the published diaries of a certain Dorothy Woolfenden (forgive my handwriting!):

1 Apr 1864, Calabria: Having risen early I stood at my window and witnessed a remarkable phenomenon – which I should certainly not believe were it related to me by any other – the weather was fine – I saw upon the horizon above the Messina Strait a gauzy haze through which I gradually perceived a

shimmering city. A great cathedral was built before my eyes, with pinnacles and arches – a grove of cypress trees which all at once bowed as if buffeted by a gale – and only for a moment a vast and glittering tower in which were many high windows – then as it were a veil descended – the vision ended – the city was gone. In my astonishment I ran to tell my companions – they had slept, and seen nothing – but believe it to have been the infamous Fata Morgana, which draws men to their doom.

Nor does the fairy content herself with ships and cities: there were phantom armies in the sky at the battle of Verviers, and the Norsemen called it the Hillingar, and saw impossible cliffs appearing on the plains.

Naturally enough there's a prosaic explanation, though as I think of it now it seems hardly less marvellous than if Morgan le Fay had followed us down to the saltings. As I understand it, the illusion is created when a particular arrangement of cold and warm air creates a refracting lens. The light which reaches the observer is bent upward in such a way that objects beneath or beyond the horizon are refracted far above their location (I am imagining you writing in one of your notebooks – are you? – I hope so!). As the pockets of cold and warm air shift, so does the lens – did you see, as I did, the ship seeming to sail upon its own reflection? Objects are not only misplaced, but repeated and distorted – something quite insignificant may be duplicated many times and form bricks from which whole cities are built!

So while we stood there baffled and bemused, I suppose that all along, somewhere out of sight, Banks was taking a shipment of wheat up to Clacton quay.

I've a tendency to sermonise, I know – but I cannot seem to let the matter rest. Our senses were deceived utterly – we stood for a moment clean out of our wits, as though our bodies conspired against our reason. And I have been unable to sleep, not because I am haunted by the possibility of a phantom ship, but because it occurs to me that my eyes are not to be trusted; or, at least, that my mind cannot be trusted to interpret what my eyes perceive. This morning as I walked for the train I saw a dying bird on the road – something about the way it flailed blindly on the path made me feel sick. Then I realised it was just a clump of wet leaves blowing about, but it was a while before the nausea passed – and it struck me that if my body had responded as if it had been the bird, was my perception of it really false, even if it had only been the leaves?

Round and round my thoughts have gone, turning as they often do to the Essex Serpent, until I begin to see how it might have appeared to us all in its various guises, and that far from there being one truth alone, there may be several truths, none of which it would be possible to prove or disprove. How I wish you might go down one morning and find its carcass on the beach, and that it would be photographed, and the picture annotated and handed about. Surely we could then be certain of things?

But it pleases me to think of you and me standing there together. Ungodly of me I am sure, but I would rather we were both deceived than I alone.

With regards,

WILLIAM RANSOME

I was there! I saw what you saw; I felt what you felt.

As ever

CORA

MAY

I

May, and the tender weather coaxes roses early from their beds. Naomi Banks peers at the moon and takes full credit for the soft rain, the mild mornings, but all the same she's unhappy. She recalls the afternoon down on the saltings when they'd commanded spring to come, but what she sees of that day is not Joanna's hand held in hers over the flames, but of something in the water biding its time. She is her father's daughter, and knows – none better – the vagaries of the tides, and how the water might buck above a sandbank, or carry in its current the severed limbs of oaks. All the same, she's grown wary of the Blackwater – will not set foot on the deck of the barge – skirts the quay as if convinced something down there will grasp her ankle as she passes.

Her teacher chides her for a lazy feckless thing, and sets her lines of punishment, but the words on the paper settle and shift like flies; instead, she takes to making charcoal sketches in which a sea-serpent – black-winged, blunt-beaked – snaps at her from the page. Then down she looks at the webbing between her fingers, and flinches at the memory of it having first been noted by her classmates, and how feared she'd been and reviled, until tall Joanna with her father's authority had intervened. But there it is – she raises her hands, and watches lamplight pick out the veins in the little pouches of skin – she is distorted, unnatural; it would be entirely in keeping for the Essex Serpent to single her out; perhaps she is its kindred. For a time she refuses glasses of water, certain that there in the liquid are particles of skin sloughed from the serpent's back.

One evening, coming home from a fruitless search for her father, she passes the open doors of the White Hare. The scent of drink is so familiar it's as if she's breathing her father's breath, and she dawdles on the doorstep. Men beckon her in, and admire her red hair, the pewter locket she wears (it contains a piece of the caul she was born with, to ensure she will not drown). She grows aware of a kind of power she had no idea she possessed; she pirouettes when asked, and laughs at their admiration of her ankles, of the white bones of her knees. To be admired is so delicious, and so strange, that she allows them to tug at her ringlets, and examine the locket where it lies on her skin; yes (she says), laughing, she is covered all over with freckles. She darts away; they call her back, and when she returns, they say, 'Pretty, pretty,' and she thinks that after all perhaps she is. Then she's drawn down onto a waiting lap, and is all at once aware that something is very wrong – she feels both afraid and outraged, but finds it impossible to move; somewhere behind her a man she cannot see makes a noise which is like that of an animal finding food.

That night in her sleep the Essex Serpent lets just the wet tip of its tail show under her pillow and breathes coldly on the closed lids of her eyes; she wakes expecting the sheets beneath her to be briny and damp. The dream seems to have something to do with the loss of her mother years before (though that had been decently done in the bedroom with the curtains closed, and not anywhere near the Blackwater), and leaves her too anxious to eat.

The Essex Serpent does not content itself with visitations to a child. It comes to Matthew Evansford as he leafs through the book of Revelation, and sports seven heads and ten horns, and upon its heads the name of blasphemy. It rains down blows on Cracknell's door in the buffeting of an easterly wind; it awaits Banks as he mends his sails and thinks of his lost wife, his stolen boat, the daughter who won't meet his eye. It winks at William Ransome from the wormy arm of its pew, and leaves him in no doubt of his failings – he reads the collect with a fervency that delights the congregation: *Lighten our darkness, we beseech thee, O Lord; and by thy great mercy defend us from all perils.* It comes to Stella in a light fever but it's no match for her: she sings to it, and pities it for a cowardly creeping thing. In the dining room of the Garrick, Charles Ambrose – having eaten too richly – puts a hand to his belly and jokes to his companion that the Essex Serpent's got its claws in him. Evidence of divine judgment in a more general sense is spotted here and there: a plague of cuckoo-spit in the gardens, a cat aborting its kittens on the hearth. Evansford hears of a death in St Osyth which the coroner cannot explain; he reserves the blood from his Sunday chicken and goes out that night to paint the lintel of every door in Aldwinter, that God's judgment might pass over them. There's a downpour before sunrise and no one's any the wiser.

Martha watches her companion for signs of wanting to return to Foulis Street, but there are none, for Cora has come to feel her happiness is rooted in the Aldwinter clay. One afternoon she goes to East Mersea and walks in a daze of joy for which she fears she'll one day be punished. The russet cliffs are wetted by a beck, and where the water runs, yellow coltsfoot grows. Down on the shore she stoops to inspect the stones and gravel sifted in the longshore drift, and finds no ammonite, no toadstone, but a smooth bit of amber that fits perfectly in the crease of her palm. At times she runs through her store of Essex memory – the dumb sheep's struggle, Cracknell whispering in the All Saints aisle, Stella tucking a confiding arm in hers, how silently the ship had sailed across the sky – and it seems to her that she must've lived there years, that she can recall no other way of being. Besides, there's the serpent to think of – she takes a boat round Mersea Island, she visits Henham-on-the-Mount, she reads the dying ode of Ragnar Lodbrok, who slew an enormous serpent and won himself a bride. She keeps before her the spirit of Mary Anning, who certainly would've pursued the rumour of a winged sea-serpent to the earth's end, and her own.

She goes often to the rectory, bringing gifts for the Ransome children: a book for Joanna, a Jacob's Ladder toy for James (this he dismantles at once), something sweet for John. She kisses Stella on both cheeks, and means it, too. Then on she goes to where Will waits in his study (there is the amber on his desk), and always at first sight there's a moment of delight, of surprise: *you really are here*, each thinks.

Side by side they sit at his desk, books opened and discarded; has he read this or that, she says, and what does he think of it; certainly he has, he says, and thinks nothing of it at all. He attempts to sketch the refracting light that gave them the Fata Morgana; she draws the parts of a trilobite. They sharpen themselves on each other; each by turn is blade and whetstone; when talk falls to faith and reason they argue readily, startling themselves by growing swiftly bad-tempered ('You don't understand!' 'How can I understand when you do not even make attempts at speaking sense?'). One afternoon they come almost to blows over a question of the existence of absolute good, which Cora denies, with reference to the thieving magpie. Will falls back on condescension, and puts on his parson's voice. Then she gleefully brings up the Essex Serpent – nothing but rumour and myth, he says, and she'll have none of it: didn't he know how in 1717 a beast fourteen feet long was washed up on the Maldon shore? And he an Essex man, too! Each considers the other to have a fatal flaw in their philosophy which ought by rights to exclude a friendship, and are a little baffled to discover it does nothing of the kind. They write more often than meet. 'I like you better on paper,' says Cora, and it is as if she carries around with her, in a pocket or threaded around her neck, a constant source of light.

Stella, passing the open door, smiles, pleased and indulgent: she herself is attended so warmly by so many companions it pleases her to see her husband fitted up with so suitable a friend. Questioned once by a curious Aldwinter wife hopeful of scandal she says, all mischief, half-tempted to stoke the ember: 'Oh, I never saw firmer friends: they've almost begun to look alike. Last week she'd got halfway home before she realised she had his boots on.' She stands at the mirror in the morning brushing out her hair and half-pities Cora, who to be sure has a handsome and costly look when the rare mood takes her but in general could never be mistaken for a beauty. She puts down the brush – her arm aches – the flu has left her a little weak, a little disinclined to go out: she prefers to sit by her window in the blue hour before dusk and watch cowslips come up on the lawn.

Luke Garrett is alarmed to discover that he has become a celebrity. There's a brief fad among surgical students for mimicking all the idiosyncrasies that once were roundly mocked: they rig up mirrors in the operating theatre, and take to wearing white cotton masks. He remains in disgrace with his seniors, who fear the corridors will grow clotted with victims of street brawls holding open their shirts for the needle and thread. Spencer – both generous, and attempting to keep his own possessions from being endlessly pressed into his friend's service – commissions him a leather belt with a heavy silver buckle, and on the buckle he asks to be engraved the snake of Asclepius coiling round its staff, by way of commemorating the medical triumph.

Uncertain what he thought might change once he'd proved it

possible to close a cardiac wound, Luke discovers things remain the same. He can still barely afford his rent, reliant on bank-notes he suspects Spencer secretes in his room; he's still a crouch-ing black-browed thing; all the accumulated humiliations of life have not evaporated with the last of the chloroform in Room 12. Besides, he didn't quite get at the heart, not quite: both blades had stopped short of the chambers; really he can hardly say it's been much of an achievement at all.

He admits to Spencer and to no-one else that he'd thought it might at last elevate him in Cora's estimation: she loves him of course (or claims to), and admires him; but he feels himself out-ranked. She's acquired new friends, and writes to tell him how the parson's wife has a face so lovely you thought flowers would wilt in shame as she passed, and how their daughter has adopted Martha, and how even Francis can bear their company an hour or two. Her move to Aldwinter astounds him: then he imagines that she's merely lapsed into the low spirits befitting a widow, and is greatly cheered at the prospect of raising them. But when they meet in Colchester she speaks of William Ransome and grows so animated her grey eyes gleam blue; really (she says) it's as if God pities her absence of a brother and has fitted one up for her at the last minute. There's nothing secretive in the way she speaks of the man, no blushes or sidelong looks; but all the same Garrett looks up and catches Martha's eye and for the first time discov-ers they're in complete accord. *What's happening?* they silently say. *What's going on?*

Spencer is immersed in London's housing disgrace. What at first had been merely a means of pleasing Martha has become an obsession: he pores over Hansard and committee minutes, he puts on his worst coat and goes walking down past Drury Lane. He discovers Parliament's habit of making policies benevolently enough, then covering its eyes and shaking hands with industry. Sometimes the greed and malice of what he sees appals him so much he thinks he must've misunderstood; he looks again, and it's worse than he thought. The local authorities tear down slums, and compensate landlords according to lost rents. Since nothing makes a tenement more profitable than vice and overcrowding, landlords facilitate both as diligently as any pimp in the street, and government rewards them handsomely. The tenants then turned out find themselves considered too immoral for a smart new Peabody home, and are left to find rooms in lodging-houses: there are times when the streets are full of firelight as tenants burn furniture too poor to be sold. Spencer thinks of his family home in Suffolk, where recently his mother discovered another room they'd never known was there, and is nauseated.

Over at World's End Cracknell turns a wary eye on the estuary. He keeps his fences thickly hung with stripped moles, and a candle burning in the window.

2

Late one afternoon, walking on the saltings with a Psalm on his tongue, William Ransome encountered Cora's son. He sought out the features of his friend in the small inscrutable face, and found none. These then were the eyes of the man he supposed she'd loved; this the plane of his cheek and chin. But the child's eyes were querying, not cruel, as he imagined Seaborne's must have been, though they were not childlike, precisely – Francis was never that.

'What are you doing, down here all alone?' said Will.

'I'm not alone,' said the boy. Will looked about for someone standing on the shingle, and saw no-one.

Francis stood with his hands in his pockets, and scrutinised the man before him as though he were a sheet of problems to be worked out. Then he said – as if the question arose quite naturally out of their exchange – 'What's sin?'

'Sin?' said Will, so startled that he stumbled, and put out a hand as if expecting to encounter the pulpit door.

'I've been counting,' said Francis, walking beside him. 'Seven times you said it this Sunday. Five the last.'

'I was not aware you've been in the congregation, Francis. I never see you there.' And Cora – had she, too, sat in the shadows, listening?

'Seven and five makes twelve. But you don't say what it is.'

They'd reached Leviathan, and Will – grateful for the pause – stooped to pick at pebbles drifted up against its bones. In all his years of ministry nobody had ever asked, and he was appalled to find himself at a loss. It was not that he had no answer: he had many (he'd studied all the requisite books). But out of doors – with no pulpit or pew in sight and the river mouth licking at the shore – both question and answer struck him as preposterous.

'What's sin?' said Francis, without the inflexion of a repeated phrase. *God! Give me strength*, thought Will, both devoutly and profanely, and handed the boy a pebble.

'Stand back a bit,' he said, 'here, by me – a step further – there. Now throw the stone and hit Leviathan – that rib, there, where we were standing.'

Francis looked at him a while, as if assessing whether he were being mocked; evidently concluding he was not, he tossed the pebble, and it fell short.

'Have another' – Will put a blue stone in his palm – 'try again.'

Again he threw; again he missed.

'That's all it is,' said Will. 'To sin is to try, but fall short. Of course we cannot get it right each time – and so we try again.'

The boy frowned. 'But what if Leviathan had not been there – what if you had not told me to stand here? If I'd stood *there*, and Leviathan had been *here*, I might have hit it, first time.'

'Yes,' said Will, feeling he'd entered deeper waters than he'd bargained for: 'We think we know where we're aiming, and perhaps we do – but morning comes, and a change in the light, and we find out we should've been trying in a different direction after all.'

'But if it changes – what I should do, and what I shouldn't – how do I know where to aim? And how can it be my fault if I fail – and why should I be punished for it?' A crease came faintly between the boy's black brows, and there at last was Cora.

'There are some things' – Will trod carefully – 'which I think we all must try to do, or else try not to do. But there are others we must work out for ourselves.' The last pebble he held was smooth, and flat; he turned his back to Leviathan and tossed it spinning at the outgoing tide. It skipped once, and fell behind a shallow wave.

'That wasn't what you meant to do,' said Francis.

'No,' said Will. 'It wasn't. But at my age, you're used to failing more often than not.'

'So you sinned,' said Francis; Will laughed, and said he hoped to be forgiven.

Frowning, the boy studied Leviathan a while. His lips moved, and Will thought he might perhaps be calculating the correct trajectory of a stone. Then he turned away and said: 'Thank you for answering my question.'

'How did I do?' said the rector, hoping he'd fallen somewhere between faith and reason, and fallen without doing himself harm.

'I don't know yet. I'll think about it.'

'Fair enough,' said Will, and wished he could ask the boy to conceal their conversation from his mother: what might she make of her son being instructed in the doctrines of sin? He knew the stormy turn her grey eyes could take.

Each surveyed the other, both feeling that the rector had done his level best under circumstances less than ideal. Francis held out his hand; William shook it; and they walked companionably on the High Road. When they reached the Common the boy paused, and began to pat at his pockets, so that Will wondered if he'd perhaps lost something on the saltings. Then Francis withdrew first a blue bone button, and then a black feather looped in a circle and tied with a bit of thread. He frowned, ran a forefinger down the feather's spine, then sighing returned them to his pocket. 'No,' he said. 'I'm afraid I can't spare anything today,' and with an apologetic look he waved goodbye.

3

Since her friendship with Martha – built as patiently and carefully as one of their houses of cards – Joanna Ransome had changed her school seat to one very nearly under Mr Caffyn's nose. Always a clever child, with a habit of raiding her father's library with particular attention to books placed furthest out of reach, her spiritual inclinations were fed one moment by Julian of Norwich and the next by *The Golden Bough*; she could give you an account of Cranmer's martyrdom in one breath, and of the war in Crimea with the next. But until meeting Martha it had all been directionless, and done as much in the hope of disconcerting her elders than with any other object in mind, and it had never occurred to her to be shamed by a friendship with an almost illiterate fisherman's daughter. Able now to name the women surgeons and socialists, satirists and actors, artists, engineers and archaeologists who were apparently to be found anywhere but in Essex, she set herself the task of joining their ranks. I'll do Latin and Greek, she thought, flinching to think of how weeks before she'd cast spells by Leviathan's bones: I'll learn trigonometry and mechanics and chemistry. Mr Caffyn had a hard time of it supplying work to occupy her at weekends, and Stella said, 'Mind you don't end up needing glasses,' as if nothing could be worse than diluting the effect of her violet eyes.

Naomi Banks felt Joanna depart from her, and mourned. She'd heard much of Martha, seen little, and hated her, feeling strongly that an adult who was twenty-five if she was a day had no business taking away her Jo. She would've liked to show her friend the serpent drawings, and explain how impossible it was to sleep; to confess what had happened in the White Hare, and ask if she ought to be angry or ashamed. But it seemed impossible: her friend had begun to look on her with pity, which was worse than dislike.

On the first Friday in May Naomi came early to school. They'd been promised a morning with Mrs Cora Seaborne, who'd lived in London and been very important, and who collected fossils and, as Mr Caffyn had put it, *other specimens of note*. Joanna had already enjoyed the reflected glory of having met Mrs Seaborne before ('We know her very well,' she'd said: 'She gave me this scarf – no, she's not beautiful, but it doesn't matter because she's clever, and has a dress covered all over with peacocks and let me try it on . . .'), and looked forward to seeing her stock among her fellow pupils rise still higher. No-one could resist Cora: she'd seen them try.

Finding the seat beside Joanna empty, Naomi slipped the other girl a scrap of paper, on which she'd written out a spell they'd concocted a few weeks before. But Joanna had moved on to algebra, and couldn't remember what the smudged symbols meant, and crumpled the paper in her hand. Then there was Mrs Seaborne herself, dressed disappointingly drably, in what was surely a man's tweed coat, and with her hair combed too severely from her forehead. She carried over her shoulder a large leather bag, and under her left arm was a file which shed a little drawing of something like a woodlouse as she passed. The only bit of the promised glamour Naomi could see was a diamond on her left hand so large and so bright it couldn't possibly have been real, and a fine black scarf on which small birds were stitched. Mr Caffyn, evidently overawed, said, 'Good morning, Mrs Seaborne: class, say good morning to Mrs Seaborne.'

Good morning, Mrs Seaborne, they said, eyeing her with slight mistrust, and Cora eyed them back, a little nervous. She'd never known what to do with children: Francis had wrong-footed her so completely that she'd come to think of them as a delightful but volatile species no more to be trusted than cats. But there was Joanna, whom she knew well, with her mother's eyes above her father's mouth; and beside her a red-haired girl whose face was all freckles; and they each sat with folded hands, surveying her expectantly. She said, 'How pleased I am to be here: I'm going to start by telling you a story, because anything that was ever worth knowing began with once upon a time.'

'As if we're *babies*,' muttered Naomi, receiving a sharp kick from her friend, but found that after all it was a better schoolday than most to listen to Mrs Seaborne tell her tale of the woman who'd once found a sea-dragon cased in mud; and how all the earth was a graveyard with gods and monsters under their feet, waiting for weather or a hammer and brush to bring them up to a new kind of life. Only look hard enough and you'd find ferns unfurling in beds of rock, she said, and footprints where lizards had walked on their hind legs; there were teeth so tiny your eye could hardly pick them out, and ones so large they'd once been worn as charms to fend off the plague.

She reached into her bag and they passed ammonites and toad-stones from hand to hand; 'Hundreds of thousands of years old,' she told them: 'Perhaps millions!' and Mr Caffyn, whose first twenty years had been spent in a Welsh Methodist chapel, coughed, and said, 'Remember now thy Creator in the days of thy youth . . .' and looked a little aggrieved. 'Any questions for Mrs Seaborne?'

How did birds end up in the rock, they said, and where were their eggs? Did they ever find humans there among the lizards and fish? How did flesh and bones become stone? Would theirs one day do the same? Was something waiting underneath the schoolyard now if they went out with spades and dug? What was her most favourite fossil and where had she found it and what was she looking for now and had she ever hurt herself and had she been abroad?

And then – voices lowered just a little – what about the Blackwater: had she heard? What about the man that drowned on New Year's Day, and the animals found dead and the things they'd seen in the night? What about Cracknell, who'd gone mad now and sat up all night by Leviathan watching for the beast? *Was something there and was it coming?* Mr Caffyn saw the turn the morning had taken, and tried his best to turn it back. He said, 'Now girls, don't trouble Mrs Seaborne with that nonsense,' and scrubbed out the ammonite sketched on the blackboard behind.

Cora had walked with William Ransome the evening before and been told, in the parson's voice he occasionally adopted if he wanted to show the upper hand, that she was not to encourage the children to talk about the Trouble. It was bad enough dealing with Cracknell, he said, and Banks's insistence that there was no herring to be had and he'd very likely starve: putting ideas in their heads would help nothing and no-one. At the time she'd dutifully thought: *You're right, Will, of course you are right*; but presented now with a dozen faces turned to her enquiringly and in places openly afraid, she felt a flash of temper. *Always being told what to do by some man or other!* she thought.

'There may still be animals alive today just like those we find in the rock,' she said, treading carefully. 'After all, there are places in the world no-one's ever walked, and water so deep they've never found the bottom: who knows what we might've missed? Up in Scotland, in a lake called the Ness, there have been sightings of a creature in the water for more than a thousand years. They say once a man was killed out swimming, and St Columba sent the beast away, only it surfaces every now and then . . .'

Mr Caffyn coughed, and with a roll of his eyes towards the youngest members of the class (a girl in a yellow dress had turned down the corners of her mouth in a grimace of delighted fear) indicated that his guest might prefer to keep to the stones and bones she'd brought in her bag.

'There is nothing to be afraid of,' said Cora. 'Except ignorance. What seems frightening is just waiting for you to shine a light on it. Think how a pile of clothes on the floor of your bedroom can seem to creep up on you until you open the curtains and see it's just the things you took off the night before! I don't know if there's anything out in the Blackwater but I do know this: if it came up on the banks and let us see it, we wouldn't see a monster, just an animal as solid and real as you and me.' The girl in the yellow dress, plainly preferring to be afraid than to be instructed, yawned delicately into the palm of her hand. Cora looked at her watch. 'Well: I've talked too long, and you've been so patient and listened so well. We have an hour left, I think – is that right, Mr Caffyn? – and what I'd like more than anything is to see how well you all draw and paint. I've seen your pictures' – she gestured to a wall of butterflies – 'and like them very much. Would you like to come and choose something to draw, and when you're done, I'll pick the one I think is best, and whoever drew it will have a prize.'

At the mention of a prize, the class clattered up – 'In single file, please,' said Mr Caffyn, watching Cora dole out ammonites and toadstones and soft pieces of clay in which sharp teeth were embedded – and fetched pots of water and brushes, and hard cakes of paint.

Joanna Ransome remained placidly seated. 'Why don't we go up?' said Naomi, itching to get her hands on some particularly beautiful rock, and show Mrs Seaborne that she, too, was worthy of her attention.

'Because she's *my* friend and I can't talk to her with you *children* all around,' said Joanna, not meaning it nastily: but in Cora's presence her old friend had seemed to dwindle in the chair beside her, and grow shabby and stupid, her clothes torn and smelling of rotten fish deep in the seams, her hair in ugly bunches because her father never could get the hang of plaits. *How can I be like Cora,* she thought, *if I talk like Naomi, and sit like her, and am as stupid as her, and don't even know that the moon goes round the earth?*

Behind her freckles Naomi turned pale. She felt slights keenly, and never more keenly than this. Before she had a chance to respond Joanna was at the woman's side, and had kissed her cheek, and was saying, 'I thought you did very well' – *Just as if she were a grown-up too, and didn't still wipe her nose on her sleeve when she thinks no-one's looking!* Naomi hadn't eaten that day, and hunger made the room begin to turn about her; she tried to stand, but Mr Caffyn appeared at her desk and set down a pot of black ink, a sheaf of paper, and something that looked like a garden snail made of grey stone.

'Oh *do* sit up straight, Naomi Banks,' said the teacher, who was not unkind, but who felt that Mrs Seaborne and her monsters had turned out to be less of an asset to the day than he'd hoped. 'You're a better artist than most of us here: see what you can do with that.'

What will *I do with it*, thought Naomi, hefting it in her right hand and then her left: she would've liked to toss it at Cora Seaborne and strike her square on the forehead. Who was she anyway? They'd all been all right before she came, Jo and her with their spells and fires. *Probably she was a witch*, she thought: *wouldn't put it past her with a coat like that; probably the Essex Serpent was a familiar she'd brought with her*. The wickedness of the idea cheered her, and when Joanna came back to her seat Naomi was circling her paintbrush in the pot of ink, laughing. *Probably sleeps with it tethered to the end of the bed*, she thought: *probably rides it*. She stirred and stirred the pot of ink, and blots appeared on the sheet of white paper in front of her. *Probably gives it her breast at night!* she thought, and laughed harder, only wasn't sure whether the laughter really had anything to do with her own thoughts, because it was so loud and strange, and she couldn't stop it, even though she saw Joanna look puzzled, and a little cross. *It's probably here – on the step – outside the door*, she thought: *I bet she whistled for it like the farmer does with his dogs*. She looked down at her own hands, with the little white pockets of flesh that linked each finger, and they seemed to her to be gleaming with salt water, and scented with scraps of fish. Her laughter shook her and grew a little high-pitched, and it was the unmistakable pitch of fear: she glanced over first her left shoulder and then her right, but the classroom door was closed. The paintbrush in the inkpot went frantically round, as if someone else were guiding her hand, and the desk jolted, and a jar of water toppled and spread across the ink-stained page. *Look at it, there it is*, thought Naomi, still laughing, still jerking her head over her shoulder (when it came she'd be the first to see it!): 'LOOK,' she said, to Joanna, or to Mr Caffyn, who appeared again in front of her, wringing her hands, saying something she couldn't hear above her own high peals of laughter. 'CAN'T YOU SEE IT?' she said, watching the water make the ink bloom, making – surely they could see it! – the coiled body of a serpent of some kind, heart pulsing through the thin skin of its belly and a pair of black wings opening. 'Not long now,' she said, 'not long now –': over her shoulder she looked, again and again, absolutely certain the serpent was on the threshold – she could smell it, certainly she could: she'd know the scent anywhere

... and besides, others could see it too – there was Harriet in her yellow dress, and she was laughing, and craning her head so far over her shoulder you'd think her neck would break, and there were the twins from across the road, who barely spoke, even to each other, and now dashed their heads left and right, left and right, snapping them back and forth, and laughing as they did it.

Cora, appalled, watched as laughter spread outward from the red-haired girl's desk, missing Joanna, moving around her like a flow of water interrupted by a rock. It was as if they'd all heard a silent joke which had passed the adults by: some girls laughed behind hands pressed to their mouths; others threw back their heads and roared, thumping the desk in front of them, as though they were older women and the joke had been a bawdy one. Naomi, who'd begun it all, had worn herself out, and sat giggling quietly, putting her hands in the water-and-ink that spilled across the paper, now and then pausing to look over her shoulder and giggle a little more loudly. The child in the yellow dress, who was nearest the door, had laughed herself into frantic tears, and instead of turning to look over her shoulder had turned her chair around and sat facing the door, her hands pressed to her cheeks, chanting *It's coming ready or not, coming ready or not* between open-mouthed gulps at the air.

Mr Caffyn, both outraged and afraid, plucked at his tie and cried, 'Stop this! Stop this!', looking furiously at their trouble-some visitor, who'd gone very white and stood gripping Joanna's hand in hers. Then a girl doubled over, laughing so violently her chair toppled and she fell to the floor with a yell that pierced the muddle of foolish laughter, which immediately began to recede. Naomi put a hand to her neck – 'It hurts,' she said: 'Why does it hurt? What have you done?' and looked around at her classmates, blinking and shaking her head, bemused at their tear-streaked faces. Little Harriet twisted the yellow hem of her dress and had a fit of the hiccups, and one or two of the older girls had gone to comfort the weeping child who cradled a swelling wrist beside an upturned chair.

'Joanna?' said Naomi, looking at her friend, 'What's wrong? Was it me? What have I done this time?'

Cora Seaborne
3, The Common
Aldwinter

15th May

Luke – You're basking in your celebrity I know and are probably up to your elbows in a chest cavity somewhere, but now WE *need you.*

Luke, something's going wrong. Today something went through the children here as fast as fire – not sickness in the way it's usually meant, something in the mind, and down they all went like dominoes. By evening all was well again but what could have done it – was it my fault?

You understand these things: you had me under hypnosis when I would not believe that you could – had me walking over the heath to my father's house while I lay there on the couch – won't you come down?

I'm not afraid. I'm not afraid of anything anymore: that all got used up a long time ago. But something's here – something's going on – something isn't right . . .

Besides, you must meet the Ransomes, and most of all Will. I've told him about my Imp.

Can you bring more books for Francis? Murder, please, and the bloodier the better.

Love,

CORA

Luke Garrett MD
Pentonville Rd
London N1

15th May

Cora –

Don't fret. There are no mysteries anymore.

One word: ergotism. Remember? Black fungus in a crop of rye – a pack of girls hallucinate – Salem hangs its witches. Check their lunches for brown bread and I'll be with you by Friday next.

Enclosed: 1 x note for Martha, with Spencer's regards. Something about housing: he bores me and I don't listen.

LUKE

George Spencer MD
10 Queen's Gate Terrace
15th May

Dear Martha –

I hope you are well. How is Essex in the spring? Do you miss civilisation? I thought of you when I saw the gardeners out in force in Victoria Park, and how neat the flowerbeds are. I don't suppose Aldwinter is growing tulips in the shape of a clock face.

I've been thinking about our chat. I'm glad you shook me out of my complacency and made me look elsewhere and ashamed it took you to do it. I've read everything you said I should read, and more. Last week I went to Poplar and saw for myself the state of their homes, and how they live, and how the one feeds the other.

I've written to Charles Ambrose, and hope he'll write back. He has more influence than me, and understands better how government works, and I think he can be useful. I'm hoping he can be persuaded to come with me to Poplar or Limehouse and see what you and I have seen. If so, might you come too?

I've enclosed a clipping from The Times I thought might cheer you: it seems the Housing of the Working Classes Act is at last making itself felt beyond the city. The future's coming to meet us!

With good wishes,

GEORGE SPENCER

4

Luke came to Aldwinter in triumph and a new grey coat. For all
that his success had not proved a cure to all his own ills, it was useless to deny that this evidence of his skill and courage gave him
stature. Over in Bethnal Green the heart of Edward Burton beat
stronger by the hour: he'd taken to making drawings of the dome of
St Paul's, and was likely to return to work by midsummer. Luke felt
Burton's heart beat beside his own, so that he walked with the vitality of two; and though he knew how pride precedes a fall, it seemed
so novel to have any distance to tumble he willingly faced the risk.

In the train from London and the cab from Colchester he'd
thought of Cora, and smoothed her letter on his knee: *we* need
you, she'd said, and scowling he wondered whom she meant by
'we': was it also this parson of hers, who peppered her correspondence, who'd drawn her away from London into the Essex mud?
The envy he'd felt watching her stoop over her husband's pillow
and kiss his greasy forehead in the final days was nothing to what
went through him when he saw that name in her handwriting.
First she'd written of *Mr Ransome*, the title keeping him at arm's
length; then *The Good Reverend*, with a mocking fondness that
had made him uneasy; then – lately, and easily, with no warning – *Will* (and not even *William*, though that would've been bad
enough!). Luke scoured the letters for evidence of any feeling
on Cora's part that might indicate a connection beyond cheerful
friendship (he grudgingly conceded she'd a right to other friends),
and found none. But even so Luke looked out at the fields scud-
ding past the window, and his own dark reflection laid over them,

and thought: *Let him be old, and fat, and smelling of dust and Bibles.*

In her grey house on the common Cora stood waiting at the door. Since the morning in Mr Caffyn's classroom she'd slept uneasily, feeling it all to have been her fault. Will had warned her not to put flesh on the bones of the Blackwater terror, and he'd been right: there's no imagination like a child's, and she'd fattened it up 'til the Essex Serpent was solid as the cows grazing under Traitor's Oak. Those girls laughing, and the snapping back and forth of their necks! It had been horrible, and she relied on Luke to find some consoling explanation.

In the aftermath Joanna had grown withdrawn, and though she still went early to school with her books under her arm she'd have nothing to do with Naomi Banks, and at the end of each day sat studying in the kitchen, where there was no chance she'd find herself alone. Worse, she had not laughed once since, afraid that if she started she might not stop, and no amount of teasing or capering on the part of her brothers could raise a smile. Cora had been afraid her new friends would blame her for the incident, and for Joanna's sombre state, but neither Will nor Stella had seen it happen, and when it was explained to them could only think that girls were ridiculous creatures and always getting the giggles over nothing at all.

Worst of all, Cora's cheerful interest in the Blackwater was soured. She didn't (of course!) think it a judgment from God – but perhaps there were soft dark places in all of them that ought not to be probed. Then came Luke, striking out over the common, clutching a case to his chest, seeing her at the threshold and breaking out, almost, into a run.

Later that same week Joanna folded her hands in her lap and surveyed the black-haired doctor with mistrust. 'Don't worry,' he said. His manner was brisk, but Jo was not entirely fooled. 'Just do as you're told and you'll be all right. Tell her, Cora.' And Cora, wearing her scarf with the birds stitched on, had said, 'It's all right – he did it to me once, and I slept better that night than in years.'

They sat in the largest room in Cora's grey house, with no lights lit. It was raining drearily, without the stormy conviction that makes for a comfortable afternoon, and Joanna was not warm. On a large sofa beneath the window her mother sat between Cora and Martha, and the women held hands: you'd've thought they were in for a séance and not a process no more mysterious (Luke said) than the removal of a tooth.

Only Martha had disapproved of the plan to put the girl under hypnosis to see what light might be shed on what she called The Laughing Incident. 'The Imp thinks of us all as nothing but cuts of meat, and you'd trust him with a child's mind and memory?' She'd bitten her apple down to the pips and said, 'Hypnosis! He makes it up. It's not even a word.'

The question of hypnosis had not been raised until certain other matters had been settled. Mr Caffyn, fearing for his career, had produced a report made in the days following, listing the names of the girls involved, their ages and addresses, their fathers' occupations and their average grades and appending a chart showing the position of each girl at each desk. He deplored Cora's presence in the village, but didn't dream of saying so. Little Harriet consented to be questioned from her mother's lap, and gave such an elaborate description of a coiled snake unfolding wings like umbrellas that she was put down as a nice child but a dreadful liar (Francis, listening at the door, thought: 'Is a dreadful liar bad at lying, or good at it?'). Naomi Banks, who began it all, refused to say anything other than that she had no idea what she'd been thinking, and could they leave her alone. Parents were delighted to have their daughters examined by a London physician, and declared one after the other in perfect health (save for six instances of ringworm, which were treated on the spot, and could not account for their hysteria).

Luke, who'd been introduced to Stella Ransome over lunch (and noted the rosy bloom on each cheek), had said, 'There'll be something at the heart of the matter – a shared memory or fear; the question is how to allay the fears when the girls cannot or will not share them?'

Stella had pulled at the blue beads looped around her wrist, and taken a liking to the scowling London doctor; *only wouldn't it be awful to be ugly*, she thought. 'Cora tells me you practise hypnosis – am I saying it right? – and that somehow it might help Joanna? She'd like it – she likes everything new. She'd write it all up in her schoolbook.'

It had been tempting for Luke to take Stella's small hand and say that yes, yes: certainly it would help; that her daughter would restfully recount what it was that had been seen and heard that day, if anything at all, and in coming to would regain her good cheer. But his ambition faltered before the blue eyes turned on him in trust, and he said: 'It might, but it might not, though I don't suppose it would do any harm.' His insistent conscience pricked him: he said, 'I have never tried it on anyone so young. She might resist it, and laugh at me.'

'Laugh!' said Stella: 'I wish she would!'

'When I was hypnotised,' said Cora, pouring tea, 'I felt swept clean as a chimney, as they say. It was restful, and I said very little. There is nothing to be afraid of: there is nothing strange; it is all just the working of the mind.' The tea had spilled in the saucer; the light had faded on the wall. 'I can almost imagine that by the time she's your age and mine it'll be so commonplace there'll be hypnotists on the High Street beside every chemist's and shoe-shop.' (At her shoulder the absent Will was gravely watching, and was ignored.)

'With pot plants in the window,' said Stella, taking to the idea: 'And receptionists in white blouses. No-one will ever have any secrets again – aren't you hot? Could we open the window? – and I'd like to see her happy again.' It occurred to her to wonder what Will might think: he'd not yet met the doctor, or shown any inclination to, and she supposed he might baulk at the thought of Jo submitting to a procedure her own mother couldn't pronounce. But then, Cora wouldn't do anything Will might dislike. It was comforting, she thought – never in her life having felt envy, unable to imagine what it was like – to think of her husband so steadfastly and loyally liked. 'Open the window wider,' she said: 'I am only ever hot, these days.'

Cora turned to Luke, who'd taken Stella's wrist in a chivalrous gesture, hoping she'd not notice he was taking her pulse (and yes – yes, as he'd suspected: it was skittish below the skin). 'Well: why don't we call Jo, and ask her, and see if she is willing?'

And since she had been willing ('Am I going to be an *experiment*?'), she lay now on the most comfortable couch, gazing up at the ceiling where the plaster had begun to peel. It was difficult to take the thing seriously, since she'd overhead Cora call the doctor an imp and could not help thinking how apt that was (he ought to've carried a pitchfork, not a Gladstone bag!).

Drawing up a chair beside her, and leaning in so that she could smell something like lemons rising from his shirt, Dr Garrett said: 'This is what will happen. You will not sleep, and I'll have no power over you, but you'll be more comfortable – more at ease – than you ever were before. And I'll ask you questions – about how you have been, and about that day – and we'll see what we can learn: how it began, and what it is you felt.'

'All right,' she said. *But there's nothing to learn about that day, and the laughing*, she thought, *or I'd have told them all I knew*. She looked for her mother, and Stella blew her a kiss.

'Do you see that mark on the wall – there above the fire where the paint is chipped? I want you to keep looking at it, however heavy your eyelids, however sore your eyes . . .'

There were other instructions, delivered murmuringly and as if from a great distance: she was to let her hands fall, her head droop, her breath slow, her thoughts wander into other rooms . . . it was impossible to keep her open eyes fixed on the mark, and when permission was given to close them she did so with a sigh and almost fell in her relief from the couch. She never knew until later what it was she said as she hovered midway between waking and dreaming (later they told her it was something about Naomi Banks, and a leviathan, but that she hadn't seemed at all afraid). What she remembered was a polite rap on the door, then the drag of it against the carpet; and then her father's voice raised in a rage she'd never heard before.

Will saw his daughter prone on a black couch with her arms hanging at her sides and her mouth half-open, while a creature bent over her and whispered. He'd come home from making his round of the parish to find the house empty, and calling for Stella found a note on his study directing him to Cora's, should he care to join them. Crossing the common he'd pictured Stella's bright head and Cora's untidy one framed in a window, lamp-lit, impatiently waiting his arrival, and his step had quickened.

He'd known, of course, that Dr Garrett was coming, and felt resentful at the intrusion. The village had had quite enough of that sort of thing, he felt: what with Londoners and serpents it had been a troublesome year; couldn't they have a moment's peace? Then he considered how fondly Cora spoke of him, and how proudly she had reported the surgery which had saved a man's life, and concluded the surgeon must be the sort of man he could come to like. He'd be short and slight and anxious, he decided, reaching the shadow of Traitor's Oak; he would have a long despondent moustache and finicky aversions to food and drink. Probably the poor fellow could do with a country break, given the state of his health.

Martha had greeted him with a curious look, not quite able to meet his eye; it was so unlike her usual directness that he felt uneasy long before he opened the door and encountered a crouching black-browed thing whispering at his daughter's side. She lay quite still, as if stunned by a blow; her head was tilted back, and her half-open eyes had a vacant gaze. He was for a moment rigid with shock and distress; when he saw Stella and Cora observing placidly from a nearby sofa, evidently complicit in the scene, he found himself tripped into a fury which not the Essex Serpent nor Cracknell nor any event of the past puzzling months had induced. Quite what he thought was unfolding in that well-furnished room with its curtains blowing out he couldn't later say, only that he felt a kind of revulsion: it was his daughter, and she was murmuring – something Latin, was it? – and laid out like a fish on a slab! He crossed the room and fitting his fingers beneath the crouching man's collar tried to tug him from his chair. But if the rector was strong, the surgeon was heavy: there was a tussle which Cora briefly found hilarious before growing afraid that Will in his righteous temper might actually do her friend harm. She thought of the sheep as it struggled in the mud, and how it raised cords of muscle on Will's forearm; she stood up and said, 'Mr Ransome – Will! It's only Dr Garrett – he's only trying to help!'

Joanna, frightened and drowsy, rolled from couch to floor and struck her head on the hard seat of a chair. She stared up at the ceiling and said, 'It's coming,' then knuckled at her eyes and sat up. Stella, who'd been half-dozing despite the chill coming in through the open window, looked at her husband in surprise ('Darling, don't drip on Cora's carpet!') and went over to her daughter. 'How do you feel – are you sick? Have you hurt your head?'

'It was just so *easy*,' said Joanna, rubbing her forehead, on which a white lump had begun to appear. She looked from the doctor to her father, and seeing how the two men stood rigid as far from each other as the room would allow said, 'What's wrong? Did I do something wrong?'

'*You* didn't,' said Will; and although he did not take his eyes from those of the other man it was quite clear to Cora where his anger was directed, and she felt a kind of contraction in her throat. Falling back on fine manners, she stood between the two and said, 'Luke, this is William Ransome, my friend.'

My friend, thought Luke: *I never heard her say 'my husband' or 'my son' with so much pride.*

'Will, this is Dr Luke Garrett – won't you shake hands? – we thought we'd help Joanna – she's not been herself since what happened at the school.'

'Help? How? What were you doing?' Will ignored the offered hand, which was held out (he thought) with a sardonic grin. 'She's hurt – look: you're lucky she didn't knock herself out!'

'Hypnosis!' said Joanna, proudly. She had been an experiment! She would write about it later.

'We can tell him later,' said Stella, patting about for her jacket: all these raised voices! Her head hurt.

'Nice to meet you, Reverend, I'm sure,' said Luke, putting his hands in his pockets.

Will turned away from his friend. 'Put your coat on, Stella, you're shivering – why have they let you get cold? – yes, Jo, you can tell me all about it later – good afternoon, Dr Garrett: perhaps we'll meet again.' As if borne on a tide of politeness Will left the room with wife and daughter in his wake, not sparing a glance at Cora, who at that moment would've been as grateful for a glare as for a smile.

'I was an experiment!' they heard Joanna say at the door: 'And now I'm hungry.'

'Absolutely charming man,' said Luke. *So much for the fat parson in gaiters*, he thought: *he'd looked like a farmer with ideas above his station and had a fine head of hair, and in his presence Cora Seaborne – of all women! – had seemed a child dismayed to find herself disgraced*. Martha rose from the sofa where she'd been silently watching and with a contemptuous look at the doctor came to stand beside her friend. 'No good ever came of leaving London,' she said: 'What did I tell you?' Cora briefly put her cheek to Martha's shoulder and said, 'I'm hungry too. And I want wine.'

5

Edward Burton sat on a narrow bed and opened the paper packet on his lap. In a high-backed chair beneath a print of St Paul's, his visitor dredged her chips with vinegar, and the hot scent roused his appetite for the first time in weeks. She wore her hair in a fair braid wrapped around her crown: she looked, he thought, breaking batter from his bit of fish, like an angel, if an angel could be hungry, and didn't mind grease on her chin and a smear of green peas on her sleeve.

Martha watched him steadily eating, and felt hardly less proud than Luke had done on closing up his wound. It was her third visit, and there was colour in his cheeks. They had been introduced by Maureen Fry, who beside a willingness to visit Burton in order to tug the stitches from his healing scar was a relation of Elizabeth Fry, and had fully inherited the family social conscience: it seemed to her the nurse's duty lay well beyond the tying up of bandages, the mopping up of blood. She'd first encountered Martha at a meeting of women concerned with Union matters, and over strong tea discovered that Dr Luke Garrett ('Of all people!' Martha had said, shaking her head) was the link between them. When Martha first accompanied Sister Fry to the house where Edward and his mother lived in Bethnal Green, she'd discovered a home which was small, certainly, with sanitation troubles that left an ammoniac reek in the air, but was pleasant enough. Little light came in, only what filtered through lines of laundry running between the houses like the pennants of a coming army, but there were always flowers on the table in a rinsed-out jar of Robertson's jam. Mrs Thomas earned her living by way of laundry, and contriving rag rugs out of scraps; these rugs decked their three small rooms and made them bright. It had never occurred to her that Edward might not recover entirely, and go back to the insurance company where he'd passed five years as a clerk, and so she faced a period of nursing him quite stoically.

That first visit had been an unsatisfactory one, with Edward Burton white and silent in the corner. Mrs Burton was battling delight at her son's unlikely salvation with a troubling sensation that the man who'd come off the operating table was not the man who'd been laid out on it: 'He's so quiet,' she'd said, wringing her hands, and borrowing Sister Fry's handkerchief. 'It's like the old Ned bled out and I've got another one in his place and I have to get to know him before I can say he's my son.' Nonetheless, Martha had found herself fretting, in the following days, that Burton would not eat enough, or test the strength of his legs by walking the length of the road, and so she had returned a week later with packets of fish and chips, a net of oranges, and several of Francis's abandoned copies of *The Strand*.

Edward steadily ate. To Martha – used to Cora's endless conversation and her sudden fits of joy or gloom – his company was peaceful. He responded to everything she said with an inclined head, considering it slowly, often saying nothing in response. Sometimes there was a sharp pain in the place where his rib had been severed – it was like a cramping of the muscles as all the fibres tried to knit – and he'd gasp, and put a hand there in the hollow where the bone was gone, and wait for it to pass. Martha would say nothing then, only sit quietly with him, and when he raised his head say, 'Tell me again how they built Blackfriars Bridge.'

That afternoon, as rain gathered in the gutters in the Tower Hamlets streets and poured from the eaves, Edward said, 'He came to see me again, the Scottish man. He prayed with me and left some money.' This was John Galt, whose tent mission in Bethnal Green brought the gospel to the city alongside temperance and improved personal hygiene. Martha knew of him – had seen his photographs recording the city at its worst – and deplored his tender Christian conscience. 'He prayed, did he?' She shook her head and said, 'Never trust a do-gooder,' disliking as always the connection between righteousness and weather-proof walls.

'It's not only that he *does* good,' said Edward, thoughtfully. He surveyed a chip before putting it in his mouth. 'I think he *is* good.'

'Don't you see that this is the trouble – that it's not a question of goodness – it's a question of *duty*! You think it's kindness to bring you money and ask if the walls are damp and leave you in God's hands, wherever they are, but it's our right to live decently, it shouldn't be a gift from our betters – oh!' She laughed. 'See how easily that came out! *Our betters!* What, because they never put money on the dogs or drank themselves stupid!'

'What are you going to do about it, then?' He said it with good humour so deeply buried that only Martha could've seen it there. She finished her meal, and wiping the oil from her mouth with the back of her hand said, 'Plans are afoot, Edward Burton, mark my words. I've written to a man who can help – always comes down to money, doesn't it, in the end? Money and influence, and God knows I've no money and not much influence but I'll use what I've got.' She thought briefly of Spencer, and his way of looking at her slightly askance, and felt a little ashamed.

'Wish I could have a hand in it,' said Edward, and with a gesture that took in his thin legs – thinner now than ever, since he could not run ten paces without losing his breath – he looked briefly hopeless. He'd taken his place in the city without considering it, until this woman with her hair like a rope and her brisk way of talking had stood on one of his mother's rugs and raged at what she'd seen in the streets. Now it would be impossible to walk from one end of Bethnal Green to the other without thinking how that dark labyrinth of mean housing had a consciousness all of its own, operating on everyone who lived in it. At night, when his mother slept, he took out rolls of white paper and made drawings of high, wide buildings that let in the light, with good water running through them.

Martha withdrew her umbrella from under the chair and unfurled it, sighing at the rain running thickly down the window-pane. 'I don't know yet,' she said. 'I don't know what I can do. But something's going to change. Can't you feel it?'

He was not certain he could, but then she kissed him on the cheek, and shook his hand, as if she could not decide which greeting suited them best. At the door she paused, because he called out after her: 'It was my fault, you know.'

'Your fault? What is – what've you done?' It was so unlike him to speak unprompted that she was afraid to move and startle him out of it.

'This,' he said, and lightly touched his breast. 'I know who did it, and why. I deserved it, you know. Or if not this – something.'

She returned to her chair, not speaking, turning away to pluck at a thread loose on her sleeve. He knew it was done to spare him, and there was a movement in his damaged heart.

'I was such an ordinary person,' he said. 'It was such an ordinary life. I had a bit of savings. I was going to get a place of my own, though I didn't mind living here: we've always got on all right. I didn't mind my job, only sometimes got bored and made plans of buildings that'll never be built. Now they tell me I'm a miracle, or whatever does for miracles these days.'

Martha said, 'There are no ordinary lives.'

'At any rate, it was my fault,' he said, and recounted how content he'd been, there at his desk at Holborn Bars, awaiting the clock's chime and the hour of freedom. He'd had a popularity he neither sought nor enjoyed, and suspected his peers were conned by his height, and by the biting wit he could barely remember possessing. The Edward who'd fallen in the shadow of the cathedral was not the silent man that Martha knew. That other man had been always laughing at this or that; his temper had been quick, hot, and soon extinguished. Since his own bad moods passed swiftly, he was heedless of the lasting harm his careless blows might cause. But the blows did fall – they did cause harm: 'It was just teasing,' he said. 'We didn't think anything of it. He didn't seem to mind. You couldn't tell, with Hall. He only ever looked miserable, so what did it matter?'

'Hall?' said Martha.

'Samuel Hall. We never called him Sam. That's telling, isn't it?'

No: he didn't seem to mind, thought Burton, but telling it now to Martha he flushed with shame. Samuel Hall, unblessed with good looks or good humour; arriving in his drab coat a minute before the working day and departing a minute after its end; resentfully diligent, entirely unremarkable. But they *had* remarked on him – lightly perhaps, and in hopes of drawing out some buried wit – and it had been Edward, laughing, always at the fore.

'I couldn't help thinking there was something so funny about how unhappy he was. Do you understand? You couldn't take him seriously. He could've dropped dead right there at his desk and we'd've all laughed.'

Then drab little Samuel Hall – behind whose glasses muddy eyes blinked resentfully out at the world – had fallen in love. In a dim bar near Embankment they'd seen him, and seen how he'd laughed, and exchanged his dull coat for a bright one; how he'd kissed a woman's hand, and how she hadn't minded. Nothing could've been funnier, it seemed: nothing – by the light of the lamps and the warmth of the beer – more absurd. Burton could not remember what it was that was said, or by whom, only that there'd been a moment when he'd had the woman, bewildered, in his own arms; that he'd been kissing her with a gallantry all too obviously mocking.

'I meant nothing by it – it was done to make them laugh – I went home that night and wouldn't even have been able to tell you where I'd been.' But all the week that followed, Hall's desk had been empty, though no-one thought to ask where he'd gone, or why; it did not occur to them that alone in his single room with its single chair all the accumulated resentments of Hall's life – all the slights both real and imagined – had united in an implacable loathing of Edward Burton.

'I'd stopped to look up at St Paul's – I'm always wondering how the dome holds up, aren't you? – and there were black birds on the steps and I remembered being told as a child how one rook is a crow, and many crows are rooks. Then someone stumbled against me – that's how it was: as if they'd lost their footing. I said "Watch out!", and there was Samuel Hall, not looking at me, just running on by, like I'd made him late.' On he'd walked in the shadow of St Paul's, and felt all at once very weary; he'd put a hand to wetness on his shirt, and withdrawn it gloved in blood. Then night had fallen early, and he'd lain down on the steps to sleep.

The room was dim; he reached for a lamp, and lit it; in the slow-bloomed light she saw the lean face turned from her in shame and shyness, and how he flushed across the high bones of his cheek.

'It's not a question of guilt and punishment,' she said. 'It's not how the world turns. If we all got what we deserved –' It felt to Martha as if he'd given her a gift that was easily broken. Something had altered between them – she owed a debt of trust. 'We cannot help it, if we are to live,' she said. 'Causing harm, I mean; how could it be avoided unless we shut ourselves away – never speak, never act?' She wanted to repay the debt, and casting about for sources of her own guilt it was Spencer's face that first came to mind, and would not be dispelled.

'If we all got what we deserved I'd be waiting for my punishment,' she said. 'It would be worse, I think; a knife in the heart would be the least of it – you did not know what you had done – but I know, and still I do it!' And she told her quiet companion about the man who loved her ('He thinks he conceals it, but no-one ever does . . .'); his shyness, and how he grasped after goodness for its own sake, and because it might please her. 'Spencer's wealth is obscene, it is obscene – he has so much he doesn't know how much of it he has! If I let him love me, and pretend I might return it, and it makes him do something good – is it really so bad? Is a broken heart too high a price to pay for a better city?'

Burton smiled, and raised his hand: 'I absolve you,' he said.

'Thank you, Father,' she said, laughing. 'You know, I always thought that was the great benefit of being religious: get the guilt over and done with, and move on to another sin. Well,' – she gestured to the window, and beyond it to the lowering sky – 'I must go, or miss my train.' When she took his hand to bid him goodbye he held it, and drew her down, and kissed her once; and she saw for the first time what vitality had once been in those long fingers, in the legs outstretched beneath the blanket.

'Come again,' he said, 'come soon'; and after she'd gone he sat for a long time in the chair she'd left, making plans of a garden for neighbours to share.

6

In Colchester the rain was mild and barely seemed to fall, only hang in the air as if the whole town were enveloped in pale cloud. Thomas Taylor had rigged up a tarpaulin and sat contently beneath it sharing cake with Cora Seaborne, who'd come to town for papers and books, and better food than could be had in Aldwinter ('It's all right for bread and fresh fish,' she'd said, 'but no marzipan to be had for all the tea in Yorkshire'). He suspected passers-by were pleasantly shocked to see so obviously wealthy (if untidy) a woman at his side, and hoped he might see an increased profit in the afternoon. In the meantime, they had a great deal to discuss.

'How's Martha?' he said, on first-name terms with the girl who, each time she came to town, contrived to disapprove of him vocally but leave him in a good temper. 'Still got those ideas?' He licked a crumb from his finger, and watched the sun look coyly out from a cloud.

'If there were any justice,' said Cora, 'which you and I know there isn't, she'd be in Parliament, and you'd have a house of your own.' In fact, he had a neat flat on the lower floor of what had once been one of Colchester's townhouses, being in receipt of a good pension and a better wage, but it would not do to disappoint his friend. 'If wishes were horses,' he said, sighing, and rolling his eyes towards the trolley that would later convey him home, 'I'd make my fortune in manure. And what about the village folk, over Aldwinter way? Has the Essex Serpent come crawling up and eaten them all in their beds?' He gnashed his teeth, and thought she might laugh; but instead she gave a frown that scored her forehead with lines.

'Do you ever feel haunted?' she said, gesturing up to the ruin, where rags of curtains hung wetly, and a mirror above a broken mantelpiece showed small furtive moments from somewhere inside.

'No such business,' he said cheerfully. 'I'm quite religious, you know: no patience for the supernatural.'

'Not even in the night?'

At night, he'd be in bed under a good thick quilt with his daughter snoring next door, and his stomach full of toasted cheese. 'Not even then,' he said: 'There's nothing here except house martins.'

Cora ate the last of her cake, and said, 'I think the whole village is haunted. Only – I think they're haunting themselves.' She thought of Will, who'd not written since the day they'd let Luke loose on Joanna, and when he greeted her did so with such extravagant politeness it chilled each separate bone in her spine.

Not having much patience for the turn the talk had taken, Taylor poked at the newspaper Cora had brought, and said, 'Why don't you tell me what's going on in the world? I like to keep my eye on things.'

She shook it out and said: 'All the usual: three British servicemen dead outside Kabul, a test match lost. Only' – she tapped the folded paper – 'there's this: a meteorological curiosity, and I don't mean this endless rain! Shall I read it?' Taylor nodded, then folded his hands and closed his eyes, willing as a child to be entertained. '"The keen meteorologist should turn a weather eye to the heavens in the weeks forthcoming in anticipation of witnessing a curious atmospheric phenomenon. First observed in 1885, and visible solely in the summer months between latitudes 50°N and 70°S, these 'noctilucent clouds' form a curious layer perceived only at twilight. Observers have noted the luminous blue nature of the

display, which fluctuates considerably in brilliance, and in forma-
tion is best described as resembling a mackerel sky. The origin
of this 'night-shining' remains a source of contention, and it has
been suggested in some quarters that its first having been observed
subsequent to the eruption of Krakatoa in 1883 is no mere coincidence." There now,' she said: 'What do you make of that?'

'Night-shining,' he said, shaking his head, a little affronted.
'Whatever will they think of next!'

'They say Krakatoa's ash has changed the world – these bad
winters we've lately had, changes in the night sky: all because
years ago and thousands of miles away a volcano blew.' She shook
her head. 'I've always said there are no mysteries, only things we
don't yet know; but lately I've thought not even knowledge takes
all strangeness from the world.' She told him what she'd seen with
William Ransome at her side: the phantom barge in the Essex sky,
and how she'd seen gulls fly beneath the hull.

'It was just the light,' she said, 'up to its old tricks. But how was
my heart to know?'

'The Flying Essex-man, eh?' said doubting Thomas: if ghost
ships were ever to take to the seas they could surely find better
waters than the Blackwater estuary. He was saved from further
comment by the arrival of Charles and Katherine Ambrose, carrying a green umbrella and a pink one respectively, their presence
on the street brightening up the town.

Cora stood to greet them – 'Charles! Katherine! You can't stay
away – you know my friend Thomas Taylor, of course – we're
discussing astronomy. Have you seen the night-shining? Or are
the London lights too bright?'

'As always, dear Cora, I don't know what you're on about.'
Charles shook the cripple's hand, dispensed several coins into his
hat without first checking their value, and drew Cora under the

shade of his umbrella. 'I have heard from William Ransome,' he said. 'You are in disgrace.'

'Oh' – she looked chastened, but he pressed on: 'I know you insist that we must all face the modern age, but it might have been polite to ask permission first.' It was very difficult to continue, since Cora looked miserable, and Katherine was giving him one of her warning looks, but he loved William, and in his latest letter he'd seemed more shaken than the incident deserved ('I wish you hadn't sent her,' he'd written: 'It's been nothing but one thing after another.' And then, following swiftly on a postcard, he'd said, more cheerfully: 'Forgive my bad temper. I was tired. What news of Whitehall?').

'Have you apologised?' he said, thanking God fervently – and for neither the first time nor the last – that he'd been spared parenthood.

'Certainly not,' said Cora, taking Katherine's hand, feeling she deserved an ally. 'I shan't. Joanna gave her permission. Stella, too. Or must we all bide our time until a man provides written consent?'

'*What* a nice coat,' said Katherine, rather desperately, looking at the blue jacket which had replaced the old man's tweed Cora wore all winter, and which made her grey eyes stormy.

'Isn't it?' Cora said absently: she could now only think of her friend, back in his Aldwinter study, thinking badly of her. She had so much to tell him, and no means of telling it. She turned back to Taylor, who was picking the last crumbs of cake from his lap and watching all three with pleasure, as if he'd paid for a ticket. 'I ought to be getting home,' she said, shaking his hand: 'Francis asked for the latest Sherlock Holmes, which he's afraid will be the Great Detective's last case, and if it is I really don't know what we'll do: write them myself, perhaps.'

'Give him this, then,' said Taylor, who knew the boy rather better than his mother suspected, since he'd had a habit of slipping out of the Red Lion unnoticed and clambering up into the ruins. He passed Cora a piece of broken plate on which she made out a snake coiled around an apple tree.

'More serpents,' said Charles. 'There seems to be a lot of it about. Cora, I haven't finished with you yet: we're staying at the George and it strikes me you could do with a drink.'

Seated comfortably in the parlour of the George, it was not William they discussed, but Stella. Her letters to Katherine had taken on a spiritual cast ('Not,' said Charles, looking horrified, 'what one expects of a clergyman's wife!'). Her God had slipped into something that had little to do with the thundercrack above Mount Sinai: she seemed instead to venerate a series of sensations she associated with the colour blue. 'She told me she meditates on it day and night – that she carries a blue stone with her into church, and kisses it – that she can only bear to wear blue, because other colours scorch her skin.' Katherine shook her head. 'Is she ill? She was always a little silly, I suppose, but cleverly so – it was as if she'd chosen to be silly because it's a characteristic so often expected of women that it's almost admired.'

'And she's always *hot*,' said Cora, thinking of how she'd held her hands when last they'd met, and of how they'd been like those of a small child in fever. 'But how can she be ill, when she grows more beautiful each time I see her?'

Charles poured another glass of wine ('Not bad I suppose, for an Essex pub'), and holding it to the light said, 'William says he called the doctor, and that she can't shake off the flu. He'd like to send her away somewhere warm, but summer is icumen in, as the old song goes, and she'll be basking soon enough.'

Cora was not so sure: Luke had said nothing to her (he'd

departed Aldwinter as swiftly as he could, as if he still felt William's hand on his collar), but she'd seen his watchful appraisal of the woman as she'd chattered amiably about the cornflowers she was raising from seed, and the turquoise drops she wore in her ears; watched him take her pulse, and frown. 'The other day she told me that she'd not seen the Essex Serpent but heard it, only she didn't know what it had said.' She drained her glass, and said: 'Was she joking, playing along, knowing I half-think there's something there after all?'

'She's too thin,' said Charles, who mistrusted anyone who did not eat. 'But – yes – beautiful: sometimes I think she looks like a saint seeing Christ.'

'Can't you get her to see Luke?' said Katherine.

'I don't know – he's a surgeon, not a doctor – but I would like to – I've thought of writing to ask him.' It struck Cora – just then, as the rain ceased and left everything quiet – how fond she'd grown of the woman, with whom she had so little in common, who doted on her reflection and on her family, who somehow knew everyone's business better than her own, and only ever meant well. *Should I envy her?* she thought: *Should I wish her gone?* But she didn't, and that was that: Will's wife was welcome to him, as far as she had him. 'Look,' she said: 'I must go – you know how Frankie counts the hours – but I will write to Luke – and yes, Charles, yes: I will write to the good Reverend – I will be good, I promise.'

Cora Seaborne
2, The Common
Aldwinter
29ᵗʰ May

Dear Will –

Charles tells me I must apologise. Well: I shan't. I cannot apologise when I don't concede I've done wrong.

I have been studying the scriptures, as you once urged me to do, and observe (cf. Matthew 18 15–22) that you must allow me a further 489 transgressions before you cast me out.

Besides – I know how you spoke to my son about sin – and I had no quarrel with you over that! Must we make battlegrounds out of our children?

And why should my mind cede to yours – why should yours to mine?

Yours,

CORA

Rev. William Ransome
The Lodge
Aldwinter

31st May

Dear Mrs Seaborne

Thank you for your letter. Naturally you are forgiven. In fact I'd forgotten the incident I suppose you allude to and am surprised you mention it.

I hope you are well.

Kind regards,

WILLIAM RANSOME

III

TO KEEP A CONSTANT WATCH

JUNE

Midsummer on the Blackwater, and there are herons on the marsh. The river runs bluer than it ever did before; the surface of the estuary is still. Banks gets a good catch of mackerel early in the day, and notes with pleasure the rainbows on their flanks. Leviathan is decked with spikes of rosebay willowherb and a rosemary wreath, and a patch of samphire grows at the prow. At midday Naomi lies alone by its black ribs with her skirt up by her hips, saying her solstice spells. Joanna has stayed late at her school desk and says she'll not move until she can recite all the bones in the human skull. (*Occiput*, she says as Naomi leaves, and the red-haired girl remembers it, to be used late one night in a curse.) The Essex Serpent recedes for a time, since how could it thrive under so benevolent a sun?

On the path above Naomi, Stella slowly walking plucks speedwell from the verge. It is blue, and so is her skirt, and so are the bands of fabric she has around her wrists. She is going home to the children. She supposes they'll want feeding, and the thought revolts her – all that soft stuff going into their gaping mouths, into that glistening hole: it is disgusting, if you think about it. She has no appetite for anything you might eat.

In his study Will is sleeping. There's a sheet of paper on the desk, and it reads, 'Dear'. Just that: 'Dear'. He writes so many letters, these days, that on the knuckle of his third finger there's a swelling he sucks now and then to ease the ache. Waking, he'll say to himself, 'Dear . . .', and at the first face coming to mind he'll smile, then cease smiling.

Martha is peeling eggs. Cora has planned a midsummer party: Charles and Katherine Ambrose are coming, and Charles likes nothing more (he says) than an egg rolled in celery salt. Luke is coming. His feelings as regards eggs are of no interest to her. There will be William Ransome, stern as he is these days, and Stella in blue silk.

Cross-legged on the playing-fields with a cheese sandwich on his lap Mr Caffyn writes a note: 'The school is quieter now than I have ever known it. The children work calmly and are expected to meet the required standards. See enclosed requisition form: order of twenty notebooks (ruled, with margin).'

At three in the afternoon Will pays Cracknell a visit. The old man's not well, and lies on a couch with his boots on: he knows the flutter in his chest will be a rattle come Christmas. 'A tincture of rosehip syrup in the evening is what Mrs Cracknell would've recommended and I'm not above taking even a dead woman's advice, Parson – that bottle, there, and the spoon.' It is a valiant attempt at courage, and Will smiles, but Cracknell does not. 'It wasn't the cough that carried her off,' he says, touching the rector's wrist. 'It was the coffin they carried her off in.'

Over in Colchester on the earthquake ruins Thomas Taylor suns his phantom feet. He does a fair trade on a fair day, and his hat is heavy with coins. Wasps have been so obliging as to make their nest in the folds of a curtain, and the papery mass – with all its sinister regularity – is quite the tourist attraction. The air hums; the wasps are too drowsy to sting. Late in the afternoon the black-haired doctor crouches over him in his good grey coat. His hands are raw in places and his skin smells of lemons. He fondles (none too gently) the flesh healed over the severed bones, and says 'A poor job: I wish I'd been here. I'd've done you proud.'

Fifty miles south as the swallow flies and London's at her

best. She knows it: she is irresistible. Children feed black swans in Regent's Park and pelicans in St James's, and the limes are incandescent in the avenues. Hampstead Heath comes over like a country fair; nobody uses the Tube. The sun is thick on the pavements while jugglers and tricksters grow rich in Leicester Square. No-one wants to go home. Why would they? Outside pubs and cafes office juniors grow impertinent, and if it's not exactly love which brews in with the hops and the coffee it's as near as makes no difference.

In his Whitehall rooms, dressed for the solstice in a new blue shirt, Charles Ambrose greets a visitor. 'Spencer,' he says, 'I have your letter here. Are you free for lunch? There are people I think you should meet.' Charles himself is more or less indifferent to Spencer's sudden philanthropic bent – it's all very much the rich man in his castle, the poor man at his gate, as far as Charles is concerned – but he likes Spencer, and so does Katherine, and one might as well do good as do anything at all.

Spencer, who's come prepared to plead Martha's cause, hopes he can remember this statistic and that, and how to mimic her habit of being both matter-of-fact and impassioned. He pictures Martha's face when he gives her good news ('And will you come when we instruct the architects, Martha, since you understand it so well . . .'). *There'll be one of her rare smiles*, he thinks: *she will see me.*

He takes a drink from Charles, and says, 'Thank you, I'd like that. I thought: maybe you might come with Martha and me, next week? We're going to visit Edward Burton over in Bethnal Green – the man Luke operated on, you know. Martha has become a friend of his, and says he makes the perfect case study . . .'

Case study! thinks Charles. He looks at Spencer fondly. The boy's too thin by half. Would there be lamb at lunch? Might there be wild salmon? 'Will you be coming to Cora's party, to see the merry widow play Persephone with flowers in her hair?' But Spencer cannot: he'll be in his white coat at the Royal Borough, setting limbs perhaps, a little relieved to be spared the ordeal of finding social graces under Martha's gaze.

Essex has her bride's gown on: there's cow parsley frothing by the road and daisies on the common, and the hawthorn's dressed in white; wheat and barley fatten in the fields, and bindweed decks the hedges. Cora has walked four miles and is not yet tired. At the fifth mile she passes a farmer stripped to the waist and unbuttons her shirt: why should her skin be disgraceful, when his is not? But there's someone on the path, and she puts the buttons back through their slots: no sense courting disaster.

She comes to a place where roses are grown for bowls and vases in dining rooms elsewhere; an acre or two of blooms laid out in coloured stripes, as if bolts of silk had been dyed and left to dry. It scents the air; she licks her lips, and there's Turkish Delight on her tongue.

As so often these days, she's thinking of Will. She cannot concede that she's done wrong, or that she deserves to be in disgrace: she faintly despises him for being so readily thrown into a bad temper. *Male pride*, she thinks: *the most tender, contemptible thing!* But all the same her conscience is pricked – has she really ridden roughshod over him? She considers prostrating herself half-ironically in apology for the pleasure of watching him try not to laugh, but no: she has her own pride to consider.

What's more, she misses the whole Ransome household – James had promised to show her the periscope he's made out of a broken piece of mirror, and Stella's gift for gossip is a fine substitute for London life. The thought of Stella casts a shadow on the path: has Will failed to see his wife's new strangeness, how she wears only blue, and puts blue flowers in her hair? How she roots around the marshes for blue sea-glass and bluish stones, and sends to Colchester for roses with their stems dipped in ink so the petals come out cornflower coloured? How she's grown thinner but more vital-seeming, her cheeks flushed, her motions hectic, her pansy eyes brighter than ever? *I'll speak to Luke*, thinks Cora: *Luke will know.*

She arrives home with her arms full of dog-roses in creamy bloom and three new freckles on her cheek. She puts her arms round Martha's waist, thinking how well they fit there in the groove above her broad hips, and says, 'They're on their way – everyone who's ever loved me and everyone I've ever loved.'

2

Late in the gentle evening Stella Ransome walked over Aldwinter common with her husband on her right hand and her daughter on her left. Back at the rectory, in the care of Naomi Banks, her boys were eating toast and playing Snakes and Ladders. Cora had called that morning on her way home from walking, carrying armfuls of roses that left little scratches in the crook of her elbow, saying, 'Come early, won't you? I never could have a party and not be afraid no-one would show up, and that I'd be left to sit up all night with bottles around me, drowning all my sorrows.'

Earlier Stella had stood at her mirror smoothing her skirt's white silk across her hip, and Will had said, 'What, no blue today?' and she'd looked down and laughed, because everything she saw was blue. The skirt's folds shimmered with it; her own skin had a bluish cast; even Will's eyes – which surely had once been the colour of the acorns the boys collected every autumn and lined along the windowsill – were blue. Sometimes she thought her eyes had filmed over with ink-stained tears.

'I think I'm blue-blooded,' she said, and lifted her arms, and thought how slender they were, and how pretty; and Will had said, 'I never doubted it, my star of the sea,' and kissed her twice.

On they walked, while house martins darted at insects over the grass, passing villagers off to set solstice fires in their gardens and on the margins of fields. Greetings chimed out across the village with the tolling of the All Saints bells: *What a night for it! What a glorious night!*

William slipped a finger inside his collar and loosened it:

he did not want to see Cora – he wanted very much to see her; he'd thought all day of her roaming the marshes, her finger-nails crusted with Essex clay – he never thought of her at all; she was the worst of women – she was his friend. Gratefully he looked down at Stella's silvery head, ringed with sunlight, gleaming, and thought: not once in all these years has she caused me unease – not once! Her little hand turned in his, and it was hot, and at the nape of her neck where her white dress was cut low he saw a sheen of sweat. The flu, the Colchester doctor had said, putting away his stethoscope: it had left her weak. She should rest and eat and sleep. The summer had come. They were not to worry.

Stella saw the grey house with all its bright lamps lit and in each window a jug of dog roses. Behind them someone was moving back and forth, and there was the sound of a piano being played. Nothing pleased her more than a party on a warm night; to be the still centre of an eddying crowd, knowing she was admired, light-ing on this person and that with her endless interest in grandsons, and ailments, and fortunes won and lost. But she felt desperately weary, as if she'd burned up her store of energy in the hundred yards they'd walked. She wanted to be home in the blue bower she'd made, counting over her treasures, lifting to the light the blue waxed paper that had wrapped a bar of gentian soap, taking in the scent, or running her finger in the curve of the robin's egg her sons had brought her in May.

Flu, the doctor had said, speaking to Will; but Stella Ransome was no fool, and knew consumption when she saw it speckle the white folds of a handkerchief. Once in her youth she'd seen a girl die the White Death (as they'd called it then, as if to name the dis-ease was to bring it into the room): she too had burned away, grown slender and *distrait*, greeting the end when it came contentedly, all her pains inside and out blunted by opium. A week before dying the girl had brought up gouts of blood that splashed her white bed-sheets.

Stella knew that she herself had not yet slipped so far into disease: when she did, she'd take Will aside, and ask to be sent to some high ward where she'd sit looking out on mountain ranges and all of their peaks would be blue. There'd been a reddish mist on the mirror once when she'd been caught by coughing one morning as she brushed out her hair – on the hundredth stroke it had come; but only once, and it had wiped away easily enough. (And why was it that blood when it came out was red, when clearly through the thin skin of her wrist every vein showed blue? It didn't seem fair.)

But she could not go away – not yet, not when Joanna was still so sombre, not while Will so often slammed his study door, not while the village still shrank from the river and the villagers still came silently to church and left without being comforted. Star of the sea, Will had said – and wasn't that also the name of the Virgin, who also only ever wore blue? She laughed, thinking: *Pray for me, Mary Mother of God, and lend me one of your robes.*

Then they were on the doorstep, and there was Cora in black silk, looking so stern and so serene that for a moment Will forgot his righteous indignation. Wrong-footed once again he took her hand and said, 'Cora, you look tired – have you been walking too far?'

Tall in her costly black, a little nervous perhaps, it seemed to him that he'd never met her before – that she'd taken on a kind of remoteness that made him want to run after her, wherever it was she had gone. He watched her greet her guests with the grace he imagined cultivated in high-ceilinged establishments in Chelsea and Westminster: she seemed to know precisely what to say, and how to say it; who to greet with kisses and who preferred her handshake, which was so like a man's. She conveyed Stella at once to a broad low seat on which a blue silk cushion was placed – 'I saw this in Colchester just last week,' she said, 'and thought you should have it; take it with you when you go.' She'd brushed her hair, and wore it loose like a girl, only pinned above the ears with silver combs; she wore pearl drops in her ears, and the lobes were red, as if they were sore from the weight of them.

When Charles Ambrose came in, blazing brightly in his new silk shirt, he held his hostess at arm's length – 'I thought you'd be decked in flowers, Cora: what a sad sight you are,' but his gaze had been an admiring one.

'You're gorgeous enough for us all,' she'd said, and kissed his plump cheek, and fingered Katherine's long-fringed shawl ('I am going to steal this later: see if I don't').

'She's getting fat,' said Charles, not disapprovingly, watching her make her way past low tables set with silverware. Then Luke was brought over, and proudly presented ('You know the Imp, of course!'), a yellow cowslip dying in his buttonhole and his black hair oiled.

'Cora,' he said, 'I have something for you: I've had it for years, and you might as well have it as anyone.' He handed her a packet wrapped in white, rather carelessly as if it hardly mattered whether it pleased her. When she opened it, Katherine Ambrose saw a small frame in which a miniature embroidered fan was set behind glass, and wondered what on earth the man was doing working with linen and coloured silk threads.

Martha, wearing green, looked a country girl born and bred, and more so when she produced a loaf shaped like a corn-sheaf and two gleaming capons dressed with sprigs of thyme. There were ducks' eggs and a clove-studded ham; platters of tomatoes sliced and dotted with mint, and potatoes small as pearls. Joanna followed her to the kitchen and back, begging to be useful, permitted to cut curls of lemon to dress the salmon. All along the table early buds of lavender were crushed by heavy dishes and made the air sweet. Charles Ambrose had brought good red wine from London, and as he opened the third bottle he lined up the crystal glasses and with a wet finger on their rims played a melody. On a wool rug Martha and Joanna lay on their stomachs poring over papers, making plans, looking very serious and sucking cubes of ice, and coiled on a window-seat Francis drew his knees to his chin and recited the numbers of the Fibonacci sequence.

What Will wanted most of all was to take his friend aside, and pull up two chairs, and tell her everything he had stored up those past weeks – how he'd found in his papers a poem he'd written when he was a boy and how he'd burned it, and wished he hadn't; how Jo had borrowed her mother's diamond ring and tested its strength by scoring her name on the window; what Cracknell had said as he licked rosehip syrup from a spoon. But he could do none of those things: she was busy elsewhere, dredging strawberries with sugar and persuading Stella to eat, and saying rather shyly to Francis that if it was numbers that bothered him most these days she had several books he could read. Besides (Will tried to rouse himself to anger again) they were in the midst of a battle, with no quarter asked, none given.

Still, the anger wouldn't come however hard he summoned: he pictured the crouching man stooping over his daughter, whispering, but after all it was only this Dr Garrett, this imp, who ought to be pitied, really, for his meagre height and the way one shoulder was surely more hunched than the other. Where were his good graces? What had Cora done with them?

He went over to the doctor, who'd taken the yellow flower

from his buttonhole and was pulling at the petals, and heard himself say, 'I was rude, that day when we met: I shouldn't have flown off the handle like that – will you forgive me?', and looked astonished at the glass of wine he held, as if it was the liquid there that had spoken, and not him. The doctor flushed, and stammered, and said, 'Don't mention it,' with something like hauteur, then the flush receded and he said, 'it was just something I like to try out sometimes – we did it to Cora once – we didn't see any harm.'

'I can't imagine anyone making Cora say anything she didn't want to say,' said Will, and for a moment the air chilled, with each thinking the other had no right at all to an opinion on what Cora was likely to do.

'She says you are a genius,' said Will: 'Are you?'

'I expect so,' said Luke, and bared his teeth in a grin. 'Your glass is empty – let me help – tell me: do you have any interest in medical science, or does your collar preclude it?' And in the minutes that followed Will could do nothing but admire a man whose ambition burned so vividly: 'Impossible to operate on the heart itself, of course: even if we could work out how to suspend the blood's flow – to isolate it, if you like – the brain would be starved of oxygen and the patient would die on the table – Martha, get us some wine, would you? – there: are you squeamish? – let me show you . . .' The Imp took out the notebook he always carried, and Will saw a drawing of a baby with the skin of its breast flayed from the bone while a cord linked the infant to its sleeping mother. 'You look appalled – don't be: it is the future! – if the mother's circulation is connected to her child's, so that her heart pumps for them both, and her breath supplies the oxygen, I could close up the hole in the heart so many babies are born with, but they won't let me attempt it, you know. You look faint.' And Will did look faint, but it was not the pipes and fluids of the body that troubled him, but the matter-of-factness of the surgeon, who spoke as if all God's creatures were to be plucked and gutted like hens. 'I forget you are a man of the cloth,' said Luke, with a delivery that made the words an insult.

Under the table Francis peeled an orange brought down from Harrods in a paper bag. He saw Charles Ambrose sit beside Stella and give her a glass of cold water; he heard them speak of Cora, and how well she looked, and how lovely she'd made the room, as if she'd summoned the garden inside. Then Stella wiped her forehead with the back of her hand and said, 'We should dance the summer in – can't someone play?'

'I can do a waltz,' said Joanna. 'Nothing else.'

'*One* two three *one* two three,' said Charles Ambrose, treading on his wife's toes: 'Shall we roll back the carpet?'

'Come out of there,' said Martha, seeing Francis in his hiding-place, tugging the carpet from under him, revealing the black boards beneath. At the piano Joanna, straight-backed, played a run that took in every key, wincing and saying, 'It's horrible! It'll sound horrible – it's been left to get old and damp!' Then she played a melody that was too fast, and then too slow; every several note rang so dull as to not be heard, but no-one was troubled. Outside the moon was full and low ('The Corn-Planting Moon,' said Francis to himself), and the estuary lapped at its banks, and for all they knew something was even now crawling up onto the marsh, but they cared nothing for any of it. *I think it could knock three times on the door and no-one would hear*, he thought, and found himself listening for it on the threshold, and imagining the blaze of its hooded eye.

Luke Garrett, leafing through handwritten pages in a dim corner of the room, set his notebook down and went to stand beside Cora's chair. He bowed like a courtier and said: 'Come on – you are almost as bad as me – a fine pair we'd make.' But Stella by the open window had other ideas: 'Since I'm too tired to dance with my husband, will my friend take my place? Will!' – imperious, laughing, she summoned him: 'Show Cora you're no ordinary parson, only ever at home with his books!'

Reluctantly, Will came forward ('Stella! You give them false hope . . .') and stood alone in the centre of the room. Without pulpit or Bible he looked all at a loss, and held out his hands a little shyly. 'Cora,' he said, 'it's not use denying her. I've tried.'

'The Imp is right,' said Cora, going to meet him, fastening a button at her cuff. 'If I dance, it will be badly. I've got no music in me.' She stood before Will, seeming somehow diminished, as if she'd gone some distance away: not since they'd left Foulis Street had she looked so unsure of her footing.

'She's right, you know,' said Martha, sighing and shaking out her green dress. 'She'll break your foot – she's heavy – won't you have me instead?'

But Stella stood, and came forward: like a dancing-master she placed Cora's hand upon her husband's shoulder. 'See how well-matched you are!' She surveyed them a while, then returned, satisfied, to sit below the open window. 'There, now,' – she stroked the blue silk cushion in her lap – 'eat, drink, and be merry, for tomorrow it rains.'

Then William Ransome put his hand on Cora's waist where her blouse was tucked, and Francis heard his mother sigh. She looked up – they stood quite still together – there was a quiet moment, and no-one spoke. Francis, watching, burst a piece of orange on his tongue: he saw how his mother smiled at Will, and how the smile was met with a steady, stern look – how then her head moved as though drawn back by the weight of her hair, and how his hand flexed at her waist, tugging at the fabric of her skirt.

I don't understand any of this, thought Francis, seeing Martha withdraw, and stand beside Luke, and seeing how perfectly her face mirrored his: they looked almost a little afraid.

'I can't keep playing it over and over,' said Joanna at the piano, rolling her eyes at Francis.

'I don't know the tune!' said Will, 'I never heard it before –'

'Shall I try one like this?' said Jo, and the piano slowed, grew rather languorous; Martha said, 'No! No – not like that.'

'Should I stop?' said Joanna, raising her hands from the keys, watching her father. How odd they looked, simply standing there! They might have been John and James, uncertain if they'd committed some little household sin.

'No: play on, play on!' said Luke, turning the sharp points of his mischief on himself and wincing as he did it: he would've liked to slam the piano shut.

Then the rector said, 'No: I can't – I've forgotten the steps.' Joanna played on – the clock ticked – still he did not move.

'I don't think,' said Cora, 'that I ever knew them.' Her hand fell from his shoulder – she stepped back, and said, 'Stella, I have disappointed you.'

'Poor show altogether,' said Charles Ambrose, looking with regret into his empty glass.

'Best stop playing now, I think,' said Will, turning to his daughter, giving her a look which was almost an apology. He made a deep bow before his dancing-partner, and said: 'You'd've been better with anyone but me – I was never trained for this.'

'Oh – please,' said Cora, 'the fault's all mine. I'm good for nothing but books and walking. But Stella, you are shivering – are you cold?' She turned away from Will, and stooped to take Stella's small hands in hers.

'I don't feel it,' said Stella, glittering, 'but I suppose Jo ought not to stay so late.'

'Yes!' said Will, rather swiftly, as if grateful: 'She certainly ought not, and we should see what havoc the boys have wrought while we were gone . . . Cora, will you forgive us if we go?'

'Nearly midnight after all,' said Charles, peering at his watch. 'The clock will strike and make white mice and pumpkins out of us all – Katherine? Where is my Kate! Where is my wife?'

'Here I am, as always,' said Katherine Ambrose. She held out his coat, and watched as Cora grew brisk, polite, her manners beyond reproach. She pressed the blue silk cushion on Stella ('Darling, you must: plainly they had you in mind when they made it . . .'), and kissed Joanna on the cheek ('I could never play a note, you know – how clever you are!'). Still, Katherine was not quite fooled. There ought to have been nothing in a brief waltz on the bare boards – nothing in those polite familiar steps to take anyone by surprise. What then had caused that curious moment, with so sudden a change in the air she'd hardly have been surprised to hear a thunderclap? Well – she shrugged, and drew down her husband for a kiss – it was late, and after all Will Ransome was a clergyman and not a courtier.

Cora opened the door and the scent of the Blackwater came in. There was a curious bluish light in the sky, and she shivered, though the air was warm. From beneath the table Francis saw how his mother held out her hands to each guest as they crossed the threshold – 'Thank you so much – thank you: promise you'll come again!' – and how vivid she seemed, how bright, as if however late the hour she'd never need her sleep.

William Ransome left with his wife on one arm and his daughter on the other, almost (Francis began to peel another orange) as though he'd buckled on a coat of armour. Cora – even brighter, more vivid – seemed somehow to sweep them all out onto the common. She closed the door, and clapped her hands together in satisfaction, but it seemed to her watchful son that a false note rang out as clearly as if Jo still sat at the ill-tuned piano. Why had William Ransome said nothing as he went out – why had his mother not offered him her hand – what caused Martha and the Imp to survey her silently now, as if she'd disappointed them? Well – he crawled out from beneath the table – what use was it to observe the human species and try to understand it? Their rules were fathomless and no more fixed than the wind.

After Francis had been put to bed, reciting the Fibonacci series as another child might a fairy tale, Martha and Luke set about clearing the tables and unfurling the carpet, crushing buds of lavender strewn across the floor. Cora had briefly been very animated – hadn't it been a good night, she'd said, wasn't Jo a clever girl, although music probably was not her vocation – then said that she was tired, and needed her bed. Her friends had watched her run barefoot upstairs and grown companionable in their fear. 'I don't even think she *knows*,' said Luke, drinking the last of Charles's good red wine: 'She's like a child, I don't think she can see it, what they've done – and all the while Stella there watching –'

'Every day his name comes up, every day – what would he think of *this*, how he would laugh at *that* – but really what *have* they done, it was nothing, no-one else saw –'

'And in her letters too – on every page! What can *he* give her? A country vicar afraid the world's changing. And besides, he already has a silly wife, isn't that enough, must he have Cora too –'

'She's collecting him' – Martha plucked grapes from their stem and rolled them across the table – 'that's what it is. She'd put him in a glass jar if she could, and label his parts in Latin, and keep him on a shelf.'

'I'd kill him if I could,' said Luke, appalled at the truth of it, flexing finger and thumb as if he felt a scalpel there – 'She's going away from me . . .'

They surveyed each other, feeling all their antipathy ebb, and how the air was thick with the uselessness of their longing, and no way for it to be spent. In the dim room the surgeon's eyes blackened; he watched Martha put her hands up to her hair – saw how her green dress pulled at the seam beneath her arm; he moved towards her, and she turned away to the foot of the stairs. 'Come with me,' she said, reaching for him: 'Come up with me.'

The windows in her room were open and light was fading on the wall. She said, 'There may be blood,' and he said, 'Better that way – better'; and it was Cora's mouth he kissed, and Cora's hand she placed where she wanted it most. Each was only second best: they wore each other like hand-me-down coats.

Across the common, in the shadow of the All Saints spire, Joanna slept with her slippers on, and Stella dozed with her head on her new blue pillow. Some distance away, approaching the marsh, Will walked alone, raging. Desire had never troubled him: he'd married Stella young and happily, and their hunger was innocent and easily sated. Oh, he loved Cora – he knew that: had known it at once – but that also did not trouble him: if she'd been a boy or a dowager he'd've loved her no less, and prized her grey eyes just the same. He was a Bible scholar, he knew its various names for various loves: he read the words of St Paul to the churches and their sacred affection summoned Cora's name: *I thank my God on every remembrance of you . . .*

But something had shifted there in the warm room seasoned with briny air and roses blooming in every corner – he'd put his hand on her waist and seen her throat move as she spoke – was that it, or how her scarf had slipped from her shoulder and he'd seen the scar and wondered if it had hurt, and how, and whether she'd minded? He thought of how he'd gripped her, of hearing his fingernails rasp against the fabric of her dress; of how she'd looked at him with her level long look. He thought she might have been a little afraid of him, but no: it wasn't fear that darkened her eyes but a challenge, or satisfaction – had she *smiled*?

He walked on to the mouth of the estuary, not knowing what to do with his desire, only that he could not take it to Stella; he knew he'd touch her and find her for the first time slight and insubstantial – he had in mind something more like fighting, and it appalled him; he went out to the water's edge and with quick movements spent himself on the black marsh with something like a bark and with a dog's joy.

3

Long after midnight, as the year slipped past the half-way mark, Francis Seaborne went out. Into his left pocket he put the silver fork taken from the Colchester ruin, and into his right a grey stone perforated with a hole into which his little finger fit. Upstairs Cora lay pressing the scar on her collarbone, willing the pain back; in a room elsewhere Luke and Martha fell apart. No-one wondered where Frankie was: if they thought of him at all, it was first with unease, and then with the comfortable certainty that this inscrutable child was keeping himself safely to himself.

No-one had ever tried to fathom Frankie's habit of night-walking; it had been chalked up as just another oddity. That he couldn't bear to be in company, but would haunt bedroom doorways in the smallest hours, was entirely in keeping with that baffling boy. If anyone had asked, he'd have told them it was only that he tried to understand the world and its workings: why (for example) did the wheels of a cab seem to turn against the direction of travel? Why was it that he didn't hear a falling object strike the earth until after he'd seen it land? Why did he raise his right hand but his reflection raise its left? He watched his mother with her mud and rocks, and made no connection between his own quest and hers. She looked down: he looked up. She was no help at all. Of all the men and women he'd met, he only had patience for Stella Ransome. He saw how she gathered her blue stones and flowers, and thought they understood each other. He also saw the too-bright colour of her eyes, and wondered why no-one spoke of it: but wasn't it just like them all, to see but not observe?

Out he went under the shadows the moon made, seeing how they lay in parallel, wondering why. The evening's muddle had unsettled him – he'd watched so carefully but found no order or reason in what he'd seen – and out alone in the night there'd be problems more readily solved. He thought he might go down to the Blackwater and see for himself what waited there in the estuary. It struck him as unjust that he alone of all the Aldwinter children had had no glimpse of the beast, not even in his dreams. Across the common, under Traitor's Oak to High Lane, heading east, while all around low voices murmured and bonfires burned to ward off what spirits braved the modern age. Someone played the fiddle; two girls passed him dressed in white; there was a nightingale in the hedge. When he reached High Lane the common fell away, and the noise of it: there was the scent of wood smoke and a delighted yelp away to his left, and then he might have been alone in the world.

He reached the salt-marsh in sight of World's End, thinking to find the point where the Pole Star pinned the sky in place, or see the moon give its counterfeit light, but encountered instead a black sheet on which a net of vivid blue was stitched. It was as if he looked not up into the vaulted sky, but down at the surface of a lake with sunlight on its ripples. From north to south above the pale horizon fine shreds of blue light hung, and between them showed the sky's dark blue. Now and then, as if caught by wind, a slow movement passed across and the bright net closed and widened. The light it gave off was not borrowed, like a white cloud ringed in sunlight, but seemed entirely its own: it might have been many fine lightning bolts fixed in place, burning inexplicably blue. Francis was transfixed with joy. It rose in him so suddenly and so completely he could do nothing but laugh, frightened at the strangeness of his own delight.

As he stood watching – craning his neck too far, so that in the morning his mother wondered why he held his head so strangely – a movement on the salt-flats caught his eye. The blue lights made the world a little brighter than it ought to have been, and the estuary surface showed oily black with pricks of blue upon the surface. Between the water's edge and the shore, not far from Leviathan's ribs, a bundle of cloth moved. There was a sound, very faint, like the snorting of an animal; the bundle shifted and lengthened on the mud, and then was still.

Curious, Francis turned to watch, peering into the dim air. If this was the Blackwater beast, he thought, it was a pitiful thing and ought to be drowned. The snorting paused a while as the bundle edged towards Leviathan, then began again, only this time it ended in what was certainly a cough, and then a long gasp at the air.

Francis, unafraid, came nearer. The bundle convulsed, then with a groan raised itself, and Francis saw the greasy layers of a black coat and dense fur collar, and above it the wild head of an old man he'd seen once or twice over at the church where the villagers were buried. Cracknell – that was it: a stinking old thing who'd once held up his sleeve and shown the boy the earwigs scuttling there. The groan ended in a fit of coughing that doubled him over again: he clutched the coat closer and fell silent.

Cracknell, with his boots at the water's edge and his eyesight failing, saw the thin boy with the black hair neatly combed and tried to call out. But it was as if the air had edges that caught at his throat as he breathed, and each time the name came to his mouth (Freddie, was it?) the coughing set up again. At last his breath returned; he called out 'Boy! Boy!' and beckoned at Francis, swaying on the path not fifteen feet away.

'I don't know what you're doing,' said Francis. What *was* he doing? Dying, possibly, but what a strange place to be dying in. His father had died with a clean white sheet pulled up to his chin. He turned away a moment to look up – there, the net widened and in places broke, and blue-black sky showed between fragments of light.

'Get someone,' said Cracknell, and after that fell to muttering at length, exasperated or amused, fixing Francis with an imploring and furious glare.

Francis crouched, and clasping his knees surveyed Cracknell with mild interest. A moth had settled in the fibres of the coat's fur collar, and elsewhere the fabric showed patches of pale stains that might even have been mould (could mould take hold on clothing? He resolved to find out). '*Ransome*,' said Cracknell, who did not quite want to make his last confession, but wouldn't have minded a kind face being the last he looked on. He put out a hand to tug the boy's coat – *please*, he meant to say – but the effort was too great.

The boy tilted his head and took in the name. 'Ransome?' he said. He supposed that made sense. The man with the white strip at his throat had visited three villagers in the past weeks (he had counted) of whom at least two had died. Did he bring death, or only ease them into it? He assumed the latter, but it was important to be sure. Examining the old man, Francis saw foam gather at the corners of his mouth and his chest rear inside his coat. Even in the near-dark it was possible to see the man's flesh take on a waxy cast, and already the bones of the sockets showed blue around his sinking eyes. It was both frightening and commonplace: probably this was always the way the end came.

Cracknell discovered he could not speak: it would waste the breath he eked out of the cool air. What was the boy doing, crouching placidly behind him, turning now and then to look up and smiling every time he did it? His heart lurched in its cavity: surely he'd go running now, and fetch Ransome, who'd come with a lamp and a good thick blanket to lay over his shaking limbs? But Francis, who knew what was coming, saw no sense in wasting time. Besides, it struck him that sharing the wonder that all the while unfurled over their heads might not halve his own pleasure, but double it. He stooped over the man, and said, 'Look,' and taking a handful of grey hair tugged at his drooping head so that Cracknell had no choice but to turn away from the black water and up to what he'd once thought was the heavens. 'Look,' said the boy: 'See?' and he saw the old man's filmy eyes widen and his mouth gape. The shining scraps of cloud were fading as the dawn came, but had gathered into a pale arc that split the sky, and as they watched a skylark flew up ecstatically singing.

Then Francis lay beside him on the marsh, not caring for the mud that seeped through his clothes, or for the reek that came off the old man's body, or the morning chill. Their two heads touched now and then as Cracknell, dazed, turned his head to take in the sight, sometimes trying out a scrap of a hymn: *it is well with my soul*, he sang, doubting it less now than ever. When the life went out of him it was on a long untroubled breath, and Francis patted his hand and said, 'There, there,' feeling quite satisfied, because what he loved above anything else was for things to go as he'd thought they would.

2, The Common
Aldwinter
22nd June

Dear Will,

It's four in the morning and summer's begun. I've been watching
something strange in the sky – did you see it? The night-shining,
they call it. Another omen!

A long time ago you said how sorry you were I'd lost my husband
so young. I remember wishing you had said that he'd died – I didn't
lose him: it wasn't my doing.

Why were you sorry? You didn't know him. You didn't know me. I
suppose they teach you these kind phrases when they give you your
first white collar.

How could I tell you then what it had been like – not just the death
(see how easy it is to say!) but everything before.

He died and I was glad and I was distraught. Do you believe it
possible to hold in your mind two sensations which are entirely at
odds and yet for both to be completely true? I imagine you don't – I
imagine your idea of absolute truth and absolute right can't take it
in.

I was distraught because I knew no other way of living. I was so
young when we married, so young when we met, that I barely
existed – he called me into being. He made me what I am.

And at the same time – at exactly the same time! – I felt so happy
I thought I'd die of it. I'd had so little happiness – I thought it was
hardly possible to live at such a pitch of it and not burn out. The

day we met I was walking in the woods and could hardly breathe for gladness.

Once I met a woman who told me her husband treated her like a dog. He'd put her food in a dish on the floor. When they went walking he told her to come to heel. When she spoke out of turn he rolled up the newspaper he was reading and struck her on the nose. Her friends were there and saw it. They laughed. They said what fun he was.

Do you know what I felt, when I heard that? I felt envy, because I was never treated like a dog. We had a dog – a wretched thing: once I picked a tick from its fur and it burst like a berry – and Michael would draw its head to his knee and not mind the drool and stroke its ear, and look at me as he did it. Sometimes he'd slap its flank over and over, hard – it made a hollow noise – and the dog would roll over in ecstasy. When Michael was dying it was his shadow. It didn't survive his death.

He never touched me so kindly. I looked at the dog and I envied it. Can you imagine being jealous of a dog?

I'm going back to London for a while. I won't go to Foulis St: it isn't home anymore. Charles and Katherine will look after me.

Don't feel you should write.

With love,

CORA

PS: Re. Stella: You should receive a letter from Dr Garrett. Please consider the offer of help.

4

Joanna went to All Saints in the morning and found her father there. It had been a good night, she thought, remembering how she and Martha had pored over plans for new homes in London where the water was clean and ran in copper pipes. She'd played the piano well enough, she'd worn her good dress, she'd eaten an orange (her nails were still stained with its peel). True, it had worn her mother out, and her father that morning had been silent, but then (he said) he always had such a lot of thinking to do.

She found him stooped in the shadows with a chisel in his hand. With furious movements he worked at the serpent coiled on the arm of its pew; over the years the Essex oak had ossified and blackened, and though the creature's folded wings had come away and lay on the stone floor, it still grinned at its adversary, baring its teeth.

'No!' said Joanna – imagine destroying something that had taken so much skill! – and ran to the pew, and pulling at his sleeve said, 'You can't do that! It isn't even yours!'

'I am in charge! I'll do what I think's right!' he said, sounding not at all like her father, but like a boy who couldn't get his own way; then as if he heard his own petulance he straightened his shirt and said, 'It's no good, Jojo, it shouldn't be here – look: can't you see it doesn't belong?'

But Joanna had stroked the tip of its tail since she could barely walk, and seeing its severed wings she wept and said, 'You shouldn't go breaking things! You're not allowed!'

Her tears were so rare that on any other day they might have stayed his hand, but William Ransome felt beset by enemies and this one at least he could destroy. All night, sleepless, they'd come to him: the crouching black-browed doctor, Cracknell with his moleskins hanging, a roomful of schoolgirls dismantled by laughter, the Blackwater parting, and there on the mud Cora standing sternly, and behind her with its heart beating behind its wet skin the Essex Serpent . . . he filed off a winking eye and said, 'Go home, Joanna, go back to your schoolbooks, and don't meddle.'

Joanna stood tall beside him and considered bringing her fist down on his bent head, feeling for the first time the helpless rage of a child knowing itself wiser and more just than its parent. Then behind them the church doors opened and the light came in, and there with her red hair burning was Naomi Banks. She was breathless with running, and her hands were coated with mud to the elbow. 'It's happened again!' she said, and her voice rang in the vault. 'It's come again: I told you it would – didn't I tell you! Didn't I say it would!'

By the time Will reached the marsh a handful had gathered round the bundle lying there. Cracknell's head was turned so far to his left – and upward, craning, as though looking into the face of his destroyer – that it was immediately apparent (they said) that his neck was broken. 'Wait for the coroner,' said Will, stooping to close the filmy eyes: 'He'd been ill a while.' There on the man's coat, placed precisely on his stomach and between two torn pockets, were a silver fork and a grey stone pierced with a hole. 'Who did this?' he said, looking up at the faces of his flock: 'Who put these things here, and why?' But they all shrank away, one after the other, not admitting to anything, saying that they knew there was something there, had known it all along, and that they'd all best lock their doors whenever the tide was high. One woman crossed herself, receiving a stern look from her minister, who long ago had trained them out of superstition.

'It's torn off one of his brass buttons,' said Banks, tousling his daughter's head, but no-one paid much attention: it was a miracle Cracknell had any buttons at all.

'Our friend has passed away only because he was ill, and now he's gone to glory,' said Will, hoping this last was true: 'He would have wandered out at night for air, or got lost and confused. It's not the time to talk of snakes and monsters – has someone sent for the doctor? – thank you, yes: cover his face – let him rest in peace – isn't it what we all hope for in the end?'

On the outskirts of the small crowd Francis Seaborne stood, now and then patting the pocket of his jacket where he'd put a shiny button on which an anchor was embossed. Someone had begun to cry, but Frankie had lost interest: he was looking out to the horizon, where blue clouds banked up all around. They were so like mountain ranges receding into mist he thought perhaps the village had been plucked up out of Essex and dropped, wholesale, into a foreign country.

Dear Cora – I saw this postcard and it called you to mind – do you like it?

I have your letter. Thank you. I will write again soon. Stella sends love.

As ever,

WILLIAM RANSOME

Philippians 1:3–11

Luke Garrett MD
c/o Royal Borough Teaching Hospital

23rd June

Dear Rev Ransome,

I hope you are well. I write with regard to Mrs Ransome, whom I have met twice. On both occasions I observed the following: a significantly raised temperature; heightened colour in the cheek; dilated pupils; a fast irregular heartbeat; and a rash on her forearms.

I believe her also to be suffering a small degree of delirium.

I would strongly advise you to bring Mrs Ransome to the Royal Borough hospital, where as you know I am employed. My colleague Dr David Butler has offered to examine her. He has considerable expertise in respiratory disease. With your permission I will attend. There are certain surgical procedures you may wish to consider.

An appointment is not necessary. You will be expected as soon as possible.

Yours sincerely,

LUKE GARRETT MD

Rev. William Ransome
The Lodge, Aldwinter
Essex
24th June

Dear Cora —

I hope you are well. I couldn't write sooner, though I wanted to — something has happened: Cracknell has been taken.

Why do I put it like that? I knew he was ill: I sat with him the day before he died. He wanted me to read to him, but we couldn't find a single book in the house, except my Bible, which of course he didn't want. In the end I recited 'Jabberwocky'. It made him laugh. 'Snicker-snack!' he said, and thought it very funny.

We found him on the marsh. The tide was coming in and had got as far as his boots. He seemed to have been looking up at something over him, though the coroner says there's no foul play. He must have been there all night. Already it looks as if World's End is sinking without him into the mud. Joanna has decided we have to keep Magog (or possibly Gog); she put a rope round its neck and walked it all the way home. It's in the back garden eating Stella's flowers. It's looking at me now. I don't like its slotted eyes.

Of course the villagers are in uproar: they're keeping their children in. The night it happened they say there was a strange blue light in the sky — one woman (little Harriet's mother, do you remember her?) kept saying the veil had been pierced, and I can't get her out of the church. She'd get up in the pulpit, given half a chance. Imagine if she'd seen the Fata Morgana, as we did! Bedlam would have been the most we could hope for.

Someone's been hanging horseshoes in Traitor's Oak (probably Evansford, who is taking a lot of pleasure out of being afraid) and one of the farmers has burned his crops. I don't know what to do. Are we under judgment? And if we are, what have we done and how can we atone for it? I accepted this flock, and tried to be a good shepherd, but something's driving them over a cliff.

Your imp of a doctor wrote. By letter he's a fine firm man: I could hardly refuse. We travel to London next week, though Stella looks better now than lately and sleeps the whole night through.

But all the same, I'm troubled. Dr Garrett showed me what he would do to infants and women if they let him, and it sickened me. Not the cuts and stitches, but how careless he is. He told me that if I believed in the immortal soul I'd have no more reverence for my own carcass than for that of a rabbit; we are all only passengers, he said. He told me that since he reverences science, since he worships the vessels and corpuscles and cells that make us up, it is I who am the barbarian!

Since you've been gone I've been reading like a student. I hope you don't think I'm too proud to sift over my thoughts, to order them. What does Locke say? We are all short-sighted. I think more than ever I need glasses with lenses three inches thick.

I won't accept that my faith is the faith of superstition. I suspect you despise me for it just a bit — and I know your doctor does! — and I almost wish I could deny it to please you. But it's a faith of reason, not darkness: the Enlightenment did away with all that. If a reasoned creator set the stars in their place then we must be capable of understanding them — we must also be creatures of reason, of order!

Cora, there is more – there is more besides the counting of atoms, the calculating of the planet's orbit, counting down the years until Halley's Comet makes its return – something beats in us beside the pulse. Do you remember the Frenchman who tied a pigeon to a photographic plate and cut its throat, and thought he caught a wisp of soul escaping through the wound? Absurd of course, and yet – can't you see him there with his knife and imagine how he thought it might be so?

How else to account for so much? How else to explain how attentive, how loving my whole being becomes when I turn towards Christ?

And how else to account for the longing I have for you? Cora, I was content. I had come to the end of everything new – I had no more surprises in store, and I never sought any. I was serving my purpose. And there you were – and from your hair which is never tidy to your man's clothes, I've never liked the look of you (do you mind?). But I seem to have learned you by heart, seemed at once to know you, had immediate liberty to say everything to you I could never have said elsewhere – and all this is to me the 'substance of things hoped for, the evidence of things not seen'! Ought I to be ashamed, or troubled? I am not. I refuse to be.

How do you like that, you rank atheist, you apostate? You have driven me to God.

With love – and with prayer, whether you like it or not,

WILL

Rev. William Ransome
The Lodge, Aldwinter
Essex
30th June

Cora, I've had no letter from you – did I speak too freely? Or did I not speak freely enough?

I'm afraid for Stella. Sometimes I think her mind wanders, then she's her old self and she tells me how St Osyth has a new vicar and he doesn't yet have a wife, or how up in Colchester there's a new shop opened and the pastries come direct from Paris.

She writes all day in a blue book. She won't let me see.

Tomorrow we go to London. Think of us both.

Yours in Christ,

WILLIAM RANSOME

5

Stella flinched under the stethoscope and breathed under instruction: as deeply as she could, and never mind the coughing. The fit, when it came, was not one of her worst, but bad enough: it threw her forward in the chair, it let loose a little urine; she called out for a fresh handkerchief.

'It's not always so bad,' she said, dabbing at her mouth, feeling sorry for the three men surveying her sombrely: how alarmed they were! Had they themselves never been sick? There was Will, who out of distress or discomfort could barely meet her eye. And there was the Imp, who stood far back in the corner, his black gaze even from that distance missing nothing. There, too – the elder of the men and the most gracious, having had longer to cultivate a soothing manner at bedsides both tawdry and grand – was Dr Butler, who withdrew the stethoscope, and with a gentle hand tugged his patient's blouse into place. 'No doubt in my mind of tuberculosis,' he said, seeing – as Luke had promised – the pretty flush on the woman's cheek: 'Though naturally we'll take a sputum sample, in order to be certain.' His full white beard compensated for a high domed head which was completely bald (it was said by his students that his thoughts moved at such a speed that over the years their friction made any hair growth impossible).

'Captain among these men of death,' said Stella into her handkerchief, whispering to the forget-me-nots embroidered there. There was no need for all this: she'd have told them months ago, if anyone had asked. The high open window showed the white sky splitting open to show a fragment of blue. 'I did that myself,' she said confidingly (not that anyone heard).

'Certain? How?' said Will, wondering if the room really did darken at that moment, or if it was only his own dread. There, beneath the couch where she lay still smiling, he imagined something in the shadows moving, and with it the scent of the river. 'How can you be sure? There has been none of it in her family – none – Stella, you must tell them.' But how could he have missed it – had he really been so blinded by what had come to Aldwinter? 'Flu, the doctor said: it had gone round the village, and everyone after was weak . . .'

'Family's got nothing to do with it,' said Luke. 'It doesn't pass from father to son. It's just the tuberculosis bacteria, nothing more than that.' His dislike for Will came to the fore, and he said with nasty precision: 'Bacteria, Reverend, are microorganisms that can carry infectious disease.'

'I'd like to be certain,' said Dr Butler again, casting a troubled glance at his colleague, who to be sure was not known for his manners but was rarely so rude: 'Mrs Ransome, can you bear to cough again – just a little – and spit into a dish?'

'I've birthed five children,' said Stella, with a little flash of temper: 'Two of them dead. Spitting is nothing to me.' It was a steel dish they brought, and in it the fragment of sky showed clearly. She obliterated it with a brownish substance drawn painfully up from her lungs, and handed it to Dr Butler with a gracious tip of her head.

'What are you going to do with it?' said Will: 'How will it help?' And how oblivious she was to it all: how calm! It was not natural – it was a kind of hysteria: shouldn't she weep, and ask him to sit by her, and hold her hand?

'We can now stain the bacillus so that it's easily visible under a microscope,' said Dr Butler, enthusiasm making him brisk: 'And it may be that we are wrong, and that Mrs Ransome has pneumonia, or a milder disease –'

A microscope! thought Stella. Joanna had taken to asking for one, wanting to see for herself how apples and onions were built of cells just as houses were built of bricks. 'I want to see it,' she said. 'I want you to show me.'

It was not an unusual request, thought Dr Butler, though ordinarily it was the young men so intent on looking the enemy square in the eye. Whoever would've thought this slight woman with her silver hair would be so sanguine. Though it was part delirium, of course: the curious state of detached peace so many patients reached had come to her early.

'If you can wait an hour, I'll bring it to you,' he said, seeing the husband begin to demur: 'Though I hope, of course, there'll be nothing to see.'

'Stella,' said Will, imploring: 'Stella, do you need to?' It was all happening so fast: surely only minutes had passed since he'd walked home in winter from World's End with Cracknell's gift of rabbits hanging from his belt, and seen his family lamp-lit and waiting, and now it was all breaking up in pieces. He closed his eyes and saw in the darkness the bright eye of the Essex Serpent, gleaming, gleeful.

'Pray for me then,' said Stella out of pity, and because she wanted it. Dr Butler left with the covered dish, and the Imp followed; Will knelt beside her chair. But what place did prayer have, there among the vials and lenses that unpicked every mystery? What ought he to pray for, besides? The disease must've lodged in there long ago while they went on in happy ignorance – should he ask that the clock's hands go back, and if so why stop there: why not ask for the raising up of every last one of Aldwinter's dead?

Was Stella really so singular and precious God might intervene on her behalf when generally He kept Himself to Himself? But there were the words of the Sunday schoolboy making mischief, he knew – their prayers were not for favours but submission. 'Not our will but thine be done,' he said. 'God give us grace.'

When they came back it was sombrely, and Will was taken aside, as if it was his disease and not hers. The message was relayed like a game of Chinese whispers, so that by the time it reached her – 'Love, you aren't well, but they're going to help' – the truth had dwindled to nothing. 'Consumption,' said Stella, animated by the news: 'The White Death. Phthisis. Scrofula. I know its names. What's that you're holding? Give it to me.' It was the glass slide on which her future was etched, and after some persuasion the microscope was brought, and she said, 'Is that all? Just like grains of rice.'

Another coughing fit took her, and left her dazed, so that lying with her cheek on the rough arm of the couch she could only over-hear her future unfolding.

'She should be isolated as much as possible, and the children should be sent away when her symptoms worsen,' said Luke, dis-pensing with pity: what use was that to a deadly disease?

'Take your time, Reverend: it's a shock, I know,' said Dr Butler. 'But modern medicine can do so much: I personally would recom-mend injections of tuberculin, which Robert Koch has recently introduced in Germany –'

Will – a little dazed still – thought of needles piercing Stella's fragile skin and fought against nausea. He turned to Luke Garrett, and said, 'And you? What do you say? Are you going to bring out your knives?'

'Perhaps a therapeutic pneumothorax –'

'Dr Garrett!' Dr Butler was shocked. 'I wouldn't hear of it

– only two or three undertaken so far and none in this country: now is not the time to test the waters.'

'I don't want you *touching* her,' said Will, feeling nauseous again, recalling how the Imp had crouched whispering over Joanna.

'Mrs Ransome, let me explain,' said Garrett, turning to the patient: 'It's simple enough, and I know you will understand. The infected lung is collapsed by the introduction of air: it lies like a deflated balloon in the chest cavity, and in doing so the symptoms are greatly relieved and a healing process can begin –'

'She is not one of your cadavers: she's my wife – you talk as if she's offal in a butcher's window!'

Luke, losing patience, said: 'Are you really going to let your pride and ignorance endanger her further? Are you so afraid of the age you were born into? Would you rather your children were all raddled with smallpox and your water full of cholera?'

'Gentlemen' – Dr Butler was distressed – 'be reasonable: Reverend Ransome, when you brought her here she became my patient, and I advise you to give injections of tuberculin your consideration. You needn't decide yet, of course – only sooner rather than later, before the haemorrhaging begins – which it will, I am afraid.'

'What about me?' Stella raised herself upon her elbow, and smoothing back her hair said, frowning: 'Aren't you going to ask me? Will – isn't this body mine? Isn't it my disease?'

JULY

Over in Aldwinter Naomi Banks is missing. She went the day Cracknell was found and she left behind a note: COMING READY OR NOT, it says, and there are three kisses overleaf. Banks sails the Blackwater and won't be consoled: 'First wife, then boat, then this,' he says: 'I'm being picked clean as a fish.' Every house is searched and nothing turns up, though the grocer says he's down a bit on his weekly takings and might she have turned light-fingered in her state of mind?

The village is wary. No amount of Colchester coroners would have them believe Cracknell died from nothing more than his old heart running out of beats: it was the Essex Serpent, sure as eggs. They seek out signs and find them: the barley crops aren't looking good, the hens aren't laying, there's a tendency in the milk to turn. Traitor's Oak's so heavily hung with horseshoes there's a danger its branches will break come wind and weather. Even those who never saw the night-shining could tell you just how it had looked that night, hanging over the common, sprinkling the estuary with blue. Up at St Osyth there's been a drowning. *Told you so*, they say: *I told you so*.

A rota of nightwatchmen is set up. They sit by small fires on the marsh and make marks in a log book: *0200 hours, wind south-easterly, visibility good, tide low. No sighting but a faint grinding and groaning from 0246 to 0249.* Banks is not permitted to join the watch, on account of how Naomi is missing and he's likelier than ever to drink.

Aldwinter's children don't take kindly to being kept indoors.

In one of the tithed cottages a boy goes quite deranged with boredom and bites his mother's hand. 'There,' she says, showing Will the wound: 'I knew something was up the moment a robin flew in. It's the serpent in him coming out.' She hisses at the rector, showing him her teeth.

Stella is home and writes in her blue book daily – *I'd like to be baptised again in blue water on a clear blue night* – and closes it up when Will comes in. She has good days and bad days. Her visitors attend her – had she heard about this woman and that thing and wasn't it funny and didn't she still look so beautiful and wherever did she find those beads so bright – and go away shaking their heads, and dousing their hands in antiseptic. 'She's not herself at all,' they say: 'She told me she hears the serpent sometimes when she sleeps! She told me it knows her by name!' Then – 'You don't think she's seen it, do you? You don't think there's something to see?'

Will finds himself treading a line. The line is narrow and on either side it's a hell of a way to fall. On the one hand he won't hear of it, this miserable superstition: was ever a whispered rumour given such wet flesh, so many bones? It is his duty to keep it at bay. He preaches brightly: 'God is our refuge and strength: a very present help in trouble,' but it's clear the villagers doubt it. The congregation does not dwindle, only grows truculent and frequently refuses to sing. No-one mentions the splintered arm of the pew where it's still possible to make out the remnants of a tail: they're glad, on the whole, that it's gone.

On the other hand he lies awake at night, with Stella too far away along the corridor, and wonders if it's a judgment. God knows he alone could be indicted on several charges (he remembers standing alone on the marsh bent double with desire); he wonders if the Essex Serpent has his name written down in a ledger.

He hears nothing from Cora. He thinks of her. Sometimes he thinks she came in the night and put her eyes in his sockets so he'd see the world on her terms: he can't look at a clod of mud in the garden without wanting to crumble it and see if there's something curled up in there. He wants to tell her everything and because he can't the fabric of the world feels thin and drab. 'There's a dragonfly in my study trapped behind a bookcase,' he writes, 'and I can't think over the sound of its wings beating.' Then he throws the paper away.

Cora reads her letters, and does not reply. She takes Martha and Francis to London: 'It's at its best this time of year,' she says, and spends irresponsibly on a good hotel, on extravagant meals, on shoes she doesn't like and will never wear. She drinks with Luke Garrett in Gordon's by the Embankment, where the walls drip into the candles, and when pressed on the subject of her Good Reverend dismisses him with an imperious wave. But Garrett is no fool, and would prefer her old way of merrily mentioning Will each second sentence.

If Luke and Martha had expected either to fall in love or to despise each other in the time after midsummer they are greatly surprised. What comes instead is an ease which is like that of fellow soldiers who've survived a common battle. They never revisit that night, not even in memory: it was necessary, that is all. It is tacitly agreed that Spencer should be kept in the dark: Luke has such a fondness for him, and Martha such a use. He has gathered about him men of political weight and financial heft: he thinks it likely that Bethnal Green might benefit from new housing to which no moral obligations are attached, and which do more than meet the barest minimum of shelter.

Martha and Edward Burton share chips down at Limehouse and scheme while the ships from New Zealand unload frozen lamb on the docks. We'll do this and that, they say, licking salt from their fingertips, companionable, without noticing that each has assumed the other's presence on some future day. 'It's just I like looking up and seeing her there,' he tells his mother, who has her doubts: Martha's a good London girl but has airs and no longer drops her aitches.

What Edward does not notice, when he goes home that night holding one of Martha's magazines, is that in the alley the man who cut him down in the shadow of St Paul's is waiting patiently. Samuel Hall has bided his time since the day Edward came home from hospital; he wears a different coat, but in the pocket is that same short-bladed knife that slips so easily between the ribs. He can hardly remember the source of his hatred – a quarrel over a woman, was it? – it doesn't matter anymore. It has become his sole purpose, fuelled by drink and aimlessness; he was cheated once out of revenge and passes the days impatiently until the task can be complete. That Edward Burton has become the pet of wealthy men and women who come so often and stay so long has only made him more implacable: they've all become the enemy. He watches Edward flick salt from his sleeve, and fit his key to the lock, calling up to his waiting mother. *Not tonight then*, he thinks, sheathing the knife: *no, but soon enough*.

Cracknell's funeral is well-attended, since no-one's as loved as the dead. Joanna sings 'Amazing Grace' and there's not a dry eye in God's house. Cora Seaborne sends a wreath judged rightly to've cost the earth.

Will has taken to walking and finds himself thinking that if only by the laws of statistics his feet might fit where Cora's have been. While he walks he unspools his thoughts behind him, and they are divided. He cannot settle his mind where Cora is concerned: he'd been so content in his love for her – he'd thought it of a kind the apostles might admire, as if in that muddy patch of earth they'd made a heaven – and then something had altered. He can still feel how her flesh had given beneath his hand, and what came after, and he is ashamed, though not (he thinks) as ashamed as he ought to be.

And then there's Stella, serene in her blue cotton dressing-gown: with the light behind her she'd shame a stained-glass saint. Sometimes she talks of sacrifice and lies quite still as if already on the altar, then she grows animated and writes at night in her blue book. What is he going to do with her? He thinks of the needle and scalpel in the surgeon's hand and all his being shrinks from it. He rejoices in the reason conferred on mankind, but mistrusts the shifting sands of man's ingenuity. This is what he is getting at: that we have always been in the habit of making mistakes. Think of the set-to when Galileo sent the earth spinning round the sun – think of the idea that a man deposited a crouching homunculus in his wife. It was all very well for science to puff out its chest and say, 'This time we have it right,' but must he gamble Stella on it?

Will bargains with God, as Gideon once did. 'If it is not your will that she endures the treatment, prevent it by some very definite means, and let that be the sign,' he prays. The logical absurdity does not escape him, but there it is: God might as well use logic as anything else. On Sunday he climbs into the pulpit and reminds the congregation of how Moses in the desert had raised up a wooden pole around which a great brass serpent coiled, and how it had given them hope.

Late in July the nightwatchmen abandon their post.

Luke Garrett
Pentonville Road
27th July

It's late and you'll think I'm drunk but my hand's steady – I could sew up a man slit from throat to navel and never drop a stitch!

Cora, I love you – listen to me, I LOVE YOU – Oh I know, I have said it often and you smile and take it, because it is only the Imp, only your friend, nothing to trouble you, not even a stone dropped in your calm water, in your horrible calm, your TOLERANCE of me – which I think you might even mistake for love sometimes when I've amused you or shown you some clever thing I've done like a dog bringing a chewed thing to its mistress . . .

But I must make you understand – I must tell you how I carry you about in me like a growth I should excise with my knife – it is weighty and black, it ACHES, it gives out something in my bloodstream, in all the sore endings of my nerves – but I could not cut it out and live!

I love you. I have loved you from the moment you came into that bright room in your dirty clothes and you took my hand and said no other doctor would do – I loved you when you asked if I could save him and I knew then you hoped I would not and I knew that I would not try . . . And I love your mourning dress which is a lie and I love you when I watch you try and love your son, and I love you when you put your arms round Martha, and I love you when you are ugly from weeping or weariness, and I love you when you put your diamonds on and play at being a beauty . . . do you think anyone else will ever know each Cora as I have known them and love each just as much?

And I have tried and tried to make something good of my love – I tried when Michael was dying like a wicked saint in that room with the curtains open, and I tried when at last he went back to where he came from. I have tried to love you in ways that won't destroy me – I have not wanted to possess you – I have left you to this new friend of yours – and all the while I cannot sleep because when I do you are there and you are shameless, you demand things of me, I wake thinking I have all your tastes in my mouth – yet all this time have hardly done more than put my hand on your shoulder . . . you think me an imp but I have been an angel!

Don't write. Don't come. I don't need it. It's not why I've written. Do you think my love will starve without your crumbs? Do you think I am not capable of humility? THIS is humility – I will tell you that I love you and know that you cannot return it. I will debase myself.

It's the most that I can give and cannot be enough.

LUKE

I am Stella stellar I am he said! Stella my star of the high blue seas!

And I've made my own missal my holy book with blue ink on the blue page and stitched up in threads blue as blue-blooded veins that are blue.

THEY HAVE TAKEN MY CHILDREN FROM ME!!!

My two blue-born babies my three that lived none of them now are found under my roof!

They want to give me things knives needles droplets and teaspoons of this and that no I said no I can't be doing with any of that no let me live with my blue things all about me all my cobalt beads my lapis my black pearls that are blue my pot of blue ink my pot of blue paint my ribbons that are indigo my skirt that is royal my cornflowers growing both my pansy eyes

Still I bear it well enough for it was promised that though I walk through the rivers they will not overflow me! Though I walk through the fire, I shall not be burned!

AUGUST

Nothing inclined Charles Ambrose to Darwinism more than walking the narrow streets of Bethnal Green. He saw there not equals separated from him only by luck and circumstance, but creatures born ill-equipped to survive the evolutionary race. He looked on their pale thin faces – which often had a sour mistrustful cast, as if expecting at any moment to encounter a boot – and felt they inhabited their proper place. The notion that if only they'd had access to grammar and citrus fruit at an early age they might have one day sat beside him at the Garrick was preposterous: their predicament was nothing more than evidence of failure to adapt and survive. Why were so many of them so short? Why did they screech and bellow from windows and balconies? And why, at noon, were so many so drunk? Turning down an alley, twitching his fine linen coat closer, he felt much as he might if viewing them through iron bars. This is not to say that he felt no compassion: even animals in zoos should have their cages cleaned.

Four had gathered in Edward Burton's rooms that August afternoon: Spencer, Martha, Charles and Luke. Their intention was to walk further into Bethnal Green, whose slums and rookeries were candidates for demolition and replacement with the good clean housing Parliament had promised. 'It's all very well passing Acts,' Spencer had said, not knowing how precisely he mimicked Martha, 'but how much higher will the infant death toll rise before policies are put in place? It's actions we need, not Acts!'

Edward's mother served lemon biscuits on a plate from which the Queen's head looked grimly out, and fretted that her son was tired. He'd been silent in such company and responded only to Martha's quiet asides – was the old wound hurting? Could he show Spencer the plans he'd been making for a new estate? 'Very feasible,' Spencer had said, though really he knew nothing about it. He smoothed his hands across the length of white paper on which Edward had drafted, with all his painstaking untutored skill, the blueprint of a tenement block set around a square of garden. 'Can I take this – can I show my colleagues? Would you mind?'

Luke meanwhile had eaten his fifth biscuit, having admired Mrs Burton's evident attention to cleanliness, and said, 'Martha won't be happy until she's seen Thomas More's Utopia encamped on Tower Hill.' He'd licked sugar from his thumb, and looked merrily out at the ranks of peaked roofs past the window. Writing to Cora had been like lancing a boil: in due course there might be further discomfort, but for now he felt only relief. What he'd written had been the truth, at least while he still held the pen: he expected nothing back, had offered no bargain, thought himself owed nothing. Probably the euphoria would last no more than another day, but it was a heady thing while it lasted, and made him benevolent. Sometimes, imagining a sealed envelope making its way to his door on the back of a postman's bike, he grew anxious: would she be amused – would she be moved – might she ignore it and go on blithely as before? Knowing her, he thought the last most likely: it was difficult to penetrate her good temper, or move her beyond a general display of affection to everyone she knew.

'Off we go then, slumming it,' said Charles rather gleefully, putting on his coat, remembering how years before he and a companion had one night been tourists of poverty, dressing in drag and loitering under streetlights, drumming up not a solitary client between them.

'You might be sold a bad oyster,' said Edward Burton, not yet well enough to take up his post over at Holborn Bars, 'but keep your wits about you and you'll all come home again.'

As they'd left it was not yet closing time in the factories and offices, and so the alleys were rather quiet, and it was possible to make out the sound of trains shunting on the tracks a few hundred yards distant. All around, high tenements blotted out the light, and laundry hanging low above them could never have been got clean. Though the summer was mild the few scraps of sunlight coming through seemed hotter there, so that before long Martha felt her clothes grow damp between her shoulder-blades, and the pavements, slicked with fallen scraps of food, gave off the sweetish scent of decay. What had once been grand houses were divided meanly into many small apartments, let at prices out of all proportion to what wages it was possible to earn. Rooms were sub-let, and sub-let again, so that what constituted a family had long been forgotten, and strangers bickered over cups and plates and their few square feet of space. Less than a mile away, just beyond the City griffins, the landlords and their lawyers, their tailors and their bankers and their chefs, knew only what was totted in the columns of their ledgers.

Here and there Martha saw reasons to hope that passed the others by, and sometimes nodded, and smiled, because all those strangers' faces were familiar. A woman in a scarlet jacket appeared from behind a lace curtain to water the geraniums on her windowsill, and tossed away a couple of spent blooms that landed in the gutter beside a broken Guinness bottle. Polish labourers had come to seek work, discovering that if Dick Whittington had been misled about London's pavements, the weather was at least more temperate in the winter and the docks never slept. They were cheerful and noisy; they leaned in doorways in pairs with their caps tipped, passing a Polish newspaper back and forth; they smoked black-papered cigarettes that gave off a fragrant pall. A Jewish family went volubly by on their way to catch a bus, and the girls wore red shoes; a moment later an Indian woman passed on the other side and in each ear was a bit of gold.

But even Martha had to concede it was frequently a miserable scene: a young mother sat on a doorstep enviously watching two children eat cheap white bread and margarine, and a group of men watched a bulldog in training for a fight hang by its jaws from a high rope. Someone had thrown aside a copy of *Vanity Fair*, and from the cover an actress in a yellow dress smiled placidly out; beside it in the gutter a clever-eyed rat flexed its little hands. Passing the men with their dog Martha couldn't suppress her distaste: she glowered at them openly; a man with sleeves rolled high to show a blurred tattoo lunged at her, and laughed as she scuttled on. Luke, more familiar with the seamy city than he'd let on, a little amused by Spencer's display of social conscience, allowed himself to grow chivalrous and walked more closely at her side.

'Will it work? – it *must* work,' she said, gesturing ahead to where Charles walked with Spencer, picking his distasteful way through a litter of rotten fruit from which a cloud of small flies puffed. 'He must see this is unsustainable, if only out of common humanity!'

'How can it not? Bit of a stupid man I've always thought, but not an unkind one – evening, love,' he said, grinning at a woman in a curled wig who leaned invitingly out of her door and blew him a kiss as he passed.

'It's no use – Spencer has tried – I'm long past redemption.' There ahead of them on the path his friend was gesticulating towards an especially narrow alley from which a sour smell came.

'He's doing all this mostly for your sake, you know. He'd give a fortune to a beggar if you asked him but otherwise would never notice they're there –'

She considered denying this, but felt that what with one thing and another the Imp had earned her honesty. 'It's not so bad of me, is it? I've never promised him anything – and besides, I'm not what his family would've had in mind! – but I can't do this alone. I'm a woman and a poor one – they might as well've cut out my tongue.'

They'd come to a kind of courtyard overlooked on all sides by tenement blocks. Luke watched his friend stand with arms folded surveying the insoluble problem of London, speaking in his quiet steady way to Ambrose, who only half-listened, distracted by a child in a fairy costume sitting on a doorstep and smoking a cigarette. 'He has joined the Socialist League, and talks of commissioning a little something from William Morris. Martha – let him down easy, won't you?' The fairy child stubbed out her cigarette and began another; her wings shed a feather and shivered.

Martha, stirred with guilt, said crossly, 'Can't I just be friendly, and that be that? He's not a puppet: he thinks well enough for himself, listen –'

'All the new housing on the Thames Embankment,' Spencer was saying, 'that they were so proud of, and use as proof of progress: have you seen it? Little better than cages. They're packed in there tighter than they ever were – some rooms have no windows and those that do are hardly bigger than a stamp – they wouldn't house their hounds so badly.' He couldn't resist a glance at Martha, who came near and let her temper get the better of her.

'Charles – look at you – you can't wait to go home, to Katherine and your velvet slippers and your wine that costs more each sip than *they* must live on for week. You think them a different species

– that they brought this on themselves because they're immoral or stupid and that if you gave them something better they'd trash it in a week – well: perhaps they are a different animal from you, because while your kind grudge each penny of your tax, here if they had nothing they'd give you half of it – no, Luke: I won't stop – d'you think because Cora taught me which fork to use for fish I've forgotten where I was born?'

'Martha, my dear' – Charles Ambrose had maintained fine manners against far worse, and besides, he knew well enough when he'd been found out – 'we all know your point, and admire it. I've seen enough, and if you let me return to my natural habitat I'll do what I can to carry out your every command.' Seeing that his ironic bow would do nothing for her temper, he said, as if confiding state secrets: 'The Bill has been passed, you know. The policies are in place. It's only a question of next steps.'

Martha smiled as well as she could, because Spencer had withdrawn a little, as if suddenly uncertain of his attachment to a woman who'd bellow at her betters in the street, and because Luke had gone impish again, and had never looked more delighted. 'Next steps! Oh – Charles: I am sorry. They tell me I should count to ten – wait, but can you hear that? What is it – what can I hear?'

They all turned, and heard from deep within a narrow alley the sound of an organ playing. An uneven melody gained speed as someone turned the handle, then became a rousing martial tune. The child ran to meet the music with her wings shivering behind her, and as the organ-player emerged others joined her as if seeping out of the bricks and mortar around them; some were barefoot, and others wore hobnailed boots that struck sparks as they ran; two fair-haired boys carried a kitten each; a girl in a white dress trailed behind, feigning indifference. Charles, keeping to the corners, saw a man of about his own age dressed in the remnants of a soldier's tunic. Stitched on the breast was the green and crimson ribbon of the Afghan War Medal and his empty left sleeve was pinned at the elbow. With his right hand he turned the organ's handle faster and faster, and began a jig of his own. The girl in the white dress spun, and laughed, and reached for Garrett's hand; one boy held his kitten high and sang to it words of his own. Martha looked at Spencer, and saw he was appalled, and despised him for it: perhaps he imagined they ought to be decently miserable in their lot, and not snatch pleasure wherever they saw it. 'Take partners,' bellowed the soldier: 'Try this one for size,' and it wasn't a military melody he played then, but with something in it of sailors on deck sighting land. Martha held out her hands to a passing lad who'd discarded his kitten on a door-step and with great strength in his thin forearms flung her round, so that Spencer saw all her hair fan out, wheat-coloured against the grimy brickwork. '*Heave me away, my bully bully boys,*' sang the girl in white, '*I'm bound for South Australia,*' and as she passed Charles she dipped her head, as though accepting a compliment he hadn't thought to give.

A little distance away, unseen in an alley, Edward Burton's enemy was watching. Addled with beer and loathing Samuel Hall woke each morning with hatred sharpening in his belly as keenly as any knife. Daily vigils outside Burton's home had given glimpses of the enemy himself, and of frequent visitors so obvi-ously wealthy it was as if Burton had entered the wards of the Royal Borough a pauper and left them a king. What could they know of his cruelty – of how he'd soured Hall's sole hope of hap-piness? Worse, there'd been mention in the *Standard* of the opera-tion that had cheated Hall of justice: two columns and a photo-graph in praise of a surgeon who looked like nothing so much as a glowering demon. His hatred for Burton doubled, and spent itself on this other man – what right did he have, to meddle in the ways of God? The knife went in – it had struck the heart – that ought to have been the end of it, and he might have had peace!

And here he was, that same man – black-browed, a little hunched, and with him three companions: a woman he recognised for her thick hair braided at the crown, and two men he did not. Hall had watched them greeted at Burton's door, and seen them framed in Burton's window; they'd passed plates of food between them, while Hall himself could not bear to eat – they'd laughed, when he'd forgotten anything but misery! He'd followed them all the way, and seen them dancing, when he himself had lost all joy – Hall put his hand in his pocket, and pricked his thumb on the blade hidden there. If Edward Burton were to remain always just beyond his reach, here at least might be a chance at retribution.

The soldier paused – his arm was tired – in the silence the dancers grew suddenly ashamed. The tenements and gutters seemed all at once more sordid and more bleak; Luke took his arm from the girl's waist and bowed as if with apology. '*They brush their hair with codfish bones*,' she sang to the soldier invitingly, but he was tired and wouldn't play more.

Charles glanced at his watch. It had been a charming display in its way, though perhaps a detail to be omitted from his report to the department; but he wanted his dinner, and before he could reach that happy conclusion to the day he'd need to bathe for an hour at least. *And possibly*, he thought, only a little ashamed of himself, *burn my clothes*.

'Spencer – Martha – have we seen enough? Have we done our duty? – but look here, who's this? Dr Garrett, he seems to want you: is this a friend of yours?' He gestured away to his right, and at first Luke saw nothing beside the children dispersing and the soldier counting out the coppers in his cap. Then the child in the fairy wings yelped and swore: she'd been pushed aside in a sudden jostling and tumbled wailing onto the stones. 'What's going on?' said Charles, drawing his coat closer – was it pick-pockets? Katherine had *warned* him to take care! – 'Spencer? Can you see what's going on?' The group of children parted, a kitten broke loose and yowled from a windowsill, and Charles saw a short man in a brown coat come at them with his head held low and one hand thrust in his pocket. Thinking the man was in distress Martha stepped forward, and held out her hands: 'What is it?' she said: 'What's happened – can we help?'

Samuel Hall did not reply, only went on running, and they saw it was Luke he wanted; he reached the surgeon, who at first was a little amused, and fended the man off with a jovial shove – 'Do I know you? Have we met?'

Hall began to mutter beneath breath sour with beer, all the while putting his hand in his pocket and drawing it out again, as if he couldn't decide what to do next: 'You shouldn't've gone and interfered with my business – it wasn't fair – I'll show you what's coming to him!'

Luke grew troubled then, but for all his strength could not push the man away: he found himself pressed against the wall, scrabbling at the brick. He cast about for help, and found it – for there was Spencer, who with his hands on the man's shoulder wrenched him away from his friend. Then the man fell to a kind of drunken sobbing that was also a little like laughter; raising his eyes upward he said, 'Again, would you believe it! Cheated again of all I'm due!'

'Poor chap's quite mad,' said Charles, watching the man in the gutter. Then he saw him put his hand in his pocket and take out a blade. 'Watch out,' he said, coming forward, feeling each hair lift on the nape of his neck: 'Watch out – he has a knife – Spencer, stay back!'

But Spencer had turned away from the fallen man, and was slow with the shock of the fight; he looked dumbly at Charles, and at his friend. 'Luke?' he said: 'Are you hurt?'

'Winded,' said Luke, 'that's all.' Then he saw Hall scrabble to his feet, and how light gleamed on the blade; saw how he raised his arm and lunged at his friend with an animal's cry. In the long moment that followed he saw also Spencer laid out upon a mortuary table, his fine fair hair falling back against the wood, and it was unbearable: he'd never felt so appalling a surge of terror. Luke hurled himself forward with hands outstretched – he reached the man – he reached the knife – they tumbled to the pavement. Samuel Hall fell first, and fell heavily: his head struck a kerbstone with a sound like that of a nut being cracked.

The soldier had moved on to other alleys, and they heard the organ playing –something like a lullaby, so that the watching children thought perhaps the black-haired man who'd danced with them was sleeping, since he lay so still. But Luke had neither passed out nor been knocked unconscious: he lay there unmoving because he knew what had been done to him and he couldn't bear to look.

'Luke – can you hear us?' said Martha, touching him with gentle hands; he roused, then sat up and turned towards them, and the colour left Martha's cheek. From collar to belt his shirt was scarlet, and his right hand and forearm were gloved with blood. When Charles came close – having seen that the brown-coated man would certainly never get up again – he thought at first the doctor was clutching a scrap of meat. But it was the flesh of his own hand, flayed from the bone where the knife had crossed his palm as he grasped it, so that it hung down towards the wrist in a thick and glistening flap. Underneath it greyish bones were visible, and a tendon or ligament of some kind had been severed and lay in among the blood like pale ribbon snipped with scissors. Luke appeared not to be in pain, only grasped his right wrist with his left hand, peering at the visible bones of his hand and reciting over and over as if it were a liturgy: '*Scaphoid – unciform – carpus – metacarpus* . . .' Then his black eyes rolled backward and he fell into the arms of his kneeling friends.

A mile or so west of that dim courtyard Cora came up towards St Paul's with a letter in her pocket. Her time in London had been dreary: friends came and went, and found her stand-offish and *distrait*. Cora, for her part, found them all too neatly turned-out and too cautiously spoken; the women's hands were white, their nails sharp and glossy; the men were shaved pink as children or wore absurd moustaches. They knew their politics and their scandal and which restaurants would serve you the latest fad, but Cora would've liked to sweep everything off the table and say, 'Yes, yes, but have I told you how once I stood by an iron grating in Clerkenwell and heard the buried river running out to meet the Thames – did you know I laughed the day my husband died – have you ever seen me kiss my son? Do you never talk, ever, about anything that matters?'

Katherine Ambrose had visited with Joanna by her side. Soon after Stella's diagnosis, Katherine and Charles Ambrose had taken charge of the Ransome children (Dr Butler, awaiting Will's decision on how his wife should be treated, urged peace, and good clean air, and the children sent elsewhere). Appalled to find his quiet home full and noisy, Charles nonetheless found himself coming home earlier than necessary and with his pockets stuffed full of Cadbury's and games of cards, which he played with them until rather too late in the evening. They all longed for Stella, but bore it bravely: Joanna was at once let loose on the Ambrose library, but also learned to curl her hair with rags; James drew devices of impossible complexity and sent them to his mother in envelopes sealed with wax.

'I'm glad to see you,' said Cora, truthfully: Joanna had grown almost into womanhood in the space of a month and wore her mother's eyes above her father's mouth. She was studying hard at Charles's books and intended (she said) to be a doctor or a nurse or an engineer, something like that, she hadn't decided; then she'd remember her mother, and how much she missed her, and her violet eyes would grow cloudy.

'What are you doing here in London, Cora?' said Katherine, nibbling at a square of bread and butter. 'What made you leave, when you were so happy, and saw so much? If ever anyone could unravel the mystery of the Blackwater beast it surely should be you! At midsummer we all said you looked a country girl born and bred, and doubted we'd ever see you get on a train again.'

'Oh, all that mud and muddle,' said Cora brightly, not fooling her friend for an instant: 'I'm a city mouse and always was – all those mad girls, that whispering about the serpent, the horse-shoes in the oak tree – I thought if I stayed any longer I'd go mad. Besides' – she listlessly crumbled a piece of bread – 'I didn't really know what I was doing.'

'But you're going back to Essex soon though, aren't you?' said Joanna: 'You shouldn't leave your friends when they're ill because that's when they need you!' Her tears came, and could not be stopped.

'Oh – yes,' said Cora, ashamed of herself: 'Jojo, of course I'm going back.'

Later, Katherine said, 'What *did* happen, Cora? Will Ransome – you talked about him so much – I was almost afraid of what was coming! But then I saw him with you and you barely spoke, and I thought you hardly liked each other . . . it seems a strange friendship but then you never did do anything the way the rest of us might – and now, with Stella as she is . . .' But Cora – who since her widowhood could never conceal a thought that passed behind her eyes – drew down the blinds and tersely said: 'There was nothing strange about it: we enjoyed each other's company for a time, that is all.'

If Cora could've explained what had gone awry she might have done, but for all the thought that she gave it – late into the night, and immediately on waking – she could not unravel things. She'd prized Will's affection because it was impossible that he might want her as Michael once had; his affection was bounded off on all sides by Stella, and his faith, and by what she'd gratefully thought was his complete failure to notice she was a woman. 'I might as well be a head in a jar of formaldehyde, for all he cares,' she'd once said to Martha: 'It's why he prefers to write to me than see me – I'm only a mind, not a body: I'm safe as a child – don't you see how I might prefer it?'

And she believed it, too. Even now, when she thought of that moment when everything had shifted, she saw the fault as hers, not his – she ought not to have looked at him the way she did, and she had no idea why she'd done it. Something in the hard flexing of his fingers against her flesh had struck something off in her, and he had seen it, and it had thrown him off-balance. Certainly his letters now were kind enough – but it seemed to her a kind of innocence was lost.

Then Luke's letter had come, and it was she who was thrown off-balance. It was not that she'd been oblivious to his love, since he cheerfully declared it so often, but that it was no longer possible to laugh, and declare that she too loved her Imp: a kind of innocence was lost. Worse, it seemed an attempt to force her hand – all the years of what ought to have been her youth she'd been in someone's possession, and now, with hardly a few months' freedom to her name, someone wanted to put their mark on her again. *I know you cannot return my love*, he'd said, but no-one ever wrote such a letter without hope.

Crossing the Strand up by St Paul's she found a letterbox and tossed in a letter addressed to Dr Garrett with a kind of contempt. From somewhere behind her there came the sound of music, and she saw on the cathedral steps a man in a torn soldier's tunic turning the handle of a barrel organ. His left sleeve was empty, and the sun picked out the medal on his breast. The melody was a merry one, and it lifted her mood: she crossed to where he sat and dropped a few coins in his cap.

Cora Seaborne
c/o Midland Grand Hotel
London
20th August

Luke –

Your letter came. How could you – HOW COULD YOU?

Do you think I should pity you? I don't. You pity yourself enough for the two of us.

You say you love me. Well, I knew that. And I love you – how could I not? – and you call it crumbs!

Friendship is not crumbs – you're not grubbing around for scraps while someone else takes the whole loaf. It's all I've got to give. All right, once I might have had more – but for now, it's all I've got.

Well, let's leave it there.

CORA

Cora Seaborne
C/o The Midland Grand Hotel
London
21ˢᵗ August

Luke, my Imp, my dear, what have I done – I wrote without knowing what had happened – Martha told me what you did, and I am not surprised – you have always been the bravest man I know . . .

And I tried to lecture you on friendship when I have never done for anyone what you have done for him!

Tell me when I can come. Tell me where you are.

With my love, dear Luke – believe me

CORA

George Spencer MD
Pentonville Road
London
29th August

Dear Mrs Seaborne

I hope you are well. I should tell you at once that Luke doesn't know I'm writing: he'd be angry if I told him but I think you should know what he has suffered.

I know how he wrote to you. I saw your reply. I would never have thought you capable of such cruelty.

But I'm not writing to take you to task, only to tell you what has happened in the days since we went to Bethnal Green.

You must know by now how we encountered there the man who stabbed Edward Burton, and how Luke intervened to protect me. The worst of it is that he grasped the knife by the blade, and so wounded his right hand. Those nearby were very kind: a girl tore the skirt from her dress to make a tourniquet under my instructions, and a door was brought so that we could carry him as if by stretcher out of the alleys to Commercial Street where we were able to hail a cab. Happily, we were very near the Royal London Hospital in Whitechapel, and a colleague there was able to attend to him at once. The wound was cleaned, since infection was our first concern. This caused him a great deal of pain, but he refused any anaesthetic, saying that he prized his mind above anything else and wouldn't have it meddled with.

Perhaps I'd better tell you the nature of the injury. Can you bear it? You are content enough with buried bones but where do you stand on living ones?

The knife entered his palm near the base of his thumb and with a movement rather like lifting cooked flesh from the bones of a fish more or less flayed the palm clean off. The muscles were cut through, but what is worse is that two of the tendons which control the movement of his index and middle fingers have been severed. The damage was laid out plain to see: the wound was so clean a student might have looked at it and then passed his anatomy exam.

He asked me to operate. He again refused anaesthetic and spoke of the hypnosis techniques he had been studying, and how a doctor in Vienna had three wisdom teeth removed under hypnosis without flinching. He told me how he'd trained himself to enter a hypnotic trance so deep he once fell to the floor without waking. Then he said again that he did not believe pain to be any more intolerable than intense pleasure (a preoccupation of his which I have never understood), and extracted from me a promise that I would not put him under anaesthetic unless he begged. I recall his words precisely. He said, 'I trust my mind more than I trust your hands.'

I couldn't ask a nurse to attend. It would not have been fair. I believe he would have prepared the room in his usual fashion if he could, but he could do nothing but lie on his own operating table and give instruction: we were both to wear white cotton masks. I was to set up a mirror so that he could see the procedure if he roused from his trance.

He ought to have had the finest surgeon in Europe attending him, not me: my skills are modest at best (in fact, he has been in the habit of mocking them since we were students together). My hands shook each time I picked up the instruments; they rattled on the tray, and I knew he'd see I was afraid. He asked me to unbind the bandages so that he could examine the wound and issue instructions before entering hypnosis, and though I cannot imagine the suffering he endured as the cloth was drawn back from the flesh he did nothing more than bite down upon his lip and turn very white. I lifted back the flap of his palm and he surveyed the broken tendons as if they'd only been those of one of the cadavers we once cut and stitched. He told me which stitches I should use to bring the two ends of the tendons together, and ensure the sheath remained intact – how I must not cause the tension in the skin of his palm to strain once the wound was closed. Then he began to whisper beneath his breath to himself, which brought him comfort: he recited scraps of poetry, and the names of chemicals, and listed all the bones of the human body. Then at last his eyes rolled towards the door, and he smiled, as if he had seen an old friend come through, and he fell into a trance.

I betrayed him. I gave him my promise and knew that I would break it. I waited a few moments, and lightly touched the flesh of his hand, and satisfied that he was more or less insensate I summoned a nurse and we administered the anaesthetic.

I operated for more than two hours. I will not bore you with details of the surgery, only say with shame that I gave it my best, and it was not enough. No-one ever matched him for the minuteness of his skill, and for his courage: if he could only have attended to it himself I believe in a year's time no-one would know how badly he'd been injured. I closed the wound, and he was brought round, and when he felt the soreness of the tube in his throat he knew at once what I had done, and I think he might have throttled me then, if he could.

He remained in hospital for two days, refusing all visitors. He insisted on having the dressings removed, so that he could examine my work. My stitching was no better than a blind child's, he said, but at least I had kept the site clean, and there was no sign of infection. When he was well enough to go home I went with him to his rooms on Pentonville Road, and it was then that we found your letter on the doormat.

Let me tell you: where the knife failed, you have succeeded. He is shattered – you have turned out all his lights! You have broken all his windows!

Three weeks have passed and there has been no good news. The tendons that give movement to his index and middle fingers have shortened significantly, and they are crooked towards the palm, giving the appearance of a hook. Perhaps he might regain a greater scope of movement if he were prepared to do the exercises he ought, but he has lost hope. You cut something out of him. He is absent. He has no resolve. I've seen it before in the eyes of dogs whose masters broke their spirit young.

Your second letter was a kind one, certainly, but don't you know him well enough to keep your pity to yourself?

I won't write again unless he asks me.

He can't write. He can't hold a pen.

Yours sincerely,

GEORGE SPENCER

IV

THESE
LAST
TIMES OF
REBELLION

SEPTEMBER

I

Autumn's kind to Aldwinter: thick sun aslant on the common forgives a multitude of sins. The dog-roses have gone over to crimson hips, and children stain their hands green breaking walnuts open. Skeins of geese unravel over the estuary, and cobwebs dress the gorse in silk.

For all that, things aren't as they ought to be. World's End sinks into the marsh and there's fungus growing in the empty grate. The quay is quiet: better to risk a lean winter than set sail on polluted waters. Rumours come from Point Clear and St Osyth, from Wivenhoe and Brightlingsea: the beast in the Blackwater was seen by a fisherman at tide's turn one night and he went clean out of his wits; a child was found half-drowned with a grey-black mark on her belly; a dog's been cast up on the saltings with its head all awry. Now and then a half-hearted watchman sets a fire by Leviathan and makes a mark in the logbook, but never lasts the night.

No sign yet of Naomi Banks. It's never said that she must've gone down one night to the marsh and there encountered the serpent, but it's generally assumed. Banks lets his fishing-nets tangle and his red sails moulder and is banned from the White Hare for putting the wind up his fellow drinkers. 'Coming ready or not!' he bellows from the doorstep, and keels into the street.

Up in his rooms on the Pentonville Road, Luke's hand knits together well enough. Spencer winds and unwinds the dressing, and admires his own needlework, and sees the crooking inward of the fingers; meanwhile Luke looks placidly out over the wet street and says nothing. He has memorised Cora's first letter from its first word to her signature: *How could you – how could you?* Her second goes unanswered for all her contrition.

Martha writes to Spencer. Edward Burton and his mother are to lose their home, she says – the rent has become intolerable. Not all the laundry and bright rag rugs in London will keep the wolf from the door. Has anything been done? Has Charles anything to report? When can she bring good news? Spencer detects an urgency there between the lines, and puts it down to her tender heart, her good hard conscience. But he has nothing to report, and cannot think how to reply.

In the high white Ambrose house the children have grown very nearly as plump as Charles. Joanna knows the periodic table and the remarkable thing about the hypotenuse and can spot a *post hoc* logical fallacy at a hundred yards. If on a Monday she resolves to enter Parliament, by Wednesday nothing but the law will do. Charles keeps from her the unlikelihood of either: she'll grow out of hope, as everyone eventually does. Now and then she remembers casting her childish spells with Naomi Banks, and guilt sends her reeling: where is her red-haired companion now? Do her curls wave in the estuary tides full five fathoms down? She still has a drawing Naomi made of their two hands clasped, and she asks Katherine if she can put it in a frame.

Katherine wakes one night, hears weeping, and finds the brothers in their sister's arms. They want their mother; they miss the village; it's agreed they'll go down to Essex by the end of the week. Besides, says Joanna, there's Magog to think of, still tethered in the garden, missing her master. They're consoled with a trip to Harrods and sufficient cake to sink a sailor.

Cora remains in her London hotel, despising the carpets, the curtains. She has in her pocket a letter from Spencer advising her not to visit and it's so polite the paper is cold in her hands. Martha sees her walk from room to room and can find nothing to say that won't receive a harsh reply. Cora has little interest in her books and bones – she's bored and bad-tempered and there's a new crease between her eyebrows. Spencer's rebuke has lodged in her and she's sulking. Her idea of herself has never included selfishness or cruelty – she has always been done to, and never doing. It's quite an adjustment. She has gone blundering about, wishing no harm and causing much.

Will's letters are prized, read often, unanswered. How can she respond? She buys a postcard from a stand at the station and writes I WISH YOU WERE HERE, but what good did it ever do, to speak one's mind? In his absence – without the possibility of walking with him on the common, of finding on the threshold an envelope (in a neat hand in which she always thinks she can spot the schoolboy) – the world grows dull and blunted; there's no longer anything in it to delight or surprise. Then she's struck by her own folly – to feel so dreary because she can't talk to some Essex parson with whom she has nothing in common! – it's absurd; her pride revolts against it. In the end, it comes more or less down to this: she does not write, because she wants to.

She tries – as she has so often tried before – to turn all her unused affection on Francis. How can it be that a mother and son should take so little pleasure from each other? She pulls every trick in the book: conversations on subjects that please him, attempts at jokes and games; she tries her hand at baking, and buys him novels she's certain he'll like. Sometimes she catches him out looking anxious, or thinks she does, and tries to console; they make frequent journeys on the Underground to destinations of his choosing. He submits with few words and less affection, and sometimes she thinks he is sorry for her, or (much worse!) finds her amusing.

Martha loses her temper. 'Did you really think you could carry on like that – you never wanted friends or lovers – you wanted courtiers! What you have on your hands is a peasants' revolt. Frankie,' she says, 'we're going for a walk.'

Will stands in the All Saints pulpit and looks out at his flock and finds himself lost for words. They are by turns mistrustful and eager: at times it seems they're ready to run pell-mell into the everlasting arms, at others they eye him askance as if the Trouble has all been his doing. Someone somewhere has transgressed, that is the general consensus; and if the parson can't be trusted to root out the wrongdoer things have come to a pretty pass.

All the while he finds himself wavering like a compass needle between the South Pole and the North: his wife whom he loves and is the sanctioned source of all his joys; and Cora Seaborne, who is not, and what's more brought him nothing but trouble. News of Luke's catastrophe has reached him via Charles. Other clergy might've imagined this swift end to the surgeon's career to have been as divinely intended as if it had been the almighty hand wielding the knife, since it delivers Stella from the threat of the scalpel. Will, of course, is not so backward in his thinking, but all the same it's difficult not to feel they've been extended a period of grace: the brutal treatment once offered by Garrett – the diseased lung collapsed in its cavity – is now impossible, since no other surgeon in England would consent to it.

Without Cora, he finds his thoughts lack direction. What, after all, is the point of observing this, of encountering that, if he cannot tell her, and watch her laugh or frown in response? He finds himself restless, uneasy; often he grows exasperated with them both, for having permitted only a lapse in good manners (this is how he frames it to himself) to cut the knot between them. Perhaps she finds herself too enraptured by her wounded friend to recall the country parson with his ailing wife – brings him rich food he ought not to eat, learns to dress the cut, to tug silk stitches from the skin. He clothes her in white and seats her at the doctor's feet, her head bent over his ruined hand, and is appalled to find himself envious. All the same (he thinks): soon enough a letter will pass either this way or that between town and country – it only remains to be seen who'll be first to unfold a sheet of paper, to lick the nib of their pen.

Behind Stella Ransome's ribs, tubercles are forming. If Cora could've seen them, they'd have put her in mind of the toadstones she collects on her mantelpiece. They send out scavenger cells; infection's setting in. The blood vessels of her lungs are beginning to disintegrate and show themselves in scarlet flecks on her blue handkerchiefs.

Of them all, only Stella is happy. It is the *spes phthisica*, which confers on the tubercular patient a light heart, a hopeful spirit. She brims with joy unspeakable and full of glory, beatified by suffering, devoutly occupied in her taxonomy of blue. Like a magpie decking its nest she gathers talismans around her, of gentian seed packets and sea-glass and spools of navy thread, and all throughout her eyes are fixed on heaven. She feels her feet have left the mud they once were mired in – she wakes in the night sweat-drenched in a light euphoric fever and has seen the face of blue-eyed Christ. Sometimes she hears the whisper of the serpent summoning and is not afraid. There was once another like it: she knows that enemy of old.

Her love for her husband and her children does not diminish, but grows distant: it is as if a fine blue veil has been drawn between them. Will is attentive in his loving – he hardly leaves her side – he sees the skin of her hands is dry and brings back from Colchester a bottle of Yardley's lotion.

Sometimes she draws his head down to her shoulder and

cradles it as though the disease were his. No more a fool now than she ever was, she's seen his attachment to Cora grow knotted, and pities him. *My beloved's hers, and she is his*, she writes in her blue book without rancour. 'When is Cora coming back?' she says that night, playing cat's cradle with blue ribbon: 'When does she leave London? I've missed hearing you talk together.'

At night on my bed I sought him whom my soul loveth I
sought him and I found him not

Once we shared a pillow and he said Stella my star my
breath is yours and yours is mine now it is fifteen steps from
my door to his so he's safe from the contagion that's in me

Ah but he has a better helpmeet! Let him kiss her with the
kisses of his mouth for his love is better than wine and she
has the stomach for it!

I understand there's a kind of blue paint they call
ultramarine, because the stones they grind to make it
are borne to us over the sea

2

A woman walked onstage alone at the Mile End Assembly Hall. Slight, dark-browed, darkly dressed, she surveyed her scant audience good-humouredly. Perhaps a hundred men and women waited whispering under the white vault: here then was Eleanor Marx Aveling, and more than her father's daughter.

Among them – breathless from his walk – sat Edward Burton, feeling dwindled down to nothing inside his winter coat. Martha fidgeted beside him: 'I met her once, you know,' she said, glinting. 'She said to call her Tussy, like her friends.'

Left to his own devices Burton may not have chosen to attend a public meeting of the Socialist League, but Martha had been impossible to resist. 'No sense just listening to me,' she'd said, pouring tea from the cooling pot. 'No sense taking things second-hand. I'll go with you – we'll walk together – you can't be forever cooped up in here with your plans.'

In the weeks of his convalescence the earth had leaned a little further from the sun; the air now was bright, gleaming, as though he viewed the world through a polished pane of glass. It had struck him lately that if his body these days was weary his mind – at last! – was not: Samuel Hall had roused him from a long slumber. It seemed impossible that there'd been years when he'd taken his allotted place without complaint, fitting neatly into the whole great grinding enterprise of London. What he saw about him now was a sick body convulsing as it shook off its fever – disease coursing in the arteries of its roads and canals, poison silting in the chambers of its halls and factories. He was awake

– painfully, restlessly so: he ate his bread wondering what long hours the dying men worked in the flour-mills; he watched his mother stitching scraps and knew her worth to be less than that of the bricks in the street. The landlord raised their rent, and he saw it not as an act of personal greed, simply another symptom of the sickness. He thought of Samuel Hall's cracked skull and his own guilt was overlaid with pity: Hall had been degraded by enslave-ment, as they all were.

This new fervour was indistinguishable from what he felt for Martha, and he made no attempt to set one aside from the other. He'd never been much in the company of women: they'd been prized objects to be bickered over, and rarely more than that. Now he sought no other company but hers, and could scarcely name the boys and men who'd once clustered round his Holborn desk. She seemed to him neither man nor woman, but some other sex entirely. How she stood in the window with a hand pressed to the scooped hollow of her back, how once between her shoul-der-blades he'd seen sweat blot her dress: these gave him a thirst he was afraid he could never drink deep enough to sate. But she was also brisk, combative, indifferent to praise – would not give ground, moved him to laughter, never tried to please, played no tricks. Edward knew himself outwitted and outgunned. That she spoke so often of Cora Seaborne in a manner by turns fond and furious seemed wholly in keeping. She was a being like none he'd ever known and he accepted her completely. His mother was wary. 'I've never known it!' she'd said (put out that Martha always left their rooms a fraction neater than she found them). 'A woman needs her own home and a man in it. A waste, I call it – and should she be here on her own?'

No theatrics from the stage in the Assembly Hall, still less the ardour of a Bible Rally preacher: the speaker's tone was matter-of-fact, perhaps a little wearied. *She has suffered*, thought Burton, certain of it. 'It's a sad and hideous story,' said Eleanor Marx, and it seemed to those watching that she grew in stature as she spoke, her masses of hair unwinding. 'This unholy alliance of masters, lawyers and magistrates against the wage-slaves . . .' Beside him Martha nodded once – twice – made marks in her notebook; in the front row a woman holding a sleeping infant sat quite still but weeping. Now and then a dissenting voice broke through and was silenced by a look: the stage seemed thronged with girls broken by machinery and boys flayed by the blast-furnace, while standing by, stout men fondled their watch-chains and watched their capital accumulate. 'These are hard times – and even harder times will come until this bad order is replaced. This is not the end of our struggle – it is the beginning!' There were cheers, and a hat thrown onstage – no bow, but a raised hand, which was a gesture both of farewell and encouragement. *Yes*, thought Edward Burton, standing, putting a hand to his aching breast. *Yes, I see: but how?*

On a bench in a small square park he ate chips with vinegar. Children dressed in party clothes stood waiting on the kerb, and behind them, *Standard* sellers bawled the evening news. 'But how?' he said. 'It makes me stupid sometimes – all I read and hear. I have anger in me and I don't know what to do with it.'

'It is how they'd have us,' said Martha. 'It's not the function of the wage-slave to think. The girls at Bryant and May, the boys down in the quarries: d'you think they've time to think, to plot, to revolutionise? That's the great crime: that no-one need be put in chains when their own minds are shackles enough. Once I thought we were no better than horses tied to the plough, but it's so much worse – we're only moving parts in their machinery

– just the bolts on the wheel, the axle turning round and round!'

'What then? I must work. I cannot escape the machine.'

'Not yet,' she said. 'Not yet: but change is slow. Even the world turns by inches.'

Weary Edward leaned against the bench. Croesus touched the chestnut trees, the oaks and London limes; his friend was by his side. 'Martha,' he said: just that, and it was enough for now.

'You're pale,' she said. 'Ned. Let me take you home.' She kissed him, and on her mouth there was a grain of salt.

Edward Burton
4 Templar Street

Martha – won't you marry me? Don't we do all right together, you and I?

EDWARD

By hand

Dear Ned –

I cannot marry you – I cannot marry at all.

I cannot promise to love, honour and obey. I obey only as my reason commands me to obey – I honour only those whose actions demand that I must honour them!

And I cannot love you as a wife's obliged to love a husband. I see the day coming when Cora Seaborne's done with me but I can never be done with her.

What now – do you think politics stops at the doorstep? Do you think it only a matter of soapboxes and picket lines, and not also a matter of our private lives?

Don't ask me to enter an institution that puts me in bonds and leaves you free. There are other ways to live – there are bonds beside those sanctioned by the state! Let's live as we think – freely and unafraid – let's be bound by nothing but affection and by holding our purpose in common.

If you cannot have a wife, will you take a companion – will you have a comrade?

Your friend –

MARTHA

Edward Burton
4 Templar Street

Dear Martha –

I will.

EDWARD

3

Little Harriet, yellow-dressed youngest of the laughing girls, woke before dawn and vomited into her pillow. In the corner her mother stirred, and rising to comfort her child breathed in the morning air, choked, and vomited also. Coming from the Blackwater on a warm west wind a vile smell had entered the room through a broken windowpane. Creeping past World's End and finding nothing there, it had passed over and come to the borders of Aldwinter, where few lights shone. Leaving the child in her mother's arms, it came to the Banks cottage, and borne on the breeze stirred the red sails of the barges in the quay. Weighted by drink Banks slept too deeply to be roused, but something troubled him in the dark, and three times he said his lost daughter's name. On it went, past the White Hare, and on the doorstep a stray dog whined for a master long gone; past the school, where Mr Caffyn – already up, marking grammar notebooks, deploring abuse of the comma – gave a cry of disgust, and ran to fetch a glass of water. Rooks had begun to gather in Traitor's Oak on the common, sensing in the reeking air a feast. At Cora's grey house it crept above the door, beneath the lintel; it seeped into the fabric of the sheets on her bed and could not find her. It skirted the All Saints tower, and reached the window of the rectory: William Ransome, sleepless in his study, thought perhaps a mouse lay rotting beneath the boards. Pressing his shirt's cuff to his mouth he went on his knees below the desk, beside the empty chair he kept beside his own, and found nothing. Stella, in a blue satin garment through which the bones of her shoulder-blades flared like hard little wings, appeared at the threshold. 'What on earth?' she said, caught between laughing and choking: 'What on *earth*?' She held a bunch of lavender to her nose.

'A dead thing somewhere,' said Will, putting his own jacket around her, afraid she'd begin one of the coughing fits which shook her small body as if it were held in the jaws of a predator: 'Something on the common? A sheep?'

'Not Magog, I hope,' said Stella: 'We'd never be forgiven'; but no – the last of Cracknell's family could be seen at the garden's end, untroubled, chewing an early breakfast. 'Will, should we light a fire – oh! Oh, it's foul, foul – you'll go out on the common and see the earth split open and sinners looking up with all their bones broken and their lips cracked with thirst!' Her eyes glittered as if the prospect pleased her, and it troubled Will more than the vile air, which he almost thought he could taste, there on the tip of his tongue: something foetid, with a horrid sweetness behind it. Ought he to go out there – perhaps he should – certainly he must: who else was there to seek out the cause of all that had lately befallen the village? He lit a fire, and shortly the reek was displaced by wood-smoke; Stella tossed in her lavender, and there was a brief and piercing scent of recent summer. 'Go on,' she said, straightening the papers on his desk (so many letters! Did he never put them away?), giving him his coat. 'Ten minutes more and we'll hear the bell and you'll be wanted somewhere by someone.'

Kissing her, he said, 'Perhaps a fishing-boat has gone aground on the saltings and spilt its cargo, and the fish is rotting – already it's a warm enough morning . . .'

'I wish the babies were here,' she said. 'Wouldn't Jojo have woken before us all, and gone down with a lamp, and seen for herself, and James done a drawing for the papers?'

Out on the High Road a crowd had gathered. Mr Caffyn had wound a white cloth about his head as if he'd been wounded; others pressed a sleeve to their mouths and peered suspiciously at Will, casting about for signs of a Bible or some other weapon concealed in the crook of his arm. It did not occur to Will until that moment – until he scented on the dim air not only rottenness but fear – that perhaps there was another cause to the foul odour besides misfortune. But there was Harriet's mother (weeping, as she so often was), crossing herself; there was Banks, not yet sober, saying he'd not go down to the water in case the beast had belched up coils of red hair. Evansford in his black shirt, looking more than ever like an undertaker bereft of a corpse, stood reciting fragments of the Book of Revelation with evident glee. Even Mr Caffyn, who each year taught his students that the 31st of October was nothing but the anniversary of Martin Luther taking hammer and pins to his 95 theses, looked (thought Will) rather green about the gills.

'Good morning, and a fine one at that,' he said: 'And what's this that's brought us all out of our beds?' No answer came. 'Now as you all know I'm no seafaring man,' he said heartily, thumping Banks on the shoulder, 'and you can't expect me to know anything about anything. Mr Banks, you know the Blackwater better than us all – what's the cause of this dreadful business, d'you think?' The wind rose, the smell strengthened: Will gagged, and said, 'Some algae perhaps, drifted in from overseas? A shoal of herring beached on the shingle?'

'Not anything I ever smelt before or heard tell of,' said Banks, muffled behind the sleeve of his coat. 'It's not natural, I know that.'

'Well: you say so,' said Will, whose eyes streamed: 'You say so, but nothing's more natural than the smell of dead things, which I suppose this must be. You and I will both smell similar, given time.' The small crowd observed him with distaste, and he rightly judged that humour was not fitted to the moment. All right: try scripture, then – 'Therefore we will not fear, though the waters roar, and be troubled, and what have you!'

'*I'll* tell you what it is,' said Harriet's mother: 'And I needn't tell you, Banks, need I? – or you, or *you* . . .' She nodded with meaning at Mr Caffyn, and at one or two women who seemed indifferent to the vileness of the air and had already begun to wander up the High Road, towards the Blackwater, where dawn had taken hold. 'It's come to us at last, the Essex Serpent, the river beast, and none of us ready for it! It came to my little one first – oh you bet, you bet! It came to her first and she's sick as a dog and nothing I say'll comfort the girl.'

Evansford remarked that after all it had been promised by the Redeemer himself there'd be weeping and wailing and gnashing of teeth, and bolstered by this observation, the woman went on, 'It's the *breath* of the thing, the very *breath* of it I tell you, and on it there's the flesh and bones of everything it ever had between its jaws – the St Osyth boy, the man washed up on our shores . . .'

'A foul miasma, as our fathers were taught,' said Mr Caffyn, 'and bringing with it disease – look! I have a fever. *La Peste!* It has begun.' And certainly his high scholar's brow was beaded with drops of sweat, and as Will watched he began to tremble, and twist his mouth into what may have been either the beginnings of a sob or of laughter.

'The sea gave up the dead which were in it!' said Banks, growing excited (if hope was gone of holding Naomi alive in his arms he at least might have the pleasure of giving her a tomb): 'And death and hell delivered up the dead which were in them!'

'Hell! Miasma!' said Will, growing exasperated, and discovering that either the smell had begun to recede, or that he'd grown accustomed to disgust: 'Serpent! Plague! Mr Caffyn, you're not ill: it's just that you could do with a cup of tea. What! I know you all for sensible folk – Banks, it was you yourself who showed me how the sextant worked! Caffyn, I've seen you teach my daughter how to calculate the distance of a storm! We're not in the Dark Ages – not children kept in line with tales of ghouls and demons – the people that walked in darkness have seen a great light! There's nothing there, nothing to fear, there never was: we will go down and find nothing but a sheep washed up from Maldon way, not some – some abomination sent for our punishment!'

But was it so great a stretch to imagine the Intelligence that once had split the Red Sea taking the trouble to send a little admonition to the sinners of a briny Essex parish? The apostle Paul had put his hand in a nest of snakes and come away unpoisoned by way of a sign: certainly the world had turned its many thousand revolutions since, but was the season of signs and wonders really over? Why had it always seemed to him so preposterous that in the estuary something was biding its time – was it a question not of failure to believe in the serpent, but of failure to believe in his God? The fear of the crowd came then to Will, with the taste of a copper penny placed on his tongue; and it was not the fear that they were under divine judgment, but that they were not, and could never be. *Cora*, he thought, finding himself grasping at the empty air as if he might somehow summon up her strong hand: *Cora! If she were here. If she were here* – 'Right then,' he said, grown angry, attempting to conceal it: 'What use is it to stand here, and choke, and imagine? I'll go down and see for myself, and you may come or not, as you like, but I tell you by sunset there'll be an end to all this, and there'll be no more talk of serpents.' He struck out east up the High Road, towards the Blackwater and the source of their disgust. Muttering and squabbling in his wake the small crowd followed; Harriet's mother took his arm confidingly and said, 'I bid goodbye to the child at the door as I left her, not knowing if I'd make my way home.'

On the common Traitor's Oak was so thick with rooks it might've been a crop of feathered fruit – Will walked in its shadow – the avid flock fell silent. The stench grew intolerable, and Mr Caffyn, seeing the lit windows of the school, peeled away to find refuge, saying that he ought not to've taken up a post in so remote and muddy a location, but that at any rate he couldn't say he hadn't been warned. Then the pitying wind relented, and changed its course; rooks lifted from the oak with a look of black ashes blown up from burning sheets of paper. With the changed air the odour began to recede, blown back out towards the estuary, where others would wake to foulness in the morning; Banks, taking courage, sang a scrap of sea shanty and took a nip of rum.

Then there was World's End, and each averted their eyes: though they'd seen the mossy tump where Cracknell lay waiting for his headstone it was nonetheless impossible to think that he could not be there behind the mottled glass, picking at earwigs on the sleeve of his coat. A handful now, that was all: William Ransome, with a mother on his left hand and a riverman on his right, and behind them Evansford, mercifully silent.

The two women gone on ahead talked cheerily enough, gesturing at scraps of cloud stained red by the sun's rising, turning to bat at the air as if they might fend off the odour which strengthened again as they drew near the saltings. Will's stomach turned in revulsion and fear: he did not believe they were shortly to encounter the Essex Serpent sunning its thin wings on the shingle, snapping its beak, regurgitating a fragment of bone – but oh, he was uneasy. '*Cora*,' he said, aloud, appalled at his own voice, which had the inflexion of a man blaspheming: Banks at his side cast up a glance of confusion, and may himself have spoken had one of the women ahead not paused on the path, flung an arm down towards the shore, and begun to shriek. Her companion reeled with the shock of it, and stepping on the hem of her dress tripped, and unable to right herself staggered down the incline, her mouth gaping in fear.

There was a moment which Will later recalled as having been fixed, as if on the photographer's plate: the falling woman – Banks arrested in motion as he moved towards her – himself, useless, in his mouth a sweet foulness that lifted up from the rising estuary tide. Then the image broke, and by some means he could never adequately explain they were all down on the salt shingle, standing by the black bones of Leviathan, looking in terror and pity at what the sea had given up.

In parallel to the lapping water's edge the carcass of a creature lay in putrefaction. It measured perhaps twenty feet in length, so that its further end seemed to taper almost to a point; it was wingless, limbless, its body taut as a drum's skin and gleaming silver. All along the spine the remnants of a single fin remained: protrusions rather like the spokes of an umbrella between which fragments of membrane, drying out in the easterly breeze, broke and scattered. The falling woman had stumbled upon its head: eyes large in diameter as a clenched fist looked blindly out, and behind them a pair of gills split away from the silvery flesh and showed, deep within, a crimson, meaty frilling that resembled the underside of a mushroom. Either it had suffered an attack, or caught against the hull of a Thames barge making its way to the capital: in places the taut hide – which gleamed where the low sun struck it with the colours of oil on water – had opened up to show bloodless wounds. Wherever it had touched the mud and shingle it had left a greasy residue, as if fat had begun to render out of its skin. Within its open mouth – which had about it something like the blunt beak of a finch – very fine teeth could be seen. As they watched, a portion of flesh fell away from the bone as cleanly as if tugged with a diner's knife.

'Look,' said Banks, 'that's all it was, that's all it was.' He plucked off his hat, and held it to his breast, looking absurdly as if he'd encountered there in the Essex dawn the Queen on her way to Parliament: 'Poor old thing, that's all it was, out there in the dark, lost, I daresay, damaged, cast up on the marsh and sucked back out on the tides.'

And it did seem a poor old thing, thought Will. For all its look of having detached itself from the illuminated margins of a manuscript, not the most superstitious of men could've believed this decaying fish to be a monster of myth: it was simply an animal, as they all were; and was dead, as they all would be. There they stood, reaching by silent agreement the conclusion that the mystery had not been solved so much as denied: it was impossible to imagine that this blind decaying thing – cast out of its element, where its silver flank must've been lithe, beautiful – could have caused their terror. Where, besides, were the promised wings, the muscular limbs from which claws protruded? Perhaps it might've coiled Cracknell in a wet embrace, out there in the Blackwater estuary, but Cracknell had died on the dry shore and with his boots on.

'What should we do?' said Evansford, looking as if he rather regretted the bright sun rising, the pathos of the corpse at his feet, the staying of the hand of judgment. 'It can't be left. It'll poison the river.'

'The tide'll take it,' said Banks, sure-footed: no-one knew dead fish as well as he. 'The tide, the gulls.'

Then – 'Something is moving,' said Harriet's mother, who'd walked a little onward, and stood at the place where the creature's belly bulged against the shingle: 'Something inside is moving!' Will came near, and saw a kind of shiver and writhing behind the skin; it paused, so that he rubbed his eyes, imagining that his vision had grown disordered by the early morning and the low sun; he opened them again, and all at once, as if slipping free of many small buttons, the belly opened up along the seam and spilled out a pale and writhing mass. The stench was unbearable: each staggered back as if struck by a blow, and Banks could not prevent himself from running to Leviathan's bones and vomiting. He could not look – he could not: he imagined that there among the white fragments still moving he might see a skein of red hair. But one of the women, indifferent to the sight, stirred at the glistening mess with her foot and said: 'Tapeworm. Look at it, yards long and still hungry. Probably did for the beast: starved it from the inside. Seen it happen before – you not going to take a look, Reverend? Found you had something to fear, after all?' Inclining his head (he knew when he was bested) Will did take a look, reeling a little; saw the worm's last movements, and its peculiar look of a length of white ribbon into which threads had been irregularly woven. What was the creator thinking of, to come up with so revolting a creature, which moreover lived off the life of others? He supposed it served some purpose.

'Banks,' said Will, suppressing the urge to deliver a short homily which emphasised his rightness in countering the villagers' superstitious fears with godly reason: 'Banks, what ought we to do?'

'Leave it,' said Banks, in whose wet eyes new veins had broken. 'High tide'll take it, due eleven or just after. Nature has her ways.'

'And no harm done to the herring, the oyster beds?'

'See the gulls? See the rooks, followed us from the common? Short work of it they'll make, and the water: come Sunday – no sign of it.'

Nothing now moved. The lens of the creature's eye grew milky; Will imagined, knowing himself foolish, that from the open mouth a last breath came. The shingle stirred, the tide edged nearer: on the toe of his boot a dark stain showed, and its edge was rimmed with salt.

Katherine Ambrose
c/o All Saints Rectory
Aldwinter
11th September

Our darling Cora,

Have you heard? What with your determination to no longer be interested in poor old Essex (really, I never knew a fad of yours fall from favour so fast!) I daresay you remain in the dark, so for once I get the pleasure of telling you something you don't already know, which is this:

THEY HAVE FOUND THE ESSEX SERPENT!

Now dust yourself down, and fetch a cup of tea (Charles, who reads over my shoulder, says if the sun's over the yard-arm you must get a glass of something strengthening), and I'll tell all. And since I am currently in Aldwinter I have it direct from the Reverend William Ransome, whom you and I both know to be incapable of transgressing so far as to exaggerate – so you must take this report to be as sober and truthful as if it came from the pen of the man himself.

Well, it happened like this. Yesterday morning the entire village was woken by the most disgusting smell. I gather at first some thought they'd all been poisoned, since it was bad enough to make them sick in their beds: can you imagine!

At any rate, apparently they summoned up the courage to go down to the shore, and there it was – the beast itself, only dead as a doornail. Quite as big as they'd feared: Will estimates 20 feet, only not at all bulky. Rather like an eel, he said, and shining like silver, or mother-of-pearl (he grows poetical in his old age). Those that saw it knew at once how foolish they'd been – no monster after all, and certainly no wings: it looked as if it might take a chunk out of your leg, but would've had no end of trouble getting out of the water to snatch a sheep or a child. I gather there was an unpleasant moment with a parasite of some kind which I do not wish to dwell on, but there you have it: a beast, I suppose, but no more strange, no more dangerous, than an elephant or crocodile.

Now, I know you'll be wondering whether it bore any resemblance to the sea-serpents which your beloved Mary Anning had a habit of digging up, and I regret to tell you that it did not. Will says it had no limbs of any kind, and that for all its size and strangeness it was quite unmistakably nothing but a fish. There was talk of notifying the authorities – Will sent a message to Charles, since we happened to be in Colchester at the time – but apparently it broke up when the tide came in and got washed back out to sea. Oh Cora! I can't help feeling rather sorry for you. What a let-down! I had high hopes for that case in the British Museum, and inside a monstrous sea-serpent stuffed and fitted with glass eyes, and there on the wall your name on a brass plate. And what a disappointment to those looking forward to judgment day: I wonder if they repent of their repentance? I know I would!

The following day we came down to Aldwinter, half-hoping to see the wretch for ourselves, so I write to you from Will's study. It's warm, and mild: the window's open, and I can see a goat cropping grass on the lawn. How curious it is to be here without the Ransome children, knowing they're back at our own home in London! All the world is topsy-turvy. And how curious it is to be here among things I recognise as yours – your letters (I didn't look, though I was sorely tempted!) – a glove which I know to be yours

— a fossil (an ammonite, I think?) which can only have come from you. I almost think I can smell that scent of yours, which is always like the first rain of spring — as if you'd only just got up out of the chair where I am sitting! Will keeps odd books for a vicar — here's Marx and Darwin, no doubt getting along very well.

Aldwinter is quite transformed. When we arrived this morning (to what frankly I've always thought a dour sort of village) a festival was taking place. The children are out to play again, since there's no danger of encountering a beast behind the hedges, and the women had laid out blankets on the grass and sat leaning against each other, gossiping no end. We finished up the summer's cider (delicious, and far better than any wine I've ever had in this county), and made short work of an entire Essex flitch of ham. Darling Stella — even more beautiful, I'd be prepared to swear, than when I saw her last (really I think it terribly unfair) — put on a blue dress and danced a little while the fiddlers played, but had to go to bed soon after. I've not seen her since, though I hear her pacing upstairs: mostly she lies in her bed, writing in her notebook. I brought her gifts from the children, and letters, but she hasn't read them yet. She does not believe the strange fish on the shore to have been the Essex Serpent, but she's had so many strange ideas in her lately I just squeezed her hand (so hot, and so small!) and said of course not, of course not, and let her put a blue ribbon in my hair. It's a cruel disease but is treating her kindly enough.

Now then, Cora. You must allow me the dignity of my years and permit me to give you a dressing-down. I've heard it from Charles that you have not yet seen Luke Garrett, that you do not write to either Stella or Will though you must know she is sick (dying, one rather assumes, though aren't we all in our fashion?), and having to do without her children.

My dear, I know you grieve. I admit I was never sure what it was that first brought you to Michael, who always frightened me just a bit (do you mind my saying so?) but it was something. And the bond is broken, and you are left untethered – and now it seems you are severing all your ties! Cora, you cannot always keep yourself away from things that hurt you. We all wish that we could, but we cannot: to live at all is to be bruised. I don't know what has come between you and your friends, but I know that none of us was made to be alone. You told me once you forget you are a woman, and I understand it now – you think to be a woman is to be weak – you think ours is a sisterhood of suffering! Perhaps so, but doesn't it take greater strength to walk a mile in pain than seven miles in none? You are a woman, and must begin to live like one. By which I mean: have courage.

All love,

KATHERINE

PS – One odd thing: all that relief, that lightness of heart – the fiddler with a flower in his buttonhole, that marvellous food – but no-one took the trouble to climb up Traitor's Oak and take down the horseshoes hanging there? As the sun went down the wind came up and there they were: turning and flashing on their bits of string.

Don't you think that's strange?

Cora Seaborne
c/o The Midland Grand Hotel
London
12th September

My dear Katherine –

I took your dressing-down on the chin and love you no less than ever. I've displeased everyone, it seems, and am used to it by now. Do you think me self-pitying? Well: I am, though I'd stop if I could find the source of it! Sometimes I think I see what troubles me but at the last minute look away, it seems so ABSURD: whoever heard of a woman brought so low by the loss of a friend?

So then: the Essex Serpent is found. A month ago I'd have been utterly furious, but I find myself generally muted these days. I suppose I did think, now and then, that I'd stand on the shore and see the snout of an ichthyosaur poking out of the estuary waters (God knows I've seen stranger things there!), but I can't remember it. It seems absurd: the daydreams of another woman. Last week I took myself off to the Natural History Museum and stood counting the bones of the fossils there, and tried to summon up the wonder it once gave me, and there was nothing.

Perhaps you know how cruel I was to Dr Garrett. Katherine, HOW COULD I HAVE KNOWN? They don't want me there: I write, and he does not reply. I am not certain that William Ransome wants to see me, either. I go blundering about – I break things – I turned out to be no more competent a friend than I have been a wife or mother –

Oh (having read just now what I have written) what self-pity! It will do me no good. What would Will say? That we've all fallen short of the glory of God, or something along those lines: at any rate he never seemed much bothered by the failings of others since it's all a consequence of the human condition, and only to be expected. Though if that is the case, he ought to bear with my failings rather better than he seems to, or at least keep me informed as to WHICH of my failings have displeased him most . . .

You see how I have become? I was never so girlish, so mournful! Even when a girl! Even when mourning!

I will write to Luke. I will write to Stella. I will go to Aldwinter.

I WILL BE GOOD. I PROMISE.

Much love, darling K – indeed you have all of it, since no-one else wants it –

CORA SEABORNE

Cora Seaborne
c/o The Midland Grand Hotel
London
12th September

Dear Stella, Dear Will —

It's usual I know to begin with 'I hope you are well' — but I know you are not. I was so desperately sorry to hear how ill you have become, and send my love. Did you see Dr Butler? I'm told he's the best to be had.

I am coming back to Essex. Tell me what I can bring. Tell me what you most like to eat. Shall I bring books? There is a man outside the hotel selling peonies: I'll bring as many as I can stuff in a first-class carriage.

I hear the Essex Serpent was found, and nothing but a great fish after all, and long since dead to boot! Katherine tells me all Aldwinter celebrated — how I wish I could have been there, and seen it.

With love,

CORA SEABORNE

4

'He's not here,' said Stella, closing her blue notebook, tying it with ribbon: 'He'll be sorry to've missed you – no, don't sit next to me: I don't much feel like coughing, but sometimes it comes when I don't expect it – and what's this? What is this! What have you brought me!'

Relief and disappointment weakened Cora at the knee; concealing it with a smile she put a parcel in her friend's lap, and said, 'It's only a book I thought you'd like, and some marzipan from Harrods: we remembered how you like it – Frankie, come and say hello.' But Francis was nonplussed, and could only stand on the threshold, surveying the room. Never in his years of accumulating treasures had he seen anything like it: he'd thought himself expert in the collector's art, but knew when he was bested. Stella Ransome lay on a white couch between two open windows hung with blue curtains. She wore a dark blue dressing-gown and blue slippers, and was decked with turquoise beads. On her hands were gimcrack rings, and on every windowsill blue glass bottles glinted: there were sherry bottles and poison bottles and little flagons for scent, shards of glass gathered from gutters and opaque nuggets tossed up by the tide. Neatly laid out on tables and chairs were items ordered by depth or pallor of pigment: bottle-tops and buttons, silk scraps and folded sheets of paper, feathers and stones, and all of them blue. Awestruck, he knelt a little distance away and said, 'I like all your special things. I have special things, too.' Stella turned her pansy eyes on him and without surprise or censure said, 'Then we share a habit of finding beauty no-one else sees' – she lowered her voice and whispered confidingly: 'It is a habit also of the angels who we sometimes entertain unawares, and lately there's been a lot of them about.' It troubled Cora to see her put her finger to her mouth in a gesture of secrecy, and to see Francis make the gesture in return; the woman had certainly grown stranger in her absence – was it the disease? Why had Will not written to tell her?

Stella then became her old brisk self; she twitched at her dressing-gown, and said, 'Now then: I have lots and lots to ask and tell. How is Dr Garrett? I couldn't bear it when I was told – I will never forget how he treated me the day I went to hospital. It wasn't the ordinary kindness you know – he spoke to me as if I were an equal – he wouldn't let them keep it from me. Will he really never operate again? I had been ready to let him do what he wanted with me, but I suppose that's out of the question now.'

Cora found that she could not speak of her Imp without a pain in her throat, and said carelessly, 'Oh: Spencer tells me he's healing well. Can it really be that bad? He didn't lose a finger, and it would take more than a street-fight to have him lose his mind. Frankie, no – those aren't yours.' The boy had begun to fetch grey-blue stones from the mantelpiece and to put them on the carpet, and ignoring his mother breathed hotly on a flat pebble and polished it on his sleeve.

'Please – let him play: he understands me, I think,' said Stella, and together they watched a moment as he set them out in the pattern of a seven-pointed star, now and then glancing up at Stella in what his mother saw with surprise to be an expression of adoration.

'They took my babies away,' said Stella, drearily, losing for a moment her lightness of heart: 'I remember their faces, of course – I have their photos here – only I forget how it is to feel their arms around my neck and the weight of them in my lap – it makes me happy to see him there – let him do what he wants.' Then she leaned against the curved wing of the chair, and Stella saw the high colour on her cheeks burn brighter. When she raised her head again her hair was dark at the roots with sweat.

'But they're coming back again – Katherine Ambrose is bringing them to me,' she said. She touched the Bible. 'Our heavenly father never gives us more than we can bear.'

'I daresay,' said Cora.

'And they say the Essex Serpent is found, and no more than a rotting fish!' Stella leaned forward – secretive, confiding – 'But Cora, do not be deceived. Just last night a dead dog was cast up at Brightlingsea with its neck broken, and no sign yet of the Banks girl –'

How gleeful she is, thought Cora: *I believe she is almost willing the serpent back into the Blackwater!*

'I hear it whispering in the night,' said Stella, 'though I never can make out the words . . .'

Cora took her friend's hand; but what after all was to be said? Her eyes glittered, as if she saw not the hand of judgment but of redemption. Stella made a few marks in her notebook, then shook her head as if waking from a light sleep and said, 'And how is Martha: cross to find herself back in Aldwinter, I'm sure.' She'd not yet lost her habit of gossip, and for a while they ran through all their mutual acquaintances while Will filled the room with his absence.

Francis sat some distance away, observing in his usual fashion. He saw how Stella clutched the notebook, stroking its blue cover; how one moment her attention fixed avidly on what his mother said, then dissipated as she grew dreamy and vague. Sometimes she'd fall to phrases that sat oddly on her tongue – 'The fact is, and I know you agree, that this corruptible must put on incorruption, and this mortal must put on immortality!' – then immediately after say, briskly, 'Magog doesn't seem at all bothered by Cracknell's death: her milk's as good as ever.' And all the while his mother's eyes grew darker, as they did when she was troubled: she patted Stella Ransome's hand, and nodded, and never contradicted; she said, 'Tell me again how it is you plait your hair so beautifully: I try, but I can never get it right!' and poured another cup of tea.

'Come again soon, won't you?' Stella said, when Cora rose to leave. 'How sorry you must be to miss Will – I will give him all your best. And Master Seaborne,' she said, turning to Francis and holding out her hands: 'We should be friends, you and me: we understand each other. Come again and bring me your treasures, and we'll compare them, shall we?' And Francis put his hand in hers, and felt how hot it was, and how very much smaller than his own; he said: 'I've got three jays' feathers and a chrysalis. I'll bring them tomorrow, if you like.'

Cora Seaborne
2, The Common
Aldwinter
19th September

Dear Will,

I've come back to Essex. The house is cold: I write this sitting so close to the radiator I have one burning knee, and one freezing one. There's a penetrating dampness coming from the walls. It feels personal. Sometimes in the night I think I can smell something like salt and something like fish – only very faintly, coming through the window – and for all they tell me it was nothing but a poor dead fish overtaken by the tides, it's easy to imagine the Essex Serpent's still there, watching and waiting, perhaps on the doorstep wanting to be let in . . .

I live in a state of disgrace. Martha is cross with me: when she brings me tea she slams it down and I'm invariably splashed. She wants to go back to London, and I can't help thinking she's going away from me somehow. Luke has asked me not to visit, though Spencer has brought him to Colchester for a change of air, and I almost think I could walk there to see him! Spencer writes, but he signs himself Yours Sincerely and doesn't mean a word of it. Katherine Ambrose has taken to giving me a kind sort of look I can't bear: it's an understanding one, as if she wants me to know that whatever I've done she'll side with me. Frankly, I'd rather she gave me a slap.

Of course I've always been in disgrace with Frankie, but now more than ever. I believe he has seen something in Stella he was always looking for in me, and never found. He respects her! Why wouldn't he? I don't know that I ever met a braver being.

And however kindly you write, I often feel I might fall from grace with you. I doubt the wisdom of so much that I have done: letting Luke loose on Joanna – that strange night in June – even having come here at all!

Martha says I've been selfish – that I've tried to tether everyone to me and not cared what they might have wanted. I said that this is how we all live or else we'd only ever be alone, and she slammed the door so hard she broke a square of glass.

Only Stella seems not to be angry with me. I spent an afternoon with her – did she tell you? – she kissed my hands. I am afraid for her mind – one moment she sinks into despair and the next she seems to have already got her foot in the pearly gates. And such a beauty, Will! I never saw anything like it – with her hair fanned out on the pillow and her eyes blazing I think any painter would run weeping for their brushes. She does not believe the serpent to have been found. She hears it, she says: it whispers, though she doesn't say what.

Tell me how you are. Do you still wake too early and drink coffee in your dressing-gown before anyone else wakes? Did you ever finish reading that awful novel about Pompeii? Have you seen a kingfisher yet? Do you ever miss Cracknell and wish you could lean on his gate and watch him skin his moles?

Can I see you soon?

Yours,

CORA

Rev. William Ransome
All Saints Rectory
Aldwinter
20th September

Dear Cora –

Stella told me you'd come. I would have known it anyway: who else would spend a small fortune on Harrods sweets? (Thank you, by the way: I'm watching her nibble it now, and I'm glad to see her eat something besides teacups of hot Bovril.)

She's very taken with Francis. She says they're soul companions; something to do with her new fad for decking the house with odds and ends. I told her I'm writing you a note and she says can he come and visit again soon, as she has something to tell him? The doctor says while her coughing's not too bad she can have visitors for a short while.

Did you feel it – the change in the Aldwinter air? I know you'll have heard how we found that poor dead thing on the shore, and how it woke us all in our beds with its stink. How I wished you'd been there – I remember thinking so at the time – I remember wondering how you could have gone away –

That night it was like May Day and the Harvest Festival come at once. All night they sat out there on the common, singing and dancing with the relief of it. I felt it myself, though I knew there'd been nothing to fear! Poor Evansford looks quite destitute without a day of judgment to look forward to. On Sundays there are a few more bare pews. Well: I don't grudge anyone a clear conscience.

Even so, it's hard not to despair. The house seems quiet as a grave. I've stopped closing my study door since no-one ever comes in. The children write nearly every day and are coming next week. When I imagine them running up the garden path I want to hang a banner up – I want a gun salute!

Stella's glad they're coming, but her heart has moved on. Sometimes she tells me she will live, and says it to console me – then she says it's eternal life she's looking for and I think she's running to the graveyard. I love her. We've loved each other so long I've never been a man and not loved her. I can no more imagine life without her than without my own limbs. Who will I be if she is gone? If she is not looking at me – will I still be here? Will I look in the mirror one morning and find my reflection gone?

And how can this be true when news of your coming made me happier than I ever had any right to expect?

Every evening at around 6pm I walk west for a while, away from the marsh and the estuary. Even now I almost think my nose will never be rid of that awful stench – I find I prefer to turn my back on the water and go into the woods.

I'd like to see you. Come out with me. You like a walk, don't you?

WILLIAM RANSOME

5

She waited on the common in her man's tweed coat, watching all the while for Will. It was too warm an evening for the collar high at the nape of her neck: autumn was as tentative as summer had been mild. But Cora had lately felt uneasy in herself, and not only when remembering the press of Will's palm on her waist: she wanted to be swathed in heavy clothes, unwomanned by lumpish fabrics and heavy shoes. If Martha had not hidden the scissors she'd've done away with her hair, and satisfied herself instead with plaiting it severely from her face like a schoolgirl in the morning.

It had been so long since she'd seen her friend she almost wondered if she'd know him – anxiety at how he might greet her made her mouth run dry. Might he show his sterner side – part chastening, part disappointed? Might he speak warmly, as once he had, or with the diffident manners that chilled her?

The wind blew over the Blackwater and brought with it the scent of salt; in the long grass mushrooms grew and their caps were pearly as oyster-shells. When he came it was silently, as if he'd stolen up like a grinning boy: a light hand touched her arm above the elbow; a voice said, 'You needn't've dressed up on my account.' The measured cadence and country slowness on the vowels was so familiar, and so dear, that she could not think why she'd been a little afraid, and spread the skirts of her coat in a curtsey.

They surveyed each other a while, unable to keep from smiling. Will had left off his collar, and with the country man's disdain for the seasons wore no coat. His sleeves were rolled back as if he'd laboured all afternoon, and his shirt was unbuttoned at the throat. His hair had lightened since she'd seen it last, and grown longer: it was almost amber in the evening light. The scar on his cheek mimicked the edge of the sheep's hoof, and his eyes seemed smudged as if he'd rubbed at them while reading an evening paper. *He isn't sleeping*, thought Cora, with dreadful tenderness.

Under his gaze she knew she'd never looked less handsome: closeting herself indoors for much of the summer had given her face a greyish pallor, and her neglected hair grew coarsely at the crown. If she consented to look in the mirror it was to see quite dispassionately the fine lines fanning from the corner of her eyes, the single crease between her brows. All this she felt acutely, and with relief. Whatever mistaken moment at midsummer had caused their breach was impossible to countenance now: she was no man's idea of a lover. The thought was so absurd she laughed with the relief of it; the sound pleased him, because it obliterated the weeks between and put him back in that warm room when first she'd held out her hand.

'Come on, Mrs Seaborne: let's go,' he said: 'I feel I've so much to tell you'; and far from feeling chastened or suppressed, Cora felt all her recent heaviness of spirit lift. They walked swiftly, matching step for step, leaving behind the village and the briny estuary breeze; they passed All Saints, and neither averted their eyes, because it did not occur to them there might be any misdemeanour in taking the evening air.

Both had saved such stores of anecdote and complaint, of tall tale and half-formed theory, that fully an hour passed without pause. Each made an inventory of the other, totting up with pleasure the well-remembered gesture or the phrases used too often, the tendency to withhold or exaggerate, the sudden veering-off into fresh pastures which the other followed at a run. They delighted in each other then as they had from the first, without thinking it indecent to smile so much and laugh so readily, while sinking in her blue silk cushions Stella raised a scrap of cotton to her mouth and withdrew it flecked with blood, and in Colchester Luke Garrett felt himself adrift. That each had felt betrayed by the other was not forgiven so much as forgotten: they'd sealed themselves up – they were inviolate.

'And after all that, nothing but a dead fish!' said Cora. 'So much for the Essex Serpent – its wing and beak! Truly, I've never felt more foolish. I took myself off to the Reading Rooms (I half-thought I'd see you there) and did my homework, like any good schoolgirl, and saw the oarfish cast up in Bermuda thirty years ago, and read how they loiter near the surface when they're dying – I must apologise to Mary Anning for disgracing both her sex and her profession.'

'But *such* a fish,' said Will, and described for her how the shining skin of its belly had split, and how its contents had writhed on the shingle.

When they spoke of Stella, Cora turned her face away: she'd shown Will her tears once before and had resolved not to do so again.

'She asked to be shown the glass slide in the microscope,' said Will, wondering again at his wife's courage. 'She looked at what came from her own body and there was death in it and she faced it better than I did. I think she'd known for months. She'd seen it all before.'

'She's the kind of woman who's misunderstood: they think because she's so pretty and wears her clothes so well, and because she gossips and chatters, that she's nothing but a ballerina in a jewellery box turning round and round; but I knew from her first letter that she'd a sharpness to her – I don't think she misses anything, not even now.'

'Less now than ever, though something has changed.' They'd entered the fringes of a wood; the track narrowed; jackdaws convened in the oaks, and brambles tugged at their clothes. Berries had been left to rot on the branch, since all through the months of the Trouble no-one had felt much like going out alone with their baskets. 'Something has changed, and they told me it would, but I never expected this. She had faith of course, or I couldn't have married her – you are horrified! But how could I ask a woman to spare me every Sunday and half the week between if she didn't serve the same God? – yes: she had a faith, but not like this. It was' – he cast about for the right phrase – 'it was polite. Do you understand? This – it's different – I find myself embarrassed by it. She sings. I wake in the night and I hear her singing from along the hall. I think she has the Essex Serpent muddled up with Bible stories, and doesn't really believe it has gone.'

'You sound more of a civil servant than a minister! Don't you think those women who went to the tomb – I forget their names – might've been a little like that – blinded by glory, already half-dead, wanting this short time over as soon as possible – no: I'm not mocking you and God knows I'd never mock her – but if you insist on your faith you ought at least to concede it's a strange business and very little to do with well-ironed cassocks and the order of service.' She felt her temper rise slightly – she'd forgotten how readily they exasperated each other, and considered letting the conversation reach unstable ground; but it was too soon for all that. 'But I do see,' she said, growing conciliatory: 'Of course I do: nothing's more troubling than change in those we love. It's a nightmare I have – I've told you about it often! – that one day I come home and there's Martha and there's Francis and they put their hands to their faces and lift them clear away like masks and underneath there's loathing ...' She shuddered. 'But she's still your Stella, your star of the sea: love is not love which alters when it alteration finds! What will you do? What treatment can she have?'

He told her of that anxious afternoon in the hospital, with Dr Butler polite on one side and Luke sardonic on the other; of how she'd given her own diagnosis and coolly taken in their prescriptions. 'Dr Butler is cautious – he wants to see her again – wants to give her tuberculin, which is the fashion these days. Charles Ambrose says he'll pay, and how can I refuse? I've not been able to afford my pride for a long time.'

'And Luke?' Still she could not quite say the name without a rise of shame that stained her cheek.

Will might, with effort, have forgiven the Imp, but since his creed made no mention of actually developing affection for those who'd wronged him he said, 'Forgive me, but I'm glad he's prevented from operating – he wanted to collapse her lungs, one at a time, to let the other heal! Don't misunderstand me – I regret very deeply his injury – but really I cannot think past Stella, and her wellbeing: it's all that matters now.' Then he flushed, as if caught out in a lie – *all that matters*, he'd said – and it ought to be! It ought to be!

'What does Stella say?' Cora was conscious of a sensation very like envy: what must it be, to be loved so entirely?

'She tells me Christ is coming to gather up his jewels, and that she's ready,' said Will. 'I don't believe she much cares one way or the other. Sometimes she speaks as if this time next year she'll be climbing Traitor's Oak with James, and sometimes I find her lying with her hands crossed over her breast as if she's already in her coffin. And the blue – the incessant blue – she sends me out for violets and I tell her it's not the season and she almost weeps with rage!'

Then he told her – shyly, because he was ashamed – of his bargain with God, and how he'd been prepared to loose his wife into Luke's hands, his needles and blades, if the signs had seemed auspicious. 'News came of Garrett's injury and if I didn't exactly think it a sign, certainly Stella did – she looked relieved; she told me she'd've had the operation if I'd thought it best, but preferred to give herself over to God – sometimes I think she wants to leave us – that she wants to go away from me!'

Cora concealed a look at her friend, who so rarely seemed less than in command that it threw her – she said: 'I remember when Michael was first taken ill. We were having breakfast and he couldn't swallow – he went rigid and red and pulled at the table-cloth, then flapped at his throat – and since he never panicked or let down his guard, not ever, we knew something was wrong. Just then a bird flew in and God knows I've never been superstitious but for a moment I thought of that old wives' tale that a bird indoors foretells a death and my heart *lifted*, and I sat and watched him choke ... then of course I came to my senses and we gave him water, and he vomited, and later that month he passed blood and Luke came – it was the first time I ever saw him and I was a little afraid of him, to speak the truth: isn't it odd, how strangers come over the threshold and you never know what they might become ... Oh!' She shook her head. 'I don't know what point I'm making – how can I compare him to Stella: they might be different species! – only that it takes us strangely, all this.' She flung out her arms, and he was grateful: what a strange habit she had, of offering up understanding out of her thorough disagreement with almost everything he knew and prized.

Evening had come quickly, and the rosy sun was caught below a black bank of cloud. Light struck only the lower part of the beech and chestnut trees and left the rest in darkness; it gave the appearance of ranks of bronze pillars bearing up a thick black canopy. They'd come to a slight rise, and the path was traversed at regular intervals by forest roots that formed a broad and shallow flight of stairs. Everywhere was thickly mossed, and it laid down a carpet of vivid green.

For all their talking and delight there'd been little of the intimacy of their letters, which spoke so readily of 'I' and 'you'; but as the wood closed around them it seemed possible to approach the heart of the matter – though tentatively, and by small degrees.

'I was glad when you wrote,' he said, diffidently: 'I'd had a bad day of it and then there you were, on the doormat.'

'I am glad I swallowed my pride.' She put her foot on the green stair, and paused, and said: 'You were so angry with me after Luke tried out his tricks on Jo – and I've never minded anyone being angry with me if I deserved it, but I didn't think I did – it was only an offer of help! If you'd seen what I saw – those laughing girls – how they laughed and snapped their heads back and forth . . .'

He shook his head, impatient. 'It doesn't matter now – what use would it be to go over it?' Then he laughed, and said: 'I always did enjoy fighting with you, but not over anything that mattered.'

'Only matters of good and evil . . .'

'Exactly – look, we are in a cathedral.' High overhead the trees stooped and made a chancel arch; a branch had sheared off a nearby oak and left behind a peaked cavity above a deep shelf. 'It looks as though Cromwell's taken hammer and chisel to a saint.'

'I see you've despatched the serpent in your church, at least,' said Cora. 'I went in the day I came back and there's nothing but a few scales left: what made you lose your patience?'

Thinking of that shameful moment on the midsummer marsh after he'd left them all behind, Will coughed and said: 'Joanna would've boxed my ears if news of Cracknell hadn't come in time – look: all these conkers lying about, and no children taking them home.' He bent to pick up a handful and passed one to her, snug in its green casing. With a fingertip in the split she prised it open, and found the nut in its white silk bed. 'I was angry,' he said: 'That's all. Now the Trouble has gone I hardly remember how it was – how folk kept indoors and we never heard the children playing, and how nothing I could say would convince them there was nothing to fear they didn't summon up themselves.'

'I felt it in the village as soon as I came,' she said. 'A change of air. I heard the school choir singing and not until I was home did I remember the day they'd laughed and laughed and something went badly wrong. To think when I first came there was rarely anyone on the common, and I thought I'd see people look at me mistrustfully – as if it were all my fault! As if it had anything to do with me!'

'Sometimes I think it was,' said Will, dropping his hands, kicking at the moss. He gave her one of his chastening looks and only half in jest.

She said, laughing: 'The Trouble might not be my doing, but I hardly helped – I made other things muddled. What you said in your letter – that you'd come to the end of new things – I realised then how I go blundering about. I forced myself in. I might as well have broken a window! Imagine saying we should write to each other when you were barely half a mile away! And all because we talked once . . .'

'There was also the question of the sheep,' said Will.

'There was that, of course.' They looked at each other, relieved to have overstepped the crack opening in the path before them. But it widened and they tripped: Will said, 'My windows were already broken – no: I left them on the latch – and why? Why was it, when I had everything a man asks, I saw you and ever since was glad of you –'

'It's not surprising to me.' Cora prised the conker from its shell and rolled it between her palms. 'Did you really think because you loved *here* you couldn't love *there*? Poor Will – poor boy! – did you think you had so little of it? Look – should I boil it, bake it, or pickle it in vinegar?' She made as if to throw it at him, but he'd turned away and moved a step or two above her.

'It's like talking to a child,' he said, exasperated: 'I know what you think of me – secretly, even secret from yourself – that I'm a God-addled half-wit fallen miles behind you, as if you've evolved past me!' She surveyed him sombrely, and (he thought) with amusement very faintly at the corner of her mouth, and it made him press home his point more cruelly than he meant: 'Look at you! Whichever Cora you are – the one in silk and diamonds or the one who wears clothes Cracknell would've thrown away; the one always laughing at us or the one vowing love to anyone who'll listen – you wall yourself away because you know as well as I do you've almost run through your youth without ever having been loved as you should have been –'

'Stop it,' Cora said. All the intimacy she'd sought by letter was unbearable out there under the black forest canopy; she wanted to be back in their safe territory of ink and paper and not here, where her colour rose and she thought she could smell, above the sweetness of a distant fire, the scent of his body under his shirt. It was indecent – he was at his best sealed in an envelope – that he was so unavoidably a thing of blood and bones made it impossible to ignore the strong pulse beating in her neck – 'Come down,' she said: 'Come back – don't fight with me. Haven't we had enough of that?' A little ashamed, he stooped beside a chestnut tree, rooting among fallen leaves for conkers, handing them to her one by one.

'I wish we were children!' said Cora, closing her fingers over them, remembering how once they'd been treasures to be bartered and prized. She came closer – she sat beside him on the moss – 'Why can we not be like children, and play together . . .'

'Because you're not innocent!' said Will – there was a strange vertiginous feeling, as if what they were saying had flung them high up and they'd not yet fallen: 'You are not innocent, and nor am I – you play at it – you fend me off –' He tugged at her sleeve, a little rough – 'd'you think because you wear a man's coat I might forget what you are?'

'And do you think I do it for *you*?' she said. 'I forget I'm a woman – I set it aside. God knows I'm no mother and was never much of a wife . . . d'you think I should torture myself with high-heeled shoes and paint out my freckles so you're kept on your guard against me?'

'No – I think you're guarding against yourself; you told me once you'd like to be nothing but an intellect, disembodied, untroubled by your own flesh and blood –'

'I would, I would! I despise it – my body only ever betrayed me: I don't live in it, I live up here, in my mind and words . . .'

'Yes,' he said, 'yes, I know, yes: but here you are too, *here*,' and moving aside the folds of her coat he tugged her shirt where it was tucked at the waist, in the place where once he'd touched her and been disgraced by it. But the disgrace this time kept its distance: it seemed to him that to keep apart from her now would be obscene; how could it be possible to seek out each fold and turn of her mind, and not grow familiar with the particular patina of her skin, the scent and taste of it? Not to touch her now would be to breach a natural law. Back she lay against the soft green stair in the thickening dusk and fixed her eyes on his, unsurprised, daring him: he raised her shirt and there in the split between the black cloth of her clothes he found her soft belly, very white, marked with the silver lines her son had made; he kissed it once, and could not stop, and she rolled against him in delight.

The sun slid down – the forest closed about them – the copper on the pillars of the trees turned to verdigris. The gilded temple was gone, and in its place there was the scent of leaf mould and long grass dying, and windfall apples splitting on the path. She met his gaze then, levelly as she always had, and felt herself go rushing to meet him like a river in spate; 'Please,' she said, pulling at her skirt: 'Please,' and he heard it like a command. He found her easily, and his hand slipped and moved in her, and her bright head drooped, and she was silent. He showed her his hand, and how she gleamed there; he put a forefinger to his mouth and hers, and they had an equal share.

6

Later that same night, hardly five miles distant, Luke Garrett walked alone beside barley fields harvested white. He'd taken it into his head to walk the River Colne, setting out in that mean time before dawn when even the lightest burden is intolerable and the prospect of sunrise laughably remote.

Though the moon had not yet set, the sky in the east was stained with light and the fields gave rise to mist. In places it thickened into scraps coming at him as he walked; they breathed wetly on his cheek then dissipated like sighs. Some time back he'd lost the Colne and neither knew nor cared where he might pitch up: if he could, he'd have walked clean out of his own skin. The Essex land to his London eye was uniform in its strangeness: all the fields were ploughed black, save here and there where barley stubble glowed pale under the setting moon, and the low hedges seethed with life. The ranks of oaks were sturdy watchmen surveying him as he passed: he was an imposter.

He came in time to an incline where grass grew thick, from which it was possible to see out across a modest rise-and-fall to a village drowsing in the hollow, and here he rested against an oak. By disease or bad luck it had shed its leaves early, and in among the branches mistletoe showed vivid green even in that murky light. He supposed another man might look up and think of mouths kissed under Christmas sprigs, but he knew it for a parasite, leaching all that was good from its host. Hanging in the bare branches the bundles looked, he thought, like nothing so much as tumours growing on a lung.

Having come to a halt he encountered many separate pains: his feet, unused to walking much beyond an urban mile or so, were rubbed raw against his boots; his knee was swelling where he'd stumbled, swearing, over a stile. Worst, he'd let his injured hand hang loosely by his side, so that blood collecting there throbbed against the healing cut. Where knife and scalpel had scored the palm, the flesh looked rather like a thin mouth stitched shut. 'There was a crooked man,' he said, 'who walked a crooked mile.'

But he could hardly resent the pains, since they distracted from the frantic misery that had dogged him since his arrival from London with a good-for-nothing hand and in his pocket Cora's letter. 'How could you?' she'd said, and he'd felt her anger, and understood it: how *could* he? Own nothing which is not beautiful or useful, she'd once said, and he was neither. A squat, glowering creature as near to being beast as man, and now (he pushed the thumb of his left hand into the damaged palm of his right, and reeled with the shock of it) useless to boot.

Since the day the knife had gone in, he'd woken each night drenched in sweat that collected in the hollow of his collar-bones and left his pillow damp. *Useless*, he'd say, beating a clenched fist against his temples until his head ached, *useless – useless*: all that gave him purpose had been taken in a matter of hours.

Sometimes he woke forgetting, and for fleeting seconds the world was spread out before him invitingly: there were his notebooks and his models of the heart with its chambers and pipes; there the letter Edward Burton wrote in the early days as he healed, and beside it an envelope into which Cora had put a piece of stone and an explanatory note in her schoolboy hand. Then he'd remember, and see it was all false as stage props, and the black curtain would fall. It was not melancholy he felt – he might have welcomed that, imagining it possible to enjoy a fading sadness that found companionship on memorial benches. Instead he veered between bitter fury and a curious deadening that dwindled his whole range of feeling to little but a shrug.

Under the oak in the coming dawn he grew calm. *If I am useless*, he thought, *can I not discard myself?* He had no duty to go on living – no obligation to walk a yard further. There was no God to censure or console: he answered to no intelligence but his own.

Over in the east a coral light struck the low cloud while Luke laid out reasons for living and found each insufficient. Once his ambition had driven him on through poverty and disgrace; now it belonged to a lost age. His mind was now muddied and slow, and besides: what use was it, matched to a mutilated hand? Once he might have let love for Cora sustain him, but he'd lost that too: her outrage hadn't extinguished it, not quite, only turned it into something secret and furtive, of which he was ashamed. Would she grieve him? He supposed she would, and imagined her putting on one of those black dresses that made her skin so pale, and imagined William Ransome looking up from his books to see her there on the threshold, her lips parted a little, a tear gleaming on her cheek – oh certainly she'd grieve: she did it so well, after all.

He pictured his mother's grief: well, she'd never yet had his photo on the mantelpiece – perhaps she'd enjoy finding a silver frame going cheap in the market, and tuck behind the glass a black curl of his baby hair. There was Martha, of course – the thought of her raised something like a smile: what they'd done on midsummer night had delighted them both, but it had also been only a poor substitute. *What a mess*, he thought: *what a mess we make*. If love were an archer someone had put out its eyes, and it went stumbling about, blindly letting loose its arrows, never meeting its mark.

No, there was no reason to continue – let the curtain fall when he chose it. He looked up at the branches of the oak, and they were sturdy enough for a gallows.

Just a moment longer there on the earth with the mist rising, then – since there was neither a hell to shun nor a heaven to gain he'd go out with the Essex clay under his nails and filled with the scent of morning. He drew in a breath and all the seasons were in it: spring greenness in the grass, and somewhere a dog-rose blooming; the secretive scent of fungus clinging to the oak, and underneath it all something sharper waiting in a promise of winter.

A vixen drew near and turned her gaslight eyes upon him, then drew back and sat surveying him a while. She cocked her head – considered his position on her territory – concluded he might stay, and losing interest nosed at the white plume on her breast. Then she grew avid and merry with hunger, and went down the hill in little leaps – sometimes spying something in the grass, jack-knifing with her forepaws crooked – and vanished down the incline with her bright brush held high. Luke felt a love for her then which almost made him cry out, and knew that no man ever had a better farewell.

7

At about the time Luke was choosing his own gallows from among the Essex oaks, Banks sat beside a fire high up the shingle, near the black bones of Leviathan, making marks in the logbook: *Visibility, poor; wind, north-easterly; high tide 6.23am*. For all that he'd witnessed the great silver fish lying beached on the saltings with its belly splitting open, Banks knew – with a certainty which had begun to obliterate all others – that the Essex Serpent had not been found. How could it, when he woke each night with its breath on his cheek – expected to wake and see himself enfolded in its wet black wing? When all of Aldwinter had celebrated, rolling out the cider-barrels and draining them dry, he'd sat at a distance, alone, thinking of his poor lost daughter and her coral-coloured hair. 'All alone out there with the flotsam and jetsam,' he'd said, 'and the mark of the Serpent on her.' Oh, there was something out there all right – he'd seen it, he'd marked it: black it was and ridged in places and its appetite unsatisfied. He drowned his sorrows in bad gin; it fended off the worst of the images that came in the night, but out there with his face to the rising tide they came vividly at him: the serpent in the Blackwater with a livid eye, its blunt snout, how it pawed at his daughter as she rolled dumbly in the shallows.

'Did what I could to keep her dry,' said Banks, growing tearful, looking about for a witness and finding none: she'd been born with a caul, had Naomi, and killed her mother coming out; and he'd done as any good sailor would and put a bit of caul in a pewter locket and she'd worn it every day to fend off water-sprites. 'I did what I could,' he said, and the fog rolled in, and dawdled by the fire.

He took a bottle from his pocket and drained it dry; the spirit stung his throat, and he doubled over coughing, and when he raised his head he saw surveying him placidly across the fire the black-haired son of that London woman who'd taken up with the rector.

'Bit early for you, isn't it?' he said. The child had always unnerved him, with his steady gaze and his habit of patting his pockets over and over. If the beast was to take any child it ought to've been this one, whose presence raised all the hairs on his neck's nape – who he'd once seen steal five blue sweets from behind the counter in the village store!

'But isn't it the same time for me as it is for you?' said Francis Seaborne. 'Did you see it?'

'What are you on about – what do you want?' said Banks, choosing to deny the serpent. 'Nothing out there, lad, nothing to see.'

'I don't think you think that,' said Francis, coming closer. 'Because if you did, why would you be here and what are you writing in your book? Stands to reason.'

'Visibility poor,' said Banks, flapping the logbook at the boy. 'And getting worse: I can hardly see you, never mind the Blackwater.'

'I can,' said the boy, and took a hand from his pocket to gesture out east where the fog banked up above the salt marsh. 'My eyes are good. Over there. Can't you see?'

'Where's your mother? Doesn't she keep you indoors – keep back, won't you – where did you go?'

Francis stepped away from the fire into the white air, and for a time Banks was alone again; then a slender figure appeared from a little away to his left, saying again, 'Didn't you see it then? Can't you hear?'

'No – no, there's nothing there,' said Banks, coming to his feet, kicking salt shingle over the fire: 'There's nothing there and I'm going home – let go of my hand! Only one child ever held it and she's gone and won't be coming back!'

The cold hand in his had a strength out of all proportion to its fingers; the boy tugged at him, trying to draw him near the incoming tide, saying, 'Look harder, look better, don't you see it?'

Banks shook him off, growing afraid, not of what lay out there on the wet mud but of the child, who stared so implacably back at him. 'I'm going home now,' said Banks, and turned away – then there came from close by the sound of something moving. It was a curious, low, muffled sound, deadened by the thickening fog; it was like the slow grinding of a jawbone, or of something scrabbling for purchase on the shore. Then there was a groan – rather high-pitched, and ending on something like a squeal – and the thick pale air lifted in the wind, and Banks saw the long low curve of something dark, hunched, in places glistening smooth and in others uneven and rough. It shifted against the shingle, and there was the groaning again; Banks called out to the boy, but the fog enclosed him in a pale shroud and he saw nothing. The glowing embers of the fire beckoned him, and he ran towards it, stumbling in the mud and the high tussocks of marsh-grass; once he fell, and felt his knee-cap shift under his skin; then he half-hobbled home. As he went, his heart lifted, despite the terror: *I was right – oh, but I was right!*

Francis, meanwhile, held his ground. He assumed he was afraid, since his palms were wet and his breath was coming fast, but as far as he was concerned that was no reason to turn tail. He rarely thought of Cora – not out of contempt, but because she was a constant, and so seemed hardly worth troubling over. But he thought of her then – of how often she bent over a fragment of rock, and sketched it; of how she'd beckon him over and tell him the names of what she'd found. Perhaps he could do the same, here, or something like it: observe a phenomenon at the closest of quarters, and make a report, and show her. The idea satisfied him; he walked on, and beyond the pale curtain the sun rallied, and the fog began to thin. The wet mud glistened gold, and water began to run in rivulets towards the shingle; there again was the sound of grinding, and a dark shape shifting a few yards distant appeared as slowly as if it were just that moment being formed out of the air. Francis stepped forward. A low gust came from the east and whipped at the fog, and there was a bright clear moment in which he saw plainly what it was that had been cast up on the shore.

He numbered his feelings as accurately as any of his treasures: first it was relief he felt, as his breath slowed and his heart's beating subsided; then disappointment; then hard on its heels came mirth. Laughter bubbled up in him and could not be suppressed; he had to ride it out like a coughing fit, or as if he were being sick. After a while the laughter died back, and he was himself again, drying his eyes with his sleeve, considering how best to proceed. What he'd seen was gone now – hidden behind a fresh bank of fog, or borne out again on the lapping tides – and it was important to settle on what he should do next. Certainly he ought to tell somebody, and it was Cora he thought of first. But no – he ought not to have been out-of-doors so early in the morning – he imagined her discarding his account in favour of explaining that he had done something wrong, and the idea was intolerable. Then he remembered Stella Ransome, and how he'd visited her in her blue bower, and how she'd let him touch her treasures, and how readily she'd understood that in his own pockets there'd been a bent coin, a fragment of gull's egg, and the empty cup of an acorn. He'd grown so used to being greeted with bemusement and suspicion that her immediate affection earned her his absolute loyalty. He'd tell her what he'd seen, and she'd tell him what to do.

Dear Mrs Ransome

I want to tell you something. Please may I visit at a time convenient.

Yours sincerely Francis Seaborne (Master)

PS I will put this through your door to save time.

8

Dr Garrett found a branch fit to bear a stocky man. Hanging would doubtless be unpleasant: he'd have much preferred a high drop and broken neck to long slow pressure on his throat; but he understood it, and knew how his tongue would loll, and his bowels loosen, and how blood vessels would lay scarlet cobwebs over the whites of his eyes, and he'd never been afraid of anything he understood. He fumbled at the buckle of his belt, favouring his wounded hand (as if it mattered now what damage was done, or how he pulled at the stitches!), and as he looped the strap through the silver buckle to form a noose his thumb moved across the ridges which formed the symbol there. There it was, the coiled snake, the sign of his profession: the darting tongue picked out with the engraver's tool, the winking eye. It was a mockery – he had no right to it – to think that once he'd walked proudly bearing the sign of gods, of goddesses! Worse, it called to mind Spencer – his long anxious face, his loyalty, his habit of seeming always to be dashing after him to prevent some disaster. How extraordinary it was that all the while he'd sat leaning on the gallows he'd chosen, numbering his reasons for living and setting each one aside, he'd never once thought of his friend. It was as if his presence was so constant, and so taken for granted, that he'd come to be barely noticed. Again he traced the symbol, resentful of its intrusion, and tried also to set Spencer aside. He was a grown man, after all, with pockets as deep as his heart was large – dull on first meeting, but generally liked: he'd miss Luke, but no more than if he'd gone to another country. But Luke knew this to be untrue. Since their days side by side at the college bench flaying open severed hands to see their bones and tendons Spencer had conferred on him a friendship more unerring than any brother could've shown. He'd patiently borne every slight and insult (of which there had been many); by wealth and good manners deflected the rage of tutors and debtors; had by his silent approval enabled every small step Luke made towards his goal. By slow degrees they'd established an intimacy more easy than that with any lover either had known: Luke remembered a time when Spencer, after too much wine, had lolled against his shoulder, and how he hadn't moved for fear of waking him, though his arm grew stiff and sore. Luke pictured him – waking now in the George, perhaps, in his absurd striped pyjamas with a monogrammed pocket, his fair hair receding, probably thinking of Martha first, then of his friend in the adjoining room; how he'd dress too neatly and come quietly down for his egg, wondering when Luke might wake; how then he'd grow uneasy, and come knocking on the door – would he go to the police, or come searching himself? Would he find his friend hanging there, with the buckle of his belt shearing the flesh behind his ear – might he scrabble at the branch to bring him down?

No – it was impossible to think that he could do such harm – and it was also unfair: must he really struggle numbly on for the sake of George Spencer? How humiliating it was that neither the hope of professional glory nor the possession of Cora Seaborne might keep his neck from the noose, but nothing more than a friend. How humiliating – and another failure, even at the end! The calm he'd felt receded, and in its place was the old familiar rage: he thrashed wildly at the grass with the belt, sending up clods of mud, while behind him in the branches of the oak something moved because it had seen the sun.

Shortly after noon Spencer stood wringing his hands at the threshold of the George Hotel and saw a cab draw up. The driver opened the door and thrust out his hand for money, and then there was Luke, with his wounded hand cradled against his shoulder and his black hair all on end. Spencer's righteous fury receded when he saw how the other man stared and stared with the whites showing all around his eyes, and a graze on his cheek as if he'd fallen.

'My God – what have you *done?*' he said, putting out his hand to draw him in; but Luke shook him off like a petulant child, and pushed past him into the lobby. The cab driver counted through the coins – 'Where was he?' said Spencer: 'How far have you come?' – but he didn't answer, only shook his head and tapped the side of his head: *Mad as a hatter, that one.* Above them a door slammed fit to rattle the windows in their frames, and Spencer went upstairs in dread and hope.

His friend stood against the window, looking down onto the Colchester streets. The whole broad bulk of him was rigid; Spencer imagined he might topple over and break in pieces against the bare floor. 'What's happened?' said Spencer, coming nearer: 'Is everything all right?'

When the other man turned to look at him, Spencer went cold at the bitterness of his black gaze: '*All right?*' said Luke, and his teeth ground against each other; he looked almost as if he might laugh. Then he shook his head, and grunted, and lunging at Spencer with his left hand struck him hard against the temple, splitting the skin above his eye. Spencer reeled against an ugly chest of drawers, and swore; his vision was speckled with stars, and behind them, Luke in his rage and misery said, 'If it hadn't been for you it would all be done with now, it would all be finished – God, stop looking at me, *I never wanted you here* –' Then, as if he'd been held by a cord suddenly severed, he fell against the closed door, and huddled there, cradling his bandaged hand; he did nothing so good and simple as weep, but instead gave out a low and rhythmic groaning that was nearer the grief of animal than man.

'I'm sorry,' said Spencer, a little shyly: 'It's no good. I'm not going to go away, you know.' Then carefully, prepared for another blow, he sat beside his friend, and keeping an English distance, patted his shoulder. After a pause he fell to rubbing it roughly, as if it had been the pelt of a dog coming out of disgrace, and said, 'I'm not going to go away – have a good cry, I would, then we'll have breakfast, and you'll feel much better.' Then, colouring violently, he bent and kissed his friend where his black curls parted, and standing said, 'You get yourself all cleaned up. I'll be waiting downstairs.'

Stella Ransome
All Saints Rectory
22nd September

Dear Francis

Thank you for your note. I never saw better handwriting!

You must visit as soon as possible, for I am always home, and I look forward very much to hearing what you have to tell me.

If, before you see me, you find anything which is blue, I would very much like to have it.

With love,

STELLA

Dear Will – How long did you stay alone out there under the beeches in the dark? When you went home, did you sleep? Are you troubled – has the guilt come yet? Keep it at bay, if you can. I feel none.

It's morning now, and there's a heavy fog that brings a curious light into the room and with it the scent of the estuary – sometimes I think I'll never escape that smell, as though I've already drowned in it. The fog is pressed so close against the window I feel as if the whole house must've been blown up into a bank of cloud.

Did I ever tell you about my parents' orchard? The trees were trained to grow in ordered rows against a kind of wooden structure; I remember thinking they'd been tortured out of their natural shape and for two full summers I wouldn't eat their fruit.

I remember eating lunch there one afternoon. I must've been a child because I can see my hair lying over my shoulders in two long braids, and it's fair, the way it was when I was young. And it must have been spring, because blossom blew into our teacups and onto our plates and I tried to make a wreath. We had a guest that day, whose name I've forgotten: one of my father's friends and such a wrinkled yellowish man he looked like an apple himself, only one that got left in the dish uneaten too long.

He took a shine to me, seeing my head always in a book, and all afternoon came out with things to please me: how to say 'checkmate' is to speak Sanskrit and say 'the king is helpless', and how Nelson never got over his sea-sickness.

What I remember most of all is this. He said, 'There are two words in the English language which are spelt the same, and pronounced the same, but have opposite meanings. What are they?' I couldn't find an answer and of course that pleased him no end: he said (with the sort of flourish magicians have when pulling silk scarves from their sleeves) CLEAVE. To cleave to something is to cling to it with all your heart, he said, but to cleave something apart is to break it up.

All last night, that word came to me as clearly as if it had been you who'd told me only hours before – the memory got mixed up with the May blossom falling and the apples in the grass and the conkers we found on the path and the tear in the seam of your shirt – I've never found ways to explain to myself what it is that exists here in our letters or when we sit together in warm rooms or go walking out in the woods, and I am not sure it's necessary, not even now when I still feel your imprint in me . . . but for now that word's the best that I can do . . .

We are cleaved together – we are cleaved apart – everything that draws me to you is everything that drives me away.

I'll send this note with Francis: he says there's something he must tell Stella. He has gifts for her: a blue bus ticket from Colchester, a white stone with a blue band. Martha says she'll walk him over the common, and she's bringing a jar of plum jam.

CORA

9

'You look well,' said Martha, truthful but also a little afraid: Stella Ransome burned with too much life. 'We're not disturbing you? Frankie wanted to come and says he has gifts. And Cora sends jam, though I'm afraid it hasn't set. Hers never does.'

Stella sat on her blue couch, wrapped in many blankets. She'd watched them come across the common: first the bobbing of torchlight through fog, then two figures circled by a glow: for a moment she'd thought she was being called home, but concluded that her summoning angels were unlikely to knock at the door. Besides, hadn't that black-haired boy said he was coming with something to tell her? 'I feel well,' she said: 'I feel my heart beating fast and strong and my mind opening out like a blue flower – I tarry only a short while here on the earth and want very much to live it vividly! Frankie' – she was pleased to see the boy: 'Sit there, by the window, where I can see you. Not too close: I've had a bit of a cough lately, though nothing too bad.'

'I've got things for you,' said Francis, and kneeling a discreet distance away laid out the bus ticket, the blue-banded stone, and a foil sweet-wrapper the colour of a robin's egg.

'Navy, cyan, teal,' he said, touching each in turn. Then he put his hand in the other pocket and took out a white envelope. 'And I've got to give you this, which is a letter for your husband from my mother.'

'Cyan!' said Stella, delighted, making a note of it: Cyan! Teal! Really there was no end to the boy's charms. Her own children were returning to her tomorrow – would they also understand?

She suspected not. 'Put your treasures on the windowsill – there, where I've left a gap – and we'll give William his letter – he'll be pleased. He missed her while she was gone.' She turned her eyes on Martha, who wondered what they saw, and what they did not.

'Is he here?' Martha said, curious: Cora had wandered home late in the cool evening, dazed as if with drink, though there'd been nothing telling on her breath; she'd said, 'We had such a good long walk,' and curling in a chair fallen immediately asleep.

'In the garden feeding Magog if he can find her in the mist – Jo will be home tomorrow and will go straight out there and want to know what she had for breakfast and whether she still pines for Cracknell – go and find him, why don't you, and take him the note?' Stella lowered an eyelid very slightly at Francis, who understood that his new friend wished them to be alone, and felt himself grow warm with pleasure.

'I've got something to tell you,' he said when Martha had gone. He stood precisely where he'd been told to stand, and no nearer; very straight, and rigid with the importance of what he had to convey.

'So I understand,' said Stella. *Suffer the little children to come unto me!* Her own babies were coming, and here in the meantime was another, and she'd cradle him close if she could – sometimes she looked down at her arms and thought she saw love seeping out of every pore! 'What is it? I won't be here much longer, you see, so you have to tell me quick.'

'I disobeyed my mother,' said Francis, a little cautiously. He did not consider this to be a sin, but had observed that it was looked on dimly in most quarters.

'Ah,' said Stella. 'I wouldn't let it trouble you. Christ came not to call the righteous but sinners to repentance, after all.'

Francis didn't know about that, but, relieved to see he was not to be told off, edged a little closer, rolling the brass button in his pocket between finger and thumb. 'I got up this morning at half past five and I went down to the saltmarsh and that man Banks was there and there was lots of fog. I wanted to see if I could see it. The serpent. The Trouble. What they said is in the water. They told me they'd found it but I wasn't sure because obviously I hadn't seen it.'

'Ah! The Essex Serpent – my old adversary, my foe!' Stella's eyes glittered, and the hectic colour on her cheek spread upward; she leaned forward and said confidingly, 'I hear it, you know. It whispers. I write it all down.' She flicked through her blue note-book and held it out, and Francis saw, written over and over in two neat columns, COMING READY OR NOT. 'It's all right,' said Stella, wondering if she'd frightened the lad: 'You and I understand each other, as I have always said we do. They have been deceived, Francis. I know the enemy. It can be placated. It's been done before.' She looked down at her palms, and read them – surely there were sores coming where the head-lines crossed the lines of memory? – she held them up, but Francis saw nothing.

'Well,' he said, pressing on, 'there was such a lot of fog I couldn't see very much, but then I heard a noise and there it was.' He flung out his arm as if the Essex Serpent might creep out from behind the dining table. 'Just there, big and dark and moving: I could've thrown a stone and hit it if I wanted! Well, I looked and looked and I tried to tell Banks but he wouldn't come. And then the fog was gone for a bit and the sun came out and I saw what it was.' He told her what he'd seen, and how he'd laughed, and how then the fog and the tide had swallowed it up. 'Oh . . .' she said, disbelieving, as he'd feared she would be, a little let down; then 'Oh – !' and she too fell to laughing, and could not stop. Francis watched, recalling how his father once had reached for his throat as if it could be coaxed into being calm. His father's illness had interested him without troubling him, but as Stella's eyes streamed with tears his own wetted in response – should he help her? He crossed the carpet, and gave her a glass of water; the fit passed, and she sipped gratefully, then clasping her hands in her lap said, 'Well, then. Well, Francis. What are we going to do about it?'

'We should show them,' he said: 'We should go down there and show them.'

'Show them,' she said, 'yes: the substance of things hoped for, the evidence of things not seen . . .' She patted at the beads of sweat which settled in the cleft above her lip: 'The people that walked in darkness will see a great light! We will deliver them out of their fear – give me my notebook, hand me my pen: I am a ready writer! Come' – she patted the vacant seat beside her, and Francis knelt there, leaning on her arm, watching her leaf through pages blotted with blue ink – 'I will show you what we'll do, you and I.' She began to sketch, her moment of weakness forgotten; her small body radiated vitality and purpose. 'It is my time,' she said: 'The sands are sinking – I have heard it calling! – I am wet to my ankles in blue water . . .'

Francis wondered if he ought to be troubled, or should call for Martha: the woman's white hands trembled – her words were tangled strings of bright beads – the black centres of her eyes had spread to the rims. But she put out her arm, and drew him to her, and Francis – who could not bear the shy attempts his mother made to pet him – leaned against her, and felt the heat rise from her shoulder and the incurve of her neck. 'I can't do it without you,' she said, confidingly: 'I can't do it on my own, and who else understands, Frankie? Who else can help me?'

She told him what she had in mind. Any other child might have been frightened, or put their head on her shoulder and wept. But as she drew in her notebook, and showed him what part he should play, he was aware for the first time of being wanted, and not out of duty. A new sensation came, which he examined, and would think about later, when he was alone: he thought perhaps it was pride.

'When shall we do it?' he said. She tore the pages from the notebook (he admired how neatly she had set out what they were to do, and the care with which she'd planned it) and put them in his pocket.

'Tomorrow,' she said: 'When I've seen my babies again. Will you help? Do you promise?'

'I will,' he said. 'I do.'

Martha in the garden watched Will try and crown Magog with a home-coming wreath: the goat, growing stout on scraps, shook it repeatedly off, giving him a sour look they both understood to convey that Cracknell would've never dreamt of such an indignity. She blinked her slotted eyes and retreated to the misty garden's end.

'When are the children home?' said Martha. 'You must've missed them.'

'I've prayed for them every day,' he said. 'Nothing's been right since they've been gone.' He looked very young, in a shirt with a tear on the shoulder and red berries from the discarded wreath caught in his hair. He'd left behind his pulpit voice and instead leaned on his country vowels; it had a curious effect, drawing the eye more than ever to the corded strength of his bare arms. 'Tomorrow on the midday train.' Martha studied him a while – dared she ask where he'd walked the night before with Cora? Had he too been a little off-kilter since then, a little restive? Perhaps it was only that his children were coming home, and meanwhile Stella burned in her blue room.

'I'll look forward to seeing them,' she said: 'Anyway, I was sent to give you this.' She gave him the letter, which he looked at without interest; 'Leave it there,' he said: 'I'd best go fetch Magog.' He gave a curious bow – half-ironic, and half-comical – and walked into the white air.

Returning to the house to take Francis home, she stood amazed at the threshold. Frankie – who even as an infant could never bear to be held – was seated astride on Stella's lap, his arms clasped about her neck; she'd drawn a blue cloth over them both, and under it they swayed very slightly back and forth.

What Martha later recalled most vividly of those last few fog-white days was this: William's wife and Cora's son, fit together like broken pieces soldered on the seam.

The blackeyed boy came and showed me the way.

Bless the LORD Oh my soul!
And all that is within me bless his holy name!

Do not let this cup pass from me for Oh I am thirsty

And Oh my tongue is dry

'Bad morning for it,' said Thomas Taylor, surveying the lamplit Colchester street. He held up the sleeve of his coat, and saw on every fibre a bead of moisture gleaming in the gaslight glow. The sea-fog was in its second day, and though the city was spared the dense and briny pall enclosing Aldwinter the streets nonetheless were queerly mute, and every now and then a passer-by stumbled on the curb or ran into the arms of a startled stranger. Behind him in the ruin, coils of mist moved across carpets and hung in empty grates, and fanciful guests at the Red Lion swore they'd seen a grey lady closing the curtains in the highest window.

Taylor was joined these days by an apprentice, who sat cross-legged on a slab of stone. He was an odd copper-headed lad, slight and silent, who soberly took instruction and, what's more, on finer mornings turned out cheerful caricatures of passing tourists, who parted readily with their coins and often came back for more.

'Can't see a bloody thing,' said the apprentice: 'Nobody knows we're here. We might as well go home.'

Taylor had found the child a month ago, curled up in what had once been the dining-room, with fallen masonry for a pillow. No amount of questioning on his part could establish where the child had come from, or where he was going: there was mention of a river, and having walked a good long way, and certainly there were sufficient blisters and bruises on foot and knee to suggest he'd had a journey, and a hard one at that. Taylor, wheeling himself this way and that on the threshold, had chivvied the lad out of the ruin with many an admonition on the dangers of trespass, then sent him over the road for two teas and as large a bacon sandwich as he thought he could manage. 'I'll not see that money again,' he'd thought, watching the slight child walk away, trailing a wounded foot, but back he'd come, with a paper packet and two steaming mugs. 'Newcomer, I take it?' he'd said, watching the lad set about his breakfast with bites both dainty and determined, but received no reply. The meal and the tea did their work; the child accepted the cleanest of Taylor's many blankets, and finding a scrap of carpet grudgingly conceded to be more or less safe slept for several hours. Taylor was delighted to discover that nothing plays so sweet a tune on the heart-strings as a sleeping child with a smudged cheek, and doubled his takings in an afternoon. Natural avarice vied with his own good heart: when the child woke, he tried once again to establish where he'd come from, and where his parents might be, and made faint reference to the local bobby. These lines of questioning were met respectively with silence and terror, so that Taylor felt quite justified in offering the boy a partnership in a thriving enterprise, together with full board and lodging. By way of demonstrating good faith he handed over a modest proportion of the day's wages, which the lad surveyed in astonishment for some minutes before counting them carefully into his pocket.

'I've got a daughter, mind you,' said Taylor, reassuringly: 'You won't be expected to care for me, though a push of the old carriage wouldn't go amiss, what with my hands getting arthritic around the knuckles. I daresay she'll like to have you about, never having managed to fetch a family of her own. Fancy telling me your name? No? Well, if you don't mind me calling you Ginger after an old tomcat of mine, we'll get along nice enough.' And they got along very nicely indeed, as it turned out: Taylor's daughter had accepted worse eccentricities, and furthermore felt that given the loss of his limbs he should be permitted the occasional lapse in judgment. Ginger never quite developed what Taylor called the gift of the gab, but once provided with pencil and paper seemed content enough, if occasionally given to making troublesome sketches, frantically scribbled, that Taylor could never make out.

'Might as well go home,' the boy said, peering into the mist; but then there was the rattle and clamour of a group coming up the pavement from beneath the spire of St Nicholas, and Taylor readied himself: 'It's a bad businessman as shuts up shop on account of a bit of weather,' he said, and rattled his cap. The group drew near, and he heard their voices – *Just for a few minutes to see how he's doing, shall we?* and *James, don't dawdle, we've a train to catch* and *I'm hungry and you promised you absolutely promised . . .*

'If it's not my old friends!' said Taylor, glimpsing a scarlet frockcoat and the gleam of a brass-spiked umbrella swung high: 'Mr Ambrose, ain't 't –' but then there was the sound of a door opening and closing, and the party vanished one by one between the glowing windows of the George Hotel. 'Damnitall, Ginger,' he said, looking about for the boy, and not finding him: 'A very openhanded gentleman that one – what is it, lad? Where've you gone?' His apprentice had abandoned his post, silently and swiftly, and sat crouched behind the marble plinth, thrusting out his bottom lip in a failing effort to fend off tears. *Children!* thought Taylor, rolling his eyes heavenward, and dispensing a bar of chocolate: he'd've been much better off getting a dog.

'Dear me,' said Charles Ambrose, surveying Spencer and Luke Garrett. The former had a split severing his right eyebrow, which was held together with fine strips of plaster; the latter, besides his heavily bandaged right hand, was ashen-faced, and had grown thin, so that the heavy bones of his brow gave him more than ever a simian look. The men stood side by side, looking rather like school-boys caught out in the aftermath of a prank. Katherine made moth-erly noises, and kissed each of their cheeks, whispering something sweetly to Luke, who coloured and turned away. They'd brought the children with them, who each in their way felt a certain heavi-ness in the air and did what they could to lighten it. 'Got anything to eat?' said John, scouring the room with a practised eye.

'John, you are a pig,' said Joanna: 'Dr Garrett, how's your hand? Can I look at it? I want to see the stitches. I'm going to be a doctor, you know. I've learned all the bones in my arm to show my dad when I get home: *humerus, ulna, radius —*'

'Not an engineer, then,' said Katherine, drawing the girl away from Luke, who'd not yet said anything, only flinched a little as if the girl had recited profanities and with a half-shamed reflex tried to put his wounded hand out of sight.

'I've got a bit to make my mind up,' said Joanna. 'I can't go to university for ages yet.'

'Or at all, probably,' said James Ransome, rather spitefully: since Jo's sudden shift from dabbling in natural magic to dab-bling (with what he felt was equal pointlessness) in the sciences, he'd felt himself deposed from his position as the family's bright spark. 'Look,' he said, turning to Spencer, and taking a sheet of paper from his pocket: 'I've designed a new sort of valve for a lavatory. I thought you could use them in your new houses. You can have it for free if you like,' he added, feeling generous: he was not immune from Martha's Marxist influence. 'I'll patent it once you've done the building work.'

'That's really very kind,' said Spencer, scrutinising the plans, which were certainly sufficiently detailed to resemble every other blueprint he'd seen. Charles Ambrose caught his eye, with what was a look of almost paternal gratitude.

'Heard from Martha, have you?' said Charles, seating himself beside the fire while Katherine took Luke Garrett to one side and with gentle, inconsequential conversation tried to coax him out. Spencer coloured a little, as he always did at Martha's name. 'She's written twice – she tells me Edward Burton and his mother stand to lose their home! The landlord has almost doubled the rent at a stroke – their neighbours are already turned out. And meanwhile we move so slowly! How good she is – to care so much about a man she barely knows.'

'I've done what I could,' said Charles, truthfully: where conscience and argument could not move him to push wholeheartedly for the Housing Bill to become bricks and mortar, the sight of Luke Garrett wounded in the gutter had. Nothing, he knew, could remedy the sudden curtailment of a life's ambition, but at least they could see that it was not wholly a waste. 'There's enthusiasm in Parliament, but what counts for enthusiasm in the Commons would look very like laziness elsewhere.'

'I wish I could give her good news,' said Spencer, wringing his hands, and failing as ever to conceal the personal motive behind his philanthropy. His long, shy face coloured, and he cuffed at a thread of fine fair hair. Charles, who'd taken a keen liking to the young man for his good nature and his lack of guile, and who'd had his own correspondence with Martha, felt his heart contract with pity. Ought he to tell the lad which way the wind blew, and snuff out the candle he held? Probably he ought, though he was scarcely certain himself what that exasperating woman had in mind, and suspected she had further shocks in store. Glancing at the children to see they were occupied elsewhere he said, gently, 'It's not only goodness that makes Martha bother herself about Burton's rent – she's throwing her lot in with his, I'm told.' The blow landed – Spencer stepped back as though to fend off another

– he said, 'Burton? But –' He shook his head like a dazed dog, and Charles in his kindness tried his hand at levity. 'We're all as shocked as you are! Ten years Cora's companion and she'd throw it all in for three rooms and a fish supper! No date set for a wedding, mind you, and one can hardly picture her in a veil –'

Spencer mouthed silently once or twice, as if trying and failing to form Martha's name; he seemed diminished, and he looked perplexedly down at his own hands as if he couldn't think where he should put them. Charles looked away, knowing the man would assemble himself in moments – there in the corner John had found a packet of crackers and ate them with contemplative dedication, while Joanna and James bickered pleasantly over who'd first found a drawing of a hip-joint corroded by disease. Turning back, he saw Spencer fastening his jacket, as if packing away whatever it was that had threatened to come out. 'I'll write to congratulate her,' he said: 'Nice, for once, to have good news.' His eyes brightened with withheld tears, and flicked towards Luke, dully staring at the floor beside Katherine, who'd grown hopeless, and felt she could do nothing but insist that he eat.

'Yes,' said Charles, discomfited by his own pity, and urging on the hands of the clock: Aldwinter beckoned, and after that a return to a peaceful home. 'Yes: it's been a bad year all round, it's true – but we're only three-quarters through.'

Spencer – who thought thoroughly, if not fast – said, slowly, wringing his hands: 'I had wondered why she was so troubled by the rise in Edward Burton's rents – it seemed such a small thing, in the greater scheme . . . Luke, did you know? Have you heard?' He turned towards his friend, with the old impulse of looking there first to be guided or mocked, but he was gone. 'Well,' said Spencer, turning back to Charles, forcibly bright: 'Will you keep me posted?' There was a shaking of hands, which conveyed a mingling of sympathy, resolve and embarrassment, and children were fetched from their various corners. They asked where Luke was, and asked again after his hand; John said he was sorry for eating him out of house and home and pointed out that if he'd been given the promised cake it wouldn't've come to that, and he'd replace the packet of biscuits when his pocket money came through.

'I am worried for our beloved Imp,' said Katherine, taking Spencer's hands, noting his pallor, putting it down to anxiety over his friend. 'Where has he gone? It's like the lights blew out.' All her maternal instinct – sleepily roused by the Ransome children – fixed now on the surgeon, who'd sat beside her concealing his right hand beneath his left as if he'd once caught it out in a shameful act. 'Does he eat? Is he drinking? Has he seen Cora?'

'Early days yet,' said Charles, helping his wife into her coat, buttoning it to the chin: he'd had more than his fair share of melancholy this past half-hour and was anxious to take the children home. 'He'll be himself again come Christmas – Spencer, come to lunch soon: we'll go over the plans – Joanna, James, thank Mr Spencer for his time; you'll see Dr Garrett again soon – goodbye, then!' John stopped on the threshold and said, suddenly remembering, 'We're going to see Mummy!' and flung his arms around his sister. 'Do you think she's better now? Will she still be pretty?'

Out on the High Street where the mist thinned under the low sun, Joanna thought of her mother, and felt her stomach turn. She'd missed her at first with the constant dull ache of an old injury; everything had been all awry. Katherine Ambrose had been kind, but not in the way Stella was kind; her room was comfortable, but not in the way Stella would've made it so. Dinner was served too early, on the wrong kind of plates; there were no African violets on the windowsill; Katherine laughed at the wrong things and did not laugh at the right ones; they had hot

milk for supper, and not camomile tea. In those early days she had
written to her mother daily, and blotted the ink more than once,
and could not sleep at night without summoning into the kitchen
downstairs a slight white-fair figure in a blue-bordered dress. But
the pictures had faded fast: the letters that came back were fervently loving and oddly phrased and rarely touched on anything
Joanna had said. Then they grew rare, and when they came were
like little devotional leaflets handed out by women in thick brown
stockings outside Oxford Street station, and they embarrassed her.
Within weeks she became a Londoner, at ease on Tube and bus,
able to look Harrods girls square in the eye, with strong opin-
ions on where to buy notebooks and pencils. Aldwinter dwindled,
became mud-bound and dull, the Essex Serpent a bumpkin beast
too dim-witted to make its presence felt. She missed her father,
but pleasantly, and felt it would do them both good: she'd read
Little Women and felt that if Jo March could manage without for
a while, certainly so could she. She had the hardness of youth, and
it stood her in good stead, save when she caught sight of a fallen
crow's feather or a spider putting a fly in a winding-sheet; then she
remembered her days of magic, and her red-haired companion,
and would for a moment be floored with guilt and grief.

So it was that when she looked across to the ruin and saw the
cripple there, and the ragged child cross-legged on a marble plinth
bending over sheets of paper, she gasped, and shrugging out of her
brother's grasp dashed blindly across the road. She was bright-lit
for a moment by the lights of a bus, then was gone behind a group
of elderly tourists headed for the castle museum. '*Joanna!*' called
Katherine, feeling instantly sick, frantic on the kerb, trying both
to reach the girl and prevent the boys from tumbling into the road.
Charles, with an unshakeable belief that no Essex vehicle would
contemplate muddying his scarlet coat, walked with measured

calm to the ruin, and was astonished to find Joanna bellowing at the crippled man, and raining down blows on his shoulder. 'What've you done to Naomi!' she said: 'Look what you've done to her beautiful hair!'

Charles interposed himself between the two, receiving a light slap on his arm: 'Joanna,' he said, 'I'm the first to admire your forthrightness but on this occasion fear you may've over-stepped the mark – sir, I am sorry for my . . . really, Jo, *what* am I to call you? . . . I am sorry you have been attacked in this disgraceful fashion! Perhaps I can make amends?' Coins rained into Taylor's upturned hat; the men shook hands. 'Now then,' said Charles, fervently wishing himself elsewhere: 'What possessed you, child?' Joanna was not listening, only stood looking back and forth between Taylor and a thin lad in a dirty jacket. She'd gone very white, and her face seemed to flicker between a woman's fury and a child's distress, and all the while the boy stood staring at the ground. Charles, baffled, put out his hand to Joanna; then she said – gulping a little at a threatened sob – 'They all said you'd been stealing from the shop, but I told them you'd never do that, and then when you didn't come we thought the Trouble'd got you and you were here all along – Naomi Banks, I should give you a black eye!' The girl looked for a moment as if she might do exactly that, then instead threw herself at what Charles by now realised was no boy, but a thin girl whose hair had been lopped short and stood out in grubby ringlets, glinting copper. She stood aloof from Joanna – now almost hysterical with weeping – crossing her arms with an expression of hauteur.

'Trouble?' said Taylor, thinking once again of dogs he might've had: 'Stealing? My Ginger? I confess,' he said, stirring at the coins in his hat, 'to be at a loss.'

'I think we can infer,' said Charles, 'that your employee here has been having you on, and is a girl called Naomi, and a friend of Joanna's.' Here ended his understanding, since no-one had thought to tell him of the boatman's missing child. The red-haired girl ran out of her store of pride, and with a choking cry returned Joanna's embrace. 'I wanted to go home, honest I did, but I was too scared to be by water and no-one wanted me anyway!' She drew back, and looked severely at Joanna, and her eyelashes were spiked with tears. 'You didn't want to be my friend anymore and everyone was scared of me because of what I did at school and that thing in the water and I didn't mean it: I don't even know what happened, just that I was so afraid I couldn't stop laughing . . .'

'Ginger?' said Taylor, summing up the situation as best he could: 'Didn't I look after you all right?' Slyly he looked at Charles, who added another coin or two to the insatiable hat.

'It's all my fault, isn't it – all my fault – I've been a bad friend . . .'

'It was that woman,' said Naomi, whose freckles showed brightly in the runnels of her tears: 'That woman came and after that nothing was all right. She put it there! She put the monster in the river!'

'Haven't you heard?' said Joanna, finding she'd grown tall enough to draw the girl's head to her shoulder: 'It's gone, the Essex Serpent – it's gone, there's nothing there, there never was – just a poor old fish, a big one, and it died in the water — come back, Nomi' – she kissed the girl's hand, feeling on her mouth the ruin's dust and the town's grime – 'don't you want to see your dad?' At this the last of Naomi's pride departed, and she fell to crying, not violently like a child, but with the steady hopelessness of a woman. When Katherine Ambrose arrived, John on one hand and James on the other, she saw Joanna seated on a marble plinth in a *pietà*, a thin girl cradled in her lap, crooning what sounded very like a child's idea of a spell.

'I'm afraid,' said Charles, looking at his watch, 'we seem to've acquired another one.'

Stella in her blue bower heard her children coming and held out her arms: she knew the rap of John's shoe on the doorstep, and James's considered tread; she knew how Joanna would throw down her coat and come running long-legged, full-tilt. Then there was Will at her door, his smile that of a man bringing gifts, triumphant: 'Darling, here they are – they've come back and tall as telegraph poles' – then, quietly, to Joanna: 'Go carefully: she's weaker than she seems.'

Joanna had dreaded seeing her mother lolling on a sickbed, gaunt and grey, listlessly thumbing at a blanket, but here was Stella starlike, with eyes gleaming and a touch of rouge; she'd dressed for their arrival with turquoise beads looped three times round her neck and a shawl on which blue-winged butterflies flew. '*Jojo*,' said Stella, straining towards them – she could not reach them soon enough. 'My Joanna,' she said, holding their names on her tongue: 'James. John.' How well she knew their particular scent – of John's hair, which had always been a little like warm oats, and of James, who had something sharper about him, keen as his wits. Joanna felt beneath the shawl to brittle bones, and shuddered; her mother felt it, and a complicit look passed between them.

'I like your necklace,' said John, admiringly, then presenting half a bar of chocolate said, 'I brought you a present.' Stella knew this for a sacrifice, and kissed him, and turned to James, who had not ceased talking since he crossed the threshold, about the *Cutty Sark* and the Tube, and how he'd been down to see Bazalgette's sewers. 'One at a time,' she said, 'one at a time: I don't want to miss anything.'

'Don't tire her,' said Will, watching from the threshold, throat aching with pleasure and sadness: he could've stood there an hour seeing Stella hold them to her breast – he wanted to feel them in his own arms, warm and compact and wriggling; and all the while he wondered how he'd frame it for Cora, by letter or word: how it would please her, how her grey eyes would blur. *God help me: I am severed*, he thought, but no – it was not that he was there in part, and in part in the grey house across the common; he was wholly present in both. 'Don't tire her,' he said, coming forward, finding himself drawn in by small hands: 'A bit longer, then let her sleep.'

'I have you all now,' said Stella. 'I have you all here now, sweethearts: be with me now before I go.'

HE calls me home to his banqueting house

          His banner over me is LOVE

HE sent the serpent to Eden's blueflowered garden
and he sends it now and the penance must be paid for as
by one man's disobedience Aldwinter's sinners are brought
under judgment so by my obedience they will be delivered

God's serpent servant in the blue Blackwater water has
come to take our taxes

I shall pay their dues and it will go back whence it came

    and I

     shall enter

       the gates of GLORY!

Down at the quay Banks sat beside his struck sails dully counting out his losses – wife, boat, child, all slipped through his hands like so much salt water. Behind the sea-fog the estuary swelled in the coming tide, and he recalled the black-haired boy by the fire in the morning, and how he'd dragged him towards the shore. 'Didn't see a thing,' he said into the dim air: 'Didn't see a damn thing'; but in his mind's eye there it was – the strange news, the Essex Serpent: bloated, arrow-tailed, pawing at the shingle. Now and then the pale mist parted and there were the lights of smacks and barges winking in the dusk; then the curtain fell, and he was alone again. He whispered the boatsman's plainsong for comfort – *The starboard light is green at night – The starboard light is on your right ...* – but what use were flames behind coloured glass when down in the deep something was waiting, biding its time?

When he felt a small hand on his shoulder it came so gently he didn't flinch or shirk it. The touch was not only familiar but possessive – no-one else could've touched him like that – it struck off memories that rose through the fuddle of drink and the thickening mist. 'Come home then, littl'un?' he said, tentatively, putting up his own hand in a searching pat: 'Come back to your old man?'

Wrapped in Joanna's cast-off coat Naomi looked down at her father's head where hair grew thinner than she remembered, and felt a new and unexpected tenderness. For a moment he was no longer her father, so nearly an extension of her own self that he hardly crossed her mind. She understood for the first time that he too felt fear and disappointment – that there were things he

hoped for, and suffered, and enjoyed. It moved her, and propelled her forward through the years: she took up her old position
cross-legged beside him on the quayside and drew a fishing-net
towards her. Expertly, she pulled it through her fingers, finding
a tear, saying, 'I'll get on with this one if you like.' It had always
been a hated task – it left welts in the webbing between her fingers
that grew sore with salt – but her hands found their old rhythm,
and there was comfort in it. 'Sorry I went away,' she said, drawing together the torn threads, turning away to let him shed tears
privately. 'I was scared of things but it's all right now. And besides'
– she reached over and did up the buttons on his coat – 'I earned
some money all on my own! We'll go home and you can help me
count it.'

Midway through the afternoon the sea-fog rallied and approached
Aldwinter from the east. It crept across windowsills and pooled in
ditches and hollows, and dampened the ringing of the All Saints
bell. Cora, restlessly walking on the common, looked the sun dead
in the eye and saw, specked on its surface, the dark sunspots of
storms raging. *Who will I tell now, if not him?* she thought: *Who
else would believe me when I speak of impossible things?*

'I'm tired,' Stella said in her blue room, 'and now I lay me down
to sleep.' Curled in the corner, James and John looked up from a
game of cards, and looked down again, incurious and content as
animals returned to their hide. Joanna, who'd read several times
a paragraph of Newton and felt none the wiser, saw how moisture gleamed on her mother's forehead, and how her hair clung
there, and was afraid. Stella, no less acute now than she'd ever
been, beckoned her child over, and said: 'I know you see it, Jojo: I
know you see what they don't. But I'm happy – sometimes even
when you were all away and the house was silent I'd think: I am

happier now than I've ever been. Do you believe me? I wouldn't
do without an hour of my suffering, because it has lifted me – it
has shown me the path of life!' She held out her skirt, and began
to pick up all her treasures, one by one – the blue mussel shells, the
fragments of glass, the bus tickets and the sprigs of lavender – and
drop them into the fold of cloth. 'I ought to tidy up,' she said, looking about the room. 'Bring it all to me, Jo – the bottles, there; all
the stones and ribbons – I want to take them with me.'

In his study Will laid a sheet of clean paper beside Cora's letter
and could not pick up his pen. *Keep guilt at bay*, she'd said, as if
it could be fended off, as if she had any idea! She'd untied herself from all that: she had no idea it was not simply a general
sense of wrongdoing, but of personal and particular wounding;
that he'd hammered in a little further the nails in foot and hand,
that he might as well have taken a length of bramble and wound
it tight round Stella's brow. *I am the chief of sinners*, he thought;
but wasn't there pride in that, another sin heaped on the first?
He thought of Cora, and summoned her easily up – the freckles high on her cheek, her steady grey gaze, her way of standing
bolt upright, queenly in her tattered coat – and was blinded for a
moment with fury (there – another sin: put it on the charge sheet,
stick it on the slate!). From the moment of opening Ambrose's
letter when the year was young he'd known the wind was changing – he ought to've buttoned up his coat and pulled the windows
shut, not turned to face the draught. But all the same it was Cora
(he said her name aloud), *Cora*, who'd grown intimate in the first
clasp of their hands – no, before then, while they grappled in the
mud – who delighted and enraged, who was generous and selfish,
who mocked him as no-one else ever did; Cora, who in his presence alone could weep! The fury receded, and he remembered the
press of his mouth on her belly, and how warm she'd been, how

soft, how like an animal at ease: it had not felt like sinning then, and hardly did now – it was grace, he thought, grace: a gift he'd never sought and did not deserve!

How long did you stay alone out there? she wrote, and it had been a long while: he'd gone down to the river-mouth, to Leviathan's black bones, and looked out at the estuary, willing the serpent up from the deep to swallow him down like Jonah. *By the rivers of Essex I sat down and wept*, he thought, and upstairs the door to Stella's room was gently closed, and footsteps moved across the landing. His heart made a painful circuit: there was Stella, his bright particular star, going out in a blaze; he was afraid she'd leave behind a black cavity into which he'd hopelessly fall. He wanted to go up to her, and lie beside her on their bed, and sleep as he always used to with her fitted to his back, but it was not possible: she wanted now always to be alone, writing in her blue book, her eyes fixed avidly elsewhere. On he sat in that dark room, unable to write – unable to pray – watching the red-rimmed sun, and wondering if somewhere Cora also watched.

Across the common Francis Seaborne sat cross-legged, watching the clock. He had in his pockets so many bluish stones that try as he might he could not get comfortable. Elsewhere his mother roamed about the house, distracted and restless, sometimes coming in to see him and put kisses on his forehead without speaking. He held the note from Stella Ransome, on which were clear instructions written in blue ink, and a picture that frightened him, though it was lovely to look at. He folded and refolded the paper – the minute hand moved slowly, and he half-wished it would move more slowly still: it was not that he doubted the wisdom of his orders, only that he wondered if he had the courage to see it through. At five o'clock precisely Francis went out to the hall where boots and jacket neatly waited, and set off into the fog. He looked up, trying to find the rising Hunter's moon, but it was hidden, and wouldn't be back for a year.

Leaving her mother sleeping, Joanna had gone to find her friend: she wanted to reclaim the old territory of their gossiping and spells, and show her how the saltings were free from the serpent's shadow. It had soon become clear that their days of magic had become a distant childish memory and one not to be recalled without a blush. Still, it was good to walk their old paths, matching step for step. 'Cracknell was there when I found him,' said Naomi, pointing to a clear stretch of shingle beside a narrow creek. 'Stretched out with his head on one side. I went over thinking maybe he'd fallen – he was so old, wasn't he? And old people do fall over – but his eyes were open. I saw something dark in them and thought maybe it was the last thing he'd seen, maybe it was the monster, but then it moved and it was only me, like they were mirrors I was looking in. They say it was because he was old and ill – funny to think we all thought the serpent did it!'

They walked on past Leviathan, feeling the air damp against their cheeks; the fog on the banks of the Blackwater was thick, particulate, full of pearly grains. A little distance away a watchman must've set a fire burning and later left his post: its embers gave off a yellowish haze that shifted as the wind moved the mist.

'It's gone,' said Joanna, 'and there was nothing to be afraid of after all, but all the same my heart is beating – I can hear it! Are you afraid? Shall we go on?'

'Yes,' said Naomi, 'and yes.' It was necessary to be afraid in order to have courage: this is what her father taught her out on the deck of his barge. 'Let's go on – mind there, it gets deep.' She knew the saltings well, and all its creeks and high tufts of marsh-grass: 'Hold onto my arm and trust me,' she said, 'the tide turned an hour ago. We're safe.' It pleased her to be there again with her friend, only with everything altered: she was not poor Naomi, slow to read, biddable, in awe of the rector's daughter – these were her elements, and she felt in command. All the same, it was a dim, uneasy evening. The sea-fog disclosed the marsh in small portions (it parted and there was an egret waiting out the mist) then closed and they were all alone. Once there was a moment where the sun beat through the fog, and they discovered they were surrounded on all sides by dabchicks whinnying and diving. 'As lost as we are,' said Joanna, laughing, and wishing she were at home. 'Let's go back now,' she said. 'What if we can't find the way?' She clung to Naomi, despising her just a little for taking charge, stumbling against the rotting posts of an oyster bed and crying out.

'What if it's still here,' said Naomi, only half-teasing: 'What if it's still here after all and has come back for us?' Out of a shameful desire for revenge she withdrew her arm and stepped backward into the mist, and cupping her hands to her mouth gave a kind of beckoning call. 'I'll summon it, shall I?' she said, frightening herself, but not wanting to stop. 'Watch out! Here it comes!'

'Stop,' said Joanna, fighting unwomanly tears: '*Stop it!* Come back – I can't find the path . . .' When Naomi appeared again, a little ashamed of herself, she struck her on the shoulders: 'You're horrible, *horrible*, I could've walked out into the estuary and drowned and it would have been your fault . . . What? What is it? Nomi – stop playing games, when you know full well it was just a great big fish . . .' Beside her, Naomi had gone very still, and put out a restraining hand. It was not towards the estuary she looked, where the Blackwater rolled out to join the waters of the Colne, but back towards the shore, where the fire still glowed coral-coloured through the fog. 'What?' said Joanna, on her tongue the copper-penny taste of fear: 'What have you seen, what is it?'

Naomi's hand on her sleeve flexed and tightened – she drew her friend nearer and put her mouth close to her ear: '*Shh* . . .' she said, 'shh now . . . look, up by Leviathan, can't you see? Can't you hear?' Joanna heard, or thought she did: a kind of groaning or grinding, coming in fits and starts, without reason or pattern. It fell silent, then struck up again, seeming nearer; from scalp to fingertips she felt a dreadful chill that left her fixed in place. It was there – it had been there all along, waiting, waiting – it was almost a relief, to think they'd not been duped after all.

Then the pale pall lifted, and there it was – fifty yards distant, no more: black, snub-nosed, bulkier than either had imagined; wingless or sleeping, blunt-tailed, with an ugly lumpish surface, not the sleek lapping scales of fish or serpent. Naomi half-screamed, half-laughed, turning to bury her face in Joanna's shoulder: '*I told you!*' she whispered, hissing: '*Didn't I tell everyone?*' Joanna took a step towards it, curiously unafraid – then it shifted, and there was that grinding again, almost of great teeth moving against each other in hunger, and she shrieked, and leapt back. The fog closed about it, and they saw nothing but a shadow biding its time.

'We have to go,' said Joanna, forcing down a yell of fear: 'Can you get us back – look, the fire's burning there on the bank – go towards it, Nomi, keep your eyes on it and don't make a sound . . .' But the fire's embers dampened, and the light faded, and for a while they stumbled helpless and blind on the shingle, each keeping back tears only for the sake of pride. '*Ready or not – ready or not –*' muttered Naomi for consolation; then the low sun pierced the fog-bank and they found they'd come hard up against it, had almost stumbled on its wet black flank. Joanna yelped, and pressed her hand to her mouth: there it was, *there*, after all this time only an arm's length away – blind, slumbering perhaps, impossibly ungainly on the bank – was it sleek in water, in its native element?

Did it go beneath the waves and grow slick and gleaming? What of the wings, outspread like umbrellas, someone had said: had they been clipped and who had clipped them? And there was something else – some bluish marking on its belly: something she half-recognised, could almost make out in the thinning mist.

Beside her, Naomi stood bolt upright, hands flung up, on the verge of the laughter that drove the schoolgirls mad. She was pointing at the markings, mouthing at the air; there was the grinding again, and she flinched, but all the same drew closer. 'Mummy,' she said: '*Mummy ...*' and for a moment Joanna thought she was calling for her mother, who lay in the churchyard under the cheapest headstone to be had. 'Look,' said Naomi, whispering, 'Look there: I know those letters, even upside down – Gracie it says – Gracie, my mum's name, the first one I ever wrote down and I never forgot it, not for ten years –' Forward she ran on the shingle, in the lifting mist, and Joanna tried to call her back. But all the fear had left her friend, and took with it her own terror, so that she too moved towards the dark shape shifting on the marsh.

The strengthening sun cast a clear light on the shingle, so that each girl saw, at the same bright moment, what had been cast up. It was a black boat, small and clinker-built, long sunk in the Blackwater and thick with barnacles which gave it the look of uneven flesh, coarse and battle-scarred. Its upturned hull had rotted and begun to sink, so that there was the impression of a blunt snout nosing at the shore; it moved in the last lap of the receding tide, causing its wood to grind against the shingle, and now and then its timber groaned in distress. It was possible to make out, beneath the draping of bladderwrack and sugar-kelp, the name GRACIE picked out in blue-white paint: Banks's boat, long since given up for lost, all the while casting up on the marsh on the whim of the tides, sending a village clean out of its wits.

They clutched each other, not knowing whether to laugh or weep: 'It was here all along,' said Naomi, 'he thought it was stolen from the quay and I said no, it's just you never tie it up right, that's all . . .'

'Think of Mrs Seaborne down here with her notebook, wishing she'd brought her camera, thinking of a case in the British Museum –' said Joanna, beginning to laugh, feeling disloyal, though certain Cora would see the humour in it.

'– and all the horseshoes hanging up in Traitor's Oak, and the watchmen, and no-one letting the children out –'

'We ought to tell my father,' said Joanna: 'We should bring everyone down here, and let them see – only what if we came back and it was gone because the tide took it, and no-one believed us . . .'

'I'll stay,' said Naomi. It was hardly possible to believe, while the low sun copper-plated the wet marsh, that they'd ever felt a moment's fear. 'I'll stay. It's practically my boat, after all.' *Gracie*, she thought. *I'd know it anywhere!* 'Go on, Jojo, fast as you can, before it gets too dark to see.'

'It's funny,' said Joanna, turning away to the path above the shingle: 'There's something blue sticking out underneath – can you see? Cornflowers, maybe, though it's late in the year for that.'

Some distance away, sitting between the ribs of Leviathan and pulling at dark splinters driven into the palm of his hand, Francis Seaborne watched – seen by neither, missed by no-one.

In his study Will drowsed dreamlessly. When he woke it was to so uneasy a mind and such vivid recollections that for a moment he was hard pushed to tell which had been sleep, and which waking. There on the desk was the blank sheet of paper, but what use was it now? There was no hope of conveying to

Cora how all the deep-sunk foundations on which he'd built his being had shifted, cracked, been rebuilt. Each phrase that came to mind was immediately contradicted by another of equal and opposite truth: we broke the law – we obeyed it; would to God you'd kept your London distance – thank God you live when I do, thank God we share this earth! The effect was to be nullified: he had nothing to say. *A broken spirit and a contrite heart Thou wilt not despise*, he thought, wishing in that case that his own spirit could be more completely broken, his heart more wholly contrite.

A sound roused him – footsteps, a gate closed and opened: he thought of Stella, waking upstairs, wanting him, perhaps, and his heart lifted, as it always did. He pushed away Cora's letter with a sound of distaste – it was a taint at worst, a distraction at best, when every thought should be directed up to where his loved one lay half in this world, half in the next. But after all, it was only Joanna, back from the saltings with the scent of it on her coat, her eyes gleaming, mischievous, merry: 'You've got to come,' she said, plucking at his sleeve: 'You've got to come and see what we've found – we'll show everyone and everything's going to be all right.'

Going quietly, afraid they'd wake Stella, they set out across the common, where in the blue dusk Traitor's Oak cast a long shadow and all the mist was gone. 'You wait,' said Joanna, making him run, refusing to answer ('I'm tired, Jojo, can't you tell me?' – 'Just you wait and see'). Then they were on High Road, which blazed wet in the last of the day; as they reached All Saints they saw Francis Seaborne running home like any ordinary boy. Then there was World's End, which had so lost heart without Cracknell it had returned almost completely to the Essex clay. 'Just a bit further,' she said, dragging him on: 'Down by Leviathan, where

Naomi's waiting.' And there was Naomi Banks with her glinting curls, and some distance away a fire set in a circle of stones.

He heard the gulls all crying out, relieved at the clear sight of land; drew in air scented with salt and the sweetness of oysters in their beds. Turnstones busied themselves in the creeks, and there was the curlew's underwater song. Then Naomi called, and beckoned, and he saw what it was they'd found: in the clear evening light a wrecked boat, heavily barnacled and decked with bladderwrack. Something in the way it was cast up, nudging at the shingle, gave it a half-alive look; he came closer, seeing GRACIE written clearly on the hull. 'After all that,' he said, turning to Naomi, 'was it really just your father's boat?' She nodded, rather proud, as if it had all been her doing, and bowing, he shook each girl's hand in turn. 'A job well done,' he said. 'You should be given the freedom of this parish.' Silently he prayed in brief full-hearted gratitude: *Let that be an end of it, then – the fear, and the whispers, and you girls half-mad at your desks!* 'Let's fetch your father, Naomi: there'll be no more of this. To think we had two Essex Serpents, and neither of them fit to harm a fly!'

'Poor thing,' said Joanna, stooping beside the boat, knocking on the wood, wincing at the barnacles sharp against her knuckles: 'Poor thing, ending up like this, when it should be headed out to sea. And look,' she said. 'Blue flowers in the stones, like they were put there, and a bit of blue glass.' She picked up the sea-blunted glass and put it in her pocket. 'Come along home,' said Will, drawing her away. 'It'll be dark before we know it, and Banks should be told.' Arms linked, companionable, feeling they'd done a good day's work, they turned their backs on the Blackwater.

Cora looked up from the book she'd not been reading, and there was Francis at the door. He'd been running, that much was evident: his fringe lay slick against his forehead, and his thin chest fluttered beneath his jacket. To see him at all out of sorts was so extraordinary that she began to rise from her chair: 'Frankie?' she said – 'Frankie? Are you hurt?'

He stood neatly at the threshold, as if afraid he ought not to come in; he took a folded sheet of paper from his pocket, which he opened carefully and smoothed against his sleeve. Then clutching the paper to his chest he said, with eyes turned to hers in an appeal she'd never – not ever – seen before: 'I'm afraid I've done something wrong.' His voice was more like a child's than it had ever been, but with no childish sniffling or gulping at the air he began very quietly to cry.

Cora felt something rise in her which was like the accumulation of every pain she'd ever felt; it clutched at her throat, and for a moment she could not speak. 'I didn't mean anything bad by it,' he said: 'She told me she needed my help and she was kind and I gave her my best things –' It took a great effort not to run towards him and attempt to take him in her arms; she'd done so many times before, and been rebuffed. Better simply to let him come to her – she returned to her chair and said, 'Frankie, if you were only trying to be kind, how could you have done something wrong?' Then there he was on her lap, suddenly, with his dark head fitting precisely between her cheek and her shoulder; his arms clutched about her neck – she felt the warmth of his tears, and how his fast heart beat against hers. 'Now,' she said – she cradled his face between her palms, half-afraid she'd see him recede from her, and never come back again – 'tell me what you think you've done, and I'll tell you how we can make it right.'

'It's Mrs Ransome,' he said. 'I want to show you, but I'm not supposed to! I want to show you, but I told her I wouldn't!' The impossibility of reconciling what he had promised, and what he desired, bewildered him: whichever way he turned, something would be knocked out of place. His grasp on the paper loosened, and she took it from him. There in blue ink on blue paper were the words TOMORROW / SIX / MY WILL BE DONE! and beneath them a childish sketch of a woman – long-haired, smiling – laid out beneath a curling wave. Stella Ransome had signed her name, and written underneath, *Put your jacket on it might get cold.*

'Stella, my God,' said Cora – but she could not frighten Francis, or toss him from her lap as she ran for the door: what if he never came to her again, her son – with his arms open, and his eyes seeking hers? Nausea came, and she bit at it, and said – conversationally, as if nothing much would come of his response – 'Frankie, did you go down with her to the water? Did you help her down?'

'She told me she was being called home,' he said: 'She told me the Essex Serpent wanted her, and I told her there was nothing there, and she said God moves in mysterious ways and she'd already stayed too long.' He put his hands over his face and began to shiver, as if he were still out there on the shingle and the sun long gone.

'All right,' said Cora: 'All right, now,' and soothed him, astonished to find that he submitted to it, that he actually turned his face towards her. She held him, as much for her own comfort as for his; she called for Martha, who came, and whose recent coolness to her friend did not last beyond the threshold.

'Take him – please, Martha,' said Cora – 'my God, my God, where is my coat, my boots? – Frankie, you only did your best, and now I'll do mine – no, no – stay: I'm coming back soon.'

Will was walking on the High Road with Joanna and Naomi by his side. *How proud they are!* he thought, smiling, wondering, as he always did, how best to tell it all to Cora, what might please her most; but perhaps that was impossible now, it had all been broken, remade, he could not make out the shape of things – then 'Cora!' called out Joanna, and waved. And there was his friend on the path running, or almost; and for a brief moment (which caused him to make a sound he could not suppress) he thought perhaps she'd come to seek him out, could not remain another hour behind closed doors.

'What's wrong?' said Naomi, stopping, touching her pewter locket for comfort. Something was wrong, that much was certain – Cora's cheeks were wet, her mouth open in distress – she clutched a sheet of paper which she waved at them as she came, like a signal none of them could decipher. She reached them, and hardly paused, only tugged at Will's sleeve and said, 'I think Stella is down there, by the water – I think something is wrong.'

'But we have come from there – it's nothing, it's the boat Banks lost –' But Cora by then had gone, the scrap of paper thrust at Will and dropped on the wet path, and for a moment he could neither move nor speak. For something *was* wrong, yes – yes: he ought to've seen it at once – it was there, just beyond his reach – he could not quite grasp it. Joanna stooped to pick the paper up. She couldn't at first take it in, then a picture formed in her mind so strange and terrible that she raised her hands as if she could bat it away from her. 'Daddy,' said Joanna, unable to keep from crying: 'Isn't she sleeping? Didn't we leave her safely upstairs?' Will, very white, reeling a little, said, 'But I heard her, her footsteps, the door closing – she said she wanted to rest . . .'

They saw Cora reach the place where the road fell down to the saltings, and how she threw off her coat to run a little freer to the marsh. Will followed, cursing a body grown suddenly sluggish, unwilling, as if it were another man's and he a possessing spirit. He was the last to reach the wreck – there was Cora, kneeling in the mud, straining against the hull, so that the muscles of her back shifted beneath the fabric of her dress. And there were the girls at her side, kneeling also, and it gave the effect of supplicants before an ugly malevolent god to whom all prayers went unanswered. He saw (how could he have missed it?) the blue-banded stones set around the ruined boat, the scrap of pale ribbon just visible, the blue glass bottle set upright in the shingle. 'She said she was tired and it was time for her rest –' he said, bewildered – what were they doing, there in the mud – their dresses heavy with it, their heads bowed with effort? 'Stella, Stella,' they called over and over, as if she were a child who'd gone walking and not come home when she was told. Their hands slipped on the wet wood, and the three women lifted up the boat, which was not so heavy after all, and disintegrated as it moved.

Lying there in the shadows, shrouded, silent, set about with all her blue tokens, lay Stella Ransome. Seeing her, Will cried out, and so also did Cora: she lost her hold on the boat, which fell away, breaking apart on the marsh. Then Stella basked in the day's last light, her thin blue dress showing all the pretty bones of her hips and shoulders. She held a bunch of lavender that still gave off its scent, and nestled around were her blue glass bottles, her scraps of cambric and cotton, under her head a blue silk cushion and at her feet her blue notebook, curling in the damp. Her skin also was blue, her mouth dusted with it, her veins marbling close to the skin; the lids of her closed eyes were touched with purple. William Ransome, on his knees, drew his wife towards him. 'Stella,' he said, kissing her forehead: 'I'm here, Stella, we've come to take you home.'

'Don't leave us, darling, not yet,' said Cora – 'don't go'; she took the woman's small white hand and rubbed it between her own. Joanna tugged at the fine hem of her mother's dress to cover her bare blue feet: 'Listen, her teeth are chattering, can't you hear it?'

She took off her own coat, and tugged Will's from his shoulders; together they cocooned her against the cool air.

'Stella, darling, can you hear us?' said Cora, in whose loving desperation was a painful unaccustomed twist of guilt – and oh, yes, yes – she could: the dusky eyelids fluttered and raised, and there were her bright eyes, pansy-like as ever. 'I was faultless in the presence of his glory,' Stella said: 'I stood at the door of his banqueting-house and his banner over me was love.' Her breath was shallow, and she convulsed in a cough that left a blood-fleck at the corner of her mouth. Will wiped it away with his thumb and said: 'Not yet though: not for a while yet. I need you – dear, we promised we'd never leave each other alone – don't you remember?' It was joy he felt, a great indecent uplifting of it: here was redemption, out on the shingle, with no thought in his mind but for her. *It is grace, again!* he thought: *Grace abounding to the chief of sinners!*

'We'll both go out on the same day like candles left by an open window,' she said, smiling: 'I remember! I remember! – but you see, I heard them calling me home and something was out here in the water and it whispered in the night and was hungry, and I thought: I will go down to the river and make peace with it for Aldwinter's sake.' At this she turned in Will's arms to look out towards the river-mouth, where the clear sky showed the evening star brightly burning. 'Did it come for me?' she said, fretful: 'Did it come?'

'It's gone,' said Will. 'Brave as a lion you sent it away – come home with us now, come home.' How easy it was to lift her, to be helped to his feet by Joanna and Naomi – as if already she'd begun to dissipate up into the blue air!

'Cora,' said Stella, quietly calling, putting out her hand – 'how warm you are and always have been – tell Francis to take my stones, my bits and pieces, leave them all behind. Give them to the river, turn the Blackwater blue.'

NOVEMBER

On turns the tilted world, and the starry hunter walks the Essex sky with his old dog at his heels. Autumn fends off the diligent winter: it's a warm clear-eyed month, with a barbarous all-too-much beauty. On Aldwinter common the oaks shine copper in the sunblast; the hedgerows are scarlet with berries. The swallows have gone, but down on the saltings swans menace dogs and children in the creeks. Henry Banks burns his ruined boat down on the Blackwater shore. The damp wood spits, the black paint blisters. 'Gracie,' he says, 'there you were, all along.' Beside him Naomi stands very straight, warily watching the turning tide. She feels herself arrested in motion, pausing for a moment with one foot in water and one on the shore. *What now?* she thinks. *What now?* Deep in the flesh that joins thumb and forefinger there's a black splinter from the boat's hull: a talisman she touches, awestruck by all her hands have done.

London capitulates too readily and hangs out her white flags: come mid-November there's frost on the windows of the buses on the Strand. Charles Ambrose finds himself playing at fatherhood again: there's Joanna, always at his desk, with an unerring taste for his least suitable books, and there's James, who at breakfast found in the gutter a broken pair of glasses and had made a microscope by supper. He conceals his particular fondness for John, in whose appetite and placid good nature he recognises himself. He lies on his stomach playing cards; on Guy Fawkes' Night he tears his coat, and doesn't mind. In the evening he catches Katherine's eye, and they shake their heads: the presence in their ordered tasteful house of these three is as strange as any number of river-borne beasts. Letters pass between London and Aldwinter with such frequency and speed they joke there's a night train in the sidings waiting just for them. John believes it, and asks if he can bake a cake to keep the train driver going.

Charles receives a letter from Spencer. It lacks the vigour of his earlier efforts: certainly he remains ethically committed to better housing policy, but is concentrating for now on prudent invest-ment of his so very burdensome fortune. Property, perhaps, he says (vaguely, though there was no need to elaborate), property's the thing these days, and Charles is not for a moment deceived. Over in Bethnal Green there's a new landlord, he'd wager, and one with a good heart and correspondingly poor business sense.

Edward Burton, not yet returned to work, looks up from his blueprints and sees Martha at the table. Cora Seaborne has given her a typewriter and it makes quite a racket, but he doesn't mind. How can he? In the space of a month he's moved from threatened homelessness to a degree of security and peace that bewilders him when he wakes in the morning. The entire tenement block has been bought up by a landlord who employed two clerks to make an audit of each home. They came with a camera and refused tea; they noted the damp window-frame, the buckled door, the creaking third stair. Within a week these were remedied, and the street took on the scent of whitewash and plaster, and over break-fast and supper, factory-workers and nurses, clerks and mothers and elderly men braced themselves for a punitive rise in rent that never came. Now neighbours gather in stairwells and scratch their heads, and it's generally agreed the man's nothing but a fool. There's a degree of resentment in public – I stand in no need of charity, more than one tenant says, bullishly – but behind closed doors they'd bless his name, if they knew it.

Martha keeps in her pocket a folded note from Spencer, wishing her happiness. 'For a long while I wondered what use I was, with only money to recommend me. I play at being a surgeon because it's a respectable way to pass the time and it appealed to me once when I was a boy but my heart's never been in it, and God knows I'm no Luke Garrett. It's because of you I've found a purpose which allows me to look in the mirror and not be sickened by myself. I do wish you'd loved me, but I thank you for helping me find a way to love you, and try to right the wrongs you showed me.' It's so humble, and so kind, that she briefly wonders whether her path might better have run alongside his. But no: in the absence of Cora it's Edward Burton she wants, with his near-silence and his clever hands, her comrade and her friend.

Her longing for Cora is strangely no greater in Bethnal Green than it was in Foulis Street, in Colchester, in the grey house on Aldwinter common. It is as fixed as the Pole Star, and she need not look for it. Nor does she resent their years of companionship: she understands the alterations of time, and how what was necessary once may be no longer needed. Besides (she looks up from her typewriter – sees Edward frowning over his plans – touches the magazine which has lately published her work) it's a poor woman whose ambition is only to be loved. She has better things to be getting on with.

In Luke Garrett's rooms on Pentonville Road a marriage of true minds has taken place. There are moments when each heartily wishes the other at the bottom of the Blackwater, but no more devoted couple can be found from one end of the Thames to the other.

Early in November Spencer leaves his home in Queen's Gate (one which he increasingly considers an embarrassment) and takes up residence with his friend. Luke feels it his duty to protest at some length (he doesn't need a nursemaid, thanks; he's got no wish to see anyone, ever; he's always found Spencer a more than usually annoying companion), but in truth he's glad. What's more, Spencer has unearthed an ancient maxim regarding the saving of a life, and points out with some regularity that since Luke prevented his dying, Spencer is both his possession and his responsibility. 'I'm your slave, in effect,' he says, and hangs a photo of his mother beside the portrait of Ignaz Semmelweis.

There's no sign of any great improvement in the mutilated hand: the stitches have been removed, the scar's no worse than to be expected, there's no loss of feeling, but the two fingers crook resolutely inward and fumble over anything finer than a fork. Luke dutifully (if ill-temperedly) submits to a series of exercises with a rubber band, but more in hope than expectation. The spectre of Cora lies always before him. He cherishes two scenarios of equal unlikelihood: first, that he'll suffer a necrosis that'll leave him a stinking suppurating wretch, and that she'll be moved to a lifetime's remorse; second, that he'll find a means to heal himself, and immediately undertake an operation of such daring he'll achieve overnight fame, earn her helpless adoration, and sneeringly discard it in a public fashion. For all the promises he once made, he lacks Spencer's capacity to love humbly and quietly with no hope of return, and his implacable loathing of Cora sustains him far more than Spencer's insistence he eat a decent breakfast ('You're thin, and it's doing you no favours . . .'). Spencer – wiser than anyone ever gave him credit for – understands what Luke does not: that a division fine and fragile as tissue-paper lies between love and loathing, and that Cora need only touch it to poke clean through to the other side.

But it's not just sentiment and loyalty that sees Luke fetching pork chops for supper, and Spencer more or less forcing his friend out of doors to study or dine. There's a practical aspect to their arrangement, which is this: Spencer has coaxed Luke back to the Royal Borough, where he has been both surgeon and patient, and proposed a solution. His own dexterity as surgeon was never anything on Luke's, it's true; but it's good enough, and better than some. What Spencer lacks (he cheerfully admits) is the courage and insight of his friend, for whom every wound and disease represents no threat but a welcome opportunity to demonstrate his skill. That being the case, he says, could they not be between them a kind of chimera, with his own hands being substitute for Luke's? 'I promise not to actually think,' he says. 'You always said I wasn't much good at that,' and he flings open the door to the operating room, triumphant, hoping the sight of it will prove irresistible. And it does: the scent of carbolic, the gleam of scalpels in their steel trays, the laundered pile of cotton masks, act on Luke like an electric charge at the base of his spine. Not since having his hand stitched up has he set foot there, thinking it'd be much like giving a starving man a dish of food just out of reach. Instead, it enlivens him – the shadow of the gallows-oak which has seemed always at his feet recedes – the half-crouched body seems once again possessed of frightening reserves of potential energy. Then in comes Rollings, stroking his beard, catching Spencer's eye: he says, diffidently, as if the thought had just occurred, 'There's a compound fracture of the tibia just come in – a bit of a mess, I'm afraid – and the man can't afford to pay. Don't suppose either of you chaps want a go?'

Sunday comes, and William Ransome's in his pulpit. He sees a cracked pane in the west window and he makes a note; he sees the dark pew with its splintered arm and looks away. It's a scanty congregation, what with no whispered terror to drive them to the mercy seat, but a cheerful one for all that: *Let us now with gladsome mind*, they sing, willing kindness on their neighbours. The horse-shoes have been taken down from Traitor's Oak, save one so high in the branches it'll likely hang there until no-one can remember what purpose it might have served. Only once has he mentioned the serpent – the double illusion of it, the falsity of their fear – con-cealing it in a kindly homily regarding Eden's garden. They leave in no doubt of having been foolish, but understandably so, and resolve to mind their tongues.

Down the narrow pulpit stair he comes (favouring his left knee, which lately has ached in the mornings), and it's a cursory greeting he gives to those who wait at the door, who pause by the lych-gate: 'Wednesday, in the afternoon, certainly I'll come – no, not Psalm 46: perhaps you're thinking of 23? – she sends love: she wishes she could've been there.' But all's forgiven. He's indulged now as he never was before: they talk still of the London woman who not so long ago seemed always at his door; they know how he cradled his wife on the marsh. They see tarnish on him, and it makes him precious: he's not steel, he's silver. Besides, they know what waits behind the rectory door, and why he rushes home – the blue-eyed wife, who circuits the common every week or so, wrapped to the ears, taking air and hailing neighbours, then returning breathless to her curtained room. They leave gifts on the doorstep of rosehip syrup and walnuts in their shells; they leave cards and handker-chiefs so small, so fine, they're no use at all.

Will takes off his collar, throws down his parson's black coat: he does it impatiently these days, though almost as hurriedly puts them back on. Stella's waiting, curled kittenish under a blanket, putting out her arms. 'Tell me who you saw and what they said,' she says, in one of her gossipy moods. She pats the bed, beckons him closer, and they're children again, or nearly – laughing, dis-missing all others, falling into half-remembered phrases that'd be nonsensical if anyone overheard. But no-one does: the house is empty, the children gone for a time, grown in their absence the stuff of legend. 'Remember Jo,' they say, 'Remember John and James,' taking pleasure in the pain of wanting them, since it's a sweet grief that'll be assuaged by a train ticket or a postage stamp. Will – always stifled by small rooms and low ceilings, whose muscles ache from under-use – turns maid and mother, sometimes putting an apron on, surprising them both with a knack for roast meat and clean sheets. Dr Butler comes down from London and pronounces himself pleased: it's a question now (he says) of management, better done here than anywhere, given appropriate precautions. He washes his hands in carbolic soap: mind you do the same, he says.

Stella remains as ever the happier of the two, feeling herself slowly unmoored, sails up for the coming wind. She aches for her children – sometimes she can't tell if it's love or disease that leaves her grasping the bed's edge, white-knuckled, gasping – but (she says) every hair on their head is numbered; and if their father in heaven knows each sparrow's fall, how much more will he see to it that John doesn't run into the path of a London bus?

When she thinks of the Essex Serpent – and she does, though rarely – it's with something like pity, forgetting that after all it was nothing but flesh and wood and fear. *Poor beast*, she thinks: *Never a match for me*. Sometimes she grows fretful, looking for her notebook with its blue bindings and blue ink, but it's gone on the estuary tide, all its fibres and filaments dissolved in the dark Blackwater.

Daily, Will walks out between fields where winter wheat sends up vivid seedlings so fine, so soft, he might as well be walking between lengths of green velvet. By an effort he thinks might one day halt his heart, he sets Cora aside so long as he's under any

Aldwinter roof, and takes her out again in the bare forest, by the Colchester road, down on the Blackwater marsh. He brings her out, as if he'd kept her concealed in his coat, and considers her by daylight and in the pearly light of the autumn moon, turning her about – what is she to him, after all? He cannot settle his mind. He does not miss her, since she seems so insistently present, in the yellow lichen wrapping the bare beech branches, in the kestrel he once saw skimming the oaks, quivering its outspread tail. Coming to the green stair – faded now, the carpet muddied – he thinks of her impatient hand on her own skirt's hem, and the taste of her, and he comes undone, of course he does; but that is not the whole or peak of it. How simple that would be, and how contemptible! But the truth is (and he remains truth's disciple) that casting about for how best to name her he can land on nothing more exact, more honest, than to say: 'She is my friend.'

For all that, he does not write – he hardly feels the need. She signals to him in the high mares' tails overhead, in the turns of phrase she has borrowed and lent, in the curled scar on his cheek; and by similar means he imagines he also signals to her: that their conversations go on, silently, in the downspin of a sycamore key.

Cora Seaborne
11 Foulis St
London W1

Dear Will,

Here I am again in Foulis Street, and I am left alone.

Martha's gone to Edward now – half-wife, and half-conspirator – but she's still here, in the scent of lemon on my pillow and the way the plates are stacked. Frankie's away at school, and he writes, which he never did before. His letters are short and his handwriting's neat as newsprint, and he signs himself YOUR SON, FRANCIS, as if he thinks I might forget. Luke heals, though more for Spencer's sake than mine. I hope I'll see them all soon.

I go from room to room pulling dust sheets from the furniture and put my hand on every chair and table. I live mostly in the kitchen, where the stove is always lit: I paint and write, and catalogue my Essex treasures. They're poor things – an ammonite, bits of teeth, an oyster-shell perfectly white – but finders keepers: they're mine.

I eat an egg for my supper and drink Guinness with it and read Brontë and Hardy, Dante and Keats, Henry James and Conan Doyle. I mark up the pages and look back and see I've underlined where I think you also might have got your pencil out; then in the margins I draw the Essex Serpent and give it good strong wings to fly by.

Solitude suits me. Sometimes I wear my old boots and my man's coat and sometimes I put on silk, and no-one's any the wiser, and certainly not me.

Yesterday I walked to Clerkenwell in the morning and stood by the iron grate where the Fleet flows, and listened, and imagined I heard the waters of all the rivers I have known – the head of the Fleet at Hampstead where I played when I was young, and the wide Thames, and the Blackwater, with its secrets that were hardly worth keeping.

Then it carried me in spate to the Essex shore, to all the marsh and shingle, and I tasted on my lips the salt air which is also like the flesh of oysters, and I felt my heart cleaving, as I felt it there in the dark wood on the green stair and as I feel it now: something severed, and something joined.

The sun on my back through the window is warm and I hear a chaffinch singing. I am torn and I am mended – I want everything and need nothing – I love you and I am content without you.

Even so, come quickly!

CORA SEABORNE

AUTHOR'S NOTE

I am indebted to a number of books for having opened the door to a Victorian age so like our own I am almost persuaded I remember it.

Matthew Sweet's *Inventing the Victorians* (2002) challenges notions of a prudish era enslaved by religion and incomprehensible manners; rather, he shows us a nineteenth century of department stores, big brands, sexual appetites and a fascination for the strange.

An obscure book by an anonymous Essex rector, *Man's Age in the World According to Holy Scripture and Science* (1865), suggests a clergy that did not see faith and reason as mutually exclusive. It amuses me to think of it on William Ransome's shelves.

In *Victorian Homes* (1974) David Rubinstein collates contemporary accounts of housing crises, venal landlords, intolerable rents and political chicanery; they would not look out of place in tomorrow's newspapers. *The Bitter Cry of Outcast London* (1883) was compiled by Rev. Andrew Mearns, and is readily available online. It draws spurious parallels between poverty and lack of moral virtue that may strike the reader as familiar from modern political rhetoric.

Those in the habit of picturing the Victorian woman as forever succumbing to fits of the vapours under the gaze of a bewhiskered husband can do no better than to read Rachel Holmes's biography of Eleanor Marx (2013). In its preface the author says: 'Feminism began in the 1870s, not the 1970s.'

In researching the treatment of tuberculosis – and in particular its effects on the mind – I am grateful to Helen Bynum, both in correspondence and in her book *Spitting Blood* (2012). Meanwhile Richard Barnett's *The Sick Rose* (2014) shows the troubling beauty that can be found in sickness and suffering.

Roy Porter's majestic work *The Greatest Benefit to Mankind: A Medical History of Humanity from Antiquity to the Present* (1999), his overview of surgical history *Blood and Guts* (2003), and Peter Jones's *A Surgical Revolution* (2007), have all been invaluable in framing the mind and work of Dr Luke Garrett. Inaccuracies and elisions in the medical aspects of this novel – as in all others – are of course mine alone.

The nature of Stella Ransome's *spes pthisica* was profoundly influenced by Maggie Nelson's *Bluets*, an exquisite meditation on desire and suffering, filtered through a lens of blue.

Strange News Out of Essex, the pamphlet alerting villagers at Henham-on-the-Mount to the presence of the Essex Serpent, is real. You may see both the 1669 original and Miller Christy's 1885 facsimile at the British Library; a copy of the facsimile is also held in the library at Saffron Walden, Essex, where it was first printed. The titles of each of this book's four parts are taken from the text of the pamphlet.

Mary Anning's 'sea-dragons' are displayed in London's Natural History Museum.

ACKNOWLEDGEMENTS

First and most loving thanks to my dear Rob, whose company is an inexhaustible supply of interest and charm, and who first told me about the legend of the Essex Serpent.

I'm profoundly grateful, as ever, to Hannah Westland and Jenny Hewson for their wisdom and support, and for their uncanny habit of knowing my mind better than I do: to work with them is a privilege and joy. My thanks also to Anna-Marie Fitzgerald, Flora Willis, Ruth Petrie, Emily Berry, Zoe Waldie and Lexie Hamblin, all of whom have done so much for me, and for this book.

Thank you to my family, who've been so kind to me, particularly to Ethan and Amelie, dauntless travellers through time and space. Thanks also to my three smallest muses: Dotty, Mary and Alice.

Thank you to Louisa Yates, my first reader and my tutor; to Helen Bynum, who was kind enough to advise me on aspects of TB; and to Helen Macdonald, for her guidance on matters floral and avian. Much of this book was drafted at Gladstone's Library, where I think a piece of my shadow lives always at the same desk: thank you to all my friends there, particularly Peter Francis.

For their patience, friendship and wisdom, my love and thanks to Michelle Woolfenden, Tom Woolfenden, Sally Roe, Sally

Craythorne, Holly O'Neill, Anna Mouser, Jon Windeatt, Ben Johncock, Ellie Eaton, Kate Jones and Stephen Crowe. I am endlessly grateful for the kindness and support shown to me by writers, many of whom I have admired for years: thank you especially to Sarah Waters, John Burnside, Sophie Hannah, Melissa Harrison, Katherine Angel and Vanessa Gebbie. To the women of the FOC, who were the first ever to hear me read from this book: my love.

I could not have written this book without the support of the Arts Council, and am profoundly grateful for their assistance, and for that of Sam Ruddock and Chris Gribble at the Norwich Writers' Centre.

AN INTERVIEW WITH
SARAH PERRY

by Rowan Mantell

A shifting, tilting world, where river meets sea and faith meets science and linear progress meet the constant ebb and flow of tides, is surprisingly familiar to Sarah Perry, whose writing is coloured by an unusual childhood.

Sarah, who now lives in Norwich, grew up in Essex. 'I really wanted to portray the county as I know it – a place of strangeness and beauty. I must have come across the story of the Essex earthquake of 1884 at some point during researching the history of Colchester and the local area, though I don't recall exactly when or where. I was immediately struck by it because it seems such a very unlikely event to happen in Essex, which is not generally held to be a place of natural wonders and danger!'

The 1890s setting is a period with which Sarah feels an unusual connection, as she grew up in a home without television or pop music, enjoying embroidery, classical music and the stories of the traditional King James version of the Bible, which was read at mealtimes. 'Sometimes I think I will only ever be comfortable in about 1895. At one point I cut my hair very short and began to wear jeans and shirts, but I felt as if I were a child dressing up, and was much more content when my hair began to grow back and I went back to my dresses and boots! That being said my husband – whom I met when I was a teenager – did set about introducing me to pop culture. And like most people who were brought up without a television I could quite happily watch it all day, though I don't think that's a bad thing for a writer, as it can be a great source of inspiration.'

'I have always been particularly interested in how faith and science sit together. My parents – along with many people I have known – are Creationists, but also extremely intelligent and educated people. My father was a materials scientist and during my childhood he did so much to educate me about astronomy, physics, chemistry and so on: he had a telescope, and a microscope, and over dinner in the evenings he'd tell us about experiments he had done in the lab during the day. I suspect that these days there's a popular belief that faith and reason are in absolute opposition, but this isn't my experience of either faith or reason. But there is I think a struggle – and so much of the book looks at this struggle and whether it can ever be resolved.'

During her childhood and youth, Sarah attended a Strict Baptist Chapel, a denomination which viewed innovations such as modern translations of the Bible, and hymns accompanied by guitars, with suspicion. 'The church had stayed very much as it would have been at the turn of the century – the nineteenth century that is!' And it was this belief that past centuries were a safer place than the twentieth century which meant Sarah's childhood was filled with classic literature, the music of Beethoven, the pictures of the pre-Raphaelites and the poetry of the King James Bible.

Far from being a culturally deprived background it was rich in words, music, art, ideas – and also in landscape. 'Aldwinter is not a real village, but I suppose it's an amalgam of many little Essex villages I've visited. For example, there's Mersea Island, a wonderful and rather strange place, where the tide goes out and leaves behind mudflats, and you can see withy-sticks sticking up out of the water to mark out oyster beds. I love places that are on the very edge of the land, and have never forgotten once visiting St Peter-on-the-Wall at Bradwell, which is one of the oldest buildings in the UK and really does look like it's the world's end. We used to go quite often to Maldon, a little seaside town on the coast where we'd sometimes see Thames barges go up and down the estuary, just as they would have done in the 1890s. I always thought them marvellously romantic. When I was a teenager I spent a few summers in St Osyth, which is mentioned in the book, and I remember one hot day walking for miles along the coastline by the saltmarshes. The use of coastal defences means that there are many thousands of acres less marshland now than there was at the end of the nineteenth century, but there are still wonderful stretches of wild coastal land.'

However, it is not the marshes of Essex, but the city of Norwich that has really captured Sarah's heart. She moved there three and a half years ago and says 'I can't imagine why anyone would live anywhere else. I walk in the grounds of the cathedral whenever I can and feel so privileged to be here – and decidedly resentful whenever I have to be away.' However, some trips away have proved fruitful, including a drive through Essex with her husband. 'We passed a sign to the village of Henham-on-the-Hill, which is where the Essex Serpent was first seen (or supposedly seen!) in the seventeenth century. He asked me if I knew about the legend, and I didn't; when he told me I knew at once that I had the beginning of a novel. By the end of the journey I had the bones of a plot – the rural vicar, and the amateur naturalist down from London with her strange son.'

Sarah's first novel, *After Me Comes the Flood*, was set in a disorientating, imagined Norfolk, part Thetford Forest, part north coast saltmarshes. A man is stranded at a crumbling country house as a searing drought and heatwave threaten to dissolve into thunder and flooding, and an atmosphere of foreboding overshadows disintegrating histories and personalities. It was longlisted for the Guardian First Book Award and won the Book of the Year title in the 2014 East Anglian Book Awards, and was highly rated by readers and reviewers. 'I think the most important impact of *After Me Comes the Flood* having had a good reception with critics, and having found readers, is that I felt free from what had been a really heavy burden of lack of self-confidence. When it came out to such generous praise I felt absolutely liberated – free to write exactly as I pleased, which I think is why *The Essex Serpent* took far less time to write. And I've been fortunate enough to have had some wonderful experiences since publication: I've met novelists I have worshipped from afar for years, and even shared a stage with some of them; I spent two months in Prague as a UNESCO writer-in-residence earlier this year; and I've been lucky enough to feel part of a community of writers, which – for me at least – is really important in what is quite an isolating profession.'

'My ambition as a writer is – more than anything else, I think – to give joy and pleasure to readers; to convey to them the love I feel for my characters, and the places they walk, and to have them feel what my characters feel.'

This is an edited version of an interview which first appeared in the Eastern Daily Press *in May 2016.*

READING GROUP
QUESTIONS

1   'I'll fill your wounds with gold', Michael says. He means both
    literally that he will make sure Cora is financially comfortable
    during their marriage in exchange for the pleasure of hurting
    her, but also that he will remake her as something more beau-
    tiful and interesting than she was before. Cora survived her
    horrible marriage, but was definitely damaged by it. What do
    you think the seams of gold are in Cora's character?

2   Many comparisons have been drawn between Sarah Perry's
    writing and the Victorian novelists who were writing at
    the time the book was set, including Charles Dickens and
    Wilkie Collins. Do you think this book feels Victorian, or
    contemporary?

3   Martha could choose to marry a very wealthy man, like Cora
    did, though Spencer is much kinder than Michael. Early in
    the novel, we are told that she views people like Spencer as
    useful but still distrusts them. She eventually chooses Edward
    over Spencer. Many of the characters have unequal relation-
    ships: Cora and Martha, Spencer and Will. Do you think that
    viewing someone as a means to an end necessarily precludes
    loving them?

4   Cora's son, Francis, might today be diagnosed as being on the autistic spectrum. Despite his difficulties, he gets a lot of pleasure from learning about the natural world. Eccentricity seems to have been more acceptable in the Victorian era, at least for men of a certain class. Do you think Francis would be happier in his time or in our own?

5   Will is at odds with the superstitious villagers, who insist the serpent is a message from God and want him to preach fire and brimstone to them. However, he is also wrangling with Cora, who is more interested in science than faith. Will is a minister of the established Church, but secretly reads Darwin. Do you think he believes faith is more about the following the words of the Bible or more about personal belief?

6   When Francis asks Will what sin is, he describes it as falling short. When Will and Cora finally have their encounter in the woods, Will's wife is still alive. Do you think Will would judge this incident by his own definition of sin?

7   Cora's physical size and mannish habits of dress are frequently commented upon by other characters in the novel. She rejects a lot of society's expectations of her as a woman, whereas Stella Ransome is the living embodiment of the perfect housewife. Despite their differences, they are friends. What do you think Perry is trying to tell us by having Cora save her love rival instead of quietly letting her drown?

8   Cora sends her angry letter to Luke at a terrible time – it arrives as all his other hopes are being dashed. If this unfortunate coincidence hadn't taken place, would we still read the

letter as cruel? Should she have expressed her thoughts more kindly or was she right to be angry?

9 One of the subplots of the novel is the disappearance of Naomi Banks. She and Joanna Ransome argued and Naomi ran away. By the end of the novel, she has returned and Joanna is trying to cope with the imminent death of her mother. Do you think they will become close friends again, for good, or are the differences between them simply too great?

10 The novel sets up Cora to choose between two men and in the end she chooses neither. Do you think this is a comment on traditional literary plots? Do you think the novel sees friendship as more valuable and enduring than romantic love?